Rust
&
Stardust

Center Point
Large Print

**This Large Print Book carries the
Seal of Approval of N.A.V.H.**

Rust & Stardust

T. Greenwood

CENTER POINT LARGE PRINT
THORNDIKE, MAINE

This Center Point Large Print edition
is published in the year 2018 by arrangement with
St. Martin's Press.

Copyright © 2018 by T. Greenwood.

The text of this Large Print edition is unabridged.
In other aspects, this book may vary
from the original edition.
Printed in the United States of America
on permanent paper.
Set in 16-point Times New Roman type.

ISBN: 978-1-64358-012-8

Library of Congress Cataloging-in-Publication Data

Names: Greenwood, T. (Tammy), author.
Title: Rust & stardust / T. Greenwood.
Other titles: Rust and starduct
Description: Center Point Large Print edition. | Thorndike, Maine :
   Center Point Large Print, 2018.
Identifiers: LCCN 2018041777 | ISBN 9781643580128
   (hardcover : alk. paper)
Subjects: LCSH: Kidnapping victims—Fiction. | Ex-convicts—Fiction. |
   Life change events—Fiction. | Large type books.
Classification: LCC PS3557.R3978 R87 2018b | DDC 813/.54—dc23
LC record available at https://lccn.loc.gov/2018041777

(Had I done to Dolly, perhaps, what Frank Lasalle, a fifty-year-old mechanic, had done to eleven-year-old Sally Horner in 1948?)

And the rest is rust and stardust.
—*Lolita* BY VLADIMIR NABOKOV

Rust
&
Stardust

Camden, New Jersey
June 1948

SALLY

The girls at school had a club, a secret club with secret rules. Beyond the playground under the trees' dark leaves, they pressed their fathers' stolen blades against their plump thumbs, watched the blood bead before pressing their flesh together and swearing loyalty. Sally Horner spied them from the swings where she dragged her shoes in the dirt, her fingers pinched by the chains. She studied them as they stood in a circle, sucking the metallic blood, tongues working over those important wounds. She strained to hear their whispered oath, this sisterhood spell. Mesmerized.

At lunch later, she peered at them from the table in the cafeteria where she normally sat alone, nibbling at her butter sandwich or peeling back the golden skin of her butterscotch pudding. But her need to understand what sort of coven had been formed underneath those red oaks was irresistible, though it took her nearly ten minutes to pick up her lunch tray, go to their table, and speak to them.

"Mind if I sit here?" she said softly to the one whose hair reminded her of the white fluff inside of a milkweed pod, Irene, who looked up at her and then turned back to her friend.

"I saw you at recess," Sally tried again, smiling.

"You didn't see nothin'," the one with the red hair said. Bess was her name.

"I did. Over by the trees. It looked like—"

"What are you, some sort of *spy?*" Irene hissed. Her eyes were icy blue.

Sally shook her head, and cast her gaze down at her shoes. This was a mistake.

"It's a club," the third one chimed in. Sally looked up, and the girl was smiling at her. She had black hair and dark blue eyes, a widow's peak. She reminded Sally of Elizabeth Taylor. "A secret sisterhood. We took an oath."

Sally thought of her own sister, Susan, living all the way in Florence ever since she and Al got married. Sometimes at night Sally would wake up, expecting to see her in the other bed, only to remember that she didn't live there anymore. It made her heart feel hollow, like an empty tin can.

"You can sit here," the dark-haired girl offered, gesturing to an empty seat.

Nervous, Sally sat down, and Irene huffed, reluctantly scooting her chair over to make room, metal feet scraping against the linoleum.

"I'm Vivi," the brunette said, and reached out to shake Sally's hand. "You're in our grade, right?"

"She's been in our grade forever," Bess said, rolling her eyes. "She's the one whose daddy got drunk over at Daly's and then—"

14

"Would you like to join our club?" Vivi interrupted.

"Really?" Sally said.

"Vivi," Irene scolded, but Vivi scowled.

"I mean, that would be keen," Sally said, trying not to seem too eager. "If you're accepting new members."

Irene sucked the last of her milk through her straw and stood up, hands on hips, elbows sharp as blades. "Well, she'd have to be initiated. Not just *anybody* can join."

"What do I gotta do?" Sally asked.

"You need to steal somethin'," Bess said.

"From the Woolworth's." Irene seemed to improvise. "After school."

"Oh," Sally said, suddenly thinking this wasn't such a good idea. What if she got caught? Once, when she'd accidentally walked out of the market holding an apple she forgot to pay for, her mother marched her back in with a nickel and an order to confess her crime and made her do the dishes every night for a week to earn that nickel back.

Vivi looked at her apologetically.

Bess snapped, "You want to be in the club, this is whatcha gotta do. Otherwise, you can just forget about it, and stop followin' us around."

Sally felt her skin flush hot. She knew she wasn't like these other girls, the ones with glossy hair and perfect smiles. Sally wore homemade dresses and hand-me-down shoes, while these

15

girls got their clothes from the J.C. Penney. The shiny copper pennies they put in their loafers caught the sun. They were the keepers of light, Sally thought. Shining and bright.

These were the girls who lived inside the pretty houses near the school, with picket fences and lacy curtains. She could practically smell their pot roasts, their buttery potatoes, hear Doris Day's sweet clear voice on the radio through the open windows. Sally imagined their aproned mothers and gentle, soft-spoken fathers inside. Sally, on the other hand, lived alone with her mother in a run-down row house on Linden Street, both her real daddy and her stepfather, Russell, long gone. She knew the stories people told about her stepfather, heard the whispered speculations. (They heard he did it with a rope, in the closet. With a shotgun, in the basement. Someone, somewhere said *no,* he just got drunk as always and wandered from Daly's Café onto the train tracks one night—this one the tender, awful truth.)

She knew they whispered behind her back, mocked her. But Sally still ached to belong, and studied those girls with the same wonder and love with which she studied the laws of the universe. She thought them the sun, and herself simply a small and quiet planet in orbit around them. And she forgave them their meanness. It was no different than forgiving the sun its heat, the moon its tidal pull. This was simply the nature of girls. She knew they couldn't help themselves, and oddly, it made her love them all the more.

School would be out for the summer in just a couple of days. Perhaps, if she was in their club, she wouldn't have to spend her whole summer alone, the long hot days ahead something to look forward to rather than dread.

"Okay," she said, nodding and then thrusting her chin up confidently, surprised by her sudden gumption. "I'll do it. And then I can be in the club?"

"Sure," Irene said, shrugging, but she wasn't looking at her. "Meet us after school."

Usually, the last bell of the school day was a reason for celebration. But now, as she descended the school's front steps to the sidewalk, Sally felt dread in her stomach like a peach pit swallowed whole.

Those girls who never noticed her teemed about her now. There were six or seven of them suddenly, their faces bright with anticipation, with something like friendliness. As they smiled and chattered like happy birds gathering around a wriggling worm, she felt the pit begin to soften.

On any other day, she would have walked to the library or all the way home, alone, satchel swinging at her side, shoes pinching her toes, thighs rubbing together uncomfortably beneath

17

her skirt. But today, she was not alone, not lonely. Instead, she was swept up in the cheery and excited swell of these girls, which carried her down North 7th Street toward Federal. They were like bees, she thought, buzzing and fairly harmless alone, but thrumming and dangerous as a group. She was caught up in the magic of this swarm as they made their way to the Woolworth's.

At the corner of Broadway and Federal, the girls dispersed. Some went into the five-and-dime and sidled up to the counter to order cherry Cokes or root beer floats. Others lingered outside on the sidewalk, kicking at loose pieces of pavement before ducking around the corner to light cigarettes stolen from their mothers' packs. Sally wished she could stay with them, waiting for some other girl to be initiated.

"Go on," Irene, said, giving her shoulder a sharp little shove through the front door.

Inside, the fans chilled her. She swallowed hard and walked slowly beyond the lunch counter, empty save for Vivi and Bess and, at the end nearest the door, a hawklike man hunched over a bowl of split-pea soup. Irene joined them, and Vivi glanced up at Sally and winked. It made her skin burn hot again, but also gave her courage.

Past the lunch counter, she noticed the garden display and thought of her stepfather and the way he used to care for the postage stamp–

sized garden in front of their row house. How he'd teased tulips from the soil, azaleas, and even once a single large zucchini. Her fingers skipped across the seed packets: radishes, sweet corn, sugar peas. One of those envelopes would be easy, wouldn't it? Though maybe too easy to count? She felt as if she'd been invited to play a game, but that nobody was telling her the rules. Metal watering cans, rubber boots, and garden gloves. She walked down row after row of toys (BB guns and Matchbox cars and a Madame Alexander doll dressed up like Jo from *Little Women*). Her hand reached out and touched the doll, wishing for a moment it were her own. But she quickly withdrew her fingers, ashamed. What was she thinking about dolls for? She was eleven years old now.

She found baby clothes and baby bottles, cloth diapers and bibs. Her sister, Susan, was having a baby soon. Sally could hardly wait to meet her little niece or nephew. She wondered if she might find something here for the baby, some trinket or stuffed toy. But thinking of her sister made her think of her mother, and the peach pit returned. Her mother with her sorrow and her pain. Usually, Sally had made it her job to not cause her any grief. She tried not to think about how all of this would hurt her mama.

Shaking the thought out of her head, she walked quickly toward the stationery aisle and studied the pens and pencils. Again, probably too easy. But then, as she ran her hands over the fat pink erasers, she got an idea. At the five-cent display was a stack of black marble composition notebooks. Something she could use later. She liked to write stories, or maybe the club would need a secretary to take minutes at their meetings. She had beautiful handwriting. Everyone said so.

She quickly peered around. The man at the end of the lunch counter was pushing a dollar bill across with his check, tipping his hat to the waitress. The girls were still giggling and swinging their legs. Vivi smiled at Sally again and nodded.

Sally glanced back at the display of notebooks, picked one up, and touched the smooth surface with her thumb. She thought about blades, about the girls inviting her into their sisterhood. How they would let her press her thumb against theirs, their blood mingling, bonding them to each other. Blood sisters. She shivered at the thought of the slice that would splice them together forever.

Before she could give it another thought, she slipped the notebook inside her cardigan sweater and, crossing her arms, hurried toward the front of the store. There. She had done it. She felt giddy, light. She could hardly wait to get outside the store and show the girls. She headed toward the lunch counter where Vivi and the others were finishing their Cokes; they looked up at her as she neared. But just as she began to make her way to the front door, the man who had been eating the bowl of soup stood up and stepped in front of her.

"Slow down there, sweetheart," he said. She kept her head lowered and nodded. But as she tried to pass, he reached out and grabbed her by the arm. When she looked up, he was staring at her, a serious expression on his face. His eyes were nearly colorless, the blue of the thin milk her mother made from a powdered mix. He was wearing a faded fedora, which partially obscured his long, thin face.

"I'm sorry, miss, but you're going to need to come with me."

"What?" she asked.

"I saw what you just did."

"I'm sorry . . . I didn't mean . . . ," she stuttered, pulling the composition book out from her sweater, pushing it toward him. "I was gonna pay, I didn't plan . . . I just forgot . . ."

"Oh, I see," he said, grabbing the notebook from her. "You didn't *plan* on stealing it, eh? You also probably didn't plan on running into somebody from the FBI, either. You know what that is, miss?"

FBI? Of course she'd heard of the FBI. They were like the police, only more important. They had something to do with the president, didn't they? Or maybe she was just thinking of FDR? The one before President Truman?

"Yes, sir?" Her heart hammered in her chest; she held her breath.

"Well, I'm an FBI agent, and you, little miss, are under arrest."

With the man still clutching her arm, Sally scanned the lunch counter, looking for the girls, for Vivi, the nice one, to help her explain. It was all just a dare. An initiation. She hadn't meant any harm. But the girls were gone. And there weren't even any other customers milling about the store anymore. Where had everyone gone? She was alone now with this man and his long cigarette-stained fingers digging into the soft, pale mohair of her sweater.

"I'm gonna need for you to come with me," he said, tugging at her arm to pull her along.

"But my friends . . ." The word seemed to mock her. Where were these *friends* now? "I can't, please . . ."

"The courthouse is across the street, you know," he said. "They'll know what to do with a juvenile delinquent like you."

"No, please, sir."

They were walking together now toward the front of the store. She tripped, and he tugged at her arm, righting her. He tossed the composition book down on a display case and wordlessly guided her to the front door, holding it open with his free hand for an old woman who was coming in.

Outside, they stood on the street; across the way, the courthouse loomed before her. Was that where the jail was?

He still clutched her arm, standing close to her before gently nudging her down the street and around the corner into an alleyway. It smelled of garbage and motor oil.

"What's your name?" he asked, his voice like gravel. "I'll need it for my report."

"Florence Horner, sir. But I'm called Sally for short. Are you taking me to jail?" She wondered if it was even possible for her to go to jail. She was just a little girl. Her stepfather had spent the night in jail more than once, put in the drunk tank. She'd heard her mother whispering into the phone. Sally had been little the first time, thought her mother had said "dunk tank," and imagined her stepfather sitting happily waiting for someone to throw a bean bag at the target and send him plummeting into a tub of cold water. When she asked her mother why he had gone to the carnival without her, her mother had shaken her head. "He ain't at no circus. Fool's got himself locked up in jail again." The only other things Sally knew about jail she learned from the pictures she saw at The Savar: Abbott and Costello, black-and-white-striped uniforms, limbs tethered to heavy balls and chains.

Suddenly, a policeman came strolling down the

23

alley, and her heart jumped to her throat. Would the FBI man hand her over? Would the policeman put her in handcuffs right there?

"Afternoon, Officer," the FBI man said, tipping his hat as the policeman passed the entrance to the alleyway and spotted them.

Sally's eyes filled with tears.

"Everything okay here?" the officer said, stopping.

"Sure thing, sir," the FBI man said.

"What's the matter, little girl?"

Sally shook her head.

"My daughter's just upset I won't buy her an ice cream. Spoil her dinner. Her mother would string me up."

The officer chuckled, and nodded. "I *see.*" He came over, bent down so he was eye level with Sally, and wagged his meaty finger in her face. "You do as your daddy says, you hear?"

Sally nodded, tears escaping and rolling down her cheeks. Why was this man lying?

The officer stood upright again. "Got three of my own," he said to the FBI man. "Got me wrapped right around their little fingers."

The FBI man threw his head back, and his laughter sounded like a gunshot.

"You two have a nice afternoon," the policeman said, and walked back to the street, whistling.

"Listen up, Sally," the FBI man said, watching the officer walk away. He smiled a little, and she noticed his crowded teeth, like long thin tombstones.

"Yes, sir?" Sally said, blood pounding in her temples.

"You are a lucky girl," he said, peering in the direction the officer had gone before looking back at her. "Very lucky indeed that it was me who caught you instead of another G-man."

Lucky? This was one thing she knew she was not.

"Anybody else would have handed you right over to the law. But I like you, Sally," he said, still grinning. "And I'm pretty sure you're usually a good girl. So I'm willing to strike a deal with you."

She nodded. She *was* a good girl. Anything. She'd do anything at all if he'd just let her go home. He didn't loosen his grip on her arm, though.

"Here's the thing," he said, glancing up and down the alley again. "I want to keep you out of the reformatory, so what I need for you to do is to check in with me from time to time. Sort of like a parole officer. Have you heard of that before?"

Sally nodded, though she had no idea. It must be something to do with the FBI.

"Where do you go to school, Sally?"

"Northeast School," she said. "I'm just finishing the fifth grade. It's on Vine Street."

"Okay then," he said, and finally released her, though it felt like his fingers were still digging into her arm. This was how she felt when her mother had a bad morning and clung to her as she ascended the stairs before returning to bed. Sometimes, she'd feel her mother's clutching fingers all day long.

"Can I go home now?" Sally asked, and immediately regretted being so bold.

His face darkened, he hesitated, and for a moment she worried he'd changed his mind.

"Here's the arrangement," he said, his voice low and gritty like dirt. "You don't say a word of this to nobody. I'd be in a lot of trouble with the FBI if they found out I'm taking mercy on you after what you've done. Do you understand me?"

She nodded, still crying.

"I'll be waiting for you outside school tomorrow. To check in."

"Okay," she said. "I promise. Can I please go home now?"

He gripped her arm again, and this time she noticed a crescent moon–shaped scar across his hand. His face was scarred, too. It made her think of the scar she had on her leg from falling out of her high chair when she was a baby. It made her think of accidents.

"Not a word, Sally Horner. Because I can change my mind any time. And you *will* wind up in the reformatory. Understand?" His mouth was

26

close to hers now, so close she could smell the split-pea soup on his breath.

"I promise," she said, nodding.

"Now that's a good girl," he said, and smirked. Then his grip on her arm loosened, he shoved his hands in his pockets, and he left her there, walking swiftly, bowlegged across the street, toward the courthouse.

ELLA

The clock ticking loudly in the kitchen said four o'clock. Sally should have been home an hour ago. Sometimes she went to the library after school, but the school year was over tomorrow. The muggy air spoke of summer. Ella Horner wiped her wrist across her forehead, releasing her foot from the treadle, which accelerated the stitches across the endless swaths of cloth. She pushed herself to standing, every ligament and joint resisting.

Ella lived in a cage of pain. Though mornings were the cruelest. When she woke, she lay flat on her back, tears running down the sides of her face as she summoned the will to rise. Because as she slept, her body stiffened: knees, shoulders, wrists. Even her ribs, it seemed, became the delicate bars of a birdcage inside which her heart beat and beat, wishing open the hatch that might set her free. She couldn't remember what it felt like to move without the complaint and resistance of every joint. At forty-one, she was already an old woman, the rheumatism rendering her bones a virtual prison.

It began not long before Russell died: started in her knees and then crept through her marrow to her hips, across her shoulders, down into her elbows, and finally into her hands. But for some reason, it hadn't been so crippling when he was still around. He'd been a master of distraction, always cracking a joke when she most needed it. It was impossible to feel self-pity when Russell was there, swooping in. She remembered when both of her knees were so swollen they wouldn't bend, and he'd swept her up in his arms and danced her across the kitchen floor. He was drunk, and he'd knocked a full cup of coffee off the counter, but she'd forgotten the pain for the full length of "Velvet Moon," which he hummed softly in her ear. But now Russell was gone. Just a wink, a blink, and he'd disappeared, and the latch on the cage was locked again.

Sitting at the sewing machine all day (and sometimes deep into the darkest parts of the night) didn't help the pain, either. Still, the piecework arrived at her doorstep weekly, and when she completed it, she had only to set it outside their door before another package appeared. On the mornings when the simplest tasks seemed to require a level of stoicism she just could not summon, she stayed in bed, but the bundles arrived with or without her. Unfortunately, she had no other income-generating skills, but this way she could at least stay at home, sitting, rather than standing on her feet all day at some factory. Be here when Sally got home from school, like the other mothers in the neighborhood, the ones who still had husbands to bring home paychecks.

When Susan was still living at home, she had been there to help take care of Sally, and later, after the rheumatism set in, of Ella herself. But now that she and Al were married and Susan pregnant, her visits were limited to family dinners and occasionally taking Sally out with them to a picture show. And Sally was still just a child. Her life revolved around school and her studies; she was the student that neither Ella nor Russell had ever been. Ella had dropped out after her first year of high school, and Russell had only made it through the seventh grade. Whenever Ella felt abandoned, alone, she had to remind herself that this was what they had wanted for the girls. Every day, Sally came home from school practically buzzing with whatever she'd learned that day. *Mama, did you know your heart beats a hundred thousand times a day? That means it's beat over a billion times! And Mama, I read that dogs can smell a million times better than humans. Can you believe it? I wish we had a dog. Maybe we could get a dog some day? Oh, Mama, maybe a dog like Lassie. Remember when we went to see Elizabeth Taylor in* Courage of Lassie *last year? I just love Elizabeth Taylor . . .*

Sally, with her infinite curiosity and enthusiasm, was the single bright light in Ella's life, a solitary shining ray in a dimly lit room. But she was also easily distracted, a dreamer. So like

Russell, even though they weren't related by blood. *Sally,* Ella would reprimand, lest the child go on endlessly, *stop with your chitchat and help me fold this laundry.*

Now with the school year coming to an end, her hope was that Sally might be able to help out around the house more. She was eleven years old and fully capable of doing household chores. Having Sally home meant help with the dishes, the floors, the beds. She thought she might even teach Sally how to sew so that when her bones became as rigid as bricks, she could help with the endless work. And she'd be there to keep Ella company as well, just a little bit of sunshine.

The clock *tick, tick, ticked.* Four thirty. Where was that girl?

SALLY

When Sally emerged from the dark alleyway, the girls were gone. She looked up and down Broadway as if they would simply be waiting there for her, in front of the Woolworth's or the J.C. Penney across the street. She'd done what they'd asked, nearly gotten herself arrested in the process, but nobody had stuck around. They had to have seen she was in trouble, but not one of them waited to make sure she was okay. Not even Vivi.

As Sally ran home, her throat raw from crying, she thought of the notebook. The FBI man had tossed it down, like he didn't care about it at all. Then why, if it was so insignificant, had he demanded so much of her? All of this trouble, and she still had nothing to prove to the girls tomorrow that she'd passed their test. *Tomorrow.* The FBI man said he'd check in with her tomorrow. She wasn't free, not really. He'd only taken pity on her. The law was still the law.

The only other time she'd ever even been close to someone official like this was after her stepfather died. They'd come to the house in the middle of the night. She remembered thinking the noise was just the sound of her stepfather stumbling home; her mother's cries the same as on any night when he came home stinking of booze and (supposedly) other women. (Sally had once locked herself in the bathroom and pressed his clothes to her face, trying to smell what her mother smelled. Perfume? Skin? The only thing she'd been able to discern was the familiar ammonia scent; he cleaned houses for a living and carried the sharp stink of bleach in everything he wore.) But when she snuck to the top of the stairs and peered down at the foyer that night, it wasn't her stepfather bumping into the walls as he tried to remove his shoes. And it wasn't her mother, shoulders shaking, fist shaking, as she spat and cried. Instead, it was a police officer holding her mother in his arms. It confused her. Was this policeman in love with her mother? Was he going to kiss her? Her body felt hot with whatever this meant. But then her mother opened her mouth and a sound came out, a wail that sounded unreal, like the feral cats who lived in the alley behind their house, the ones that cried out in the night.

It wasn't until a week later, after the funeral, when she understood that her stepfather had gotten drunk and walked out in front of a train. People had seen him, said he did it on purpose. When she asked her mother if he was in heaven now, her mother had shaken her head, and said St. Peter didn't let in suicides.

• • •

The whole way home from Woolworth's, she rehearsed the story she'd tell her mother to explain why she was late. *Some girlfriends and me, we went and had cherry Cokes at the lunch counter. On account of it almost being summer, you know?*

Who?

You know, the usual gang . . . Bess and Vivi mostly.

And as she fabricated the dream, she could almost see herself sitting at the lunch counter, swinging her legs, sipping a syrupy soda pop through a red-and-white-striped straw. She imagined whispering something into Vivi's pink ear and Vivi flashing her a bright smile and a wink.

Or, perhaps, she should just tell her mother the truth. Tell her exactly what happened at the Woolworth's, explain that she'd only wanted to join their club. That she hadn't meant any harm. She might be a thief, but she didn't need to be a liar as well.

But when she let herself into the house, her mother wasn't waiting. She was upstairs in the bathtub; she could hear the water sloshing as her mother eased herself in. The hot baths were the only thing that brought her mother's body relief. Sally knew that when the water went cold, she'd call for her to help her out. It was embarrassing for them both, but they didn't talk about that. Or anything else that brought them shame.

SALLY

The next day, the last day of school, Sally sat in the front row of her fifth-grade class. She liked to be close to Mrs. Appleton, who was sweet and smelled exactly like green apples, which Sally thought was maybe how she'd gotten her name. Mrs. Appleton always called on Sally when she raised her hand and often asked her to come to the chalkboard to work out a math problem or diagram a sentence. Sally loved school, loved learning. She was always the first to raise her hand in class (though never with answers, only questions, questions), ignoring the collective rolling of her classmates' eyes.

Yes, Sally? Mrs. Appleton might ask.

How many stars are there? In the Milky Way? Has anyone counted?

No one knows for sure. Millions, I suppose. Does anyone else have questions?

Sally's hand would shoot up again. *Why are some of them brighter than others?*

Well, distance, for one. Stars that are closer to us seem to shine brighter. But some are simply more luminous.

And Sally would carry this knowledge with her, the word "luminous" at the tip of her tongue.

"You look *luminous,* Mama," she might say

to her mother, Ella, as she worked at her sewing machine at home, leaning in to embrace her hunched shoulders.

"Oh hush, Sally. That's ridiculous."

"It's *luminous*," she might say to Susan, as she painted the nursery a bright lemon yellow. And Susan would smile and touch her round belly. "Why, yes it is, Sally. That's exactly what it is."

At school, Sally liked to be front and center, where her view was unobstructed by anyone or anything. It had been her habit since she first started school. But today, Sally wished she could disappear into the back of the room, because it felt like *she* was the obstruction and twenty pairs of eyes were boring through her skull.

Vivi sat next to her (by assignment, not by design). She was always in the periphery of Sally's vision, but Sally never dared turn her head, to be caught staring at her. Though now, as Mrs. Appleton rifled through her desk drawer for something, Vivi leaned over and whispered in her ear.

"Did that old man take you to the police?" she asked.

Sally felt her face redden; her ears were so hot they itched. She shook her head. The girls *hadn't* forgotten her. At least Vivi hadn't.

Sally turned to look at Vivi, whose face seemed full of genuine concern. Perhaps she could tell her what the man had said, about reporting to him after school. Maybe she could share the promise she'd made to meet him, so that he wouldn't send her to a reformatory. But she had *sworn* to him that she wouldn't say a word. She hadn't even told her mother. Would he know if she told Vivi? She was then struck with the thought that he'd gotten hold of Vivi, too, and this was part of the test. Or worse, what if the man wasn't with the FBI at all, but rather someone Bess and Irene had convinced to trick her? What if this initiation was all a cruel joke? She didn't know which would be worse.

"Well?" Vivi insisted, but then Mrs. Appleton found what she'd been looking for and scowled at the girls over the tops of her dusty glasses.

"Tell me later?" Vivi asked, and Sally nodded.

But later, at recess, at lunch, and when the final school bell of the year rang out, Sally didn't say a word. She couldn't bring herself to tell Vivi, or anyone, what had happened, as if saying it aloud might conjure him again. Perhaps, if she never spoke of it, she could somehow undo it. Make him disappear back into the ether from which he came. And so when the final bell rang, she hid in a stall in the bathroom until the girls were all gone, until the hallways were empty, until she was pretty sure that no one but she and the teachers and the janitor remained. Then she slipped down the hall to the front doors. It crossed her mind that she might be able to hide here for the whole summer while school was out. She could eat in the cafeteria, sleep on the lumpy couch in the teachers' lounge. She would be safe here. Safe and sound. She shook her head. She was being silly. She needed to just go home.

As she walked out the front door, she gasped when someone grabbed her shoulder from behind.

"Sally," Mrs. Appleton said. "Have a wonderful summer, dear."

Sally muttered, "Thank you," then took a deep breath and peered up and down the street. She expected he'd be standing by the big cherry tree, maybe with a police car or whatever the men from the FBI drove. But the only car on the street was covered in rotting blossoms. It hadn't moved in weeks.

Was it possible he *wouldn't* come for her? That he'd only meant to scare her? She was a child, after all. Just a girl. The realization of this made her feel ashamed at her silliness, at her gullibility. Maybe it *had* all been a trick played on her. A cruel one, but just a prank.

She looked down the street again and, with a shuddering sort of cry, she wiped at her eyes and started to walk home. With each step farther away from school, the more certain she became. A rotten trick. Bess and Irene, such vicious girls. But Vivi, at least, had been considerate, the only one to check on her after. Vivi lived just a few blocks away from Sally's house; Sally thought maybe she'd walk down and knock on her door one day soon. See if she might like to go to the swimming pool at Farnham Park. She'd need to get a new swimsuit, though; the one from last year was busting at the seams. She wondered if Vivi liked to go to the movies. Sally adored the picture shows. *Homecoming* with Clark Gable and Lana Turner was in the theaters now. Clark Gable was so handsome. But not as handsome as Cary Grant. She saw *The Bishop's Wife* just last year with Susan, and they both swooned.

She began to skip. It was summer vacation. The months ahead held nothing but possibility.

When she got to the corner where she normally turned to head home, she briefly considered going on to the Woolworth's, where she was now almost positive Bess and Irene and the others were laughing at her expense over dripping hot fudge sundaes. She could imagine Vivi reprimanding them, defending Sally. Saying that Sally was actually really pretty keen. How wonderful would it be to show up, to sit down next to them, and say, *You got me!* Wouldn't that be grand? She giggled thinking of it, even pantomimed their surprise.

"Sally," he said, stepping in front of her.

Her heart stopped like a cork in her throat.

He was wearing the same pale blue shirt and black jacket as yesterday, his tie knotted loosely.

In the bright sunlight she could see his face more clearly now, though he still wore the broad-brimmed fedora. The scar on his face she'd noticed before was also sharper, slicing his cheek in two like a jigsaw puzzle.

"Listen up. There's been a change of plans. The government says I've got to deliver you to headquarters."

Sally felt her knees weaken. Bile rose to her throat, but she was too afraid to spit it out, and so she swallowed it back down, burning. She shook her head.

"To the courthouse?" she asked.

He laughed and patted her on the back. "If only it were that easy, darling. You see, they're at the shore. Atlantic City."

"Oh no," she said. "I can't leave Camden, my mama would never let me. She's sick. She needs me to help at home." Sally shook her head. "My sister's about to have a baby."

But then he pulled back his coat, and Sally could see the butt end of a gun sticking out from his waistband. Her vision started to darken around the edges.

"Here's what you're gonna do," he said.

ELLA

Ella was hunched over the sewing machine in the dusty dining room when Sally ran through the front door.

"Mama," she said, coming to her and throwing her arms around her.

"Careful, careful," Ella said, wincing. Sally loved her mother with an intensity that embarrassed Ella. Since she was a small child, she'd clung to her in a way Susan never had. Perhaps it was because she didn't have a daddy; after Russell died, it was as if the love Sally had felt for him needed a place to be directed, and Ella became the vessel into which Sally poured her giant heart. Sally's affection was like something liquid. Brimming.

"What's the matter with you?" Ella asked, shrugging her off, aware that both her words and this gesture came out meaner than she meant for them to.

Sally hesitated and then sat down in the chair next to Ella.

"I've been invited. To the shore," she said, her eyes imploring. "To go with my friend's family."

Ella scowled. Sally never talked about girlfriends before. Never had anyone come over, never had she been asked to play at anyone's

41

house. She was a lonely girl, just as Ella had been as a child.

"What friend?" Ella asked, taking her reading glasses off and setting them next to her sewing machine. She still had hours to go, a million stitches.

Sally bit her lip and looked around the room almost nervously.

"What's the matter with you?" Ella asked. "Lord, you are acting strangely."

"Vivi?" Sally said, eyebrows raised. "Vivi Peterson?"

"I don't know no Petersons," Ella said, shaking her head.

"They're real nice," Sally said. "And they've invited me on their family's holiday. To the shore." Sally was sweating; Ella watched the beads of perspiration form on her upper lip.

"Take your sweater off," Ella said.

Sally slipped her cardigan off and hung it over the back of the dining room chair. Poor Sally, this moonfaced girl with dull hair and pale eyes; so plump and earnest. So eager to please. *What would become of this girl?* Would she wind up the way Ella had, marrying the first boy to give her a compliment only to be left ten years later with two young children to raise? Would she be duped, as Ella had been, by a charming drunk who wrecked everything he touched?

"Who's gonna help me around the house while you're away?" Ella asked.

"Susan?" Sally said, though she had to have known that was unlikely. Susan was caught up in her own new life. Not just married now, expecting, but also helping run her husband's family's greenhouse. Sally's voice sounded peculiar as she continued, "Vivi said the shore's so lovely this time of year. We're going to stay at a fancy resort hotel right on the boardwalk."

Ella slipped her glasses back on and peered down at the stitches she'd made; sometimes after she'd been sewing for a few hours, they started to look like train tracks. Two parallel lines moving endlessly across the vast fields of fabric, those rolling hills of brown and green.

"How long they keepin' you?" she asked, softening. A vacation at the shore. It did sound lovely.

Sally shook her head. "I don't know, Mama. Maybe a week?"

She couldn't give Sally much, but she could give her this. After all, she *was* still just a child. And now someone was showing an interest in being her friend. How could she deny her this?

"What did you say her name was again? Peterson?"

"Yes, Mama. He said he'll call you tonight. I gave him our telephone number. We'll take the bus to Atlantic City tomorrow."

"Who?"

"Mr. Peterson," Sally said, blinking hard, speaking slowly. "Vivi's father. Vivi and her mother are already there. He had to stay behind in Camden for work one more day."

"They go to our church?" Ella asked, though after Russell's funeral she'd been too ashamed to show her face in church, suffering through the whispers and stares only on Easter and Christmas.

"I don't know, Mama."

Ella looked up at Sally, whose eyes were now spilling tears down her cheeks. It embarrassed Ella to see her like this, and so she pressed her foot on the treadle and busied her hands. "Let me talk to this girl's father."

SALLY

The next morning, Sally packed the little red suitcase her mother found in the downstairs coat closet, wondering how one packs for a courtroom trial. Because that was where he said he was taking her. He was going to deliver her to the FBI headquarters in Atlantic City to stand before a judge, where she'd get a chance to plead her case. If the judge took pity on her, he might release her then and there. Let her go. She could get back on a bus to Camden straight away. Her mama would never be the wiser.

"I'll testify on your behalf, of course," he'd said. "But you still need to be prepared for the worst-case scenario." He'd warned her the judge might not show any leniency at all; she was a felon, after all. "You got any idea what the punishment is for stealing? Larceny's a federal crime."

Clean white blouses, her school skirts, bleached bobby socks, and her hairbrush. She sobbed as she closed her suitcase, which did not seem to want to be shut. She peered around her room, the one she and Susan had shared. Where they'd huddled together during thunderstorms and suffered through summer heat. (Susan gathered bowls of ice and situated them in front of the one feeble fan they shared; they stripped down to their underwear and lay sweating on top of their bumpy chenille spreads.) In this room, she'd watched Susan put makeup on and carefully select the dresses she wore when she went out on dates. Those nights, Sally stayed awake, waiting for her to come home. When she did, Sally tried to guess where she'd been simply from the scent she carried with her: the faint buttery smell that meant a movie, the fresh grass scent of a midnight picnic, and once, a musky, meaty scent she didn't recognize. That night Susan had scribbled furiously in her journal for nearly a half hour before turning out the little pink glass lamp on her nightstand. Sally swore she could hear Susan's heart beating that night, though perhaps it was only the rhythmic clacking sound of the wheels of the train. Susan's bed had been neatly made since her wedding to Al. That night, when she and her mother had come home from the reception, Sally had carefully untucked her mother's hospital corners, slipped into Susan's bed, and cried until the pillowcase was damp.

If she were in the club with those girls, she might have one of them come to stay over. If she hadn't gotten caught stealing the notebook, she might be planning to invite Vivi over for a sleepover right now instead of packing her suitcase to go to jail. She looked at the empty bed, and it seemed to mock her.

"Hurry up, Sally," her mother hollered up the stairs. "We're supposed to meet Mr. Peterson at the bus depot in fifteen minutes."

Sally stared at her reflection in the mirrored vanity where Sue once demonstrated how to make hunter's bow lips. *Oh Sally, you look just like a young Lauren Bacall,* Susan had marveled, and Sally had blushed so deeply she didn't even need the crème rouge Susan offered.

"Sally!" her mother hollered again. "It's time to go."

ELLA

Ella and Sally made their way to the bus depot, each step causing agonizing pains to shoot up Ella's legs.

"You okay, Mama?" Sally asked.

Ella nodded. She'd learned a long time ago that complaining didn't do anybody any good. And it certainly didn't take the pain away.

"Are you sure you're gonna manage okay without me?" Sally persisted. "Because maybe I don't have to go."

"You call me when you get there," Ella said. "I'm sure the hotel has a telephone. Just ask the operator to reverse the charges."

Ella had gotten dressed that morning with extra care, powdered her face, and put on her Sunday clothes, noting that the buttons struggled to stay inside their respective buttonholes; the fabric stretched and complained. She'd tried to recall the last time she'd walked this far and couldn't. When she spoke to Mr. Peterson on the phone, he said he was so pleased his daughter would have another girl to pal around with at the shore. He seemed like a real gentleman. When he suggested Ella walk Sally to the bus depot, where he would meet them, she was too embarrassed to explain her poor health, and instead agreed.

It was a lovely June day; she expected they'd have beautiful weather at the beach. When she and her first husband, Bobby, were courting, he'd taken her to Atlantic City once. She'd basked in that glorious sun and gotten such a terrible sunburn, her skin had bubbled and she'd had to bathe in oatmeal for a week.

"You got a sun hat?" she asked Sally.

"Yes, Mama," Sally said.

"You make sure you use an umbrella at the beach. And watch out for the undertow. It'll suck you right under if you ain't careful."

Sally was staring at her feet as they scuffed along the sidewalk. What on earth was wrong with this girl?

"You be polite. You say 'please' and 'thank you,' and you keep a napkin in your lap during meals, you understand?"

"Mama, I'm not feeling so well. Maybe, maybe I should stay home?" she said. "I can always go to the shore another time."

Ella stopped walking and scowled. "What is the matter with you, Sally Horner? You act like you're walking to your own funeral."

Sally's lip quivered. There'd be waterworks soon if Ella didn't put her foot down now.

"Just imagine all the amazing things you'll get to see, Sally. You're a lucky girl. Don't you

49

forget that. And don't forget your manners, either."

At the bus depot, the man, Mr. Peterson, was standing with a pretty young woman in a peach-colored suit, her shiny blond hair done up in two victory rolls. He set down a battered valise next to his own suitcase, tipped his hat, and extended his hand.

"Pleasure to make your acquaintance, ma'am," he said, smiling. "This is my assistant, Miss Robinson. I've asked her to come along, since Miss Sally here is a minor and all. It wouldn't be proper, otherwise."

Ella nodded. *Yes, what a gentleman,* she thought. How nice for Sally to be associating with such people. But Sally clung to her when the bus arrived, her body trembling. This was what she wanted, wasn't it? A girlfriend to spend time with? It was what Ella had wanted at that age. What she wouldn't have given to spend a week at the shore with nothing more to worry about than keeping the sun out of her eyes.

"Come on now, Sally. You're making a spectacle of yourself," Ella said, blushing at Mr. Peterson, who stood patiently waiting and pretending not to notice this display.

"I'll be home soon, Mama," Sally said, as Miss Robinson reached out for Sally's bag.

"You call me soon as you get there," Ella said,

nodding. "Thank you for having her along, Mr. Peterson."

"Please. Call me Frank," he said, and held out his hand to help Sally onto the bus. "And the pleasure's all mine."

SALLY

Sally and the lady in the peach suit sat side by side on the bus to Atlantic City. The FBI man sat across the aisle from them smoking, and the lady read a *Life* magazine. Sally leaned her head against the warm window and squinted until the trees became a blur of green, rehearsing what she would say to the judge when she got a chance to plead her case.

"You like magazines?" Miss Robinson asked, offering it to her.

Sally nodded, though she preferred *Photoplay* and *Movie Life.*

The lady had bright white teeth and a dimple below her eye that was shaped like a tiny star. Sally thought maybe she would be able to convince her she wasn't a bad girl. A criminal. That it had all been a terrible mistake. And maybe Miss Robinson could explain to Mr. Warner, that was what he said his name was, though now she was confused, because she'd been calling him Mr. Peterson for her mother's sake.

The magazine had a picture of a girl about Sally's age on the cover, sitting Indian style, wearing a long-sleeved shirt with a hood attached and shiny sandals. She was on a beach, a swath of white sand and a battered fence behind her. Was this what girls were wearing at the beach these days? She'd only ever been to the ocean twice: once last summer with Susan and Al and once when she was still a baby (she didn't remember that trip, but there was a photograph she'd found in the back of her mother's closet when she was snooping). In the photo, there was a man with huge hands holding her, but his head was outside the photo's frame. The man was their real father, Bobby Swain, but she had no memories of him. He left them just a few months after that picture was taken, and then her mother had met Russell. She couldn't remember her real father's face, and wondered if he might look like one of the movie stars she loved. Jimmy Stewart maybe, or Humphrey Bogart? She told her mother once that she could remember him singing to her, but her mother said that was impossible. She must be confusing him with Russell. First, because her real daddy took off when she wasn't even two years old, and second because *Russell* was the musician; Bobby Swain couldn't carry a tune. That phrase had captivated her. It made it sound like music was something you could hold in your hands.

"You ever been to Atlantic City before?" Miss Robinson asked, startling Sally.

Sally shook her head.

"Me neither," she said. "I hear there's a diving

horse. It leaps from a platform two stories up. Can you believe it? Maybe you can go see it with your girlfriend?"

Sally scowled, confused.

"Frank told me that you all are going to the beach to meet his family. That you and his daughter go to school together."

Sally struggled to make sense of what she was saying. This was the story he'd told her to tell her mother, the lie so that she wouldn't know what a terrible thing Sally had done. It was to protect her, he said. How ashamed would her mother be to know she had raised a juvenile delinquent? But Sally had assumed that Miss Robinson, as his assistant, knew that she was being arrested. Why would he lie to her if she worked for the FBI, too?

She had been afraid to look at Mr. Warner, who hadn't said a word to her the whole way there. She stole a glance now. His hat was tipped down to cover his face, his bony hands folded in his lap as though he'd fallen asleep while he was saying a prayer.

"I'm most excited about the shows, of course, seeing as how I'm planning on becoming an actress. All the talent agents from New York City summer in Atlantic City, you know. Looking for girls. Frank says he can help me get all the way to Broadway, if you can imagine that. No way I'm gonna be dancin' for dimes my whole life."

Words popped from Miss Robinson's mouth like soap bubbles.

Sally was completely puzzled. What was she talking about? Did she plan to quit her job with the FBI to become an actress? Sally looked at Mr. Warner again, and she was close enough to hear the soft rumbles of a snore. She turned back to Miss Robinson, who was peering at her reflection in a cracked compact, moving her head this way and that to see herself from all angles.

"Ma'am?" Sally said, and felt tears stinging her eyes; she'd promised herself she wouldn't cry. That she wouldn't pity herself; it was nobody's fault but her own what happened at the Woolworth's.

"Oh, don't cry, sweetheart," Miss Robinson said, gazing away from the mirror to look at Sally.

Sally lowered her voice until it was barely a voice at all. "It's just that my sister's having a baby soon. I'm going to be an aunt. She told me I could babysit for her. That she'd pay me so that she and Al could go out dancing every now and again. If I miss it . . . if I'm not there . . ."

"How lovely," Miss Robinson said, seeming confused. She hesitated, then pulled a handkerchief from her blouse, offering it to Sally. "Are you homesick already, sweetheart?"

Sally nodded. She took the handkerchief and caught the tears before they fell.

"I'm a little homesick, too," Miss Robinson said, and squeezed Sally's hand. "I come from Philadelphia. That's where my people are."

Sally glanced at the man again. His small chest rose up and down, his snores like soft whistles.

"Do you know how long they might keep me?" Sally said softly, just barely above a whisper.

"What's that, doll?" Miss Robinson asked, clicking her compact closed.

"How long I gotta be locked up?" she whispered. "I'm supposed to start the sixth grade this fall."

Miss Robinson cocked her head. "Whatever do you mean?" she asked. *"Locked up?"*

Sally's stomach somersaulted. Didn't she know Sally was on her way to the courthouse? What sort of awful place would he be taking her if his own assistant couldn't know?

But just as she was about to explain, across the aisle, Mr. Warner let out a loud snore, which startled Sally and rattled him awake. He plucked the hat from his face and turned to them; Sally felt faint. He looked at his watch and leaned across the aisle.

"Just another half hour to go," he said.

Atlantic City, New Jersey
June 1948

⤮

SALLY

ATLANTIC CITY: AMERICA'S FAVORITE PLAYGROUND, the sign said as they stepped off the bus. And Sally thought of the playground at school, of those girls and their sisterhood beneath the trees. How could she have been so foolish? What she wouldn't give to go back to that moment when she sat on the swings, watching them from afar.

Carrying their suitcases, she and Miss Robinson followed Mr. Warner down the crowded boardwalk along the beach. He walked quickly, a few paces ahead, and she had to practically run to keep up. Miss Robinson smiled at her sympathetically, though she was the one wearing heels, and Sally just had on her old pair of loafers.

Shops and restaurants lined one side of the boardwalk, and on the other was the beach, the Atlantic Ocean as vast and blue as the sky. The beach was filled with people, the sand littered with colorful umbrellas. The boardwalk was bustling with activity as well, and Sally looked around anxiously at all the people, families and teenagers out for a day of fun. A group of girls about her age was walking their way, each of them holding a towering cone of pale pink cotton candy. They leaned into each other, giggling and skipping. She felt a surge of longing as they passed by her as if she were nothing but a ghost.

"Coming through!" someone hollered, and to Sally's left a man pushing a bright yellow wicker cart rushed by her, nearly knocking her over. Her hand flew to her chest. The female passenger in the cart looked back over her shoulder at Sally and mouthed, *Sorry!* The woman looked just like her sister, and Sally's wildly bobbing heart became a lead sinker.

"You two hungry?" Mr. Warner asked as they arrived at a vendor selling franks.

"No, thank you," Miss Robinson said, smiling. "I'm watching my figure."

"I'll take one," he said to the vendor. "Extra onions and mustard. Sally?"

Sally felt too sick with worry to eat. She was hungry, however, and so when the vendor handed her the little paper cup of Italian ice and winked at her—*on the house*—she nodded and accepted it. She used the flat wooden paddle to scrape at the cherry-flavored ice. But it was too sweet and melted too quickly in the muggy heat.

When they arrived at the Hotel Clarendon, Sally couldn't believe how beautiful it was. How grand. It looked like a castle, with turrets and red-and-white-striped awnings. This was where they'd be staying? Mr. Warner had said it might be a few days before she was able to see the judge, but she had no idea where he would keep her until then. Maybe it wouldn't be so terrible after all. She could at least *pretend* she was on a lovely vacation at the shore.

In the cool lobby, he said to them, "Wait here," then marched up to the counter.

She and Miss Robinson sat on a velvet circular settee that was soft against her bare legs. She hadn't realized how tired she was until she sat down. If she were to lie down on this soft cushion right now, she might just fall asleep. She peered at Miss Robinson and thought about asking if she knew when she would get to see the judge. Mr. Warner had assured her that if she just told the judge how sorry she was, all of this mess would be over. She'd get back on the bus and head home to her mother in no time. She felt terrible about lying to her, but it was better this way. Her mama would never know the truth.

"As soon as I'm checked in I'm going to go see what's happening at the Steel Pier," Miss Robinson said, touching up her lipstick again in her compact. "All the best performers play there. Tommy Dorsey. Peggy Lee. *Frank Sinatra.* Do you like music?"

Sally thought of her stepfather. He had cleaned houses during the day, but at night, he played trumpet in a jazz quartet. He loved music. He was always humming something. When he died, her mother dragged his old Philips record player out onto the porch, along with his collection of 78s. They sat out there all summer long until one day Susan salvaged them, brought the record player and the collection up to their room. But when she put the record on, it sounded ghostly. The vinyl had melted, warped, in the heat. When they listened to Duke Ellington and Johnny Mercer, the strange mournful lament of those damaged records, it was like all their sadness was trapped in the grooves.

"Got you a room with a view!" Mr. Warner said, dangling a key from his finger. "The talent agent will meet you here in the morning to conduct the audition. I got a good feeling about this, kid. Make sure you get your beauty rest tonight."

Sally had no idea what Mr. Warner was talking about.

"Will I be staying with Miss Robinson?" Sally asked hopefully. She liked Miss Robinson. She was gentle and kind. Perhaps they could go together to listen to music on the pier. *Frank Sinatra.* She'd seen him with Gene Kelly in *Anchors Aweigh* a couple years ago. Was it possible he was here in the very same city she was?

"Well, of course not," Mr. Warner said. "We're meeting my wife and daughter at the other hotel. Not quite so fancy as this one here." He winked at Miss Robinson, who smiled coyly.

Wife and daughter?

"Well, my dogs are certainly tired," Miss Robinson said, slipping off her shoe and rolling her ankle.

"I always say nothing cures tired dogs like a good cat nap," Mr. Warner said, and chuckled.

"Pleasure to meet you, Sally," Miss Robinson said. "I hope you get to see that diving horse."

Sally's stomach turned. Why couldn't they stay here? This hotel seemed so nice. And wasn't Miss Robinson here to chaperone?

Outside, Mr. Warner grabbed Sally's arm. He steered her up Virginia Avenue and then turned onto Pacific Street, walking briskly eastward. Alone with Mr. Warner now, she felt anxious, scared. She wondered if she'd see Miss Robinson again. She was his secretary, after all. Or was she?

As they walked, she realized she could see the shore from here, and a towering structure ahead at the corner of Pacific and Vermont.

"That there's the Absecon," he said, noticing her looking up at it. "One of the oldest light-houses in the country."

Sally had read about lighthouses but had never seen one in real life. Lighthouses were made for sailors, the beacons of light to guide them home. She thought about home; maybe this shining light might lead her mother to her. It was foolish, she knew, but the idea brought an odd, momentary comfort.

"Been out of commission for years. Real eyesore as far as I'm concerned."

Eyesore. At the word, Sally's eyes stung and blurred.

"Sir?" she asked.

"Yeah?"

"When are you taking me to the courthouse?"

He stopped short, and she nearly tripped over him. He turned to her, his milky eyes softer now. "Well, you see, there's been a slight change of plans."

Maybe the change in plans was that he would take her home. Maybe that was why they didn't check into the hotel. Was this the way back to the bus depot?

"Mister, I'm real sorry about the notebook, sir. I swear I'll never ever steal anythin' from anywhere ever again." She didn't even care about that stupid club anymore. She just wanted to go home.

At this, he chuckled, and for a moment she thought he might just pat her on the back and say, *I know it, Sally. I hope you learned your lesson.* But instead, he gestured to a rundown house across the street, the brass numbers *203* nailed to the front, a cardboard sign in the window: ROOMS FOR RENT. Could this be where his wife and daughter lived? Or was that not a true story? She could barely keep track of the lies anymore.

"There's been a bit of a delay in scheduling the

hearing. Meanwhile, we're going to stay here."

"Here?" she asked, looking at the dilapidated row house.

"Now, you come with me, and let me do the talking."

He ushered her across the street and took the steps up to the front porch two at a time, gesturing for her to follow. He rapped his knuckles against the door, and a large woman with large hands and legs like the trunks of a tree answered the door. Was this his wife?

Mr. Warner thrust out his hand. "Name's Frank Warner. This here's my daughter, Florence."

The woman put her hands on her hips and tilted her head, like she was waiting for the rest. She peered at Sally, who looked down at her feet.

"Her mother's just passed, you see," Mr. Warner continued. "Couldn't bear to be in the family house no more. We're in need of a place to stay for a week or so. I thought a little holiday at the beach might cheer the poor girl up."

Sally looked up again. The woman in the doorway was taller than most men, but she seemed to soften, if only momentarily. She spoke with a heavy accent. "I am Mrs. Krauss. Rooms are twenty dollars a week. No gambling, no music, no guests."

Mr. Warner nodded and reached for Sally's hand, gripping it so tightly her fingers ached.

"My mother died when I was just a girl, too,"

she said to Sally. "You're lucky to have your father still." And with that, she opened the front door, wide enough for the two to pass through. Frank took Sally's suitcase in one hand, his in the other, his valise tucked under his arm, and followed Mrs. Krauss into a kitchen and then up a narrow stairwell to the second story.

The whole house smelled of cabbage and vinegar. The wallpaper was yellowed and curling; the floors felt almost soft beneath their feet. The air was damp. A toilet flushed, and pipes moaned behind the walls.

"Breakfast is included, but not the other meals. There's a washroom down the hall with a bathtub and toilet. Be considerate of the other guests, and if you don't want nothing stolen, keep the door locked. I try to keep the criminals out, but better safe than sorry."

She reached into her pocket, pulled out a key, and handed it over to Mr. Warner. "Lock's a double-key deadbolt. You'll need the key on the inside and the outside, so don't lose it." Then without another word, she waddled back down the hallway and disappeared into the stairwell.

"Here we are," he said, as he fitted the key into the lock and opened the door, which creaked on its hinges. The room was small and dusty, musty. Twin beds, a small desk and chair, a braided wool rug on the floor, and a window that looked out toward the lighthouse. Mr. Warner set their suitcases down, and Sally stood still, unsure of what she should do next. Her chest felt heavy.

"Sit down," he said, pointing to the bed. Sally sat at the foot of the farthest bed and crossed her feet at her ankles like she'd been taught to do in church.

Mr. Warner paced back and forth across the floor. She noticed his shoes were scuffed, the hems of his slacks frayed. He took off his hat and set it on the bureau, taking a cursory look in the beveled mirror hanging crookedly above, running his hand over his sparse hair.

"Listen up, Sally," he said, turning to her. "Until your court date, you're officially under arrest. You're in my custody, do you understand?"

Sally didn't understand. Not at all. But she nodded, because she was too afraid to ask him the questions that were burning on her tongue. Like why weren't they staying with Miss Robinson? And when *exactly* would she see the judge? Where would he sleep?

"I gotta go out for a bit. I've got some business to attend to," he said. "But while I'm gone, I'm gonna need you to make sure you don't get any funny ideas about escaping."

"No, sir," she said, shaking her head. "I promise I won't go anywhere. I just want to see the judge and tell him I'm sorry."

Mr. Warner stopped pacing and turned to her. He squatted down so that he was eye level with her. He was close enough that she could smell the onions from his lunch.

"I trust you, Sally," he said, cocking his head. "You got to understand, I know you're a good girl in your heart. Seems to me you just got caught up with some delinquents. Way I see it, this is a *learning lesson.* If I had my way, if *I* were the judge, I'd give you a good talking-to, a little slap on your wrist, and send you on your way."

She nodded. *Please, please,* she thought. *Please let me go?*

"But," he said, standing up abruptly. "I'm just the one that enforces the law. I took an oath, Sally. You understand what that is?"

An *oath.* That was what the girls had called it, the girls with the blades. A blood oath, swearing to be sisters forever.

"A promise, sir?"

His face brightened and he clapped his hands together. "Yes, ma'am. A promise. I'm bound by my oath to uphold the law. Which means, I got to do whatever I can to make sure you don't run away before you meet the judge. No matter how much I trust you, and I do trust you, Sally Horner, I got to do this, because it's my sworn duty." And with that he went to his valise, unlocked it, and pulled out a thick rope. It made her think of the skipping song the girls sang. She could practically hear Irene with her high sweet voice as she stood at one end of the rope while

Bess stood at the other: *Not last night but the night before, twenty-four robbers came knocking at my door* . . . And her heart beat, *knock, knock.*

He motioned for her to go to the chair by the window and gently pulled her hands behind her. *As I ran out, they ran in, knocked me on the head with a rolling pin.* Vivi would jump out, then in.

"Am I hurting you?" he asked.

She shook her head and squeezed her eyes shut. The rope was tight around her wrists.

"I won't be long," he said. "I promise. And I'm real sorry I got to do this. I know you're a good girl. I know, I do. I'm just doin' my job, see?"

She opened her eyes when she heard him shuffle over to the door. He glanced at her and smiled apologetically. *I asked them what they wanted and this is what they said . . .*

He came back over to her and squatted down again, reached out, and tucked a stray curl behind her ear. She flinched at his touch, felt her body flushing with heat. Tears filled her eyes.

"Oh, please don't be sad, Sally. What can I get for you? I'll bring you a treat. On account of you being so agreeable. Saltwater taffy maybe? Something sweet for my sweet girl?"

SUSAN

When they pulled up at Susan's mother's house for dinner on Friday night, Al had to help her out of the car. The baby wasn't due until August, but she had already gained nearly forty pounds. Everything was swollen: her hands, her fingers, her ankles. The night itself seemed bloated. She was miserable in this sticky heat. It was only June; she couldn't bear to think of what July and August might bring. And while she was excited for the baby to come, she sometimes wondered if it was too soon. After the war, Al came home and they'd gotten married right away. She was barely a wife; she could only dream of what it meant to be someone's mother.

"Don't forget the pie," she said.

"Got it," Al said, reaching into the backseat. He held out his free arm for her, and they walked up the steps to the door. "Ready?"

Ready as she'd ever be for another Friday night with her mother. She and Al had only been dating for a few months when he got called up to the Navy, but back then Friday nights were reserved for going out, for getting *away* from this house. And while Camden wasn't Philadelphia, it had its share of things to do: dinners at Jake's, movies, or a show. Every now and then they'd go dancing at Jimmy's Tavern. Before she got pregnant, Susan was a good dancer. And Al was the best. As they Lindy Hopped across the floor, she knew they turned heads; she saw the envy in other girls' eyes as he gazed into hers as if she were the only pretty girl in the world. At least he still looked at her the same way, even though she felt like a Macy's Thanksgiving Day Parade balloon.

"Oh, this looks just awful," Susan said, gesturing to the little dirt plot in front of the house. It had been a few weeks since they'd been to visit; it had been busy at the greenhouse now that summer had arrived. "We really need to remember to bring her some annuals at least next time. Maybe some zinnias?"

People came from all over to buy seedlings for their gardens, potted plants, flowers, shrubs, and trees from Al's family's greenhouse. Since they took over the business, Susan had become somewhat of an amateur botanist. Before, she'd never known the difference between an annual and a perennial; now she could tell you the growing season for everything from cabbage to corn. She spent her days helping people pick out the best plants to grow in the shade, the best bushes to attract butterflies, and the best houseplants for cat owners. She loved the greenhouse, the way it smelled like earth and all things fertile. She didn't mind getting her hands dirty, although it meant a permanent thin black line of dirt under her nails even after going at them with an old toothbrush and soap each night. She felt useful at the nursery.

Russell had loved gardening, too. He'd turned that tiny front yard into something magical; hummingbirds used to come by the dozens, wings beating, tiny bodies vibrating and trilling at the geraniums that grew in crimson bursts in the window boxes. Fireflies hid in the bushes he planted. Children from the neighborhood plucked strawberries from the plants that crept near the sidewalk. But after Russell passed, her mother let the weeds consume the tiny plot, and eventually most everything but the stubborn perennials died.

Susan had few memories of Bobby Swain, her real father, and the ones she had were like those fireflies flickering in the hedges: just bright flashes, illuminating the night before being extinguished again. Memories of Russell were the ones that lingered, that buzzed and thrummed like a hummingbird before flitting away again; she recalled dancing on his feet across the kitchen floor, the clink of ice in his glass, the way he made silly faces at her in church until she could barely contain her laughter. The sound of his trumpet rising up from the basement where he and his bandmates practiced until all hours of the night. Sally had adored Russell, too. He'd play Go Fish with her, Chinese jump rope. Hide-and-seek. *One, two, three,* he'd count, covering his eyes with his hands as Sally looked for a hiding place in their small house. *Where could she be?* he'd ask, opening the icebox door, the medicine cabinet, as she tittered inside the linen closet or hamper. Sally and Susan had both loved Russell as if he were their real father. They'd felt just as betrayed as her mother had when he did what he did. But it had been five years now, more than enough time to grieve. Life would move on, *had* moved on, without him in it, but her mother seemed stuck in the muck of her heartache.

"It's still warm," Al said, smiling at her, lifting the rhubarb pie to his nose and inhaling.

"You know she's going to complain about there not being any strawberries in it."

Susan had used Ella's recipe for the crust with cold butter and ice water to make it flaky. Ella had taught her how to navigate a kitchen, and she was grateful. Her best friend, Cynthia, didn't even know how to turn on the oven when she first got married. If it hadn't been for the local diner down the street, she and her husband might have starved to death that first year. Ella might not have been warm and loving like other mothers, but she had made sure Susan had the knowledge she would need later in life. But now Susan had gone and forgotten the strawberries, and so the pie seemed like a big mistake.

It felt odd ringing the doorbell at her own home, but since she'd left the house, it hadn't felt right to just barge in anymore, and so she and Al stood at the doorstep like visitors instead of family. Sally was the one who usually greeted them, skipping down the steps or running from the back of the house, skidding across the wood floors in her socks, so she was surprised when her mother opened the door.

"Come in, come in. Don't let the mosquitoes inside," Ella said.

"Hi, Ma," Al said, and kissed Ella's cheek. He took the pie to the kitchen, while Susan hugged her mother and studied her face to gauge the pain. Her mother's rheumatism had gotten worse in the last few years since Russell died, as if all that bitterness she felt about his suicide had seeped into her marrow. Al (wonderful Al) had offered to take her to see a specialist in Philadelphia, someone who might know how to alleviate the pain, which varied from mildly irritating to crippling depending on the day of the week, or the weather. But Ella had dismissed the idea as she dismissed anything she didn't want to think about.

"Where's Sally?" Susan asked as she slipped off her shoes, the delicious relief of which she couldn't have anticipated.

"At the shore. With a girlfriend."

Susan looked up, surprised. Despite being such a sweet, happy girl, she knew Sally didn't really have many friends. She spent most of her time reading books. On the weekends she and Al took her to the movies with them. If Sally hadn't seemed so content, Susan might have felt sorry for her.

"What friend?" she asked.

"Vivi Peterson," Ella said. "From her grade at school. Now come sit down. Supper's ready."

They ate dinner quietly, the Windsor chimes marking the quarter hour and then the half. Susan shifted uncomfortably in the hard-backed chair. The baby's foot or elbow pressed at her side, and she pushed back gently at whatever appendage it was that was poking her from the inside out.

"When will Sally be home?" Al asked. "I promised her I'd take her over to the Farnham pool one afternoon this summer. She's old enough to go in the deep end now."

"I got a call from her today, said they're staying on another week to see the Ice Follies."

"Who's this friend again? I've never heard her talk about anyone named Vivi," Susan said.

"Peterson," Ella said again. "Vivi Peterson. Her father seemed like a very nice man. Even paid her bus fare, escorted her himself."

"Hmm," Susan said, pushing her potatoes around her plate. Every swallow was difficult, acid rising up. She'd have heartburn later, have to sleep propped up. "Wonder how they can afford that?"

She couldn't imagine how a family from this

neighborhood could manage to bring another child on vacation with them. Especially on a trip to Atlantic City. She and Al had gone to the shore for their honeymoon, and between the hotel and the food and entertainment, it had cost them almost every dime they got from their wedding.

"It's vulgar to talk about money." Ella *tsk*ed, wincing, but Susan didn't know if it was due to the pain of her bones or the pain of her own financial situation. Of course, she and Al helped her out, as much as they could, anyway. But because Ella rented this house, it was as though she had an endless mortgage. Susan and Al had bought their place. Susan was determined not to fund a greedy landlord her whole life.

"She went with the girl's father, you said?" asked Al.

"Yes, he and a lovely woman assistant of his."

"Oh, what sort of business is he in?" Susan asked.

"Well, I don't know that," Ella answered. "I told you, it's rude to ask those sorts of questions. I got a postcard from her yesterday, said she was having a wonderful time."

Susan scowled. It seemed to her that if Sally were her own daughter, she'd have asked a few questions before sending her child off with a stranger.

Ella, probably sensing Susan's consternation,

76

got up from the table and went to the other room. She came back with a postcard that said GREETINGS FROM ATLANTIC CITY on the front, with a picture of the beach. She slapped it down on the table almost angrily.

Susan took the postcard and studied the writing on the back.

Dear Mama,

I am writing to tell you how much fun I'm having here in Atlantic City. We are staying at a fancy hotel called the Hotel Clarendon right near the beach. Today I got to meet Mr. Peanut at the Planters shop on the boardwalk. I even got my photo taken with him, and Mr. Peterson bought me a paper cone filled with hot peanuts.

"She doesn't like *peanuts,*" Susan said, feeling her stomach flip (or maybe it was just the baby that tumbled like an acrobat after a meal). Something about this filled her with unease.

"I'm sure she was just being polite," Ella said defensively. "I told her to mind her manners."

Still, Susan studied the postcard; she saw an odd tremble to the handwriting, which usually was so clear and smooth, like stitches in fabric.

I miss you. Love to you and Susan and Al.

"See, she's having a lovely time . . . ," Ella said, but Susan could hear the worry in her mother's voice. It was the same thing she'd heard every time Russell was late coming home from Daly's.

They ate the rhubarb pie in silence. After several minutes, Ella set her fork down. Pursing her lips before wiping at them with a napkin, she said, "Awfully tart. You know it'd be sweeter with some strawberries."

Susan sighed.

After coffee, Susan felt her eyelids growing heavy. Her body growing heavy. The heat outside, the muggy air, was relentless. Al clasped her hand, nodded.

"Ella, thank you for dinner. But we really need to be getting home," he offered, helping Susan up. "Saturdays are our busiest day at the greenhouse. Can we bring you a strawberry plant next time, Ma? Maybe whip you up a *strawberry* rhubarb pie?"

Susan loved him more than she could say, because for just a moment, her mother's face softened, the lines between her eyes disappearing. But then a shadow crossed her face. "Russell used to grow strawberries," she said.

On the drive home, Al shook his head. "So strange about your sister," he said.

Susan nodded, feeling relieved that she wasn't alone in thinking this was very, very strange. Suddenly, and inexplicably, her eyes began to water. She'd been emotional ever since she got pregnant, but most of the time it was over nothing. She'd even begun to sob once while listening to an episode of *The Guiding Light* on the radio. But this felt different.

"Aw, sweetheart," he said. "I can drive to the shore if you want. Bring her home?"

Susan shook her head and batted her hand in front of her face. "Oh goodness, I'm such a nervous Nellie. Mama doesn't seem concerned. I'm sure she's being well cared for. Otherwise, she wouldn't be writing home. Right?"

SALLY

"This here's just so she won't worry about you," Mr. Warner said, handing Sally a pen, as though he were doing everybody a favor. He bought stacks of postcards, and had her send one to her mother every few days, assuring her everything was okay. He even let her call home once, to tell her mother they'd be staying on a little bit longer to see the Ice Follies, though he never did take her to see them. But as much as Sally hated lying to her mother, she also didn't want her to be concerned. And so Mr. Warner dictated, and Sally transcribed.

Dear Mama,
I am having such a wonderful time. You would love Atlantic City. There are so many things to do and to see. Mr. Peterson took me to the Steel Pier and we watched a revue of performers dancing and singing, and they were all children! One of the girls played the accordion and sang in French. Her name was Concetta Franconero. Isn't that a pretty name?

"Can I tell her the rest myself?" Sally asked.
"So long as you let me read it after," he said.

Sometimes I go to Shriver's to watch the saltwater taffy being pulled. I'm sending some to you real soon. I think you'd like the lemon flavor the most. On Tuesday we went to a museum where there are figures made completely of wax, but they look so real! The Phantom of the Opera and Henry VIII. My favorite was Sleeping Beauty behind glass. She looks just like a real lady, and somehow they even made her breathe!

"Mr. Peterson let me ride the carousel ten times until I caught the brass ring," Mr. Warner said, nudging her shoulder, and she wrote it down, adding:

I miss you so much, but Mr. Peterson is treating me very special. Later today, he's going to take me for a ride on the diving bell submarine. For 25 cents, you go inside and they drop you thirty feet down into the ocean. I've only ever watched it before. If you stand on the pier, they have speakers so you can hear the people inside as they go under the water. Sometimes they laugh, but mostly they scream. I'm a little bit afraid, Mama. What if something goes wrong and I go in but don't ever come up again?

Your daughter,
Sally

For three weeks, Mr. Warner and Sally waited for the judge to schedule the hearing, and she didn't see Miss Robinson again. Mr. Warner told her that his assistant had returned to Camden, to attend to business matters there. Sally had so many questions, but most of them went unanswered. As generous as Mr. Warner could sometimes be—bringing her paper bags filled with creamy taffy wrapped in waxed paper, taking her to Randy's Waffle shop for strawberry waffles, buying her trinkets from the boardwalk shops—he also had a temper and didn't suffer her questions well. At home, at school, she asked questions as soon as she felt them bubbling up on her tongue: *What makes thunder? When do birds sleep? How long is infinity?* But Mr. Warner didn't tolerate her curiosity. "What do you think this is, *Break the Bank*? I look like Bert Parks?" he'd ask, laughing that gunshot laugh of his. And so the questions swelled inside her. *Who is the judge? Is he nice? If he does send me to jail, how long before I get to go home?* She wondered if this was what Susan must have felt like, with that baby taking up so much space inside her.

During the day, Mr. Warner took her all around Atlantic City, as if they really were on a vacation. He made her hold his hand as they walked along the boardwalk, said this way they would appear as though they were just a father and his daughter. No one would become suspicious. These little outings weren't allowed by the FBI. They'd both be in a lot of trouble if they were caught. He gripped her hand the way her mother did when they crossed the street.

"Good morning!" he'd say brightly each day as he rose from the second twin bed where he slept. He'd strung up an extra bedsheet between the beds for privacy, using thumbtacks Mrs. Krauss gave him. ("You know I'd never hurt you, Sally. This is strictly a professional arrangement," he'd said, though she didn't really know what he meant.)

"What would my sweet girl like to do today?" he'd ask, pulling back the heavy blinds from the window.

I'd like to see the judge, she thought. *I'd like to go home, please.*

But every day there was some new delay, and so instead they went to the beach, to the Million Dollar Pier, to the Steel Pier, where they watched the diving horse Miss Robinson had told her about. They sat in the stands, captivated by the horse as it contemplated its fate. Standing on the platform, which hovered forty feet above the pool of water below, the poor horse was unable to back up. It had nowhere to go but down. It hesitated, resisted, but then, inevitably, it became oddly resigned. It was only then, its will and spirit broken, that it lowered its head, put its feet forward, when it slid down the chute, and—for a single terrific and terrifying moment—*flew*.

Afterward, he took her to get her portrait taken, in a brand-new dress, and promised she could send the photograph to her mother when it was developed.

By the time they arrived at the rooming house each night, Sally's feet ached from all the walking. After supper in Mrs. Krauss's dining room, she and Mr. Warner retired. She changed into her nightclothes in the lavatory and slipped between the sheets while he was occupied with his own nighttime routine on the other side of the divider.

If he had to go out again, as he often did, though mostly at night, he tied her up, apologizing for the trouble, explaining it was just part of his job. He always made sure to feed her dinner before he left, and had her use the bathroom. He'd also leave a glass of water on the night table, close enough to reach, with a straw so she wouldn't need her hands, which he tied to the bedpost, apologizing for having to do so. "Tomorrow I'll take you to the beach, Sally. To ride the carousel!"

She hated being tied up, the hours ticking by so slowly. Finally, she got up the courage to ask if he'd mind leaving on the radio real soft, so at least she wouldn't have to listen to the clock, the second hand beating out each agonizing second. He agreed, though he kept the volume low, and when she closed her eyes she could almost imagine herself at home in her room, listening to the little mint-green Bakelite clock radio Susan had: Dinah Shore singing about *rings and things* and *buttons and bows.*

She didn't know where he went or what he did, but he always came home stinking of liquor the way her stepfather once had. Sometimes, he had pockets full of money, which he stuffed into one of his socks in the dresser drawer. His eyes were unfocused, his words slippery. Once, when the knot had been too tight and the rope had rubbed her skin raw and red, he dropped down to his knees and pressed his lips against the inside of her wrists. *I'm sorry. I'm sorry.* The feeling of his lips against her skin made her stomach clench. *I'm fine,* she'd said, startled. *It doesn't even hurt.* It scared her when he behaved like this, even more than thinking about jail. When he got close to her, close enough that she could feel the summer heat coming off his skin, close enough that she could smell him, she felt as if he wanted something from her. Hunger, like a dog eyeing a bone.

They went under the sea in the diving bell, and he took her on the carousel, the enormous one with the thousand painted ponies. He let her ride and ride, buying her enough tickets to ride until she was dizzy. When she finally caught the brass ring, he cupped his hands to his mouth and hollered out, "Make a wish, Sally!"

She squeezed her eyes shut and made her wish, but instead of redeeming the ring for another ride, she put the ring in her pocket. Back in the hotel, she strung it on a piece of string that she'd found in the rickety dresser drawer. She tried to tie it herself but couldn't quite reach to make a knot.

"Here, let me," Mr. Warner said, and moved behind her. "What did you wish for?"

She shook her head. You weren't supposed to tell. Not wishes on stars, not wishes on birthday candles, not wishes on carousel ponies.

"I bet *I* know," he said. His knobby fingers grazed the back of her neck, and the little hairs there stood up. "And I have a feeling that wish just might come true."

"The hearing?" she whispered hopefully, despite the chill running along her back. "Do I get to see the judge?"

"You'll just have to wait and see," he said.

That night on the other side of the sheet, she could hear the sounds of his sleep. The labored breath interrupted by fits of coughing or snoring.

She was awake until the sun began to fill the dark room with light, touching the cold brass ring at her neck. *Please,* she thought. *Please let today be the day I get to see the judge.*

ELLA

Ella was still asleep when Susan called. She'd been dreaming of Russell again, though if she had to explain it, she wouldn't be able to. The dream was a dark room, only shadows. A haunting sort of melody played under water. Muffled. Suffocated.

"Mama?" Susan said, and Ella pulled herself from the depths.

"What's the matter?" Ella asked, and then fear set in. "Is something wrong with the baby?"

"No, Mama. The baby is fine."

"Then what's the trouble? The sun's hardly even up yet."

"Mama, it's about Sally."

Ella sat up, her spine a ladder of pain. "What about Sally?"

"She's not at that hotel. The Hotel Clarendon. Al got the idea to call last night and ask for a Mr. Peterson, but the clerk said there wasn't anybody by that name staying there."

"Maybe I got the name wrong then, of the hotel," Ella said, shaking her head, though she recalled that the first letter from Sally had been written on a piece of stationery with the hotel's name embossed at the top. *The Hotel Clarendon.*

That was the only one, though; the others had been postcards, and the most recent one had been written on a piece of notebook paper with a ragged edge.

"Maybe it's against the hotel's policies," Ella said, feeling her chest constrict. "All sorts of movie stars and such coming through Atlantic City. I imagine they can't just give out information about who's stayin' there."

"Sally is not a movie star, Mama. She's a regular girl, and there's nobody at that hotel named Peterson. Al's dropping me off at the house. I want to see the letters."

Ella rolled her shoulders a little, her joints cracking and aching as she did. The pain was so bad that morning, she wasn't even able to pull her nightgown over her head, and so she stood up and simply put on a robe and her house slippers.

"You okay, Mama?" Susan asked when Al dropped her off an hour later, scowling at the ratty robe she wore.

"Just a little under the weather," she said, wrapping it tightly around her.

Susan sat down across from her at the kitchen table, studying the letters that lay spread before them like a pack of fortune-teller cards.

"This one just came yesterday," Ella said, pointing at the most recent letter. Susan read through it.

"But look, Mama," Susan said, tapping her finger on the page. "She doesn't make any mention of that girl, Vivi. Not once in any of the letters and postcards you got. It's just *Mr. Peterson this* and *Mr. Peterson that.* It's been more than three weeks already. It's time for her to come home."

Ella nodded. She still hadn't been able to shake that dark feeling lingering from her dream.

"Do any of these have a return address?" Susan asked, peering at the envelopes.

Ella hadn't thought to look. Of course the postcards didn't, but the letters must.

"Give me that one," Susan said, and Ella handed her the envelope. She turned it over and over in her hand before holding it up to the light. She gasped loudly.

"What is it?" Ella asked.

"Oh, sorry, Mama," Susan said. "Just the baby kicking." She put the envelope down on the table, and Ella grabbed it. No return address. Nothing. The postmark said ATLANTIC CITY, NEW JERSEY. That was all.

Ella swallowed, and it felt like there was a sharp stone in her throat. She needed water, but as she tried to stand, her hip joints resisted, pain shooting down both legs.

"I need some water," she managed to say, and Susan stood up, leading the way to the kitchen with her belly, hand pressed against her lower back.

"Rinse a glass from the rack, and don't be reaching up into the cupboard. It'll wrap the baby's cord right around its neck." Ella's own mother had lost two pregnancies this way. (Never mind Levi and Ashur, the two who died before they were even a year old, and little David who only made it to twelve.) It seemed to her a miracle that any child endured into adulthood.

Ella picked up each postcard again, looking for something, anything to hold on to, to make sense of why this Peterson family had taken Sally on like she was some sort of orphan. When the phone rang, she felt the stone in her throat become dislodged, plummeting to her stomach like that diving bell Sally wrote about.

"I got it, Mama," Susan said, and went to the front hall where the phone was.

She could hear Susan talking softly in the foyer. It must be Al, Ella figured. Calling to find out when he should come pick her up. He had some business in Camden to attend to, said he'd come by afterward and join them for lunch. Ella had made deviled ham. Susan and Sally both liked deviled ham sandwiches on white bread, a little bit of yellow mustard and some pickles.

"Mama?" Susan said, leaning into the doorway, eyes wide. "It's Sally on the phone."

Sally. Thank God. See? All of this had been silly. Sally was fine, fine. Probably calling to say exactly when she was coming home.

Forgetting her hips, her shoulders, her hands, she lurched out of her seat and, wincing, made her way to the hall where she grabbed the heavy black receiver out of Susan's hands.

"Sally?"

"Yes, Mama," she said. "It's me."

"Where are you?"

"Still at the shore, Mama."

"Listen up, Sally," Ella said, her voice trembling even as she willed it still. "I want you to come home now. You need to tell that Mr. Peterson your mama needs you back home. He can put you on a bus if he insists on staying. What kind of man can be out of work for near to a month anyway?"

Sally was quiet on the other end of the line.

"You still there, Sally?"

"I'll tell him, Mama, but I think he said something about maybe staying another week?"

"Sally Horner, listen here. I don't know who this man is and why he thinks I would ever agree to this. You have obligations at home. Your sister's havin' her baby soon, and I don't like the idea of that man spending his money on you for all this time. You're not some charity case." Ella felt like the dam had broken, the river of all of her worries rushing forth.

"He's very nice, Mama. And I'll be home real soon."

"Is he there? Can I speak to him? How would he like if somebody was keepin' his own daughter?"

There was silence at the other end of the line, and Ella worried they'd been disconnected. But then she heard Sally sob.

"I miss you so much, Mama," she cried.

"Well, I miss you, too, Sally," she said, forgetting her anger and frustration for a moment. "What hotel are you staying at? Al called the place you told me, but they said you weren't there. Tell me where you are, and I can ask Al to drive me there. We can come get you and bring you home."

"It's not a hotel, Mama," she said. "It's a rooming house."

All of a sudden, there was the sound of rustling at the end of the line, and she could hear Sally crying and the gruff sound of a man's voice. Ella pressed the phone hard to her ear, as if this might help her decipher whatever was going on at the other end of the line. But soon there was nothing but the raspy sound of someone breathing.

"Mr. Peterson?" she said. "This is Mrs. Ella Horner, Sally's mother . . ."

There was a loud clank and a buzzing dial tone.

Ella looked to Susan, who cradled her belly with one hand and clutched the door frame with the other.

"What's the matter, Mama?" she said, and Ella felt her knees go soft, the rigid cage of bone turning liquid.

"Something's not right," she said.

SALLY

Y ou're in some trouble now," Mr. Warner said, and yanked Sally's arm harder than he had at the Woolworth's. He'd been standing next to her at the pay phone at the corner, hovering over her just as he had the other time she'd called her mother. She hadn't meant to tell her they weren't staying at that hotel, but her mother had sounded so worried, so upset.

"I thought you were a good girl, Sally," he said as he marched her back to the rooming house around the corner.

"I *am*," she cried. "I just miss my mama. My sister."

"I imagine your daddy's to blame. Maybe if you'd had some proper discipline at home you wouldn't be so damned disobedient. Didn't your daddy ever give you the belt?"

Sally flashed on her stepfather. He could never stay angry long. One time when she was little, she'd broken his reading glasses when she was playing with them. She'd been pretending to be him: reading the newspaper, wearing his slippers, one of his unlit cigars sticking out of the corner of her mouth. He'd yelled at her, of course, told her those glasses cost nearly a whole week's pay. But when she'd started to cry, the anger had slipped out of his eyes, and he'd motioned for her to come to him. He'd scooped her up into his arms, kissed the top of her head, said it wasn't anything a paper clip or a piece of tape couldn't fix.

"I don't know my real daddy. He left when I was a baby. And my other daddy's dead. Killed by a train," she said angrily, as if it were his fault.

He shook his head, huffed. "Here I was all ready to stand up and plead your case to the judge. Court date was set for *tomorrow,* and then you gone and done this."

"Tomorrow?" *She was going to see the judge tomorrow?* Weeping, she pleaded, "I'm sorry, sir. I didn't mean to say nothin'."

Inside the rooming house, the sour smells of cabbage and vinegar still coming from the kitchen at the back of the house made her eyes sting. Mrs. Krauss was in the kitchen, occupied with cleaning up after dinner. Mr. Warner practically pushed Sally up the stairs. Could she run to Mrs. Krauss? Cling to her faded housedress, lean into her voluminous waist? What would Mrs. Krauss do if she told her that upstairs, inside that small and dusty room, Mr. Warner kept her tied like a dog? Would she call the police? But Mr. Warner *was* the law. He'd told her again and again that either she did what he said or she was going to jail. She'd broken the law, and now she was his prisoner, this room her makeshift cell.

Inside the room, Mr. Warner shut the door and locked it.

"Sir?" she said.

In the darkness, she could practically hear her heart beating, and then he disappeared behind the curtain. She heard him open the dresser drawer, the metallic rattle of something inside.

"You and me had an agreement," he said, and she could see his dim outline on the other side of the sheet. "You were to play along. I gone out on a limb for you and this is how you repay me? You were not to tell your mother where we were."

"I'm sorry, sir. I didn't mean to say anything. It was an accident."

"I've been like a father to you, and this is what you go and do."

"No, no, no," she whispered, and then startled as he yanked the curtain separating the beds down, a thumbtack glancing off her arm, and she realized what the sound in the drawer had been.

Click, click. Her body stiffened as she felt the cold metal muzzle of the gun at her neck.

"Please don't hurt me," she said, trembling.

"Shut up. Don't you see? You've ruined everything. What am I supposed to do now?"

She shook her head. What was he talking about?

He backed away from her and paced back and forth, looking out the window at the street below.

"Well, we can't stay here anymore," he muttered.

A tiny flicker of hope sparked in her chest. Maybe he'd take her back to Camden. There must be a judge in Camden that she could talk to.

"Can I go home?" she asked, but he charged at her, still holding the gun, and used his free hand to cover her mouth. She could taste the salt of his skin.

"I said, *shut up.* I need to think."

She stifled a cry, and he backed away.

He coughed, and it sounded like a crackling fire in his chest. He looked out the window. "You ever been to Baltimore, Sally?"

She shook her head, which still pounded and ached. She tried to sit up but felt dizzy.

"I'm going to call my people in Baltimore," he said. He coughed again as he ran his hand over and over his head.

"Baltimore?"

He nodded, distracted. Then he turned to her. "Yeah. FBI's got offices there, too. I'll see if we can go to the courts there."

"Sir?" she asked. "Where's Baltimore?"

"Baltimore's in Maryland," he said. "Don't they teach you nothing in school?"

"Only the capitals," she said. Annapolis was the capital of Maryland. She didn't know where Baltimore was.

"I gotta go make a call. If you so much as move

an inch, I'll use this gun for what it was intended to do," he said. He moved toward the valise where he kept the rope. "Understand?"

Tears slipped down either side of her face and she nodded.

There was a knock at their door.

"Not a word," he said to her. He shoved the gun in his pants and went to the door. He stepped into the hall, leaving the door open just a crack.

"Everything okay in here?" Mrs. Krauss's voice said.

"Everything's fine," Mr. Warner said.

"Someone said they heard your girl crying."

"Florence is a little under the weather. She gets headaches," he said. "I'm just headed out to get her some aspirin. I told her to try to get some sleep."

He closed the door behind him, and their voices were muffled in the hallway. Then she heard the stairs creaking beneath their feet.

Mr. Warner never left her alone in the room without tying her up; she was free! As soon as she heard the sound of the front door slamming shut, she scrambled out of the bed, ran to the door, and grabbed the doorknob. And, miraculously, it turned in her hand. He hadn't locked the door from the outside, either!

She ran to the window and could see him walking down the street below. She sat on the bed and tried to think. Her head was pounding in time with her heart. He'd told her before that if she tried to escape, she'd be a fugitive. The law would find her. But maybe then, at least, she'd finally get to see a judge. She just knew if she could explain, about the girls, about how sorry she was, the judge would have to listen. She was a good girl. She'd never been in trouble before, and she would never do anything like this again.

She tried the door one more time to make sure she hadn't imagined it, then ran back to the window. She could see Mr. Warner huddled in the pay phone booth at the corner. She hurried to the bureau and found a notepad, quickly tore off a sheet, and scrawled a note to her mother. She reached for an envelope and stuffed it inside, pilfering a stamp from the roll Mr. Warner kept and licking it, then addressed the envelope. Mrs. Krauss had a basket for outgoing mail in the foyer. She just needed to get the letter downstairs without Mr. Warner seeing her. She looked out the window again. He was still at the pay phone.

Quickly, she opened the door and slipped into the hallway. She took the stairs two at a time, clutching the bannister so she wouldn't fall. She could hear Mrs. Krauss in the kitchen. She quickly dropped the letter in the basket by the door, facedown, so he wouldn't see, and then she turned and ran all the way back up the stairs. She opened the door to their room and shut it quickly behind her, her heart beating in her ears.

Deafening. Then she heard the front door open and the stairs complaining under Mr. Warner's feet.

She leapt into the bed, trying hard to slow her breath. Would he know she'd escaped? Would he get out the gun again?

When the door swung open, her blood pounded in her temples.

He came straight to where she lay in the bed. She imagined herself turning to stone, and she wondered if that was where the word "petrified" came from. When she felt his hand touch her back, she stiffened and had to will herself not to cry.

He stopped. But she felt his body coming close to hers. She closed her eyes so tightly they burned. And his breath was hot in her ear. "I'm sorry, Sally. I didn't mean to scare you."

"My mama's gonna worry," she whispered, "if you take me away."

He touched her face, and her body stiffened. "Don't worry about your mama, Sally. They'll forget about you soon. It'll be like you never was."

VIVI

It might have been true, for those other girls at least, Vivi thought. Bess and Irene and the others. After that last school bell rang, Sally probably slipped from their memories like smoke from the end of a stolen cigarette. Vivi, however, did *not* forget Sally or what they had done to her that afternoon. The way they'd left her at the Woolworth's, clutching that stupid notebook beneath her sweater. How they'd abandoned her weighed on her conscience, her guilt like a sliver, burrowing deep in the tender skin of her palm. It was always there, just under the surface of things, failing to work itself out. She became inflamed by it, flesh reddened and hot with a sort of infection.

One Sunday in July, she knelt in the dusty confessional at St. Luke's and told Father McFarland about that afternoon at the five-and-dime. But instead of counsel, he simply dealt her penance (three Hail Marys and a Lord's Prayer), as if she'd only confessed to disrespecting her mother. Though, as she recited her prayers, kneeling on the cold hard pew kneeler, she didn't feel exonerated. She only felt like she'd just gotten away with something terrible. She knew she needed not just God's forgiveness but Sally's as well.

And so on Monday morning, she walked all the way to Sally's house on Linden Street. She thought to apologize and offer to buy Sally an ice cream, maybe even go back to the Woolworth's to sit at the counter where they'd ignored her when she needed them the most. She had three weeks' allowance in her pocket, plus a quarter she'd gotten for her birthday.

When she knocked on Sally's door, she hoped it would be Sally who'd answer. If Sally had told Mrs. Horner what the girls had done, what they had made Sally do, Vivi had no idea what wrath she might face. Her own mother might answer the door to a girl like her with a wooden spoon in hand. She was frightened when Sally's mother opened the door.

"Mrs. Horner?" she said. "I was wondering if Sally was home."

The woman's face looked pinched, as though she'd just bitten into a lemon.

"Sally ain't home yet," Mrs. Horner said. "She's gone to the shore with a friend."

"Oh," Vivi said, relief as hot as molten wax in her veins. "When's she coming home?"

The woman seemed to catch her breath, and Vivi watched as her hands clutched at her skirt.

"Who should I say came callin'?" she asked.

"My name's Vivian, ma'am. But I go by Vivi. Vivi Peterson."

The woman, whose face was already the color of paper, grew even paler. Nearly blue. And she clutched her hand to her chest.

"She's with you?" she asked, stepping out onto the porch and peering over Vivi's shoulder. She breathed a series of quick shallow breaths as she grabbed onto Vivi's shoulder.

"I'm sorry?" Vivi asked.

Mrs. Horner came out all the way onto the porch, wincing as she made her way down the steps, taking each one like a much older woman.

"Where's Sally?" she asked, staring down the street.

Vivi thought of her grandmother, the way she sometimes got confused, asked for her even as she was standing right there.

Vivi shook her head. "Mrs. Horner? I don't know where Sally is. I just came to see if she might like to go to the Woolworth's and get an ice cream."

Mrs. Horner was standing on the sidewalk now.

"She ain't with you? You and your daddy?"

Vivi shook her head now, terrified, as she watched the woman's legs buckle. It was like watching a house of cards fall over. Right there in the middle of the sidewalk. What should she do?

Mrs. Horner was sitting in the middle of the sidewalk, legs splayed out in front of her, and Vivi felt even sadder and more frightened than she had ever been.

Thankfully, the mailman had just turned the corner and was headed up Linden Street. When he saw the woman, collapsed on the ground like a broken toy, he dropped his mailbag to go help her up as Vivi stood paralyzed.

"I gotta go home," Vivi said, rushing past them both. "I'm sorry. I'm so sorry."

At home later, she would take the rosary beads she'd gotten for her first communion, and clutch them in her hands, reciting the prayers again and again, until her tongue felt numb with them, until her fingers ached, the sharp crucifix digging into the soft skin of her palm.

Mea culpa, mea culpa, mea maxima culpa.

ELLA

"M rs. Horner? Are you okay? Here, let me
help you up," Fred Hummer, the mailman
said, offering Ella his hand. He helped pull her to
her feet and walked her slowly back to her house.
"Are you okay? Maybe I should call a doctor for
you?"

Ella shook her head, disoriented and dizzy. *Vivi
Peterson?*

"Here," he said. "Lean on me." He helped her
up the stairs and held the screen door open as she
made her way to the kitchen. Inside, the lights
were too bright. Everything smelled of bleach;
the scent of it made her think of Russell. Dear
God, Russell. How could he leave her alone?
Raising two girls all by herself? If he were here,
he'd know what to do. He'd have gone and
brought Sally home weeks ago.

"Thank you," she managed, before going to the
sink and turning the faucet on.

"You sure I can't get somebody on the phone
for you? You look like you seen a ghost."

Ella threw her aching shoulders back and
turned to him, felt the corners of her mouth rise
involuntarily. Like the hinged jaw of Charlie
McCarthy. Her voice, too, seemed to come from
outside herself, a ventriloquist's dummy.

"I'm fine, Fred. Just a little light-headed. It's this heat, you know."

"Okay, if you say so," he said, and hoisted his mailbag up over his shoulder, making to go, but then stopped. "Oh applesauce, I almost forgot. I got a letter here for you. From your little girl."

Ella felt her world upending again. Somehow she made her way through a sea of stars to the kitchen chair while Fred riffled through his sack.

"Here you go," he said. "Now you have a good day, and maybe take a little nap. A nice cold compress on your forehead will cool you right down. Loretta swears by a bag of frozen peas."

The screen door slammed shut behind him, and Ella reached for the envelope on the table. The pencil marks were barely legible on the paper, as if Sally had been afraid to press too hard, to commit the words to the paper, wraithlike on the page: *Mr. Warner says we're going to Baltimore.* In the left corner was an address almost too faint to see: *203 Pacific Street, Atlantic City, New Jersey.*

Mr. Warner? Who was that? She sprang from the chair, her body with a will of its own. She watched her fingers dial the numbers, heard the voice come from her mouth. "Camden Police Department, please." And then, after she was connected: "This is Ella Horner. And my daughter . . . Sally . . . somebody's keeping her, and it's time for her to come home."

AL

Al answered Ella's door and led the two detectives, Burke and Morrow, inside the house. Ella had barely spoken a word since he and Susan arrived earlier. All the color gone from her face, she sat at the kitchen table staring at the clock on the wall. Susan sat across from her, holding her hand, speaking to her softly.

"Ma," Al said gently as he came into the kitchen, the two men in tow. "These gentlemen need to speak with you. About Sally."

Susan looked up, her shoulders stiffening. And slowly Ella turned away from the clock, as if waking from a dream.

"Did you find her?" She stood up, grimacing.

"No need to get up, ma'am," Burke said, gesturing for her to sit back down. He was tall and thin, with glasses and a friendly face.

"Where is Sally?" she asked, her voice cracking.

"We're going to try to figure that out, ma'am," Morrow, the other detective, said. He was more severe, with sharp features and a deep cleft in his chin. "But we're going to need your help. We have some questions for you."

Burke sat next to Ella, but Morrow remained

standing, nodding and scratching at his pad as Ella recounted her meeting with the man, the father of one of Sally's friends, who had taken her to the shore.

"So you put her on the bus with this fellow, Peterson, you say? But you'd never met him before?" Burke said gently, but it still sounded like an accusation to Al.

Ella wrung her hands and stared past him blankly. When she finally spoke, her voice was low. "He told me they'd be going to the shore, and what a delight it would be to have Sally along." Ella shook her head, and still did not look at either the detectives or Susan. "It was a chance for Sally to have a little vacation. I couldn't afford to give her one. She sent postcards. She even sent a box of lemon taffy. I have it here somewhere," she said, and again started to rise. Al watched as the pain gripped her.

"Don't worry about it, Mama," Susan said. "Just give them the last letter."

"I was going to go down there myself," Al said to Burke. "To bring her home." And he would have if Susan hadn't made him wait to speak to the police. Atlantic City wasn't far. He could have had her back home by supper. They had an address now. He wasn't sure why Ella had called the police department instead of calling him and Susan first. Whatever this mix-up was, he didn't think anything about it was illegal.

"Now, let's leave this to the professionals," Burke said. "We already put a call into the local PD in Atlantic City. Told them the address Mrs. Horner gave us and asked them to go by and see what they can find out."

"Who's this *Mr. Warner?*" Burke asked, peering through his glasses at the letter, at Sally's faint handwriting. "I thought you said the man you met was named Peterson?"

"I don't know, I don't know," Ella said, her hands curling into fists. Her knuckles were swollen, bent, crippled by her arthritis. "She ain't with the Petersons. That Peterson girl, Vivi, didn't know nothin' about a vacation at the shore. It's been over a month already. Who takes someone's child away for a whole month? I don't care how rich you are."

"Warner," Burke said, single eyebrow lifted, nodding to Morrow, who looked up from his pad. He quickly stuffed it in his breast pocket and reached for the book he had brought in with him. He flipped through it, opened it to the first page, and set it down in front of Ella.

"Ma'am, we're going to need you to look at each of these photos carefully," Burke said. "Do you recognize any of these men?"

"Who are they?" Ella asked, shaking her head, confused.

"We just need to know if you recognize any of them. Do any of these men resemble the man you

110

met at the bus station? The one who claimed to be this Mr. Peterson?"

Ella studied the photos before her. She shook her head as she carefully turned page after page after page.

"I really don't understand," she said.

Al moved to look over Ella's shoulder at the book. The photos, Al realized, were mug shots, a rogues' gallery of criminals. Carefully written notes about each felon were etched beneath: descriptions of their persons, their aliases, and their crimes. Criminal after criminal; he felt sick. Was it possible that Sally was with one of these degenerates?

Ella looked up at Al, scared.

"Go slowly, Ma," he said softly, putting his hand on her shoulder. "Are any of them the man you met?"

She shook her head, turned the page. Then suddenly, she stopped. Her eyes widened, and she pointed at a photo. "That's him," she said.

Both detectives leaned over to study the photograph.

"Are you sure?" Burke, asked. *"Frank La Salle?"*

"He was very charming," Ella said, her jaw set defensively. "And courteous."

"I'm certain he was," Burke said sympathetically. Morrow scooped the book up.

"Who is he?" Susan asked.

111

"I should have listened to my heart," Ella said, to no one in particular, shaking her head. "I felt uneasy letting her go with that man."

"No one's blaming you, ma'am," Burke offered, patting her shoulder.

"You're positive . . . ," Morrow said impatiently, holding the book up now, open to the photo of the hawkish man. "That this is the man who kidnapped your daughter?"

"Kidnapped?" Susan cried out, and stood up.

Kidnapped? Al thought. Al went to her and put his arm around her, her shoulders shaking, her body trembling.

"Al, what do they mean?" Susan asked, looking up at him, terror in her eyes. He worried about her getting so worked up; it couldn't be good for the baby. "Sit down," he said, and ushered her back down into her chair.

"That's him. The one that took Sally on the bus." Ella nodded. "I remember the scar on his face."

"Do you need some water, Sue?" Al whispered, but she shook her head.

"Well, who is he?" Ella said. "And what does he want with Sally? We don't have no money to give him for . . . what's that called? Al? Like the Lindbergh baby?"

"Ransom?" The idea was ludicrous. All of this, insane.

"Can I speak to you?" Burke said, motioning for Al to follow him out into the foyer.

112

"I'll be right back," Al said to Susan, and she sat down again.

In the dimly lit hallway, the man took a deep breath and opened the book to the photo. "This man. His name is La Salle. Frank La Salle. Also goes by Patterson, O'Keefe. *Warner.*"

"Who is he?"

Burke leaned toward the kitchen, as if to see if either Susan or Ella were within earshot. "This is just between us for now, okay? No need to get the women all riled up till we know for sure."

Al felt his stomach pitch as he nodded.

"He's an ex-con, just out of state prison in Trenton since January. We were worried it might be him. He's got a history."

"Of?"

"Of," the detective said, his freckled cheeks turning red. "Sex crimes. Against young girls."

SALLY

They were leaving soon. Going to Baltimore like Mr. Warner said.

But for now, Mr. Warner sat at the table by the window and played solitaire with a battered deck of cards, drinking straight from the bottle labeled CRACKER JACK STRAIGHT APPLE BRANDY. It made her think of the boxes of Cracker Jack caramel popcorn Susan used to get at the movies. Sally picked out the peanuts, but Susan always offered her the toy or riddle inside.

What is it that no man ever yet did see, which never was, but always is to be? She'd read the riddle aloud as they waited for the movie to begin.

"I don't know, Sally," Susan said, shrugging.

"I know! *It's tomorrow!*" Al said, slapping his hand on his knee. Al could always figure out the riddles.

Three days had passed since Mr. Warner pulled the gun out and scared her, since she sent the letter home telling her mother that he was taking her to Baltimore. It was dark now, and it made her think of that diving bell at the edge of the pier. The room transformed into a watery tomb.

Her body stiffened when she heard him slam

114

down the empty bottle on the table. The room smelled sweet, sickening.

"You awake?" he said.

Sally held her breath.

"I *said,* are you awake?"

His words blurred together. This was the way her stepfather sounded when he came home from Daly's. Now, she pretended she was asleep, pressed her hand against her chest, feeling her heart beating against her ribs. She heard him moving around the room, the scraping of his chair leg against the floor, though she could only make out his dark silhouette. She held her breath and gripped the blanket in her fists.

Then.

"Get undressed," he said, his voice made not of water but of sand. He was standing on the other side of the curtain, which he'd hung back up.

She froze. "What?" She closed her eyes and conjured the diving bell, that subaqueous crypt.

"I said, take your blouse off. Your skirt."

She hadn't changed into her nightclothes yet.

"I been real patient with you, Sally," he said, and then he yanked the sheet dividing their beds down again, and she gasped. He loomed over her, swaying. Waiting. But without the sheet, she wasn't sure where she was supposed to change.

"I been treating you real nice, haven't I?" he asked, his face close to hers.

"Yes, sir," she said, tears welling up in her eyes.

"Most girls would consider themselves lucky to be treated so nice. I ain't been nothing but a perfect gentleman." He wagged his bony finger near her face, and tears fell hot down her cheeks.

"You've been real good to me, sir."

"Here," he said. "I'll help you." And he began to unbutton her blouse, his fumbling fingers poking at her. Frustrated, he yanked at her clothes. A button flew off, landing on the floor.

"*No, no, no,*" she pleaded, her words made of water. Spilling, spreading, seeping. A salty sting, and she wondered if the little round windows of the diving bell had burst (an explosion of glass and the cold saltwater rushing in). She clung to the edge of the mattress so she wouldn't drown, the weight of him, the weight of the entire ocean on her chest, compressing her ribs, her lungs filling with the sea.

The room was so still, like it must feel like to be deep underwater.

Time stilled. Stopped.

What are you doing? she wanted to scream. *Mama!* But there was no air left in her lungs. And he pressed his hand against her mouth.

And then there was nothing but pain. She shook her head, felt herself plummeting. Sinking. She was drowning.

But then, just when she was certain she had hit the bottom, the ocean floor, the weight suddenly lifted from her chest, and she was light, ascending, dizzy and disoriented. The sky of water becoming a sky of stars. She was suspended, floating. But was she above the pain, or below it?

Mr. Warner stumbled off her, and she surfaced. He backed up, zipping his trousers.

She felt her pulse between her legs. In her temples. Moving only her aching head, she peered out the window, where the defunct lighthouse stood, dark. She felt a sob trying to escape her lips. Mr. Warner was right. The lighthouse was dormant, casting nothing but long shadows during the day. No beacon of hope, no signal guiding lost sailors home.

"Why?" she asked, the word bubbling to the surface. Irrepressible. "Why are you doing this to me? My mama, she'll send someone looking for me. My sister. Her husband." She sobbed.

He laughed, his voice full of grit. "Then I'll arrest her, too, for being an accomplice. Lock you both up and throw away the key."

When I turn around once. What is out will not get in. When I turn around again. What is in will not get out. What might I be?

A key, she thought. A key. She needed to find the key that would set her free. When she turned her aching head, she thought about the letter. *Please, let them find me,* she thought. *Before it's too late.*

SUSAN

When Susan answered the knock at her mother's door that early August morning, she knew they'd come with bad news. The two detectives stood on the porch, holding Sally's little red suitcase. But no Sally. Cleopatra, the neighborhood stray, wound herself between his legs, purring.

"Mama!" Susan hollered into the house, and Ella came to the door.

"Where is she?" Ella sobbed, clutching her chest as if to contain her heart. When the detectives didn't answer, she turned to Susan. "Where is your sister?"

Inside, they showed her and her mother the photograph they'd found in the empty boarding-house room. In the photo, Sally was wearing an unfamiliar dress with white lace and ruffles. Like a child bride. She was sitting on a swing, her hands clutching the ropes on either side. There was a painted window behind her, a window box filled with flowers. "Is this your daughter?" they asked Ella. "Is this Sally?"

Susan felt like her world was turned inside out. She had to sit with her head between her knees, breathing into a paper bag, for nearly ten minutes before she could compose herself enough to speak to the man from the county who showed up at the house a few minutes later and said he'd be taking over from here.

"Who *is* he? This man Frank La Salle?" Susan asked the county man, Detective Vail. "I don't understand any of this."

When she'd asked Al what the Camden detectives had told him, he said not to worry. That they would find her. She suspected now that Al had been keeping information from her. Protecting her. Now Al paced back and forth across the kitchen floor, and her mother sat, once again, expressionless at the kitchen table as Vail explained that Frank La Salle had, indeed, *kidnapped* her sister.

"He's got about five different aliases he's been using. He's been going by Warner since he took your daughter. The owner of the rooming house where they were staying said he registered under Warner. He said he was her father."

"She has no father," Ella said. It was the first time she'd spoken since they arrived.

Susan could only breathe shallow breaths, and she didn't know if it was the position the baby was in or something else. It felt like her lungs had shrunk in size, like she was a swimmer coming up for air that wasn't there.

"So he's not associated in any way with one of Sally's friends?" Susan said, knowing even as she asked how ludicrous this question was.

119

Something about all of this had seemed fishy to her from the start. She tried to understand how it was that her mother had handed her own child off to this criminal. She'd walked her to the bus depot, delivered her to him like a gift. She couldn't understand how Ella had been so gullible, so stupid. But the even greater mystery, she thought, was Sally herself. What on earth would have made her agree to go with him, this fiend?

When her mother got up to use the powder room, Vail took a deep breath, straightened his shoulders, and spoke softly to Al and Susan. "I'm not sure what they told you about La Salle, but you should know that just eight months ago he was locked up in Trenton. He'd just gotten out and was staying at the YMCA downtown. Looks like they kicked him out right around the time he met up with Sally."

"What was he in jail for?" Al asked.

Vail looked at Susan apologetically, and grimaced a little. "Statutory rape. Five little girls, all of them between twelve and fourteen years old. Sally's age. Before that he was wanted for the kidnapping of another girl, a teenager named Dorothy Dare. He wound up marrying the Dare girl, though, made it legal. They even had a baby. But she kicked him out, and he was right back to his old ways."

Susan's vision blurred. La Salle wasn't just a

grifter, a con man, but a *monster*. And now Sally was with him, who knew where. The letter had said they were going to Baltimore, but if that was true, would he really allow her to send it? Had he forced her to write this, as he clearly had forced her to write the others? A pile of unsent postcards the police had found in the room sat in front of them on the table covered in fabrications: *Dear Mama, Today we went to the beach. I am getting freckles on my nose from all this sunshine. Dear Mama, You would love it here. I miss you, but I am having so much fun. Dear Mama , I . . .* This one illegible, the words run together. Something had spilled. A glass of water? Dear God, poor Sally's tears?

Ella returned to the kitchen, and Susan couldn't bring herself to look at her.

"What do we do now?" Susan asked, as it appeared her mother had all but slipped away, sitting silently again, wringing her knotty hands.

"We've got a warrant out for his arrest. Because we believe he's taken her over state lines, the FBI will be in charge of the manhunt." *Hunted.* Like an animal.

"What do you think he plans to do with to her?" Susan asked, and immediately wished she hadn't.

The county man rubbed his face with his hands, his mouth twitching as he shot a glance at Ella, who was staring blankly at the door again, as if Sally might just walk right back through it.

121

"Let's try not to worry about that. For now, we're going to focus on getting your sister home," he said. But when he smiled, his eyes betrayed both his doubt and the truth that whatever Frank La Salle planned to do to Sally, he'd likely already done.

Susan sent Al home that night, staying with her mother. Ella could barely make it up the stairs, and in the tiny bathroom, Susan had to help her undress, help lower her into the tub. Something about this filled her with anger. As she ran the washrag down her mother's bony spine, she wondered, where had her mother gone? A mother was supposed to take care of her children, protect them. Not the other way around.

"I didn't know," her mother said, as if she were reading her mind. "How was I supposed to know who that man was?"

Susan breathed deeply to keep from saying all the things she wanted to say. "I love you, Mama," she said instead, though she felt herself seething. "We'll find her. I know we will."

When her mother retired, Susan went to the room she used to share with Sally and lay down on her old bed. She could have been sixteen years old again, but she wasn't a girl anymore. She was about to be a mother herself. As she lay flat on her back, her belly made a steep hill beneath the blanket. The baby was still tonight. She touched the taut flesh of her stomach and thought: Ella had once lain like this, first with Susan and then with Sally inside. Still a part of her. Still safe. Suddenly, Susan didn't want to have this baby. She wanted to keep her child inside her. The world was a terrifying and dangerous place, a world that could convince you to offer up your own child to the devil without even thinking twice. What if she, like Ella, wasn't able to protect this child?

ELLA

Ella thought of all the stolen things.

She recalled her childhood marble collection and the way the boy at school had stolen her favorite blue moonie. It looked as she imagined the Earth might look from far away. Holding it in her palm made her feel like she had the whole world inside her fist. The boy had asked her to see it and then pocketed the beautiful blue marble. It was the first time anyone had taken anything from her, and the sick pit it left behind, that wild sense of injustice and longing, plagued her for days.

Later: a favorite doll left at a park, a pair of shoes lent to a friend. Borrowed books never returned. She could track her entire life in things she'd been too careless to keep. Thieves prey on those who trust; this was a lesson she could never seem to learn. One she was afraid she hadn't managed to impart to Sally.

Even Russell knew she was an uneducable fool. "When will you learn?" he'd asked once, playfully, but his smile belied a sort of baffled frustration. After they'd married she'd had money stolen from her pocket at the market, and once her purse, which she'd left sitting on a chair at the beauty parlor. Recipes, a new hat (plucked from the pew at church of all places). And later, he himself proved to be the worst thief of all; he took everything when he took his life. Just walked out the door one night as though he weren't about to steal her entire future, rob the girls of the father they deserved. They'd already lost one daddy, and now this.

Her life had been filled with thieves. How did she not see this coming? Though this man had hardly *stolen* Sally. Ella had practically given her to him, handed her over as easily and stupidly as she handed that beautiful blue marble to the boy who plucked it from her palm and put it in his pocket.

SALLY

The rumble of the tracks was like a lullaby to those passengers who could actually sleep. But Sally didn't dare to close her eyes, was too afraid to give in to her exhaustion. They'd boarded the train in Atlantic City at dawn and then changed trains in Philadelphia. Now they were hurtling toward Maryland. When they were in Atlantic City, she'd at least known that they were still close to home. Every night in that rooming house, she'd comforted herself with the fact that home wasn't so far away. And what he said couldn't be true; of course they'd come looking for her. But Maryland? Baltimore? It was a world away, a big city, she was sure. Even if the letter had reached her mother, how on earth would they find her? Tears seared two tracks down her cheeks.

"Come on," he'd said that morning before the sun even came up. "Time to go."

"Am I going *home?*" she'd asked hopefully. She'd been half asleep, curled up at the edge of the bed like a pill bug in her stepfather's garden.

"*Home?* Don't you think if they *really* missed you, they woulda come looking for you by now?

It's been over a month, Sally. They've known where you were at the whole time."

She shook her head. That wasn't true. He'd made her lie about where she was. He didn't know about the letter she'd sent that awful night, the one with the rooming house address, the one telling her mother that he planned to take her to Baltimore. Though that was days ago. Surely, her mother would have gotten it by now. But if she had the address, why hadn't they come looking? *No, no, no.* He was confusing her.

"Just get up," he said. "We got a train to catch."

"I won't tell nobody what you done to me. I just want to be with my mama. She's sick. She needs me."

"I said, get up," he repeated, and this time he reached out and grabbed her arm, yanked her up out of bed. He shoved her toward the bureau. On top, leaning against the mirror, was that photo he'd had taken of her on the boardwalk. He'd promised she could send the photo home to her mother. She touched the picture, tears streaming down her face.

"Leave it," he said, yanking open the drawer where he gathered his stash of money and his gun. He opened the next drawer and threw a couple of pairs of trousers and some undershirts into a paper bag, then reached into her drawer for the few items he'd bought for her and did the same.

"Leave that, too," he repeated as she knelt to get her suitcase from under the bed. "This way we'll just look like a couple of day-trippers. Won't call any attention to ourselves."

"We're on the run now, Sally," Mr. Warner had explained. They had to go undercover unless she wanted to find herself in a penitentiary for the rest of her life. Taking her to Baltimore was for her protection, he said; he promised he'd do whatever was necessary to keep her safe. He was going out on a real limb for her, he said. Really sticking his neck out. She could almost picture it—Mr. Warner climbing out on a tree limb, neck stretching as he did, like a *Tom and Jerry* reel played before the main picture. The image almost made her laugh until what he was saying actually registered. *They were leaving New Jersey.* She'd never been anywhere outside New Jersey before. Not even Philadelphia.

Now, as the interior lights on the train dimmed and Mr. Warner started to drift off to sleep in his seat next to her, Sally felt in her pocket for the cold metal ring. She touched it, this talisman, closing her eyes.

They'll forget you, Sally. It will be like you never was.

She'd made a wish. After she had her photo taken, Mr. Warner had let her ride the carousel, that massive merry-go-round with the terrifying painted ponies with bared teeth, around and around trying again and again to catch the brass ring. As she leaned out, clutching the pole that impaled her horse (the pale purple one with the pink mane) with one hand, she'd whispered before grabbing at the brass ring with her other, *Please, don't let them forget.*

She knew that it was easy to forget people once they were gone. Without Susan living at home, it was easy to forget what it had been like to share a room with her, the way she laughed in her sleep. She'd forgotten the scent of Susan's perfume, the way she smoked cigarettes in their room, the open window doing little to keep the smoke from hovering above them. She'd forgotten the way she always left her bed unmade, her clothes on the floor, her makeup strewn on the bureau. It was like pulling a rock out of the sand; the water just filled the empty space when it was gone. Like it had never been there at all.

Even her stepfather's absence eventually stopped feeling like a tear in the fabric of her world after a while. She was only six when he went to Daly's for a drink and never came home, and it seemed that almost immediately her memory of him started to fade. It was his face first. She remembered lying in bed, trying to remember his smile. But she came up blank. She concentrated hard, working on remembering one detail at a time. But the memory was like confetti in a kaleidoscope, fragments (*nose, chin, grin*), never to be assembled correctly again. There were so few pictures. And the photos felt like imposters anyway. Who was that man who'd once lifted her on his shoulders to watch the Fourth of July parade? Who was that man holding her up to pick an apple from a tree? Who was that man standing next to her mother holding the knife in front of the beautiful cake? She remembered trying to recollect the sound of his voice, the tenor and timbre. He'd had two voices really: the soft slurry one after he came home from Daly's (the one that was light and happy, words tumbling and bumping into each other) and the other voice, the voice that had edges. The one that scared her just a little. But once he was gone, she might have been able to describe the sound, but she couldn't *hear* it anymore. It was like trying to explain a melody without being able to recall the music.

As her body gave in to exhaustion, lulled by that odd locomotive lullaby, she thought again, *Please, don't let them forget.*

Baltimore, Maryland
August 1948

SALLY

"Your name is Florence Fogg now," he said, his breath hot in her ear. "Understand?"

Florence. Florence had been her name once, long ago. Florence was the name her real father had given her. *Florence Swain.* But when he went away, she became Sally, a name she chose herself. It sounded friendlier to her than Florence, like the name of a happy girl who was always smiling. When her mother remarried, her stepfather had wanted her to take *Horner,* his last name. But now this man, Frank (*Warner? Fogg?* She hardly knew what to believe anymore), was changing her name again. She was to pretend that *he* was her father. She wondered if her life would always be like this: always changing who she was, to whom she belonged.

No, she thought angrily. He would not steal her name. *I am Sally Horner.*

When they arrived at the house in the Barclay neighborhood of Baltimore, Mr. Warner told Sally to keep her mouth shut and play along.

It was hot and so humid her clothes clung to her back, legs, neck. They stood at the steps of the ramshackle row house for so long she figured that it must be unoccupied, when suddenly the door swung open, and a large bald man, half

133

dressed and smoking a cigar, filled the doorway. His trousers were beltless, his undershirt stained. He was twice the size of Mr. Warner, and the skin of his cheeks and nose had the same veiny blossoms of red that her stepfather's had had.

"Sammy!" Mr. Warner said.

The man, Sammy, looked confused at first, as if Mr. Warner might be trying to sell him something. A vacuum cleaner? A set of encyclopedias?

"Frankie!" he exclaimed. "You old son of a bitch!" He reached out and shook Mr. Warner's hand, pumping it up and down and shaking his head in disbelief. "Wow! Your little one sure has grown since I last saw her. I thought you said Dot gave you the old heave-ho."

"Old lady took off, left us to fend for ourselves," Mr. Warner said conspiratorially, and Sally wondered who Dot was. "Then she comes back wanting the kid. You still got that room to rent? Like I told you, Dot's on my tail, and we need a place to stay."

"Sure thing. Hot as hell up there, but it's all yours."

"And you know of anybody looking for a mechanic?" Mr. Warner asked. He'd sweated straight through his suit jacket. She could smell him, and her eyes burned at the stink.

"I'll ask around. Shops are always lookin' for a good wrench. Come on in," the man said.

Inside, the air in the small kitchen hung heavy

with cigarette smoke. A tobacco fog. They followed him up one narrow stairwell and then another to an attic room. The sun shone in a bright beam, illuminating a single bed. Dust particles spun lazily in the light. It had to be over a hundred degrees in that room; she felt dizzy and put her hand against the wall to steady herself. *No, no, no.*

"I got an extra mattress if you wanna give me a hand getting it up the stairs," the man said to Mr. Warner. "You can give the kid the bed."

Sammy turned to Sally and said, "Bathroom's downstairs. Second door on the right. No lock on the door, so I'll make sure to knock. Been a long time since there's been a lady in the house." He winked at her, and she started to see stars again.

"I need to sit down," she said, to no one in particular, as her legs began to fail her, joints melting in this unbearable heat. Her stomach turning. She couldn't stay here.

"I got a fan I can bring up. And it cools down some at night," the man said, concerned. Sally wondered if she could maybe trust him. If he was good. Though she wasn't sure what *good* was anymore.

He took her elbow and led her to a hardback chair. She sat down and bent over, her ears filling with a loud buzzing. "She okay?" he asked Mr. Warner.

"Been a long trip from Jersey," Mr. Warner said,

135

but it sounded like his voice was underwater. She was inside that diving bell again, plummeting, the walls closing in.

"Why don't you get some rest, Florence," Mr. Warner said.

That name, *Florence,* also felt like something far away. Something both familiar and completely foreign. She looked up to find both men nodding and smiling.

"Funny, she don't look nothing like Dot," the man Sammy said. "But she's gonna be a real looker one day."

The shadows in the new room scared her; the branches of a linden tree outside the window became creeping fingers. That night, she sat on the bed with her back pressed against the wall, her knees to her chest. Sammy had been wrong. The room didn't cool off at night, save for a few degrees. Her forehead was slick with sweat, her hair drenched.

"When do I get to see a judge?" she asked, boldly at first, but then her voice breaking. "You promised I'd see the judge at the shore. I could get my punishment, and then I could go home. Is there a judge here in Baltimore?"

Mr. Warner sat down on the edge of the bed, leaning toward her.

"Listen up," he said, stroking her hair out of her eyes. He cupped her chin in his hand. "I'm putting my career at risk for you. If we get found out, it won't just be you who's sent to prison. And if they take me, then there will be nobody left to speak on behalf of your character. You understand? You'll be all alone."

Sally shuddered as a cloud passed over the moon outside. "I don't understand. I just want to get my hearing. I'll do whatever they say. Take my punishment."

He laughed, and then he scowled. "Don't you understand? When are you going to get it through your thick skull? You're a *fugitive* now, Sally. You know what that is?"

She shook her head.

"You're *wanted*." His fingertips tiptoed across her shoulder. Then he whispered into her ear, and her body tensed electric beneath him. "Won't matter to them. Understand? Dead or alive."

ELLA

"*Mrs. Horner,*" Loretta Hummer, the postman's wife, cooed, taking Ella's arm as she made her way to the front doors of St. Paul's for Sunday services.

Ella had not been to church since Russell died except on holidays, and then only because she figured Sally's soul should not be at the mercy of her own personal gripes with the Lord.

"How *are* you?" Loretta continued. She smelled of pie, eye-burning cinnamon and nauseating apples. "I read all about poor little Sally in the paper."

As soon as the FBI got involved, the reporters had come knocking at Ella's door. Vultures, every last one of them, pecking, pecking at her. *Why Sally?* they asked. *Why do you think he chose her?* As if she were a pot roast at the market, a ripe peach in the produce bin Frank La Salle had plucked out. Though that was easier than the other questions: *You'd never met him before? Weren't you suspicious?*

Finally, Al got them all to leave, told them she wasn't feeling well. That she wouldn't conduct any more interviews. She had no idea that the articles they wrote would wind up anywhere other than in the pages of *The Courier-Post*. That anybody outside Camden would give two hoots about what happened to her little girl. But when Al and Susan came for supper on Friday night, Al brought a half-dozen papers from Philly to New York City, with that photo of Sally on the swing and that horrid man in his fedora. An eight-state manhunt, the headlines announced. And below the headlines, her horror (her agony, her heart) captured inside the tidy margins of those justified columns.

"It's a good thing, Ma," he said. "The more people that see her face, the more likely it is that somebody might see her and recognize her. If she's in Baltimore, like they think, her picture has been all over *The Sun*."

He was right, of course, but Ella couldn't help but feel like she'd left her dirty laundry out on the line to dry. She could practically smell it the second she started up the steps to the church that morning.

Ella grunted as she reached the door, and tried her best to ignore Loretta's probing.

"I can only *imagine* what you must be going through," Loretta said, frowning and shaking her head. "Your daughter, your *little girl,* who-knows-where with that, with that . . ."

"Thank you," Ella said, and yanked her arm away from Loretta.

She was here for one reason and one reason

139

only. To make her peace with God, before he exacted any more of his vengeance.

Because nobody was expecting her at church, nobody noticed at first as she started slowly up the aisle. She might have been mistaken for any other middle-aged woman with aching joints and squeaky shoes. But all it took was recognition by one observant congregant for whispers to begin to gather and heads to turn toward her.

For a moment, just a single moment, she could have been a young bride again, walking up that aisle to meet her husband. She felt delirious, caught between two times in this single place of colored sunlight and incense. But this time, there was no veil to hide behind, and the faces looking back at her weren't filled with love and admiration. This time, she was clearheaded, and the eyes that returned her gaze offered nothing but horror, pity, and blame.

She could hear their whispers, felt them slither.
Sally.
Stranger.
Fresh out of prison. Vile things, with children.
Rapist.
Rapist.
Rapist.
Reaching out to grab the end of a pew, she knew she couldn't continue in this nightmarish procession of shame, God be damned, and so she stopped and turned before moving, as

quickly as her failing knees would allow, toward the open doors that spilled out onto Market Street, followed by the horrified gaze of the congregation, hearing the venomous hiss in her ears all the way home.

SALLY

After Mr. Warner fell asleep at night in that attic room, her body aching, her *heart* aching from what he'd done to her, Sally didn't dare move. He was a light sleeper, and once when she'd gotten up to put her nightclothes back on, his arm had shot out and grabbed her by the throat. The next day, his fingers had left faint blue prints on her skin. So she lay as still as she could. Sometimes, she was too afraid to breathe even, and so she held her breath, her vision filling with stars.

Two weeks they'd been in Baltimore. Two long weeks, the sweltering August days melting one into the other. Mr. Warner had gotten a job at a garage down the street, so he was at work from nine until five most days. Sammy worked graveyard at the Coca-Cola bottling plant, which meant he was gone all night and asleep downstairs all day. Until school started in September, Mr. Warner said she had to stay in the room while he was at work.

"School?" she'd asked. "I'm going to school *here?*" She thought of Mrs. Appleton, the scent of chalk, the playground. Those girls. How had the whole summer passed already? At home, summer felt like a tiny eternity, days as long as seasons. Every sunlit hour swollen.

"Well, we gotta keep up appearances. Unless you want to add truancy to your rap sheet."

In Atlantic City, at least she'd been able to go outside. Mr. Warner had taken her everywhere with him, during the day anyway. But now that he had a job, he had no choice but to keep her locked up while he was working. At least he didn't tie her up anymore. After breakfast, he made her use the bathroom before ushering her back upstairs. He'd leave her with a loaf of bread, a can of salty sardines, and sometimes an apple. He'd fill two water glasses, but the one time she drank them, she'd had to use the bathroom so badly she'd practically wet herself waiting for him to come home. And so despite the unbearable heat and the thirst that came with it, she didn't drink a drop of water until he returned and unlocked the door each night. There was no key to this door, and so instead he used a coin, wedged into the door frame. She'd heard it clatter to the floor and marveled that a single copper coin, like the ones those girls put in their loafers, could be the one thing between her and her freedom.

She tried several times to see if she could get the door to open, waiting until after Mr. Warner had been gone an hour or more. Just in case he came back. But the door wouldn't budge. She worried that the racket would wake Sammy up;

he was friendly enough, but she also knew that he was *Mr. Warner's* friend first and foremost, and if he caught her trying to sneak out, he would be sure to keep her from walking out the front door.

The attic window offered no chance of escape, either; even if it weren't painted shut, she'd fall to her death from that height. And so she spent most of her time locked in that room escaping into the books she pilfered from Sammy's shelves downstairs. All day long, she'd lose herself inside the covers of the battered paperbacks with titles like *Special Detective* and *Mania for Murder.* There were other books, too, but they made her face burn with shame, the women on their covers wearing only lingerie and lipstick. *Ladies in Hades*, *Bury Me Deep*, and *Sex before Six.* The one time she'd dared to peek inside one of these stories, she'd felt sick: the characters doing the things Mr. Warner did to her, dirty awful things. It felt like somebody had written down her worst secrets; she'd wanted to tear the pages up. After that she'd made sure to only choose the books with detectives or pirates on the covers.

Because he worked the graveyard shift, by the time Mr. Warner came home at night, Sammy would just be getting up. Most nights, Sally was charged with cooking supper for all three of them. Mr. Warner had told her it was part of earning their keep. She didn't know how to make much besides hamburgers and fried eggs, but nobody seemed to mind. At least it got her out of that room, if only for a while. After the dishes were cleared, Sammy and Mr. Warner might play a hand or two of cards while she washed the dishes, and then Sammy would put on his uniform and get ready for work. Though, no matter what they'd had for supper, she'd feel it turning in her stomach. Because once Sammy left, she and Mr. Warner were alone.

He never used the gun again to threaten her. He didn't have to. Though she knew exactly where he kept it. She also knew what was coming, and it paralyzed her. She couldn't have fought back if she wanted to. Her limbs were useless. Even her voice caught inside her throat. And so instead of fighting, she slipped away. Just like she did when she was reading those detective stories. She *disappeared.* Vanished into her imagination.

Sometimes, she conjured her stepfather playing "Take the A Train" on his trumpet while her mother washed the dishes, pretending not to listen, but her hips swinging just a little beneath her aproned skirt. This was a rare vivid memory of him, as clear as a bright star in a dark sky. Sometimes, she dreamed herself into her bedroom, when Susan still lived at home, and recalled the simple happiness of the sound of rain on the roof and the way Susan sighed in her sleep. But mostly, she thought of her mother, tried

145

to imagine what she was doing at home. In that narrow bed in the darkest part of the night, she pictured Ella hunched over the sewing machine, face illuminated by the weak glow of her desk lamp. She saw her hands, the swollen knuckles and wrists as they pushed and pulled the endless yardage of fabric. Oddly, though, she realized she had no idea what it was that she had been sewing. Clothing? Bedding? Parachutes? Sally had never seen any finished project, no product, only *process*. An infinity of dark gray cloth, the expanse of her whole life. She thought that when she finally got home, she'd ask her what it was that she'd been making. She might offer to help her. How difficult could it be? She vowed she'd be less troublesome; she'd be helpful. A better daughter. A good girl.

It was her mother she continued to summon, when he finally left her alone at night. The only thing that could comfort her as her body stung. She closed her eyes and dreamed her mother's wrist against her forehead when she was sick. Transformed the thin blanket on the bed into her mother's worn housedresses. She ran her fingers along the edge of the coverlet, conjuring the hems of her mother's skirts. She clenched her legs together and wished herself into her mother's dreams. She recited the address of Sammy's house, dreaming the numbers out the open window into the air, wishing them onto the backs of the stars. Sending these imaginary missives home.

She read a book once about pigeons that carried messages, traveling to the recipients bearing news of war, news of disaster. As the pigeons congregated outside the attic window, she wondered if they might carry a message from her, alerting her mother of this disaster. *Homing,* that was what they were called. *Home, home, home,* she thought, the words pounding in time to the throbbing between her eyes, between her legs. She needed to figure out a way to get home.

Tonight, she lay on her back wide awake, his arm slung over her like something dead. She started to roll over, to face the wall, slowly, slowly, but the moment he felt her moving, his arm turned to lead across her chest, pinning her down again. She could hardly breathe.

There was a boy in her grade back in Camden who got polio and was in an iron lung. The whole class had gone to the hospital to visit him; they'd lined up like they were at a zoo exhibit. He was smiling and happy to see his friends. The nurse had hung pictures of his mother above him, to comfort him, Sally imagined. As they each walked past, he said *hello* and *thank you for coming.* The boys in the class asked the nurse if they could crawl inside one of the empty lungs to see what it was like. The girls had covered their mouths with their hands in a sort of giddy horror, leaning into each other and whispering. Sally, however, had lingered, watching as the contraption breathed for him. She tried to imagine what it would be like to be stuck inside a machine, one you were depending on for your life.

"How long do you gotta be in there?" she'd whispered to him when it was her turn to say hello. But he'd only shaken his head. She'd looked at the photo of his mother hanging above him and felt her heart break. "Are you ever gonna get to go home?"

ELLA

It had been nearly two months since Sally left. For Ella, each day was identical, excruciatingly so, to the previous one. Calls to and from the detectives. Checking the mail for a letter, for some clue. Staring at the phone. At the door. And underneath it all was the undercurrent of pain, though Ella could hardly tell anymore if the ache was inside or outside her heart. Susan was nearing the end of her pregnancy; her skin was taut, her ankles thick. She wasn't able to help much at the greenhouse, so while Al worked, she stayed with Ella at the house. Waiting for news. They were both irritable, prickly. Nerves raw and ragged.

"The weather's turning," Ella said, massaging her throbbing knee as she bent down to get a pie pan from the cupboard. "I can feel it."

The summer heat actually alleviated some of her pain, made it sufferable, even as the sticky humidity was not. She felt the onset of fall in her bones. The threat of fall resided in her marrow. She knew Susan felt it, too. The baby was due soon. Things were coming to an end. Summer would be over. But this morning as Ella moved slowly around her home, she wished it to stay. It was illogical, of course, but she thought that

149

as long as the seasons didn't shift, if she could hold off autumn, then Sally would be safe. But as soon as the air crackled cold, as soon as she felt the biting chill as she pulled the covers off in the morning, it would mean that the world was moving on without her.

"Mama, it's been three weeks already, since you heard from Sally," Susan said as if she were reading Ella's thoughts. "Are the police only looking in Baltimore still? The FBI? What did that detective say last?" She was standing at the counter rolling out a thin sheet of dough. She could barely reach the rolling pin, her belly setting her back at least a foot from the counter.

Ella nodded. "The government men are looking other places, too."

The county detective had assured her that since the FBI was involved now, it was only a matter of time before they found Sally. But she didn't buy it; there hadn't been a single article in the papers after that big one at the beginning of August. As much as she'd hated the reporters and their hungry questions, she felt abandoned now. Forgotten.

"I'm sure he'll be sending her back home soon," Ella said, nodding. "Before school starts." As if, indeed, this had simply been a vacation.

Ella heard Susan sigh, exasperated, as she worked the pin across the dough the way that Ella had shown her when she was still just a girl.

She hadn't taught Sally how to make a piecrust yet. She hadn't taught her how to make a good vegetable stock or how to darn a pair of socks. She was still a child; there were so many things she had yet to learn.

Ella looked out the kitchen window at the backyard. It was overgrown. The swing set was partially obscured by the tall grass. Soon, though, the lawn would be covered with dead leaves and, eventually, snow. Ella used to send Sally out there to play; she loved that she could do her kitchen chores and still see Sally from here. In the summer, she'd watch as she played alone in the backyard, talking to herself, making up games. It embarrassed Ella at first, as if she were witnessing something private. But after a while it didn't seem so strange at all anymore. She felt grateful that Sally could entertain herself, that she had such a vivid imagination. How could she interrupt that innocent reverie with meat loaf recipes and methods for getting stains out of yellowed collars?

She watched as the piecrust stuck to the wooden pin.

"Al's got a friend from Baltimore, you know," Susan said.

"Here, let me do that," Ella admonished, and grabbed the roller from her. "You need more flour."

"He's been talking about heading down there.

Maybe bring a photo of Sally? Ask around to see if anybody's seen her?"

Ella closed her eyes, and thought of that awful photo of Sally on the swing. Felt her heart begin to bottom out. She gripped the edge of the kitchen counter until her fingers ached, her wrists throbbed, until the pain in her body overwhelmed the pain in her chest.

"Mama?" Susan said, and took the pin back, rolling it furiously across the dough. "God, somebody's got to do *something*."

SALLY

*H*ere?" Sally asked meekly as they stood on the street staring at the Woolworth's sign, so similar to the one back at Camden where this all started, and he pushed her gently through the door.

As they walked down the aisle of school supplies, she felt sick. Her gut was gripped by pain so intense she started to double over. He held on to her elbow tightly. She thought that even if she collapsed, she wouldn't fall, he was holding on to her so forcefully.

They were buying items for school. That morning, he'd taken her to the Catholic school on Greenmount Avenue, just around the corner from Sammy's. The school year was starting up in just a week. He'd told her to keep her mouth shut. Let him do the talking.

"I'm Episcopalian," she'd said softly, shaking her head.

"I don't care if you're a kike," Mr. Warner had shot back. "You follow my lead."

He told the secretary at the desk that his name was Fogg, and that she was his daughter, Florence. That her poor mother, bless her soul, was dead. That she was to be in the sixth grade.

Now, with his free hand, he put the items into

their basket: pencils, erasers, a small cardboard box to keep them in. When they arrived at the counter where the black-and-white composition notebooks were, her stomach cramped again, and she gasped with pain.

"Well, looky here!" he said, sneering in that way he had that made her shoulders tremble. "I seem to recall you have a preference for this kind of notebook, eh, *Florence?*"

She took a series of shallow breaths, willing the pain away.

"You want to pay for this one? Or would ya rather steal it?" He chuckled, gripping the notebook tightly in his hand, waiting for her to answer.

"Pay for it, sir," she said.

"You sure?"

She nodded, tears filling her eyes.

"Well, that's a good thing. Because from my experience, it's the repeat offenders who wind up getting sent up the river. You could even get the electric chair if you get caught stealing again. Just like they're gonna do to that nigger lady and her boys down in Georgia. You heard about that?"

Sally shook her head. She didn't know what an electric chair was, but it sounded terrifying. Pain shot through her abdomen again, and she grabbed her stomach.

Mr. Warner threw the composition notebook

into the basket and yanked her arm. She concentrated on the muscles down there, clenching them as tightly as she could.

"The school's got a uniform, but you'll be needing some socks and new underclothes," he said, and she felt sweat start to bead on her forehead. She caught her reflection in a mirror as they walked to the clothing department, and she barely recognized herself. She looked ghostlike, pale. Sickly. Would her mother even know her now?

When they got to the counter with their things, she couldn't stand it anymore. It felt like the time she'd gotten the stomach flu when she was nine. The cramping was unbearable. She needed to find a restroom. The lady at the counter was pretty, with rosy cheeks and shiny blond hair held away from her face with a rhinestone barrette in the shape of a peacock. Purple and green glass feathers.

"I need to use the powder room," she whispered.

The lady at the register looked at her and smiled. "It's right down past the lunch counter, sweetheart."

Sally looked up at Mr. Warner, pleading with him to let her go without saying a word. Back at the house he walked her to the powder room and stood outside the door. In case she tried to squeeze through that tiny window overlooking the backyard, she supposed. She'd thought about it, of course, but even if she got outside, where could she go? She couldn't go home; Mr. Warner told her that the FBI would take her mother away if they found out she was hiding her. That there were laws against harboring a fugitive. She could barely go to the bathroom sometimes, knowing he was there on the other side, waiting. Listening to her.

"We're heading home in just a minute. Can't it wait?" Mr. Warner smiled at her and at the lady at the counter.

Sally shook her head. "I'm feelin' sick," she said.

"Oh," the saleslady said. "Please go then."

Mr. Warner didn't let go of her arm, his fingers still pressing deep into her flesh.

"It's nothing," he said, and pushed the items on the counter toward the woman. Sally looked at the marbled composition book and blinked as her eyes filled with tears. "Always complaining, this one. Probably just nervous about startin' school."

But despite his smile, the shop girl looked at him sternly, as if he were the child, and walked out from behind the counter.

"Follow me, sweetheart," she said. "I'll show you the way."

And reluctantly, Mr. Warner released her arm.

As they walked down the aisle, Sally felt her head pounding with possibility. She could tell this lady (with her high heels and pink powdered cheeks). She could tell her her real name, that this man, this FBI man, was keeping her, doing terrible things to her in that attic room. She could barely think about it without feeling dizzy. As she followed the lady to the restroom door, staring at the backs of her heels (there was a small run in her stocking, a scuff), she thought maybe, if she could convince her to come with her into the restroom, she could tell her what was happening. That she might take pity on her. But as they approached the door and the woman turned to her, Sally's stomach cramped so hard, she started to see stars.

Her panties felt wet, and she worried her bowels were starting to release. The thought that she'd soiled herself, like a baby, filled her with horror and shame.

Sally practically ran into the ladies room, closing the door behind her. She lifted her skirt and tore down her panties.

Blood.

So much blood, coming from down there. She felt her vision vignetting: blackness at the edges and then stars.

"Miss?" the woman said on the other side of the door.

Was she dying? Had whatever Mr. Warner done to her torn something deep inside her? She held her breath and studied the bright red bloom in her underwear, the toilet bowl filled with blood. She thought she might vomit.

Knock, knock.

"Miss? I have something for you," the woman said.

Sally stood up, feeling woozy. She slipped the soiled panties off and rolled them into a little ball before stuffing them into the bottom of the waste bin. She opened the door to the restroom just a sliver, and the lady's arm reached in. In her hand was a brand-new pair of clean white underwear as well as some sort of bandage and a pink box that said MODESS: SANITARY BELT. The picture on the cover looked like one of Susan's garter belts.

"I wasn't sure what you needed," the woman said on the other side of the door.

Maybe she could invite her in now, beg her to please take her to the hospital. To keep her from dying. To maybe even take her home with her and hide her from the law, from Mr. Warner with his bristly face and sharp hands. (Each night, she recalled the blades, the blood of girls swirling together.) She looked down at her leg where a single blood drop traveled down toward her sock and sucked in her breath.

"Go ahead, sweetheart. Take them," the woman said.

"Ma'am . . . I . . . I'm scared . . ."

"Oh, poor baby." Her voice was gentle, and Sally almost pulled the door all the way open. She imagined embracing her, the lady stroking her hair as Sally told her everything that had happened since the last time she was in a Woolworth's. That Mr. Warner had done something bad to her, and now she was dying. But then she was struck with a terrible realization. Maybe this was a trick. Had Mr. Warner set her up? Had he done something to her to see if she would steal something again? The underpants still had the price tag attached. She looked at the pair of panties, felt the cool air on her bare flesh beneath her skirt. It felt so strange to be without her underthings. But she couldn't take a chance; if she was caught stealing again, she might never get home.

She shook her head, though the woman couldn't see her.

"Is this the first time your monthly visitor's come calling?" the lady whispered.

Sally stiffened. She'd heard Susan say that before, curled up in her bed with a hot water bottle pressed to her belly. Sally had been so worried about her, but Susan had just smiled and said, *It's the curse.* Horrified, Sally had wondered how her very own, sweet sister had been cursed. And by whom. But then Susan had laughed, and said, *It's just my monthly visitor, Sally. I'm fine.*

"Just attach the pad to the clips on the belt, and then put it on like a garter belt. Wear these panties over them." Her voice was low. "When

159

you get home, tell your mama what happened."

Trembling, Sally took the items from her, readying herself for Mr. Warner to come barreling through the door. She quickly cleaned herself up, including the tears, which ran hot down her cheeks, and the thin river of blood on her leg. She tried to get the bloodstain out of her sock, but it just blurred pink, the sock cold and wet against her ankle. When she came out, Mr. Warner was waiting, as he was always waiting, pretending he was only looking at a rack of lady's blouses.

"For her mother," he said to the shop girl, plucking a hanger from the rack and examining the fabric.

Sally choked back a sob as she thought of her mother, tried to imagine her in that pale yellow blouse. She even thought for just a moment that he meant to send her home now, with a gift for Ella. She'd tell her mother about the helpful shop girl, and then ask her what she was supposed to do. How long she'd keep bleeding. If she could die if she lost too much blood.

"It's lovely," the shop lady said. She looked at Sally and winked.

But Mr. Warner replaced it on the rack. "Too small. We'll just take the other things, thanks."

Outside the heat made her swoon as they walked, his hand returned to her arm like a vise. As they walked briskly back to the house, she was aware of the bulky pad between her legs beneath her skirt; what would Mr. Warner do if he discovered that she'd taken the new panties without paying? Would he still believe she was a good girl who did what she was told? That she could be trusted? If he found them, he might never let her go home.

AL

"Excuse me? Do you know where the closest service station is?" Al leaned out the open passenger window and asked an elderly gentleman who was walking a small dog.

"There's a Sinclair station over at East Twenty-fifth and Kirk," he said.

"That way?" Al asked, and the dog started to yap.

"Near the Coca-Cola bottling plant," he said. "Come on now, Buster. *Heel*."

Al had never been to Baltimore before and didn't really know where he was headed, nor what he might be able to find once he got there. As he parked the car on the blighted street in East Baltimore, he reached for the photo the police had found in that rooming house in Atlantic City, that oddly disturbing picture of Sally sitting on a rope swing, wearing a dress neither Ella nor Susan had ever seen before.

He'd gotten his nephew to keep an eye on things at the greenhouse today, and he'd left Susan behind reluctantly. The baby was coming any day now. She hadn't slept right in weeks, tossing and turning all through the night. During the day, when she wasn't on the phone, comforting Ella, she was consumed with readying the house. He'd caught her going at the grout in the bathroom with his old toothbrush and a cup of bleach just the other morning. Sun hadn't even come up yet.

He wanted nothing more than to be able to bring Sally back home to Susan. To Ella. But where should he even begin? He'd asked Buzz Murdock, a buddy of his from high school who'd lived in Baltimore for a spell, if he knew if there were any pool halls, any places where a criminal like Frank La Salle might go.

"You know they call it Mob City these days," Buzz had chuckled. "You sure you want to go stirring up that hornet's nest?"

Buzz was right; hunting down criminals wasn't exactly in Al's wheelhouse.

The police had said La Salle was a mechanic by trade. Al figured he'd start by stopping at all the garages, show Sally's picture around. He also had La Salle's photos from the papers, though he could barely bring himself to look at his face. The cops were pretty sure that La Salle didn't have a vehicle, so Al thought he might speak to some folks at the train station, at the bus depot. Though if that failed, he wasn't sure what he'd do. Maybe just start knocking on doors?

"Be careful," Susan had implored. Her voice was muffled, as she disappeared under the sink looking for God knew what. Ammonia maybe.

"Of course," he'd said, and offered her his arm

163

as she struggled back up to her feet, clutching a rusty green can of Comet.

"And you'll be back tonight by supper?"

"I'll try. If not, I'll find a phone and give you a call."

He studied the city maps he'd picked up at three different service stations: Shell, Gulf, Sinclair. He figured he'd start here, stopping at every service station noted on the maps, asking if anybody had seen the man in that photo. The little girl on that swing. Now, he opened up the car door and stepped onto the street, could feel sweat rolling down his sides as he made his way toward the bright green-and-red Sinclair sign.

All day he searched, but no one had seen La Salle. Sally, either. He'd show the photo of La Salle first, the one from the papers. "You seen this guy? He might have come by looking for work?" A collective shaking of heads, shrugging of shoulders. "How 'bout this girl?"

You'd think somebody would at least have recognized her from the articles in the paper. This was the photo they'd all used. But not one person had any idea who she was, never mind where she might be.

He'd gone to the bus station, the train depot. To three rooming houses and six different bars. He'd stopped by the police station as well, and they'd told him they were actively pursuing all leads. That he should let law enforcement do their job. But the lieutenant he spoke to seemed more concerned with his sandwich than he was with Al's lost sister-in-law.

He'd been a fool, he thought, to think he could find her here. That it would be as simple as showing her photo, asking around. Foolish to think a guy like him was capable of saving anyone. He was no hero; he never had been.

Al had spent exactly two years in the U.S. Navy, aboard the USS *Alabama,* where in February 1944, he'd been in the head when his best friend, Robert Lee Langston, was incinerated. While repelling enemy air attacks on their way to the Marianas, there was a malfunction in one of the gun turrets, causing a five-inch gun to fire back into another turret on the ship. It killed five of his shipmates and wounded eleven others. When it was over, he'd vomited first and then wept. He'd been seasick (he'd actually been sick since the minute he'd come aboard), and Bobby Lee had offered to take his spot at the guns. The only thing left of his friend was his boots. He'd gathered them, smelling of ash and sweat, kept them with his personal belongings for a whole year. After the war, he delivered them to Bobby Lee's mother, and she'd looked at him with such hurt in her expression, he knew he'd made a terrible mistake. Bobby Lee had died because Al was busy puking his guts out, and all he had to offer his poor grieving mother was a pair of blackened boondockers. Al still dreamed the smell of burning flesh and metal. The look in that woman's eyes. He couldn't bear to have another mother look at him with the same disappointment. He wanted to bring Sally home. In the flesh. Alive. And if he couldn't do that, he at least wanted to be able to give Ella and Sue *something,* some small bit of hope.

After six hours, his feet hurt from walking; he must have walked a hundred miles already. His clothes were nearly soaked through with perspiration. He hadn't stopped for lunch even, and now his stomach was howling with hunger. He figured he'd grab an early supper and then head back home. If nothing came up, he'd have two hours in the car to come up with a plan for what to do next. There had to be something. He felt in his pocket to see how much money he had for his meal. Just a single, crumpled dollar and some change.

Money. Maybe a *reward* would help to motivate people. *Yes,* that was it. Why hadn't he thought of it before? Feeling a jolt of inspiration, he walked into a Woolworth's on the corner and made his way to the lunch counter. The waitress said they were closing down the kitchen, but then she took pity on him and said she had some leftover fish she could warm up. He was starving and devoured the tepid fried fish platter and side of canned peaches and cottage cheese.

"Can I get you a nice slice of pie for dessert?" the waitress asked. He'd seen the Boston cream pie in the glass display, but now as he looked at his watch, he figured he'd better check in with Susan and then head home.

"Looks delicious, but I'll pass today. My wife's gettin' ready to have a baby, and I best be makin' my way back."

He paid his bill and left a generous tip on the counter. On his way out the door to go find a pay phone, he saw a display of baby items.

"Can I help you find something?" a shop girl asked.

He smiled. "I'd like to pick up a little something for my wife. She's due any day now," he said.

"Oh, how exciting!" she said, clapping her hands together. She was young and pretty, bright eyes and flushed cheeks. "We just got in some new baby books, you know, places to keep track of things. Put their birth certificates and footprints and such."

"That would be perfect!" Al said, and followed her to a display, noting that her hair was secured with a pretty peacock hair comb, its feathers made of colored glass. "Do you sell those here?" he asked, gesturing to the hairpin.

"Oh no," she laughed, touching the barrette. "This was a gift from my fiancé."

He paid for the baby book and left the store. She'd told him where to find a pay phone, and he used the rest of his coins to call. As he was dialing, he thought that after he checked in with Sue, he'd go back and show the ladies at the Woolworth's Sally's photo. The waitress, the shop girl. Maybe one of them had read about her in the papers.

But when Sue answered, he forgot all about Sally and Frank La Salle.

"Oh my God, Al, where are you?" Sue asked.

SUSAN

Susan had woken from an afternoon nap and known right away that something was wrong. Pain pulsed through her body, and for one awful moment, she thought that perhaps the same thing that had taken hold of her mother's body had somehow now taken hold of hers as well. In a slumber-induced stupor, she felt the same terror her mother must have felt each and every day when her body conspired against her.

It wasn't until sleep left her, and awareness and memory crept in, that she realized it was the baby. It was coming.

For months she had tried to imagine this, what it would feel like and how she would know. Everyone assured her that there would be no question when it finally happened, that true labor pains could not be mistaken for anything else.

"Al," she'd said, reaching across the bed as another contraction made her body pulse with pain. But then the realization hit her that Al wasn't home. He was still down in Baltimore looking for Sally.

"Oh my God," she said, feeling panicked. The fingers of pain gripped her so tightly she cried out. And as she did, her water broke, soaking the sheets, her legs, the bed.

Al had promised he'd try to be home by six or seven o'clock. It was only four now. By the time he finally called to let her know he was on his way, the contractions were coming every few minutes. Hardly enough time to catch her breath in between.

"I'll call Davey," he said. "Get ready. I'll have him come get you right away. I'll meet you at the hospital."

In her brother-in-law's car, she closed her eyes, leaned her head back, and held her breath through the waves of pain. She thought of the beach, of the time they took Sally with them to the shore: the waves backing away and then coming and crashing against the sand. Sally had marveled at them, somehow surprised each and every time the waves returned. Sally had looked at Susan, who was sitting on the beach, reading a magazine, as if to confirm that this was really possible: that the push and pull of the ocean would go on endlessly. The look of wonder in her face made Susan smile.

Sally. The pain of her absence was not predictable like this. It didn't have a cadence, a rhythm. Instead it was like a pit, a hollowness, a *hole* that opened up abruptly when she was least expecting it. A bottomless well she fell down, grasping at the sides to hang on. The fear she felt about the baby was petty, small compared to this. It was like trying to imagine the depth of the universe, infinity.

"She's having a baby," Davey said to the woman at the counter. (As though the woman wouldn't know this by simply looking at Susan, hunched over and cradling the bottom of her belly like it was a basket of ripe fruit she was trying not to drop.)

"Oh God," Susan cried as the pain gripped her harder. She felt the pressure bearing down on her pelvis. The baby was coming; she felt herself aflame.

"Her water's already broke," she heard Davey say to the woman.

She wanted nothing more than to fall to her knees to the floor, to crawl like an infant herself, her body rocked by the rhythmic ache. But just as she was lowering herself to the blessedly cold linoleum, someone came behind her with a wheelchair, and then she was being rushed down a brightly lit corridor. God, where was Al?

The old nurse, whose hands and words were rough, brusquely situated her and her enormous belly on the bed.

"No time for an enema, I don't think," the nurse said, almost scolding. "When was the last time you ate?"

Susan reached out and grabbed the nurse's wrist. She wanted to tell her that she just needed to get down onto the floor, onto her hands and knees. But her words were gone.

"Now, that's enough of that," the nurse said, peeling Susan's fingers from her arm. Another nurse entered the room, and the older nurse called her over.

"We're going to need to tie this one down."

The new nurse nodded. She was young and pretty, with dimples.

"Please," Susan pleaded. "Help me!" But the younger nurse only shook her head, her face filled with pity, and as the other nurse tied her hands down to the bed, Susan had the unbearable sense she was being imprisoned, held captive by not only this pain that enclosed her, but this sadistic nurse as well.

Sally. She thrashed, trying to free herself. "No!" she screamed, and the next wave of pain crashed over her.

"Calm down now, you're not the first person to ever give birth, you know," the cruel nurse said as the other one offered gently, "I'm givin' you something to ease the pain now, and I promise you won't remember anything later. But you've really *got* to hold still."

As the needle entered her arm, she tumbled, her body sucked under by an undertow.

The doctor entered.

"Is she out?"

And she drifted, first on those receding waves of pain and then farther out to sea. She was alone. Adrift on an unending expanse of black water, black sky, starless, terrifying. She knew Sally, the baby, Al, and her mother were all out there somewhere, and she woke screaming and reaching for them, her cries mixing with the sound of a bird screeching in that dark sky.

She fixed upon the squawking bird, that bloody bird in the doctor's large white palms before she felt another prick of pain and another hot rush of oblivion.

SALLY

Sally lay on the bed, waiting to die. She hadn't stopped bleeding. She'd soaked through the pad the shop girl had given her at Woolworth's, and had wound up stuffing one of her old socks into her panties in Sammy's bathroom when they got home. She was certain now this wasn't just a *monthly visitor* but rather something awful, the pain crippling. She thought of her mother. Of all that pain she suffered. How did she even get out of bed? It made Sally feel selfish, the way she'd been so impatient sometimes when her mother complained. She swore, if she survived this, she'd never be touchy with her mother again. She'd take care of her.

She could hear Sammy and Mr. Warner talking downstairs. Sammy was getting ready for work. She'd heard the pipes groaning as he took his shower. Mr. Warner had stayed downstairs after supper, drinking and smoking cigarettes. Listening to a Cubs/Dodgers game on the radio. Mr. Warner had mentioned something once about growing up in Chicago with Sammy.

She curled her kness to her chest. When she heard the front door slam shut, she held her breath. Wished on the single dim star she could see through the foggy window that he'd stay downstairs until the baseball game was over. For a while, it seemed that maybe her wish had been granted. She could still hear the radio. And after a couple of hours, she started to slip into an uneasy sleep.

The sound of the door opening startled her, and she sat up, backing into the corner as Mr. Warner staggered into the room. She gripped her blankets with her hands. A wave of pain washed over her.

Wordlessly, he came to her. She closed her eyes as his hands pulled at her, rolled her over, as the rough pads of his fingers stroked her neck. She held her breath. But when he pulled down her bottoms, he stopped.

"Goddamn it! What the hell?" He reached over and turned on the little lamp that sat on the nightstand next to the bed. It was too bright. "Jesus Christ," he said, jumping off the bed, staring at the blood on his hands.

"I think I'm dying, sir," she managed. "I think you gone and killed me."

At this Mr. Warner scowled. "You're a god-damned fool, Sally Horner. You ain't dying. You're a *woman*."

ELLA

The call came in the middle of the night, Ella's phone jangling like an alarm. She shot up in bed, her mind trying hard to connect this sound with its meaning. Was it Russell? What had he done this time? Had he been arrested again? First there was fear, then anger, and then the sudden shocking realization that Russell was *dead*. That he'd been dead for five years already. How many times would she have to relive this? That particular tragedy was long passed, though it was still the first place her mind went. Usually, when consciousness came, her mind settled again but now it had another place to leap to.

Sally.

God, had they found Sally? Al had gone down to Baltimore to look. He said he'd show the photos, see if anybody had seen her with that man. She leaned over to the side of the bed, her shoulders crying out in anguish as she reached first for the light and then for the heavy handset of the telephone.

"Hello?" She grimaced.

"She's here," the man said, his voice lilting with excitement.

She felt acid filling her mouth. She shook her head. "Sally?"

Silence.

"Ella, it's Al. The baby came tonight. It's a girl. You're a grandmother."

"The baby?" she asked, her throat enflamed.

"Seven pounds. Her name is Dee."

"Susan?"

"She's still asleep," he said. "I'll come get you in the morning after she wakes up."

Ella hung up the phone and sat at the edge of the bed, head hanging between her knees, the hot rush of blood to her head pulsating. Not Sally. Sally was still gone. No amount of joy could change that fact. Ella's shoulders hunched in shame at her next thought: she envied Susan. The dark truth was that first feeling, the hungry pang of envy. Because Susan had been given a daughter, when Ella's had been stolen.

SISTER MARY KATHERINE

On the first day of school, Sister Mary Katherine stood behind her desk and stared at the empty seats, so tidy in their neat rows. The chalkboard gleamed, not yet wearing its hazy scrim of chalk dust. Each piece of chalk was still white, intact, pristine. She felt a tremendous sense of satisfaction at this vision: the world and everything in it somehow right.

In a few moments, the children would arrive in a chaotic plaid flurry of hair pulling and gum smacking. Scabby knees and black eyes and all the other battle scars of summer. Knee socks and headbands and loose-buttoned shirts. The uniformed group anything but uniform. They would be loud and unruly, and it was her job to bring them to order, to coerce them into compliance with a firm sort of kindness, a gentle type of discipline. She knew this was the greatest challenge any teacher would meet: how to garner both respect and love. From her limited experience, she knew it was generally one or the other most teachers elicited.

She noticed the new girl right away. Her clothes looked as if they'd just been plucked from a rack, her shoes shiny of both leather and buckle. Her hair, however, was a tangled mess. And she clutched a composition notebook to her chest like a shield.

Sister Mary Katherine loved her the moment she saw her, something about her inspiring not pity but *worry*. Her clothing was immaculate, but her eyes (those downcast light blue eyes) were full of sadness, suggesting to the sister that she had been neglected in some fundamental way.

A motherless girl. That was it. She had the eyes (and uncombed hair) of a child who had lost her mother. Sister Mary Katherine could spot one from a mile away; before she became a teacher, her first appointment had been at an orphanage. Could she be an orphan?

"Quiet down, quiet down," she said as the din of the children's voices came to a crescendo. "Take your seats."

The children did as they were told; that was the most wonderful thing about Catholic children, the way they would sit and rise on command.

She had already memorized the roster; she took great pride in knowing not only all the children's names in her classroom, but in most of the other classrooms at St. Ann's as well. Even a few years after teaching a child, she was usually able to conjure their names when she saw them in the market or at the movie theater. It was a gift she had, and further evidence that teaching had been an even louder calling than the one she'd received from God.

"My name is Sister Mary Katherine. I will be your sixth-grade teacher. When you hear your name called, please answer 'present'—not 'yes' or 'here.' Present, because you are now and will be in every moment in my class. *Present,* meaning fully engaged. Now let's begin."

"Elizabeth Adams."

"Present."

"Anthony Bertelli."

When she called Florence Fogg, there was silence. The girl's gaze was out the window.

"Florence Fogg," she repeated, more loudly this time.

"Yes?" the girl answered, seeming to snap out of her haze.

Two girls in the third row giggled, leaning toward each other and whispering. Sister Mary Katherine took the ruler she'd been holding in her hand and cracked it against the desk. Both girls looked startled. Here was where she would establish her rules, and this sort of girlish cruelty would not be allowed. (She knew well the propensity for small brutalities among little girls, had been both witness and victim to it herself as a child, and did not tolerate it in her classroom.)

"Present," Florence Fogg corrected herself as Sister Mary Katherine raised an eyebrow (a skill she had mastered just this past year but now a key expression in her arsenal of disciplinary tools).

She completed the roster and then asked a meek and exceptionally tiny boy with the unfortunate name of Richard Small to hand out the sixth-grade readers.

Florence Fogg, what an odd little girl, and what an odd name, like something from a novel. Like an imaginary girl.

VIVI

In Camden, those other girls returned to school as well, but the seat up front and center where Sally always sat next to Vivi remained empty, her absence like a missing tooth, tongue worrying over it again and again and again.

By then they all knew that something terrible had happened to Sally, that she had been kidnapped like that Lindbergh baby before they all were born. Plucked out of his crib, a ransom note demanding money for his return. But Sally's family was poor, so what would that man want with her? Bess said her parents whispered about Sally after she had gone to bed and that her mother held her more closely—so close she could feel her heart almost pounding its way out of her chest. *Be careful. Do not talk to strangers.* Irene's father didn't allow her to walk home alone from school anymore. *You girls need to stick together,* he said to them, shaking his head.

Only Vivi had dared to ask her mother why a grown man would steal someone else's little girl.

"Well, Vivi . . . it's because . . . ," she had started, and the expression on her mother's face was one Vivi had never seen before, so full of angst and fear and something like pity. And that had scared her more than any admonishments to steer clear of strange men.

"Don't worry yourself," her mother finally offered. Or pleaded. "You're too young to concern yourself with this. You're just a girl." She returned to the afghan she was crocheting, the yarn in a bundle in her lap like a kitten.

"I just feel so bad," Vivi persisted even as her mother had ended the conversation. "For her poor mama." She'd never shake the image of Mrs. Horner on the pavement, legs splayed out in front of her. When she'd left her, the mailman struggling to help her stand, she'd been overcome with the same guilt she felt when she left Sally at the Woolworth's. What kind of terrible girl was she? "We should do something. For her family."

"There's nothing that can be done," her mother said, lips tightening, hands working furiously. "Those are private matters."

SUSAN

It was a beautiful service, Mama," Susan said, kissing her mother's cool, pale cheek. "We really wish you could have been there."

Ella huffed. "Well, come in and have something to eat now."

It was early October, and they had just come from Dee's christening at St. Stephen's in Beverly. The leaves had begun to turn, and the air felt blissfully cool and crisp. Ella had made a spread with three kinds of finger sandwiches: tuna salad, chicken salad with peeled grapes, pimento and cheese. Sugar cookies and iced tea. It was just the three adults and the baby, but there was enough food for an entire ladies' luncheon.

Ella reached out her arms for the baby.

"You sure, Mama?" Susan asked, but she was so grateful to have her arms free, if only long enough to eat a finger sandwich or two.

The baby was asleep, still wearing the christening gown Ella had made for her. Susan had told her she didn't need to make anything new; didn't she still have the one that she and Sally had both worn? But when Ella found the old gown in the depths of the upstairs closet, it was riddled with moth holes and yellowed with age. The new one was simple, just muslin with some pin tucks, but Susan was touched by her mother's efforts, though Ella had refused to attend the christening itself.

Ella had barely left the house since Sally disappeared four months ago. Al had been bringing her groceries, and, until the baby arrived, Susan had been helping out with the housework. The past six weeks since the baby was born were a blur, though—midnight feedings, a million soiled diapers. She figured she'd walked at least a hundred miles pushing the stroller up and down the sidewalk. Never mind the hours of simply watching Dee sleep. Surely Ella remembered what it was like to be a new mother. How consuming it could be?

Susan hadn't known what to expect. Of course, she'd imagined herself holding the baby in her arms, pinning diapers, and sterilizing glass bottles. She'd once practiced with her sleepy-eyed baby doll. But this, the way her body ached with longing. This odd, tender bliss took her by surprise.

Delirious, sleepless, she studied the baby's fingers, the paper-thin nails, the shivery lines of her palms, and the soft soles of her small feet. Even as her body burned and throbbed in the aftermath, she had never felt so happy in her life. Not even when she and Al fell in love. Though this was similar.

It wasn't contentment she felt, rather a sort of

185

restless love. She didn't know how to contain it. How to hold on. For even as she felt almost swollen with love, it seemed fleeting. Like trying to hold on to breath or fog or the warmth of a beam of sunlight. Strangely, it made her feel bad for Al. She couldn't explain it, but she felt like she was experiencing something he couldn't possibly grasp. It made her pity him even, though he was oblivious. Of course, he loved the baby. Took pleasure in holding her, felt pride when their friends said how much she favored him. But his was a faraway love, an abstract affection. This love she felt seemed embedded in every inch of her flesh. Every molecule. She'd heard people talk about God in this way: as if their bodies were *made* of love.

It was for this reason she couldn't understand her mother's odd refusal to talk about Sally. Whenever she and Al tried to bring it up (the investigation, Al's own search efforts), Ella clammed up, simply shook her head. And with each day that passed, she seemed to become more and more dismissive. It infuriated Susan, made her feel almost ill. Now that she was a mother herself, she knew that if anyone harmed *her* daughter, she was certain she could, and would, kill them with her bare hands.

Ella rocked the baby in the glider while Susan and Al ate. Susan had to slow herself down. She hadn't been able to eat a meal uninterrupted in so long, she was ravenous. She piled her plate high with sandwiches and went back for more when they were gone.

"Ma?" Al said, and Susan stopped.

She had warned Al not to bring it up. Not today, but he couldn't seem to help himself.

"Ma, we're thinking we need to put up a reward. To help find Sally."

Ella stopped rocking. Pursed her lips.

"You know I don't have no money."

"We know that, Mama," Susan said, trying not to lose her patience. She was exhausted; she hadn't slept more than two straight hours since the baby was born.

"Susan and I have a little nest egg we've started, but with the baby here now, we'd rather not get into that. We were hoping there might be something you'd be willing to sell? A piece of jewelry maybe? Something you don't wear?"

Susan would have laughed if it hadn't been so sad. Besides her engagement ring from Russell, all of her mother's jewelry was made of paste. She and Sally used to like to rummage through her jewelry box. Clip-on earrings so heavy they pulled their earlobes down. Strands of fake pearls.

"She doesn't have anything," Susan said, so her mother wouldn't have to.

The baby began to stir, her small mouth opening and closing like a baby robin waiting for a worm. Susan left the last tuna salad sandwich on her plate and stood up, went to her mother, and lifted the baby from her arms before her soft cries turned into something louder. She pressed the baby to her chest and bounced up and down, rocking her in her arms, assuring her that she was safe. That her mother was there.

"We should get home," Susan said to Al, who was still sitting expectantly at the edge of his seat.

"Wait," Ella said, and rose from the chair, slowly making her way to the stairs. "Just hold on."

ELLA

Ella sat at the edge of her bed, with her jewelry box sitting next to her. Inside, there were tangled necklaces, some costume brooches, and a half-dozen single earrings. She wasn't sure why she kept them. The missing ones never showed up.

She lifted the small diamond engagement ring from its velvety bed and attempted to slip it onto her finger, though it wouldn't go past her first misshapen knuckle. She still didn't know how Russell came up with the money to buy it, and speculating on it made her stomach twist.

Come dance with me, he'd said, pulling her up by her two hands. He was drunk (though at the time it had made him charming, fun). She'd resisted at first, but finally, reluctantly, she had given in, rising to her feet and rolling her eyes and letting him lead her onto the dance floor.

I'm no dancer, she protested.

I'll teach you, he countered.

The music was bright, and he was already pulling her tightly against him.

I got two children already, she warned.

I love *kids!* he parried.

He held her as their bodies moved across the floor, her feet recollecting other rooms, other rhythms. He smelled like Old Spice and cigarettes. Heady. Intoxicating.

I'm divorced, she said.

You're free! he challenged. He pulled her closer then and whispered into her hair. *You're free.*

She plucked the ring from its nest. It wasn't worth much, but it was the only thing of value she had. Al said that a reward might loosen lips, might jog people's memories. He'd take out ads in all the Baltimore papers, he said. Hang Sally's photo on every light post, every tree.

She knew exactly what Russell would want her to do. He, like Al, would have given anything he had to help Sally. He'd loved that child as if she were his very own. He'd have traded his very soul if it meant she'd come home.

It's just a rock, El. How was it that she could still hear his voice in her ear, as clear as a bell? *Just a bit of coal.*

She examined the tiny diamond, the way the gold band had softened and bent over time to fit her finger, how it had worn thin. *It's just a trinket,* she thought. Just a symbol, after all. And a silly one at that; every promise it had meant to signify had been broken. The idea that it might be exchanged for her little girl seemed foolish, but what else did she have? So she put it in the pocket of her apron and headed back downstairs.

SALLY

On Halloween night in Baltimore, Sally longed to be like the other children at St. Ann's, going out trick-or-treating in their costumes. Hobos, and cowboys, and clowns. Last year her mother had made her a gypsy costume, purple chiffon with tinkling coins sewn into the hem. Her mother always made Sally's costumes, refusing to spend money on the cheap plastic Ben Cooper masks they sold at the Woolworth's. Before Mr. Warner took her, she'd already planned out what she wanted to be this year: Dorothy from *The Wizard of Oz*. Back when she first started talking about it, her mother had promised she'd make her a blue gingham pinafore dress. Her mother had an old pair of heels she thought she might cover with red paint and glitter. They wore the same size. Sally had even entertained the idea that some of the other girls might like to join her. Perhaps Irene, Bess, and Vivi could have been the Scarecrow, the Tin Man, and the Cowardly Lion. Maybe her mother could make costumes for all of them.

But now there was no one to make her costume, and no girls to play along. Though even if there were, she knew there was no way Mr. Warner would let her go door to door with the other children. As it was, she was never on her own. He walked her to school on his way to work at the garage down the street and was there waiting for her when she got out, taking a late lunch break to walk her back to Sammy's house. At the house, he locked her in the attic room, where she did her homework until six o'clock when he got home from work. Then he would let her go wash up in the bathroom on the second floor before sending her to the kitchen to cook supper. And the three of them would sit at the table, making small talk.

"You getting along with the other kids okay?" he'd asked not long after school started in September, his jaws grinding away at the piece of meat she'd cooked.

She'd nodded, though this was a lie. She was too afraid to talk to any of the children, the other girls. He'd told her that under no circumstances was she to tell the other children at the school where she was from, her real name. *Fogg,* this was her name now. Florence Fogg. (This name made her think of those opaque dreams she had sometimes, the world obscured by a dense haze.) He told her that it was for her protection. They were undercover, fugitives. Unless she wanted to get dragged out of class in handcuffs, locked away forever, she would be exactly who he said she was. She was so terrified of slipping up, she'd decided it was easier to simply stay away from the other children. During class, she never giggled and whispered with the other girls when Sister Mary Katherine turned her back to face the blackboard. During recess, instead of jumping rope or playing games, she sat on the cold stone steps and wrote in her composition book. It didn't take long for her silence to register not as a product of shyness but of oddness. And curiosity turned to cruelty.

Little Florence Fogg, sitting on a log. Daddy's a bum and mama's a hog. They'd push their noses up and make oinking noises. She kept her head down and pretended not to hear them. She became not only a mute but deaf as well. *Florence Fogg sitting in a daze, how dumb is she? Let me count the ways. One, two, three . . .* This one hurt the most, because she wasn't dumb, not at all.

"You doing well in your subjects?" he'd asked, and she noticed the shine of grease on his thin lip.

She nodded. She was a straight-A student. Sister Mary Katherine lent her books, as many as she could carry. She selected stories she thought Sally would like and set them aside for her. It was wonderful to read books about children rather than the grown-up stories in Sammy's paperbacks. But just as at home, she didn't have any friends. So on Halloween night, instead of trick-or-treating, she stood at the stove, listening to the crackle of the cube steak; he liked it loaded up with pepper, which made her eyes water.

It was a Sunday, so Sammy was off work, and he and Mr. Warner were half in the bag already by the time they finished supper and started to play cards, a game called Machiavelli. It wasn't a betting game at least, so they never argued the way they did when they played cribbage or gin.

After supper, Sally stood at the sink washing the greasy dishes, the window open to the cool autumn night to let out the smoke from their cigarettes. Outside she could hear the neighborhood children excitedly going from door to door, ringing doorbells, hollering out "Trick or treat!" When she pulled back the curtains, she could see the groups moving in packs, the white sheets of ghost costumes glowing in the night. And she thought about the Dorothy costume that never was. Those red slippers. At the sink, she closed her eyes, stood on her tiptoes, and clicked her heels together three times.

Sammy, not wanting to be bothered by the doorbell, had turned out the porch light, a signal that there were no treats to be had here, but every now and then the doorbell would ring anyway, and one of the men would cuss. "Go away! Goddamned kids."

"Sir, I'm going to wash up," she said, drying her hands on a tattered dishrag, and Mr. Warner looked up from his plate at her. Winked.

She made her way down the hall, the smoky air

seeming to follow her down the dark corridor. In the bathroom, she moved the hamper against the closed door since there was no lock. She raised the lid to wedge it under the knob, and the smell of gasoline wafted out of the hamper, turning her stomach. She ran the water in the sink and washed her face, her hands. She tried not to look in the mirror, because seeing her reflection made her unbearably sad.

They didn't talk about what happened with the blood even once. But a whole box of those pads appeared on the back of the toilet in the bathroom the next day, and it was a good thing, because just last week it had happened again. The box was in the linen closet now where she'd put it, something about it making her feel deeply ashamed.

Ding dong.

"Trick or treat!" the voices rang out in the night. She heard the chair legs scraping against the linoleum and the heavy footsteps as one of the men went to the front door.

"Git!" Mr. Warner's voice said. "Ain't nothing here. Now shut up and keep moving."

This was followed by a trail of squeals and giggles.

Sally went to the bathroom window and peered out at the street below. Groups of witches and cowboys and princesses scurried along. It would be easy to get lost in one of these crowds. To slip in among the robots and the nurses and vampires. If she had a mask, she could be any other child.

Sally checked to make sure the hamper was secure under the doorknob and went to the window. Slowly, she lifted it, a gust of cool autumn air rushing in. She looked down below, noting for the first time that there was a fire escape; its metal bones had been right there all along. It would be just a short drop to the landing, a climb down the cold rungs, and then she could be free. Her breath grew shallow as she considered the possibility of escape.

"Florence!" His voice was like metal. The doorknob turned back and forth and the hamper jumped. Then, in that scary, slurry voice, slippery as gasoline, he sang, *"Trick or treat!"*

SUSAN

Right away there were phone calls from folks saying they'd spotted Sally.

Saw her at the supermarket.

A girl matching that description come to my door looking to sell Girl Scout cookies.

Goes to my church, always sits in the back pew with a man I thought was her daddy.

Though hopeful, Susan thought it sad that until five hundred dollars was on the line, nobody had come forward with information about Sally. Now everybody and their brother were weighing in about her whereabouts.

With the first few calls, even Ella had become hopeful. Truly believed that someone somewhere might have actually seen Sally. But as the weeks went by and the newspaper stopped running the ads, the calls became fewer and fewer and further and further in between.

Saw a girl like that on the playground, darker hair, though. Taller.

Mighta caught a glimpse of her in a shop window.

But by the time Thanksgiving came and went, the phone calls had almost stopped altogether.

Al was determined, though.

"Man's *gotta* have a job. How's he supporting

197

her if he hasn't got a job? I only made it to about a half-dozen service stations when I was there. Thought I'd call all the ones in the book. See if they've had any new employees over the last six months. Anybody matchin' his description."

While Susan fed the baby, he sat at the secretary in the living room, searching through the Baltimore phone book he'd stolen out of a pay phone booth when he was there in August.

Watching Al scour the phone book, scribbling numbers down onto the yellow legal pad they kept by the phone, Susan felt an overwhelming surge of gratitude, the distinct feeling that despite the tragedies in her life so far, she was undeniably *blessed*.

"Christmas can't come and go without her coming home," Al said. "It will kill your ma."

Susan nodded. It was true. Ella had been buoyed by the phone calls, the so-called tips. But after they all proved to be dead ends, Al and Susan regretted that they'd gotten her hopes up. Ella seemed even further resigned and defeated.

"Christmas is just a few weeks away, Al," Susan said.

"I know."

Susan was struck by a memory of a Christmas a few years before, when Sally was still little. Five or six maybe? She'd asked Russell if Santa was real, said one of the older boys at school said he was made up. And so Russell put on a Santa suit

198

he borrowed from a family he worked for and climbed up on the roof. He'd told Ella and Susan to play along.

"What's that sound up there?" Ella had said, winking at Sally. There was the faint sound of footsteps above them. The distant jingle of sleigh bells.

"I don't *know,*" Susan said, shrugging her shoulders.

"It's awfully early still, only eight o'clock. You don't think it could be Santa already, could it?"

Sally's eyes had widened.

"We should go look at the upstairs window," Susan said conspiratorially to Sally, and reached for her small hand.

They ran upstairs to Ella and Russell's bedroom and peeked out the window. Sure enough, there was "Santa," a giant sack slung over his shoulder, making toward the chimney.

Sally had nearly cried. "I knew he was real. I knew it the whole time."

At the time, it had made Susan's heart soar. They'd salvaged Christmas for Sally, at least for another year. But thinking back on it now, it felt almost cruel. Getting a little girl's hopes up like that. For nothing more than a borrowed costume and an empty potato sack.

SALLY

Sometimes, when the weather was too cold, Sister Mary Katherine would let Sally stay in the classroom during recess. She didn't have a proper coat anymore. She thought of the one her mother had made for her last year, the light gray princess coat with the scalloped trim. She had picked out the Butterick pattern at the fabric shop in Camden. Her mother had even let her choose the soft wool from the giant bolts in the back. Because Sally was often so cold, her mother made a special lining inside of light pink flannel.

One day, as Sally was lost inside the pages of *Misty of Chincoteague,* Sister Mary Katherine had come to her with a bright red woolen coat.

"Florence? This has been sitting in the lost and found for over a year. Would you like to have it?"

It was the color of a fire engine with big shiny black buttons and black velvet cuff and collar. The lining was black satin, cold but silky soft, as Sally stood up and slipped her arms into the sleeves.

Sister Mary Katherine stood back as if to appraise her, but Sally's chin dropped to her chest.

"I can't keep it, Sister," she said softly.

She could already imagine exactly what Mr.

Warner would say. That she wasn't a charity case, that he'd buy her a new coat before Christmas and that prancing around in a bright red coat was calling attention to herself. A fugitive of the law must blend in.

"Why not, sweetheart? It's only forty degrees outside. Soon it'll be colder than that. Please, whoever left it there has forgotten all about it by now."

Lost and found. She felt a sudden affinity with this coat—left on the playground or in the classroom, waiting for its rightful owner to come claim it. How lonely it must have been, waiting for whatever little girl had been so careless with it. She imagined it, folded and expectant in the giant wooden crate where all the lost things went. She'd be no better than Mr. Warner if she were to take the coat as her own. What if that little girl one day recalled what she'd lost and went looking for it only to find it wasn't there anymore?

The coat was the most beautiful shade of red. The color of candy apples, of plump summer strawberries. It was soft and so gently worn.

Sally had looked up at the nun and studied her face. She wasn't old like the other nuns at St. Ann's. Her face was so pretty. Like Donna Reed in *It's a Wonderful Life.*

"Consider it a Christmas gift. Wouldn't it make a lovely coat for the holidays?"

Sally shrugged off the shoulders of the beautiful

coat and handed it to her. "My father won't let me take charity," she said.

Sister's face darkened then, and her eyebrows pinched together.

"Perhaps if *I* spoke to your father," she started, and Sally trembled. She didn't know if it was just the chill of the classroom or the fear that caused it.

"He works days," Sally said, and thought of him at the garage down the street. The stink of his skin at night. *Gasoline.* The smell filled the attic room, made Sally dizzy. It gave her a headache. No amount of soap and water could cut through that awful smell. It lived in his skin, in his hands as they pressed against her mouth so that she wouldn't scream.

"Well, if you tell me where he works, perhaps I could go visit him. Explain that it's improper for a child to go without a coat," she said sternly.

"Please don't," Sally said, and shook her head.

Sister's face had softened, and she reached out for Sally's hand.

Sally was flooded with memories of her mother's hand, reaching for hers as they crossed a busy street, on her forehead as she lay sick in bed.

"Are you having some troubles at home, Florence?" Sister asked.

Sally felt her throat grow thick, swollen, pushing back the words. It felt like her body was filling with all those words she wasn't allowed to say. She pictured them inside her, scrambled together in her belly: "fugitive," "wanted," "kiss," "mama." She had no words, however, for what happened in that room after dark. The punishment it seemed that Mr. Warner meted out. She had no way to articulate the pain. *Gasoline, gasoline, gasoline.*

"You can trust me," Sister said again.

Sally nodded. But *could* she trust her? She had trusted Mr. Warner when he told her that she would be safe as long as she checked in with him from time to time, but he had punished her anyway: taken her away from her family. She'd trusted him when he told her she'd be able to plead her case to the judge. But he never even talked about the judge anymore. Her own stepfather had promised he'd be her daddy forever and ever—she'd asked him once; she remembered peering up into his face as he came to tuck her in. Not a year later, he'd walked out onto the railroad tracks and stood there waiting for the train that would take him away.

Sister Mary Katherine had squatted down so that she was looking Sally in the eye. "I promise, your secrets are safe with me."

Sally was not Catholic; her mother was Episcopalian. But she knew that nuns were not supposed to lie. That the promises they made to God were sacred. She felt galvanized by the possibility of opening up her mouth and letting those words out. But all the words were trapped inside. Mr. Warner had made a prisoner of not just her body, but her thoughts. Her words held captive.

Sally nodded, tears running down her cheeks.

"Your father . . . ," Sister Mary Katherine started. "Florence, has he done something to hurt you?"

She felt dizzy, the same sinking diving-bell feeling she'd felt when Mr. Warner found her slipping that composition book under her sweater that day. God, it felt so long ago. It was only June then, and here it was nearly Christmas. Six months ago. The seasons were moving on without her. She recalled the carousel in Atlantic City, the way it spun on and on and on, barely slowing to let other riders on. (She still wore that brass ring, the cold metal wish pressed against her skin underneath her blouse.)

Her own voice barely seemed to belong to her. It was low and seemed to come from a dark place inside her chest as one secret escaped. "He's a bad man, Sister."

"Okay," Sister said, nodding, ignoring the tears that welled up in her own eyes. Nodding, squeezing Sally's hand. "It's okay. I'll help you. I promise."

SISTER MARY KATHERINE

F orgive me, Father, for I have sinned. It has been one week since my last confession," Sister Mary Katherine whispered at the wrought-iron grille in the confessional.

Outside the church, the other sisters were staging the nativity scene. She could hear the parishioners hammering the makeshift stable.

"Yes, Sister," Father said. She had rehearsed her confession quietly in her room the night before. Snow falling softly outside her window, she had asked God for the words that might explain the ways in which she was failing.

"I actually came today to ask for your advice, Father."

"Go on, Sister."

"There is a child, one of my students. She is new this year, Father."

Sister Mary Katherine was certain there was something dark happening in that child's life. She'd seen sorrow in a child's eyes before. She'd seen little boys whose fathers' belts regularly met their behinds, little girls whose mothers neglected them. But the depth of Florence's burden scared her. It wasn't just that the girl had no coat, that the skin of her hands was chapped, that she never, ever smiled. It was that the mere mention of her father made the child's eyes go vacant. All the light gone.

Father's silhouette on the other side of the confessional was familiar to her now. How many times had she sat here and sought forgiveness for all of her small sins?

"I believe she is . . . ," she started, and felt her head begin to pound.

Father coughed, as if to urge her on, she supposed. She imagined he wanted to be outside with the others, drinking hot cocoa and assembling the manger. There was so much joy this time of year; usually it made her feel lighter. The world so full of possibility and peace.

"I worry that she is suffering, Father. At home. That, perhaps, she is being mistreated."

Father paused.

"How so, Sister?" he asked.

"She lives with her father. Alone. He is widowed. I fear that in his wife's absence, he may be . . ."

He coughed again.

"What are you insinuating?" the priest said. He sounded not only impatient but angry as well now.

"I am concerned that with her mother gone, and her growing into a young woman, that he is tempted, Father . . ."

"This is not your confession to make, Sister," Father said abruptly.

Stunned, her mouth fell open.

"But Father . . ."

"For the sin of impure thoughts, your penance is twenty Hail Marys. Do you understand?"

She felt suddenly hot beneath her habit. Sweat trickled down her sides, causing her to shiver.

Before she could argue, Father stood up, leaving her alone in the confessional. She heard his footsteps as he made his way to the vestibule and then outside where he would join the other men in building the nativity scene. Where for the next seven nights before Christmas, the parishioners would dress up as Mary and Joseph. Where the miracle would be reenacted: the star of Bethlehem leading the wise men to the newborn baby, who would cry out into the dark night.

SALLY

W here is Sister Mary Katherine?" the girl who sat next to Sally whispered.

It was the first school day after the Christmas recess. Sister's desk at the front of the classroom was empty. The children were restless and waiting for direction.

"I heard she got transferred over to the Sacred Heart," a boy on her other side said. "My cousin Rudy goes there."

Sally looked toward the door where every morning Sister Mary Katherine came into the room like a beam of sunshine. When a squat, serious nun whisked into the room, Sally felt tears springing to her eyes.

No.

"Good morning, children," she said, scowling at them. "I am Sister Bernadette. I will be your new teacher."

Sister Bernadette was stern and spoke to them sharply. She got rid of the books that Sister Mary Katherine had collected and didn't allow the children to stay inside during recess, not even when the air felt like knives. She looked at Sally with disgust rather than compassion when she saw that she still did not have a proper coat and forced her to wear a boy's scratchy woolen jacket salvaged from the lost and found. Insisted she wear it during recess.

That winter of 1949, Sally felt herself slipping away, disappearing. Like her namesake, she was only Fogg, now. Only mist. With each passing day in the classroom during the day and that drafty attic room at night, as she both waited for someone to find her and struggled to figure out how she might escape, she felt herself, somehow, evaporating.

Whenever she began to feel this wraithlike, vaporous sensation, she closed her eyes and thought of home. Of her mother, of Susan. At night when the bed creaked and groaned beneath her, and his heartbeat pounded against her chest, she turned those sounds into the sounds of her mother's sewing machine, dreamed herself back into the house on Linden Street.

She began on the cracked sidewalk and walked up the steps to the porch with its rusted wrought-iron railings. There she imagined the stray cat she called Cleopatra, on account of her shiny black fur, slept curled up on the turquoise patio chair on the porch. Through the door and into the dim foyer. She dreamed the wallpaper roses, the smell of a baked ham or chicken soup. She could taste the chalky pink mints her mother kept in a tiered crystal candy dish on the console table where the telephone sat. She woke herself up crying sometimes, the scent of her stepfather's Old

Spice still wafting from the medicine cabinet. (Her mother could never bear to throw away that milky white bottle.) And all the while, the sound of the sewing machine's needle going up and down, in and out of the fabric, those endless yards of fabric, resounded. Then, when he was finished, when he climbed off her and disappeared down the stairs to the bathroom below, locking her inside the room, she dreamed herself back into her bed at home. Chenille spread, soft pillow with its heady clean smell of Oxydol.

It was the only way she could keep from vanishing.

"Please," she'd whisper, her breath, her words, forming in vaporous puffs in the still, cold air of the attic room. "Please God, let me go home?" But these words, too, dissipated, as if they'd never been spoken at all. Her pleas, her dreams, her prayers evanesced.

SISTER MARY KATHERINE

Sister Mary Katherine vowed to herself, to God, she would find out where Florence Fogg lived. Go to her. She had promised the child that she would help her, and the thought that she had failed to do so was unbearable. That winter, in her small, fusty room at the Sacred Heart, she scoured the Baltimore phone book, but there were no Foggs in its pages. It was as if Florence Fogg had never existed at all. She mourned her like a mother who had lost a child to tuberculosis or rheumatic fever. She wrote her letters *(Dearest Florence, I hope this finds you; Dearest Florence, I haven't forgotten you)* and addressed the envelopes simply, *Florence Fogg, Baltimore, Maryland,* hoping some benevolent postman might find her, but the letters came back to her, stamped RETURN TO SENDER.

Then one morning in March, she dreamed of that red coat, lying empty in the snow. She awoke in a cold sweat, and the aching sense of helplessness she'd felt in the dream would not go away.

She had to take three buses to get back to St. Ann's. If anyone at the Sacred Heart knew what she was doing, she could have lost her job there as well. But she couldn't stop thinking of the dream or of that child, the fear in her eyes. *He's a bad man,* Florence had said, her voice deep with fright.

"Good morning, Vanessa," she said, smiling as brightly as she could at the St. Ann's secretary, a bitter woman who manned the desk in the school office like a prison guard. "I have a favor to ask of you. I was hoping you might give me the address for the Foggs? Florence Fogg was one of my sixth-grade students."

Vanessa scowled at her over the top of her cat-eye glasses.

"You see, she left something behind, and I'd like to make sure she gets it back," she said, her blood pounding in her ears as she lied. "It's her coat, you see. I found it in a box of my things. I didn't realize I had it until just now."

"Sister, you know that student records are confidential. I am under strict orders to protect the privacy of our students. I am certainly not giving out this kind of personal information to a *former* teacher here."

"*Please,* I intend no harm. It's just that it's been such a terribly cold winter . . ." Her voice hitched. "I'm concerned about Florence."

Vanessa peered at her over the rims of her dark spectacles, and Sister thought she might acquiesce. But then she snapped, "Sister, Florence Fogg is no longer your concern."

. . .

She left St. Ann's in a fury. Marched through the cold to the bus stop, where she stood waiting for the bus to return her to the other side of town where she had been banished.

"Buses are all running late today," a gentleman sitting on the bench offered. "On account of the ice."

The roads were sheer ice, treacherous. It had been a frigid winter, the temperatures well below average. It was the middle of March, but the air was bitter and it felt like winter might never end.

"How long?" she asked, and the gentleman shrugged.

There was a newsstand across from the bus stop. She almost never read the newspaper—the horrors of the world were too much for her to bear—but she'd forgotten to bring a book along and thought she might pick up something to read to bide her time until the bus arrived and then for what would likely be a long journey home. She didn't know what to do about Florence. She'd tried everything to find her, short of knocking on all the doors in the Barclay neighborhood.

Sitting on the cold bench, she was grateful for once for her woolen habit. She read the headlines of *The Baltimore Sun*, shaking her head at the news of murder and fire and strife. She flipped to the back of the paper, looking for birth announcements, any bit of news that wasn't full of tragedy. And there, in the very back pages, was a small article: FRANK LA SALLE INDICTED IN KIDNAPPING OF FLORENCE "SALLY" HORNER. No photo accompanied the article, but Sister Mary Katherine, somehow, knew. It was *her*. The girl in the article, the little girl stolen by a mechanic. The same age. That accent she hadn't been able to put her finger on. New Jersey! She swore that Florence told her that her father worked at a repair shop.

She crossed herself, her hand flying to the crucifix at her chest.

Florence. Florence Fogg. Could it be?

"Do you have a nickel?" she asked the man sitting next to her.

"Sure," he said, and pressed the cold coin into her hand. "For charity?"

"To call the police," she said.

SAMMY

The knock at the door came as Sammy was going to bed. Nine a.m., the sun coming up, and he'd just gotten home from his shift at the Coca-Cola plant. He lived his life backward from the rest of the world. Upside down. Nighttime became day, and day night. He'd never get used to it. Had to drink two quick shots of whiskey to knock himself out each morning, his body exhausted but resisting sleep.

Frankie had already taken off for work, but the girl was still upstairs, sick with a cold. No wonder, the poor kid didn't even have a proper coat. Frankie said not to worry about her; he'd given her some cough syrup, and he expected she'd sleep most of the day. Sammy wondered if some of that Lix-a-Col could knock him out, too.

Frankie's kid wasn't much of a talker, but it was nice to have a female presence in the house these last six or seven months. She was a smart girl, a sweet girl. It made him a little bit sick to think that her mother, Dorothy, was out there somewhere looking for her. But again, it wasn't his place to ask questions. Wasn't his job to meddle in a lovers' quarrel.

"Can I help you?" he said to the two cops who stood on his porch.

215

"We're looking for someone named La Salle," the first one said.

"Might go by Fogg," the second one chimed in. *Goddamned Frankie.*

"Sorry," Sammy said, feeling a prickle at his spine. Must be Dot finally caught up with him. "I never heard of nobody by that name."

"Well, that's odd, because your address was the address on record for one Florence Fogg at the St. Ann's School. We have reason to believe she's Sally Horner. Little girl kidnapped last year in Jersey? There's a reward out." With that he produced a newspaper clipping, with a photo of Frank next to one of Florence. REWARD: $500. He shook his head, felt the hairs on the back of his neck prickling. He *knew* the kid didn't look a thing like Dot. But if she wasn't Frankie's kid, what the hell was he doing with her?

"Did you try next door? Think there's a girl over there. Maybe they got one of the numbers in the address wrong?" He was sweating despite the chill coming in through the open door.

"Have you been drinking, sir?" the first officer asked, leaning toward him, inhaling.

"I work the night shift. I just got home," he said.

One of the cops, the one with the bad skin, rose up on his toes a little and stretched his neck, trying to look past Sammy into the house. "Mind if we come in? Kinda cold for March out here."

"Listen, fellas. I've been on my feet for the last eight hours. I was just about to go to bed. I don't know anybody named Fogg. Or La Salle, for that matter. And I ain't seen no girl."

Suddenly, there was a loud sound, almost like barking, from upstairs. It was the girl; she'd been so sick.

"What was that?" the shorter cop said.

Sammy tensed. If they found Florence upstairs, he'd be a goner. Just when he'd gotten back on track.

"That? Oh, that's just Lola, my Pekingese," Sammy said with a laugh. (Lola was his mother's Pekingese. Dead ten years already, hit by a truck.)

"All right, but we may be back. Next time with a search warrant," the tall one said, and the short one nodded.

As soon as they were gone, Sammy ran to the kitchen, grabbed the phone, and dialed the garage number Frank had scratched on a pad.

"Frankie," he said. "I don't know what you done, but you can't stay here no more."

SALLY

When she heard the yelling, Sally woke in a haze; her chest ached from coughing and her head pounded. She tried to sit up, but her body was heavy, though her head felt light. The shades were pulled shut; she didn't know whether it was day or night. How long she'd been asleep. She stood up, feeling dizzy, and walked to the bedroom door. She pressed her ear against the cold wood, leaning into it for support.

"What the hell, Frankie?" Sammy said. "You told me she was your kid."

"Jesus H. Christ. She *is* my kid. What the fuck is wrong with you?"

"I knew that girl didn't look nothin' like Dot," Sammy said. "I don't know what your game is, but she says one word to somebody and you're toast, Frankie. We both are."

"She ain't gonna say nothin' to nobody. Stupid fool thinks I'm with the FBI."

Were they talking about her?

"FBI?"

"Long story," Frank said.

"What are you doing with her, Frankie? She ain't nothing but a little girl."

218

"I told you. She's my kid. My stepkid, okay? Another story for another day."

"Five *hundred* dollars," Sammy said. "They put up a reward."

Reward? she thought. *For what?* He'd said they were fugitives. Did this mean it was true, that there was a reward to capture her? Her head spun trying to recollect the conversation. Sammy sounded like he was accusing Mr. Warner of something. *She ain't nothin' but a little girl.* Did he know what he did to Sally in that attic room? She felt like she might vomit. Was he not really with the FBI? Then how could he arrest her at the Woolworth's that day?

"The police say . . . ," Sammy went on.

"Her mother's *crazy,*" he said. "She's trying to get me locked up again. She's a . . . oh, forget about it. We'll get outta your hair."

She heard him bounding up the stairs, and she ran to the bed and lay down, feigned sleep, stifled the cough that was rumbling inside her chest.

The door burst open.

"Wake up," he said.

"What is it?" she asked, breathing fast, but sitting up slowly.

Mr. Warner paced back and forth across the floor. This was exactly the way he'd acted right before they left Atlantic City. It made her body tense, her muscles clench.

"Listen up, the FBI has asked me to go to Dallas

219

to investigate some things. It's nothing to worry about, but it means we need to pack up. Today."

"Dallas?" she asked, sitting, coughing again. "Where's Dallas?"

"Texas," he said incredulously. "You didn't think we were going to stay here forever, did you?"

No, no, no. She scooted backward slowly on the bed.

"But you don't . . ." she whispered.

"What's that?" he said. His hearing wasn't great in his right ear, and so he tilted closer to her.

"But you don't work for the FBI," she said, louder this time.

" 'Course I do."

"But I heard you, downstairs . . . ," she started, and then summoned every bit of courage she had. Asked the single question that had been burning inside her like a hot coal. "Sir? If you work for the FBI, then why you gotta fix cars?"

Mr. Warner stopped pacing and almost shouted. "I'm *undercover.* I told you that."

She shook her head, crying. "But I heard you tell Sammy I'm just a stupid fool thinks you work for the FBI." She coughed again, and the cough racked her whole body.

Mr. Warner bristled, the tendons in his neck straining as he seethed.

"Your ears musta been playin' tricks on you,"

he said, forcing himself to laugh, making a twirling motion with his finger by his temple. "Medicine's made you loopy."

No. She shook her head, gripping the sheets in her fists.

"I heard Sammy say there's a reward. That people are lookin' for me."

Mr. Warner took a deep breath and walked toward the bureau. She thought about the gun. But instead of opening the drawer, he paused, turned on his heel, and ran his hand over the top of his head. His mouth twitched, and he took a breath.

"Listen," he said, eyes darting all around the room. "I ain't sure how to tell you this."

"What?"

"I swore I wouldn't," he said, frowning.

"Tell me," Sally pleaded.

"Your mama, she'd be so angry with me," he said, shaking his head solemnly.

"Mama?" she said, the word like a lozenge in her sore throat.

He nodded, then came to the bed and crouched down. He leaned forward and swiped at a tear on her cheek with his callused thumb.

"God, I ain't seen you since you were just a little thing."

Sally's stomach pitched, and she tilted her head. Hungry for whatever he could offer her about her mother.

"What about Mama?"

Mr. Warner's thin lips spread into a smile, those long yellow teeth bared.

"Don't you see, Sally? Your mama been keepin' me from you all these years," he said.

Perplexed, Sally shook her head.

"I'm your real daddy, baby. And I come back for you."

ELLA

Despite the cold snap up and down the Eastern Seaboard, Russell's tulips erupted from the earth that spring like a violent reminder of time's insistence on passing. Those bulbs he'd planted so many years ago were like bombs in the soil; their explosion each spring never failed to shock Ella.

It had been nearly nine months already since Sally disappeared. When the garden wasn't reminding her of this cruel truth, her grandchild was. With each milestone Dee met, Ella realized that somewhere Sally was also reaching milestones, growing up—unless she *wasn't* growing up. What if the man to whom Ella had given her child had grown tired of her (how many times had she herself wearied of Sally's constant chatter?) and discarded her?

On March 17, 1949, St. Patrick's Day, Ella received word from the detectives that Frank La Salle had been indicted a second time for kidnapping. He'd been indicted earlier for Sally's abduction, a charge that carried a maximum of three to five years. Five years for destroying Ella's life. She'd been so angry, she hadn't been able to speak without screaming. This new indictment, the prosecutor assured her, would find him behind bars for thirty to thirty-five years as soon as they were able to find him. But there was the rub. An indictment meant nothing without an arrest. It was like a promise that could never be kept. Like promising your own child that you will never die.

Susan and Al had come for dinner that night, Al abuzz about the indictment.

"This is good news, Ma," he said, reaching across the table for her hand. "Once we find him and Sally, he's going away for good. He'll rot in prison. For what he's done."

Susan nodded, her eyes brimming with tears.

"We still have the reward money. Maybe now the police will put up some as well. The FBI. Maybe a bigger reward will get folks to come forward. Somebody's gotta have seen her, Ma," Al said, squeezing Ella's hand.

Al was a good man. Susan didn't know how lucky she was. When he spoke to her this way— impassioned, earnest—she almost let herself hope that he was right.

That night, after Al and Susan took the baby home, long after Ella had retired for the evening and Daly's had closed, the St. Patrick's revelers were spilling onto the street, singing "Danny Boy" at the top of their drunken lungs. Outside her window, they cussed and crooned: *"Oh, Danny Boy, the pipes, the pipes are calling . . ."*

She pulled herself out of bed, her skeleton

resisting, the revelers persisting, *" 'Tis I'll be here in sunshine or in shadow . . . "* She stood and pulled her robe tightly around her before flipping on her lights and descending the stairs slowly, her knees crying out in pain with each step.

At the front door, she looked at the mat where Russell's old pair of shoes still sat next to a pair of Sally's boots, and she felt the sorrow she'd buried deep inside clawing to the surface. She bent over and picked up the shoes and held them to her face, feeling the soft worn leather against her cheek. When she set them back down, she grabbed her own pair of shoes and slowly slipped them onto her feet.

How many times had she woken, alone in her bed, listening for the sound of the front door? For the sounds of Russell returning from the bar. His drunken stumbling, singing in the foyer. How many times had she felt not annoyance but relief that he'd returned? Dozens? Hundreds? Until the one night he didn't.

". . . And if you come, when all the flowers are dying . . . And I am dead, as dead I well may be . . . "

She opened the door and watched the huddled mass of drunken men staggering down the street. One of them must have seen her in the bright porch light, because he took off his hat and tipped it at her. "Good evenin', ma'am!"

In that midnight garden, the tulips with their

upright spines, their violent joy, seemed to mock her.

She returned inside and went to her sewing box and grabbed a pair of shears. Armed, she stepped back outside and marched down the steps to that ridiculous garden, where she started to lop off the heads of those tulips, one by one. But when that did not satisfy her, did not ease the ache that she now could no longer differentiate from the war being waged in her joints, she dropped to her knees and began to dig. She used her wretched fingers to turn the soil, to burrow in like an animal, seeking those buried bombs. The very roots of those persistent bulbs. She dug until her knees roared with pain and her spine was alight in fire. Then she grabbed the bulbs and hurled them like live grenades into the street where the drunken Irishmen continued with their song, staggering home to their wives, to their daughters.

"... I'll simply sleep in peace until you come to me."

"Go home to your wives," she yelled. "Go home, go home, go home."

"Ah, shut your cake hole, lady! Go back to bed!" one of the men screamed, making an obscene gesture.

And then she wept, alone in the ravaged garden.

SALLY

S it closer," Mr. Warner said, patting the seat next to him.

He told Sally he'd bought the pickup truck from his boss. For two months, he'd stayed at the garage after work, fixing it up. "All of this," he said almost proudly. "I done for us."

Sally looked out the truck window at the smudge of green as they drove through Virginia, Tennessee, Arkansas. She felt stretched, somehow, as if she were holding on to home with one hand while her body was torn, tugged, pulled away. She could feel the ache of it in her shoulders, sinews strained to the point of almost snapping. It was the same feeling she recalled having when her stepfather died. She'd refused to leave the grave, her mother pulling at her arm. Was this why it was called "longing"?

They had been driving for days. Three? Four? They stayed at roadside motor courts, checking in long after nightfall. Mr. Warner—she couldn't bring herself to call him Daddy like he'd asked—would tell her to lie down across the truck's bench seat as he checked them in. He'd always request a room that was farthest away from the motel office. Then, when he was sure no one was watching, he'd usher her from the truck and into the room. They kept the shades closed. They woke before the sun did each morning, Mr. Warner pulling her from the safety of her dreams and back into the truck. By the time the motel manager awoke, they were long gone.

"We're *both* wanted now," he told her.

And she'd thought about want. Wasn't it *want* that got her here in the first place? She'd only wanted to be friends with those bright-eyed girls with their white teeth and shiny hair. She'd wanted it so badly (this simple, stupid thing), that she'd broken the law. *Wanted.* Now she only wanted not to be driving away so far away from home, with this man, her *daddy,* and his awful hands (her body recounted the bones: knuckles, fingers, wrists) and grinding jaw.

"Wanted?" she asked, still peering out at the never-ending green, the impossible, oblivious sky.

"By the law. That's what the reward's about. Your mother wants to keep us apart. I been trying to get back to you for years, but she been keeping me from you. She put up the money to have me arrested."

"But Mama didn't know you at all when I got on the bus to the shore."

Mr. Warner scowled. "You really think that, Sally? That she didn't know her own ex-husband? 'Course she knew *exactly* who I was. She was happy to have you off her hands at first. One less

228

mouth to feed. It was just when we decided to go to Baltimore, she changed her mind. Didn't want you out of state. But I'm your daddy. You belong to me, just as much as her, you see. Now stop thinkin' 'bout all that grown-up business and scoot closer," he said, patting the place on the seat next to him again.

She slid across the seat, and he put his hand on her leg, squeezing. She flinched.

"Now lean your head on my shoulder and get some sleep, Sally. We got a long way to go before we stop again."

Reluctantly, she did as she was told and leaned against his hard knobby shoulder, trying not to breathe in the gasoline stink of him. He hadn't worked at the garage in two weeks, but he still carried the smell of it. It was in all his clothes. In his skin.

A man and woman in a bright blue convertible drove behind them for nearly three hours that day. She thought about what they might see: the back of Mr. Warner's head, his battered fedora, and her spill of curls as she leaned against him. *A father and his daughter.* They couldn't know, of course; it wasn't their fault. Yet Sally blamed them. She blamed all of them: the cars passing them by, the managers of the motel courts, the gas station attendants as they swiped their rags across the glass. Why didn't anyone see what was going on inside that cab? Why didn't anyone try to save her? It didn't matter one bit if this man was her real father like he said he was. She wanted to go home, and he wouldn't let her.

"We'll be in Dallas by tonight," Mr. Warner said. "I'll take you out for a nice steak dinner. Would you like that? Maybe a chocolate milkshake?"

She nodded, but her stomach was still upset. Dallas, Texas. So far from Camden, from home.

That couple in the car had been behind them all the way since Little Rock. Perhaps she could give them a signal, write *Help me* in the dust, in reverse. She looked over her shoulder out the back window, but there was nothing but an endless stretch of highway, unfurling like a dirty hair ribbon behind them.

Dallas, Texas
April 1949

SALLY

"This is where we're gonna stay?" Sally asked, peering through the windshield. The sign said GOOD LUCK MODERN TRAILER COURT, with a flashing neon horseshoe. The trailer sat on a dirt plot just off a busy street, a faded and tattered green awning and a couple of lawn chairs out front.

"I know it ain't no palace, but the court's got a swimming pool and a canteen. You can swim every day this summer if you want," Mr. Warner said.

"Where am I gonna go to school?" Sally asked, thinking of Mrs. Appleton back in Camden, of Sister Mary Katherine at St. Ann's.

"Only a couple months to summer now. Way I figure it, you start your vacation early this year. We'll get you enrolled in school in the fall," he said. When she scowled, he added, "I already talked to the school. They said you'll catch up."

Sally shook her head. "But I'll be behind the other kids," she said.

"Listen, you want me to take you back to Camden? That what you want? To a mama who wanted to get rid of you, but was too much of a coward to say?"

At the mention of her mother, her chin sank to

233

her chest. She thought about her mother putting her on the bus, knowing full well that he had no intention of bringing her back. Whenever she thought about her mother now it was anguish she felt, not solace. Still, maybe she *had* changed her mind. Sally knew they were looking for her. That was why Mr. Warner said they had to leave Baltimore, because they were *wanted*.

"You said she changed her mind," Sally protested softly. "There's a reward for me."

"Because you're an *outlaw,* Sally. A fugitive. How many times do I have to tell you that before you get it through your head?"

Sally leaned against the window and closed her eyes, and tears rolled down her cheeks. He reached over and brushed them away. His voice softened. "I'm sorry, Sally. It's just after all I've done for you . . . ," he said, looking hurt.

"I'm sorry, sir," she said.

"Listen, let's stop with all this fuss and go take a look-see."

The trailer was small, but it had a couple of beds, a kitchenette with a cookstove and an icebox, and a heater and a small lavatory. When they came out of the trailer, a woman was leaning out the open door of the trailer in the next space over.

"Hi there!" she said, waving at them. She had dark auburn hair and milky skin. She was dressed in a pair of dungarees and a man's white button-down shirt, and she didn't have any shoes on. The lady looked so friendly; something about her reminded Sally of Susan. "You our new neighbors?" she asked.

"Yes, ma'am," Mr. Warner said, stepping in front of Sally with one hand extended and the other tipping his hat. "Frank," he said, eyeing the cactus plants on either side of her doorway. "Frank LaPlante. This is my daughter. Florence."

"I'm Ruth," the lady said, smiling with big white teeth. To Sally, she said, "How old are you, sweetheart?"

"Almost twelve," she said softly.

"Well, it's so nice to meet y'all. My husband just called and said he's gonna be workin' late. I got a pot of chili cookin' on the stove. Would y'all like to join me for dinner?"

Sally nodded even though she knew Mr. Warner had said they were going out.

"And *Mrs.* LaPlante . . . ?" Ruth said, leaning forward a little and looking past them, as if Mr. Warner's wife might be hiding behind the pickup truck.

"Her mama's passed," he said. "Horrible accident. She don't like to talk about it much."

Sally felt her chest prick. Each of his lies felt like one of those cactus spines.

"Oh, sweetheart," the woman said, clutching her hands to her chest in pity and then quickly opening them to her, motioning for Sally to come closer. Without thinking at all, Sally went to her, let this stranger's arms enclose her, and felt, for the first time in nearly a year, almost safe. Ruth seemed surprised. Her heart sped up under Sally's ear. "Well, welcome home, hon."

RUTH

W hat brings y'all to Dallas?" Ruth asked the man, Frank, as she served up two heaping bowls of her famous chili for him and his daughter.

The Good Luck was the temporary home to the homeless: migrant farmworkers like her husband, traveling salesmen, and circus folk. Drifters and grifters. Evacuees and refugees.

"Following the work," Frank said, nodding and accepting the bowl and then a piece of corn bread from the steaming basket.

They sat outside at the picnic table where Ruth and Hank ate supper most nights, but tonight Hank had picked up an extra shift at the restaurant and wouldn't be home until after midnight.

"You and your husband been here long?" he asked her.

"Not too long. Six months?"

She and Hank had been on the road for years it seemed, so long Ruth had forgotten what *home* meant. From peas to strawberries to sugarcane, she and Hank had followed the crops across thousands of miles. They'd wound up in Texas because somebody had said they were looking for men for the wheat harvest. But they'd arrived too late, and so instead Hank had ended up washing dishes at the Sky-Vu, a busy nightclub and restaurant down the street. The clientele at the Sky-Vu was mixed: both locals and some high-rolling Dallas types. But they were all there for the same thing: good music, dancing, and stiff drinks. Hank's boss, Joey Bonds, was married to a showgirl named Dale Belmont. She was the headlining act most nights, a singer with a pinup girl body, backed by Johnny Cola and a five-piece band. Hank didn't talk about it, but Ruth knew that there were darker things happening at the Sky-Vu, too—bound to happen any place where gangsters congregated. She'd heard the talk.

They'd been in Dallas since last October, but she knew it was just a matter of time before they took off again. Ruth was no gypsy, but she was living the life of one, her caravan a 1940 New Moon camper. It wasn't what she planned, what she'd dreamed of as a girl. But really, how many women get what they dream of anyway?

Hank barely made enough to pay for their little lot at the trailer court, so Ruth cut hair on the side for the other ladies who lived at the Good Luck. She'd have preferred to work at one of the fancy salons in West Dallas (everyone said she was good enough to do so), but she couldn't afford a chair rental, so her clientele had to sit in the tiny trailer on an adjustable stool Hank had found at the dump. She loved washing hair, cutting it, and setting it in rollers. Nothing made her happier than making other women feel beautiful. It was her calling, she thought. With a pair of shears in her hand, she felt useful. These women trusted her, and they were the closest things she had to friends. But like her and Hank, the rest of the residents at the Good Luck were transient, and every time she started to get friendly with someone, it seemed Hank was ready to up and leave again, following this crop or that dream to somewhere else.

"Do you have any children?" the girl, Florence, asked hopefully, peering toward the trailer door as if a gaggle of young'uns would just tumble out.

"No," Ruth replied sadly.

There were no babies yet, though not for lack of trying. But after three pregnancies and three miscarriages, she'd figured a baby just wasn't in the cards for her and Hank. Still, each time her monthly came, she felt a distinct snag of disappointment. She'd even thought for a while when they first arrived at the Good Luck that their luck might turn. But six months had gone by, and she'd been right on time every one of them.

But now Florence and Frank LaPlante had arrived, and the second that curly-headed girl fell into her arms, she felt the giant hole at the center of her start to fill up. This poor sweet motherless girl, and her, a childless mother, she couldn't help but think they'd be a match.

Plus, the girl had the most wonderful head of hair. Naturally curly hair could be a blessing or a curse, depending on what you did with it. Ruth could hardly wait to get her hands on those locks. She studied the girl the way an artist studies her subject. She was at that in-between age, such a fragile place to be even *with* a mama in the picture. Her body was on the edge of blooming, but her face still bore the sweet fat of child-hood. Smooth complexion, round cheeks. Still, something about her looked tired, the kind of fatigue you usually saw in women four times her age. Grief had that effect on people, she knew. She wondered what sort of horrible accident had taken her mama's life. Car crash? Train wreck? So many possible disasters.

"You know," Ruth said to the girl. "You have the prettiest hair. You need a trim, of course. I do hair, maybe I could give you a new 'do?"

Florence looked up from the tin bowl of chili and smiled, her mouth twitching nervously.

"She got her mama's curls," Frank said, whisking his hat off his head, revealing a head full of gray stubble. He looked old enough to be her grandfather without his hat on. He ran his hand across his head and laughed.

"Mama says I'm fortunate to have naturally curly hair. That ladies pay a lot of money for permanent waves," the girl said softly.

"Said," Frank corrected her.

Florence's brow furrowed. Confused.

"Your mama *said* you were lucky." He lifted his chin to Ruth. "Hard to think of her in the past tense. It ain't been that long."

"She's right, your mama," Ruth said, feeling sorry for this poor unhappy girl. "It's lovely. The kind of hair girls would kill or die for. You come over any time, and I'll see what I can do for you."

When the sun went down, Frank and Florence retired to their trailer. Ruth had found the waterlogged copy of *A Tree Grows in Brooklyn* by the pool, and she figured she'd try to read while she waited for Hank to get off his shift. Sometimes, he'd stay late at the Sky-Vu and have a drink or two with the kitchen staff. She knew more often than not, he was really next door at Pappy's Showland, catching the strip shows. Other women might be infuriated by their husbands' wandering eyes, but she also knew that the second she started thinking about that she'd drive herself crazy. They'd stuck together through a whole lot; no hussy twirling a pair of tassels on her titties was going to change that. He had a gypsy heart, but no matter where that heart (or the rest of him, for that matter) strayed, it always came back to her eventually.

She clicked on her reading light and opened to the dog-eared page. The main character in the story, little Francie Nolan, reminded her of Florence. Same age as her and from back east, too. Maybe she'd like to borrow the book when Ruth was done. Ruth was a slow reader, though, reading just a few pages or two each night before her eyelids grew heavy. Tonight as the words began to swim on the page, she flicked out the light and snuck a peek through the slatted venetian blinds at the trailer across the way. It was dark and still and quiet. She wondered if Florence ever had bad dreams. If her old daddy had any idea what went on inside a young girl's mind. The neon sign flashed GOOD LUCK, GOOD LUCK, GOOD LUCK. She hoped that at least for Florence, this was true.

SALLY

Sally couldn't sleep at night in Dallas. As much as she hated the attic at Sammy's, at least there she was inside four solid walls. Sleeping in a trailer felt like sleeping inside the truck. They'd been on the road for so long to get here, sometimes at night when she did manage to find sleep, she woke convinced that they were still moving. That Mr. Warner had hitched the trailer to the truck and was pulling her across the desert. Only the thunderous sound of his snores in the next bed assured her that they were not barreling down Route 66 anymore. The thin metal walls that separated them from the world also did little to keep out the night sounds. Beyond Mr. Warner's snoring and the traffic on Commerce Street, the otherworldly cries of frogs and toads calling out to each other at the nearby river and the screech owls in the trees haunted her. The trailer practically vibrated with all that night music.

While she lay awake waiting for sleep that wouldn't come, her mind raced as she ruminated on what she should do now. Maybe that lady Ruth could help her. Maybe if she told her what happened back in Camden, she'd know what to do. Maybe she'd go with her to find a police officer, a judge, and together they could explain this whole mess. Here was what she knew: she'd been caught stealing, but Mr. Warner wasn't an FBI man (or was he?). He said he was her real daddy, Bobby Swain. He'd come for her, and her mother had handed her over, *lied* to her. When she got to this part each time, her heart ached. But no, now her mother had changed her mind and wanted her to come home. Put up a reward for her even. But Mr. Warner had said the reward was because she was a fugitive. Wanted. Not by her mama but by the police. Why did it all have to be so confusing? By the time she got to this part, her thoughts were swirling like the cyclones she'd read about in a book that Sister Mary Katherine had lent to her. Why hadn't she said something more to Sister Mary Katherine when she had the chance? When she was at least still in the same longitude as Camden. Instead, now here she was thousands of miles from home living in a tin can in a dirt lot between the city and a river. She dream-walked along the edge of the water, peering into the murky depths, only to see Mr. Warner's crooked smile leering back up at her.

She needed to find out if he was who he said he was. If he was lying to her about being her daddy, then maybe everything else he'd told her was a lie, too. She thought the answers might be inside his valise. It had accompanied them from

Camden to Atlantic City and then to Baltimore. She'd assumed at first it was something official. Maybe his FBI briefcase. But if he wasn't with the FBI, what could be so private? If he was her real daddy like he said, he'd have to have something with his real name on it. Maybe it was where he kept his official papers. A birth certificate maybe? Maybe his marriage license to her mother? All night long, she thought about what she could do. How she might get into that locked valise, and what to do if she found out he wasn't who he said he was. Or worse, if he was.

Her mind spun through the night, every night, until her body gave up and fell asleep. Though every morning, she woke up having lost any of the resolve she'd conjured in the middle of the night. All her machinations and plans like hazy dreams.

"Wake up," he said one morning a few weeks after they'd arrived. His breath smelled of coffee and cigarettes. She rubbed the sleep from her eyes, blood pounding in her ears. "Sally, wake up. I have something for you."

He opened the top drawer of the nightstand where he kept the gun. She felt dizzy and sick. She shook her head, *please no,* but he only pulled out a small flat box, handing it to her.

Confused, she hesitated and then took it.

"Open it," he said.

Her mouth twitched. The stockings lay in a

nest of pale pink tissue, as slippery as a wish. She lifted them out, and they unfurled. Stockings made for a grown woman, like those ladies on the covers of Sammy's dirty paperbacks. She felt sick.

"They're made of nylon," he offered. "No seams. I didn't know what color to get. The saleslady said this is what all the girls are wearing."

"Why—" she started.

Mr. Warner put his hands on his hips and shook his head. "Why, you didn't forget your own birthday, did you Sally?"

SUSAN

On April 16, 1949, Sally's twelfth birthday, Susan parked the car and unbuckled Dee, lifting her onto her hip. She'd gotten so big. Susan could hardly believe that in just four months they'd be celebrating her daughter's first birthday. Somehow, being a mother—watching her infant grow and change practically with each breath—made her aware for the first time of the fleetingness of it all. If she wasn't careful, she knew that this odd longing could have the power to cripple her. Was this what adulthood was? Mourning every lost moment? Still, the baby brought joy to her mother. *Wistfulness*— that was a better word. The baby was bittersweet.

Susan had brought one of the new bare root rosebushes they'd just gotten in at the greenhouse: American Beauties. In bloom, they were among the most fragrant and brightest roses the greenhouse sold. She thought she'd help her mother plant the bush on the south side of the house, where the sun would hit the plant nearly the whole day. With her free hand, Susan picked up the pot, closed the car door with her hip, and made her way to the door. She noticed her mother's tulips, beheaded, and their brown stalks lying in a cluttered heap like a child's game of pick-up sticks. A small fury burned inside her. Who had done this? Neighborhood kids? It made her worry for the fate of the roses.

She rang the doorbell rather than knocking, just in case her mother was upstairs. Sometimes Ella took a morning nap when her rheumatism was flaring up. She'd sounded a bit pained on the phone when Susan had called earlier, though she didn't know how much of that had to do with her joints and how much was because of Sally's birthday.

She tried the doorknob. They never used to lock the door, but since Sally disappeared, her mother had taken to locking the deadbolt, not only when she was gone but when she was home as well.

Dee wriggled and fussed.

"Shh, shh," she said, rocking her back and forth. She set the plant down and dug in her pocketbook for the key to the house. She rang the doorbell one more time before unlocking the door and stepping into the dark foyer.

Generally, her mother would be sitting at the sewing machine, working. But today the sewing machine was still, and her mother was nowhere in sight.

"Mama?" she called out as she entered the foyer and flicked on a light.

The console table, which usually held the mail, the tiered candy dish, her mother's gloves, and the telephone, was stacked high with packages from the factory. At least three weeks' worth of piecework, untouched.

Susan's heart began to race. She hadn't been to visit in a while, but she'd only spoken to her mother a few hours ago. Where was she? She didn't drive. Her knees were so swollen lately, she wasn't able to walk more than a block.

Then the smell registered. The sweet, almost cloying smell of a cake baking. The tang of lemon zest strong enough to make her eyes water. It was the lemon blossom cake her mother made every year for Sally's birthday, the one with the tangy glaze. (There was a photograph somewhere, wasn't there? One of Sally, tiny elbows propped up on the table, her five-year-old face aglow in the light of the candles.)

"Mum-mum," the baby hummed, burying her head in Susan's chest.

"Mama?" Susan said, and went to the kitchen.

Ella was sitting at the table, head in her hands. The cake sat on a wire rack on the small counter, a large yellow chunk of it still stuck in the cake pan.

"I've ruined it," her mother said apologetically.

"No, Mama," Susan said, handing the baby to her.

Ella looked at the baby like she'd forgotten what to do with her.

Susan went to the counter and, using a spatula,

worked the missing chunk of cake free from the pan.

"We'll just put some frosting here and piece it back together," she said, as she replaced the missing piece like a jigsaw puzzle.

The baby cooed.

"Mama, are your hands bothering you again?" The last time she'd been unable to sew because of her hands was a couple of years ago.

"No," Ella said. She was studying the baby's face intently now. Dee chewed on her own fingers and stared back at her grandmother.

"Can I help you with some of it?" she asked. "The sewing? I saw you haven't gotten to it lately."

Ella still wouldn't look at her. She was shaking her head, peering intently at the baby.

"She never cried," Ella said.

"No, she's a good baby. Only cries when she's hungry," Susan said, smiling. She went to the icebox and got the milk, searched through her mother's cupboard for confectioner's sugar. She bent down and opened the cupboard where her mother kept the bowls.

"Your father was worried there was something wrong with her. That she was deaf. Or an idiot," her mother said. "Brain damaged from how long she took to come out."

Susan froze.

"I kept telling him she was perfectly normal,

but I was so afraid he was right. She just lay there. As happy as could be. You could do anything, and she wouldn't make a sound. Not even when she was sitting in a soaking wet diaper."

Susan stood up and carefully set the bowl on the counter. Dee was lying contentedly in the cradle of her grandmother's arm, tiny fists rubbing at her eyes.

"Bobby would try to startle her, make her cry. He'd pinch her little arms when I wasn't looking. I saw the marks."

Susan felt her chest heaving. She didn't like to think of her real father. He'd left Ella alone with two children to raise on her own. He'd left them all.

"And she just took it. He used to say that he could have set her on fire, and she would have just sat there smiling."

Susan poured the confectioner's sugar into the bowl too quickly, and a puff of sugary smoke rose up, making her cough. She drizzled a little bit of milk into the bowl, stirring quickly, until it was the right consistency for frosting. She'd fix the cake, and everything would be okay. She'd clear away the pile of rotting tulips. She'd help her mother finish sewing the pieces and get them set out for pickup. Plant the American Beauties.

"What's wrong with a girl that won't cry even when someone's hurtin' her?" Ella said, her voice breaking.

The sound of it made Susan think of cracking bones. Quickly, she spread some of the frosting on the broken piece and pressed it against the side of the cake.

"There, Mama," she said. "Once we frost the top, you won't even be able to tell."

Susan sat down next to her mother at the table and reached for the baby.

Her mother looked up at her, her eyes glossy with unspilled tears. "Why'd she let him do it? Why'd she let him take her?"

Susan felt her chest burning. "Mama, what is wrong with you? She didn't *let him take her.*" Then, as her mother shook her head, the words escaped, as violent as a slap. "*You* did."

ELLA

Funny thing, sorrow is. For most of her life, Ella had thought it an indulgence. Like sweets or liquor, a luxury someone like Ella could little afford. She's always managed to deny her own sadness. Abstain from the self-pity that so many others seemed to bask in. She'd considered herself a sort of ascetic, a martyr, a saint even when it came to misery. But with each day that Sally was gone, her resolve weakened. It was so enticing, the allure of her bed. Of sleep. Of shutting out the world and slipping into the dark corners of her grief. Of embracing it, of just letting it wash over her like water. For the first time, she understood Russell's inclination to bask in his own delicious misery.

Nobody knew, of course, about the melancholy days, those flat notes that disrupted the melody of their lives. They were unpredictable, sudden, and somehow always took Ella by surprise. The first time it happened wasn't but a few weeks after they got married.

The wedding was at City Hall. Ella had sewn herself a fine dress using an old set of drapes she found in a musty box in the attic of the new house on Linden Street. Russell had rented the house and said that as soon as they were married, Ella and the girls could move in. The wedding was a modest affair on all accounts, a civil ceremony followed by a reception at the house. Ella made the canapés and cake, borrowed a cut-glass punch bowl from a friend. Sally was still just a baby, cutting her first tooth; Ella had spent most of the afternoon trying to get her to stop fussing. But Russell was joyful. They didn't have any furniture yet, so he and the rest of his band set up in the living room and played for the few guests in attendance. One of the other band members' wives held Sally as Russell spun Ella around the room. She'd batted at him, told him to stop, but she'd felt a wave of happiness that she was powerless against. Life had been such a damned struggle; it felt good to just let go.

"It's you and me against the world, kiddo," Russell whispered, and winked, his eyes twinkling. Something about this had comforted her. As if she hadn't just gotten a husband but an *ally*. In a hostile world, this seemed more valuable somehow.

But not a week later, after they'd settled into their new life together, the first sour note struck.

Russell cleaned houses, and he'd once apparently had a whole string of families he worked for. But lately, there seemed to be fewer who could afford to hire outside help. He relied mostly on the businesses: the churches, the schools. Nevertheless, he and Ella both rose with the sun every morning; she cooked breakfast, and he gathered his supplies. After coffee and a long kiss stolen in the kitchen before Susan pattered down the stairs, he took off up the street, a skip in his step, whistling as though he didn't have a care in the world. But this morning, neither of them woke early. Sally had caught the croup and had been up all night coughing. Ella had spent most of the night sitting in the bathroom, the door shut, the hot shower running to create steam. Her hair was muggy with it. When she finally got Sally to sleep, she'd curled up in bed exhausted and fallen into a deep sleep.

Her first thought was that he was dead. What else could explain the fact that he lay still as a stone at the edge of the bed? She shook his shoulder in a panic.

"Not feeling well," he'd said, and she'd nearly cried with relief.

"Take the day off," she said. "I'll make some soup."

But after three days, he still hadn't gotten out of bed, and she worried that maybe he *was* dying.

"You should see the doctor," she'd said, though she had no idea what he'd tell the doctor. He didn't have Sally's barking cough. When she pressed her wrist against his forehead it was cool. He wasn't using the toilet any more than usual, either.

After a week, she started to grow impatient.

"We need money for the market; we're nearly out of food. I've been mixing the baby's milk with water."

He'd gotten angry then, muttering under his breath as he pulled on his clothes, and headed out the door carrying his cleaning supplies like he was carrying the weight of the world. He was gone the whole day and didn't come home for supper, either. It wasn't until nearly midnight that he finally returned to the locked front door. "Ella, let me in!" he'd hollered, and she'd felt her knees weaken: with relief first and then anger. "I'll huff and I'll puff . . . ," he bellowed in laughter.

She flung the door open and looked down the row of houses to see four or five heads poking out of their own doors, trying to see what the fuss was about.

"Get inside," she said to him, pulling at his sleeve as he stumbled through the door, rheumy-eyed and reeking of whiskey. He pulled her into a long embrace in the foyer, holding on tight, until she managed to wriggle free from his grasp.

"I'm sorry, El," he said, his unfocused eyes watering. "Everything's going to be better now. You hear? It's all gonna be A-OK." With that he'd reached into his pocket and pulled out some change. Clearly, he'd spent most of his day's wages at the pub, and his meager offering felt like an insult. She'd plucked the coins from his sweaty palm and wordlessly pocketed them. What else could she do?

All night, as he slumbered loudly next to her, she'd thought of the words she'd say, imagined the heft of her foot as she put it, firmly, down.

But in the morning, he'd risen with the sun again. She heard him singing in the shower, his clear sweet voice like a balm smoothing over so many wounds, old and new. He drank his coffee, lightened with that weak milk, found a penny hidden behind Sally's ear as she was serving up the eggs, and held Ella an extra minute in the kitchen, kissing the top of her head, before heading out the door. There was a spring in his step, and he tipped his hat at all those busy-body neighbors. Like the last week had never happened. But not three months later, he'd taken to bed again.

Bed, then bottle, then back to business. For five years, this was how Russell lived his life. Until the pull of sorrow was like the long siren song of that train. Irresistible.

She understood now, what it felt like to be seduced by sadness. Because not only was Sally gone, but her other daughter blamed her, shamed her for it. And worst of all, Susan was right. It was all Ella's fault.

SALLY

"Listen here," Mr. Warner said as he pulled his shirt on and peered at his reflection in the mirror. "I got a job in town. I'll be working Monday through Friday now, which means you're gonna be on your own here. Just like at Sammy's place."

Sally nodded. He hadn't left her alone for more than an hour or two since they'd arrived over a month ago already. When he went to get groceries or to look for work, he jimmied the trailer lock so she couldn't get out. She hoped to God he didn't plan to lock her inside the trailer all day. She thought of those long awful hours in Sammy's attic, eating sardines and holding her bladder all day. It was early June, and the heat was already unbearable inside the trailer during the day. Ninety-nine degrees according to the Diaper Dan thermometer on the kitchenette counter; the little Negro figurine's diaper changed color depending on how hot it was. She wondered who had lived here before her; Frank only said an old friend named Joey had arranged for them to stay there. A man who owned the Sky-Vu, the nightclub down the street from the trailer park.

"Do I gotta stay inside all day?" she ventured,

then thought maybe she should have just kept her mouth shut.

He cocked his head and studied her. "Well, I guess that all depends," he said.

To keep the questions from bursting out of her, she bit the side of her tongue. It was the only way sometimes to keep from crying out.

"I'm gonna talk to Ruth. See if she can keep an eye on you. She's got a phone, which means she can call me if she catches you doing something you shouldn't be doing."

She felt her heart open, the heaviness in her chest release. *Ruth.* Of course, Ruth could watch her.

"You understand, though, if you did get any funny ideas about doing something you shouldn't, it wouldn't just be your fault."

But she *didn't* understand.

"If Ruth's in charge of you, and you were to do something, like say wander off, then a bit of the blame would fall on Ruth now, right? I'd hate to have to punish Ruth for *your* bad behavior."

She shook her head. He'd do something bad to Ruth?

"You step out of line, even a little bit," he said, wagging his crooked finger near her face, "and your friend Ruthie *pays.*"

AL

"Hello," Al said. "This is Al Panaro. I'm just calling to see if there's any new information in the Sally Horner case."

Every week through that spring and early summer, Al called the police stations in both Camden and Baltimore, inquiring if there had been any progress in the investigation. And every week, the detectives politely yet firmly told him they'd call just as soon as there was any news to share. Still, Al checked in. Because with every passing week, Ella seemed to grow more and more despondent and withdrawn. She'd essentially stopped working, and Al knew it was only a matter of time before she wouldn't be able to pay the rent anymore. Three or four days a week he would drive Sue and the baby all the way to Camden so Sue could help Ella out. The baby was crawling now, getting into everything, and he knew Sue was exhausted. Al felt like he was spinning his wheels, but what choice did he have? He couldn't just give up.

"Baltimore County Sheriff's Office," the woman said. "How may I direct your call?"

Finally, in early June he got through to someone.

"Nobody's called in with any information?

Nobody at all?" he asked, desperate for anything.

"You know, come to think of it," the Baltimore officer said. "I seem to recall there was somebody. A nun. Called in about a girl over at St. Ann's School over in the Barclay neighborhood. East Baltimore."

East Baltimore? He'd been there! He'd driven up and down Twenty-fifth Street for nearly an hour, searching for any signs of Frank La Salle. Was it possible they'd been there, right under his nose?

"Didn't pan out," the officer explained. Al could hear him shuffling through some papers. Sally's file, perhaps. "Yep. Here it is. Address for the girl on file at the school turned up nothing when we sent a couple officers over to check it out."

"When was that?" Al asked.

"Not long after La Salle got indicted again. The sister read about it in the papers and thought there might be a connection. Says here around St. Paddy's Day."

"March?" Al said in disbelief. "That was months ago! Why didn't anyone call me? What is the address? Who lives there?"

"Guy named . . . uh . . . here it is . . . Sammy DePaulo. But I told you. Nothing turned up. She wasn't there."

"What was her name?" Al asked, trying to

261

keep his voice steady. "The child at the parochial school?"

"Hold on," the officer said. "Fogg. That's it. Florence Fogg."

Florence.

"She goes to that school?" Al asked, jotting down *St. Ann's* on the notepad he kept by the telephone.

"Well, it's summertime now, sir. School's been out for a couple of weeks already."

Damn it. And sure enough, when he called St. Ann's the phone just rang and rang.

"Come to bed, honey?"

Sue had just put the baby down; she was finally sleeping through the night now. Probably the only one in the house who was.

Al had been scouring the news clippings he'd collected again, looking for something, anything that he'd missed before. His gut told him Frank La Salle and Sally weren't in Baltimore anymore. But when he tried to think about where they would have gone, his mind drew a blank. The sad fact was that they could be anywhere. Anywhere at all.

He ran his finger down the column again. What was he missing? What clue? Then he saw the name that had popped up in a few of the lengthier articles following Sally's disappearance. *Dorothy Dare.* The other girl Frank La Salle had kidnapped, the one he'd gone and married to keep from going to jail. Just a child herself when La Salle had stolen her from her own family. One of the news clippings said she was from Philadelphia. Philadelphia was just across the river. Thirty minutes away.

"Al," Susan insisted. "Please come get some sleep."

SALLY

"Good morning, sunshine!" Ruth said to Sally as she stepped out of the trailer into the bright sunlight of a hot June day, carrying a basket of Mr. Warner's dirty laundry.

The rules were she was only allowed to go to the canteen, over to Ruth's trailer, and to the pool. That was it. Mr. Warner told her that if she abused these privileges, there would be hell to pay. He'd promised her that if she even *thought* about venturing beyond the perimeter of the Good Luck, he'd make sure she never saw the sunshine again. That she never, ever saw her mother again. But that Ruth would be the one to suffer the consequences the most.

Today Ruth was sitting in her chaise longue, reading, a steaming mug of coffee sitting on the ground next to her. She was wearing a red gingham sleeveless shirt with a bare midriff and high-waisted white shorts. She looked like a movie star to Sally.

"I wanna see that picture," Sally said, gesturing to the book. *A Tree Grows in Brooklyn*. Peggy Ann Garner got an Academy Award for that role. Mrs. Appleton, her fifth-grade teacher, once told Sally she looked a bit like the actress, only with curls.

"Oh, but the book is so much more wonderful. I'll give it to you if I ever finish," Ruth said, sitting up. She wiped her forehead with the back of her wrist. "God, it's just so hot. And it's only June," Ruth said. "I can hardly believe this heat's only gonna get worse."

June. It had been a full year now since Mr. Warner had caught her shoplifting. A whole year they'd been running, though she wasn't sure anymore whom they were running from. *Twelve months*. It felt both possible and impossible. She knew that her clothes and shoes no longer fit. That the books she'd loved back then she found childish now. Even her own handwriting had changed. There was an angry slant to it lately, one she recalled seeing in her mother's hand.

She practiced writing her new name, Florence LaPlante, in the composition book she'd brought with her from Baltimore. She also drafted letters home, telling her mother exactly where she was and what she was doing (or rather what was being done to her). When she wrote these words, her writing was small, scared. Some of the words were so shameful that afterward she went over them again and again, blacking them out with a thousand dark squiggles from her pen. Still, it felt good to release them like this. To put them on the page got them out of her brain. Even the ones that it hurt the most to write.

~~Mama, he says he's my real father. That he's come back for me. But I don't remember him. And how could you let him take me? I know I'm trouble to you sometimes, talking too much, not helpin' out the way you need me to. But I promise, if you bring me home I'll be good. I'll be better, Mama. I promise. Maybe you can explain to the police? Maybe tell them it's all been a big mistake?~~

Sometimes instead of writing the truths, however, she wrote her dreams. Imagined herself into someone else's life. Gave herself a new name. *Today,* she might write, thinking of Bess with her strawberry hair, *I rode my uncle's horse, Lucky, for ten miles. I carried sugar cubes in my pocket, and let him eat a bright red apple from my hand.* Or Irene: *I went shopping with my mother today at Hurley's. She bought me a brand-new pair of shoes. Mary Janes. They're so soft, almost like a baby's skin.* But most of the time, she became Vivi: *I am having the most beautiful life,* she would gush on the page in a rush of ink. *Sometimes, when I look up at the sky and watch the clouds passing across the sun, or when my mother brushes my hair or my father lets me lean over and steer the car for a minute, my heart is so full, I feel like it might explode.*

"How do y'all like Dallas so far?" Ruth asked,

picking up her coffee mug. "You ever miss home?"

Sally nodded, her throat swollen with this truth. "My mama especially."

Sally didn't dare ask Mr. Warner when she could go home anymore. The last time she did, he punched the wall of the trailer so hard, it left a dent in the metal. He was angry a lot lately, and his temper terrified her. It was worse when he was drinking, and he was drinking more than before, it seemed. He worked all day at a garage in town and then went out; he'd come back to the trailer some nights smelling so sickeningly of grease and liquor, she had to hold a blanket over her face so she wouldn't vomit. The only blessing was that on those nights when he came crashing through the door, he usually was too drunk to bother with her, and he would fall asleep on his own bed, and she was safe.

Last night had been one of those nights; she'd heard him outside the trailer throwing up, the retching making her nauseous. In the morning she'd found his soiled clothes in a heap; he'd just left them there before he went back to work again. She'd need to use bleach to get those awful stains out.

"Well, I should be getting the laundry done," she said to Ruth.

"Sure thing, sweetheart. Come by later if you'd like. To get the book. I only got a couple chapters left."

• • •

When Sally opened the canteen door, she heard the sound of swishing water and sighed. There was only one washer that everybody at the trailer park shared. It was eight o'clock on a Saturday morning. Who on earth would be doing laundry so early?

She went past the cigarette and candy machines to the laundry room and peeked her head in. Someone was sitting on top of the folding counter, legs crossed, reading *Glamour* magazine. Oh, how she missed magazines. The movie magazines she loved and the fashion ones Susan read. Susan always spent her extra money on *Vogue* and *Mademoiselle*. When she was finished with them, she'd give them to Sally, though Susan had often torn pages out and tacked them to her wall, so Sally always felt like she was missing something important as she thumbed through the glossy pages.

"Hello," Sally said, and the lady looked up. Except that she wasn't a lady at all. She had a long beard and a handlebar mustache. Sally audibly caught her breath, and then blushed, ashamed.

"Good mornin', sugar," the lady said. (She was a lady everywhere but her chin, Sally noted.) She turned the magazine to face Sally. "You like fashion?"

"I suppose." Sally shrugged.

"I find it tiresome," the bearded lady said dramatically. "Though I do appreciate the way a pair of heels accentuates my calves." She jumped down off the counter.

"Are you . . . ," Sally started, not entirely sure what she was even asking.

"Hungry?" the lady asked, eyebrow raised. "I'm *starving*."

"No, I mean . . ."

"Lena," the lady said, extending one perfectly manicured hand.

"I'm . . ."

"Delighted?" Lena said, laughing.

"Florence. Florence LaPlante."

"Pleasure to make your acquaintance, Flo." Lena reached into the washer and started to put her items through the wringer one by one, tossing the damp dresses and dungarees and underthings into her basket, which she hoisted under one arm, a pair of pink panties falling off the pile.

"Would you mind?" she asked, and Sally bent down, plucking the underwear from the floor, pinching them together with her thumb and finger like the stem of a flower. She deposited them in the basket and Lena turned back around.

"Come meet the rest of the crew," she said, and without waiting for Sally to answer, she swung her hips wide to avoid the counter and made her way to the back door.

Sally peered at her own basket of clothes, then

269

back at Lena, who was holding the door open for her with one foot.

"Coming! Let me just get my laundry in the machine."

She dumped the load into the machine, followed by a cup of the powdered soap. She threw the lid down, turned the knob, and ran through the back door to the walkway, where Lena was waiting for her.

Sally followed Lena to the far end of the motor court, where she found a cluster of trailers, their inhabitants loitering outside. Two women, acrobats, crab-walked past her as she stared, openmouthed, at a baby elephant, drinking water from a child's swimming pool.

"That's Peanut," Lena said, motioning to the elephant, who raised his trunk as if in greeting. Sally felt her heart swell with delight.

"Maisy and Daisy," she said as the acrobats returned to standing. They curtsied to Sally, and she clumsily curtsied back.

Strung between two trailers was a wire, and a man wearing nothing but a pair of tights traversed it, holding a long bamboo pole to help himself balance.

"Breakfast!" a tiny little man said, as he swung open the door of the largest trailer in the cluster.

"That's Oscar," Lena whispered. "Our ring-master."

Sally was speechless. There was so much to see. At a picnic table, an enormous lady in a yellow dress was eating a pile of pancakes, and a small boy with hands like claws was plucking strips of bacon from a pan. Tiny dogs wearing tutus walked on their hind legs, begging for scraps, and a woman wearing a silver turban held a very long cigarette holder and blew smoke into the morning air.

"You all live here?" Sally asked in disbelief.

"One big happy family," Lena said, and winked.

RUTH

"D o they come every year?" Florence asked
Ruth as Ruth raised the stool several inches
with the press of her foot.

"Who's that, sweetheart?"

Ruth's kitchen was filled with bright light, and
the air hummed with the three fans she'd situated
to combat the stifling heat.

"The circus people. Did you know there's a boy
with lobster claws for hands?" Florence's eyes
were wide, beaming (for the first time since Ruth
had met her, she genuinely bore the expression of
a child).

"Look straight ahead," Ruth said. It had taken
her nearly an hour to comb the tangles out of
Florence's hair. Something about those knots had
made her heart ache. How long had it been since
her mama had untangled those curls? Ruth took
the comb and ran it down the back of her scalp,
making a clean white part.

"Does your daddy know you've been spending
time with them?" Ruth asked. The circus folk
usually kept to themselves. She was surprised
when she saw the bearded lady sitting at the edge
of the pool with Florence the other day, both of
them kicking their feet in the pristine blue water.
Florence's daddy kept her on a short leash. Most

of the time when Florence went swimming, he went along with her to the pool and sat at one of the small tables poolside, smoking his Luckies while she dog-paddled back and forth across the pool. He must have been afraid she might drown, and she added that to her list of possible disasters Florence's mother might have suffered.

"I don't gotta tell him everything, do I?" Ruth felt Florence's shoulders stiffen at her touch.

"Well, of course not. A girl's entitled to her secrets," she said, and Florence's muscles relaxed. "Now turn this way just a bit; good."

Ruth listened as the girl prattled on about the tightrope walker and the trapeze girls who weren't much older than she was.

"She told me they swing a hundred feet above the ground!" Florence exclaimed. "I'm just dying to go see them."

Ruth had seen the acrobats, twins, cartwheeling across the brown grass behind the circus caravan of trailers, with their thin legs and fishnet stockings. The contortionist who twisted her body into a pretzel, ankles touching her ears. Since the circus folks arrived, the whole trailer park was littered with sequins, reflecting the sun like stars.

"Have you never been to the circus before?" Ruth asked, stunned.

Florence shook her head. "My daddy was gonna

take me once, but then he . . ." Her shoulders stiffened again, and she shook her head.

Ruth had never heard her refer to Frank LaPlante as "Daddy" before. It was always "My father says" or "Father says . . ."

"I'm just gonna trim off the dead ends here," Ruth said.

"No," Florence said. "I want you to cut it short. Like Elizabeth Taylor."

"Really? You have such gorgeous curls. Just a trim to get the dead ends off?"

Florence shook her head again, and Ruth shrugged. She knew that sometimes a girl needed to reinvent herself. Every time she and Hank moved, she considered changing her name, starting over. Illinois, Florida, Texas. She could have been anyone she wanted to be. But inevitably, she lost her gumption and went back to being plain old Ruth.

She had to admit, when all those curls lay on the linoleum, like so many parentheses, Florence looked like a new girl. The cut took the weight from her hair and her curls bounced lightly around her face. Her eyes were bright as she looked in the handheld mirror that Ruth held up.

"Just like Elizabeth Taylor." Ruth winked. "You look all grown up."

SALLY

G oddamn it."

Sally woke up at the sound of Mr. Warner just outside the trailer. Like most Friday nights since they got to Dallas, he'd been down the street at the Sky-Vu for a few hours and a few more highballs. She knew that was where he was because she was always finding the Sky-Vu matchbooks in his pockets when she did the laundry. On Friday nights, he came home stinking of liquor, the smell of it coming off him like vapors. Usually, she just pretended she was asleep and he'd just tumble into bed, where he'd promptly fall asleep.

But tonight when he got home, he crawled into bed next to Sally.

"Hey, pretty girl," he slurred in her ear. But when he stroked her hair in the darkness, his hand stopped short where her hair ended. He reached for the lamp and clumsily clicked it on. Sally blinked against the glare, her hand automatically shading her eyes.

"What'd you do to yourself?" he asked.

She cried as he pulled at her arm, dragging her out of bed. She struggled to stay upright as he pushed her through the narrow entrance to their

275

bedroom and out into the tiny bathroom, where a mirror hung crooked over the sink.

"Who did this to you?" he hissed, peering at both of their reflections in the mirror.

Sally shook her head. Tears ran down her cheeks.

"Was it that circus freak?" he asked. "What's the matter with you? You gotta ask me before you go and do something like this."

She shook her head, bracing herself for what was coming. Still, it stunned her. He hit her, like a man would hit another grown man, and her skull clanged like a gong. She fell backward with the force of it, striking the kitchenette counter with her hip and then crumbling into a shuddering heap on the floor. Her vision was a night sky, swirling constellations.

"Sally," he said. "Sally, sweetheart. I'm sorry. I didn't mean to . . ."

Still on the floor, she scooted backward, afraid of him. "Don't touch me," she said, shielding her face. "Please."

He put his hands at his sides and shook his head. "No, course not. I'm sorry, sweetheart. It's just that, it's just that you look so much older now. I'm not ready for my little girl to grow up just yet."

The next day, Sally stayed in bed. She refused to speak to Mr. Warner when he brought her a plate with eggs and toast. A cup of milky coffee, even though he usually forbade her from drinking his Chase & Sanborn, said little girls shouldn't drink coffee.

"No, thank you," she said, and turned to face the wall.

"Can I get you some ice?" he'd asked, and reached to touch her face, but she flinched at his touch, and he moved his hand away.

"They need me at the garage today. Scully's out sick. But I'll be home right after work tonight," he said. "I'll bring home some of those burgers you like. Extra pickles?"

She could feel her heart beating dully in her temple where he'd hit her. Her head pounded, and later when he finally left for work, she looked in the mirror and barely recognized herself. Between the new haircut and the shiner that swallowed her right eye in a bloom of purple and blue, she could have been someone else. Florence Fogg. Florence LaPlante. Sally Horner, where had she gone? She wondered if she were to see her mother right now, if Ella would even know Sally anymore.

She thought of going to Ruth, of pleading with her to take her in, to keep her safe. If Ruth had any idea of what really happened inside the walls of this trailer, surely she would help her escape. Or would she? Those awful dirty things Mr. Warner made her do. What kind of father would do this to his own daughter? She couldn't ever tell anyone the things he had done and said to her. The secrets her skin kept now, the horror that flowed in her veins. Her marrow poisoned. Maybe Lena, who lived in a world that embraced the strange and sinful and vulgar, wouldn't judge her.

She returned to the bedroom, thinking she'd put on her swimsuit and go to the pool. Find Lena, maybe swim in that cool blue. The water might ease the aching at her temple, might soothe her. Sometimes she just floated for hours on her back in the pool, staring up at that wide blue sky. But her suit wasn't in the drawer where she kept her clothes. She searched the laundry basket, then crouched down to see if maybe it had gotten pushed under the bed.

As she peered underneath the mattress, the blood flowed to her temple, and the pain pounded hard and loud, nearly blinding her. She felt dizzy and closed her eyes. When she opened them, she realized she was looking at his valise. Shoved far under the bed. She'd nearly forgotten about it.

She reached under the bed, her fingers spider-walking across the filthy floor, trying to grasp onto the handle. When she finally had it, she stood up, setting it on the bed carefully. It was covered in dust. The leather battered and worn. She tried the rusted clasp, but it was still locked.

She wondered where Mr. Warner might keep the key, and then figured it was probably on the ring he kept in his pocket.

Sally found Mr. Warner's toolbox under the sink. He'd had it out just the other day when he was fixing a drip in the kitchen faucet. She searched through the tools for anything that would help her break the lock. Hammers, needle-nose pliers, a rusty wrench. Finally, she found a pair of bolt cutters buried under a box of screws.

Back in the bedroom, she positioned the little padlock between the blades and, using all of her strength, squeezed them. She was startled when the blades closed together and the lock snapped, and she felt sick as she thought about what might be inside.

Knock, knock.

"Florence?" Ruth was at the door. She must be wondering why Sally hadn't come out yet. It was already almost noon.

"Hold on," Sally hollered.

She carefully lifted the lid. Inside the valise was a manila envelope, with a delicate clasp. When she bent the tines back, they snapped off, and she caught her breath.

She shook the envelope's contents onto the bed.

Sally trembled as she shuffled through the photos. There must have been a hundred snapshots. All the pictures were of girls, girls who didn't seem to know they were being

279

photographed. The photos appeared to have been taken from a distance: girls sunning themselves on the beach, girls huddled together at a street corner. One of them bent over scratching her ankle. They made her feel strange.

There was also a stack of photos, these banded together with a crumbling rubber band that disintegrated in Sally's fingers, the photos tumbling onto the bed like a loose deck of cards.

Knock, knock. Sally glanced at the door and quickly shuffled through the photos.

Captured inside the scalloped borders: a blond girl, with pouty lips, wearing only a slip. Bare feet and painted nails. There must have been twenty photos of this same girl. In some of them, she wasn't wearing anything at all, and Sally's face burned with shame. Who was she? What did any of this mean?

"Sally, honey? Everything okay in there?"

She turned one of the photos over, and read in handwriting she recognized as Mr. Warner's: *Dot, Atlantic City, '39.* Then, underneath the photo, was a small yellowed newspaper clipping. Sally picked it up and studied the faded newsprint:

WANTED: FRANK LA SALLE IN KID-NAPPING OF MERCHANTVILLE MINOR, DOROTHY DARE.

AL

When Al rang the doorbell at the address in Philadelphia he'd located in the phone book under *D. Dare,* he wasn't sure what he expected, but it wasn't this.

A child. Maybe ten or eleven years old with curly blond hair and bare feet. She had small, close-set eyes and a severe expression.

"Mama's not here," she said behind the screen door.

"Oh," he said. "Are you all alone?"

"She just went to the market," she said. "She'll be right back. She's gettin' groceries."

"Oh," he said.

The porch was littered with toys, a rusty pair of roller skates, a dozen scattered jacks.

"You mind if I wait here?" he asked, motioning to a mint-green metal patio chair. It was exactly like the one Ella had on her front porch. It felt like a sign of good luck.

The girl shrugged.

He brushed some dirt from the seat and sat down. The door opened slowly. The girl emerged, and she sat cross-legged on the porch floor and scooped up the handful of jacks.

"And your daddy? He at work?" Al asked.

281

"My daddy's an old son of a bitch," the girl said, and Al had to stifle a laugh.

When he saw the woman walking down the sidewalk toward the house, he stood up and took off his hat.

"What're you doing outside?" the young woman said to the girl, grabbing her arm, the girl scrambling to her feet. "I told you to keep the door locked." She turned to him and glared. "I don't wanna buy nothin'. I got a working vacuum, and I don't need no encyclopedias or Bibles neither."

"I'm sorry, ma'am," he said. "I ain't sellin' nothing. I'm actually here because I was hoping to speak to Dorothy Dare?"

The woman's thin, plucked left eyebrow lifted skeptically.

"You see, I was hoping to talk to you about your husband?"

"I ain't married," she said. "Not anymore."

He nodded. "I know that, ma'am. I read it in the papers. Have you *seen* the papers?" he asked, reaching into his pocket and pulling out the article, the one with the photos of Frank La Salle and Sally.

"Get inside and get washed up," she said to the child, who grudgingly obliged. The woman reached out her hand, and Al handed her the clipping.

"I ain't seen Frank since they hauled him off to

jail the last time," she said, not looking up from the article. "Thought he was rotting in prison."

"This here's my wife's sister," he said, pointing the photo of Sally. "She's only twelve years old."

The woman's face softened then, and he wondered if she was thinking of her own daughter, the one he could hear singing softly to herself on the other side of the screened door now.

"They think he's in Baltimore," Al said. "You know if he knows anybody in Baltimore?"

"I don't think so," she said, shrugging, handing the paper back to Al.

"Oh," Al said, feeling hope seeping out of him like air out of a tire.

"Wait. There *is* one buddy of his I met once. He came and stayed with us in Atlantic City not long after the baby was born. Sammy something. Something Italian. Frankie knew him from Chicago, he said. But I remember he said he was, from Baltimore. I remember 'cause he brought a big bag of soft-shell crabs with him, made a real mess of my kitchen. *DePaulo.* That's it."

"Sammy DePaulo?" Al repeated. He could barely contain his excitement. "In Baltimore."

She nodded. Smiled even.

"Thank you," he said. "Thank you so much."

The woman cocked her head. "I went to the market, but I didn't have enough money when I got to the register," she said. She stuck her palm out and tapped her foot. "Came back to dig around in my piggy bank."

"Oh," Al said, understanding, and reached into his wallet. He pulled out a crisp dollar bill and held it out to her. She leaned forward and made as if to see how many more bills were hiding there. He plucked another one out, and she stuffed them both down into her blouse. He noted that her sternum was sharp, her collarbones like a hanger. When she smiled, he noticed that she was missing one of her eyeteeth. Just a black hole where bone used to be.

Back at home, while Sue stood wringing her hands, Al called the Baltimore police and told them about his conversation with Dorothy.

"You gotta go back to that house, the one where Sammy DePaulo lives," he said. "Please. Sally's been there."

SALLY

"Ihat pup's too young to be away from his mama," Lena said to Sally. "They need their mamas to teach them how to be in the world."

She and Lena were sitting at the pool, drinking bottles of Pepsi that Lena had bought from the machine at the canteen. The new puppy was curled up on the pavement, asleep in the sun, a rope tied around his neck hardly necessary. He hadn't left her side since Mr. Warner gave him to her.

Mr. Warner had come home that Saturday, long after she'd returned the photos to his valise, after she'd shoved it back under the bed, hoping he wouldn't retrieve it and find the lock smashed to smithereens. After she'd racked her brain trying to figure out what it all meant, why he'd lie about being her daddy, and wondered about that girl Dorothy. Sally had been pretending to read the book that Ruth had given her, but the words swam across the page. The only words she could see were the ones burned into her brain: *WANTED. Kidnapping. Frank La Salle.*

She'd slammed the book shut when he came into the bedroom. She wanted to ask him what those photos meant, who Dorothy Dare was. She wanted to know if he really took that girl. If he was Frank La Salle, not Frank Warner, not her real daddy like he claimed.

"Listen here," he said. "I got something for you. A couple of things, actually. First off, I'm taking you to the circus next week. See what all the hullabaloo's about. Also . . . ," he said, reaching for something inside his shirt.

Mr. Warner had tucked the tiny pup there and offered it to her, a gift. An apology. He said that another mechanic had come across the mama on his way to work a few weeks ago, and that she whelped her litter in the backseat of his car.

"He don't have a name yet," he said, setting him down on the bed.

She was startled. She hadn't expected this, this little puppy whose ribs she could see through his dull brown fur. He rolled over onto his back at her touch, licked her hand when she reached for him.

"I never had a dog before," she said softly.

"You gotta feed him with a bottle," he said. "He ain't been weaned yet."

Sally looked up, blinked hard, and looked back down at the puppy again. She picked him up and held him to her chest. His heart pulsed beneath her fingers, small but steady.

"I'm gonna love you like your mama would," she whispered, cradling the pup in her arms. "I promise I'll take care of you forever."

She named him Tex.

"I had a dog once, got separated from his mama before his eyes were even open yet. He was afraid of everything. You couldn't hardly take a step without him pissing himself in fear. Felt bad for the little guy. Couldn't take him on a walk even. Spent most of his time curled up underneath the kitchen table," Lena said.

Sally nodded.

"You certainly are an unusual little girl," Lena said, scowling.

"Am I?"

"Well, I never see you with any other children. Don't you have any friends?"

Sally shook her head, ashamed. Of so many things.

"Your daddy do that to you?" Lena asked, gesturing with her bearded chin at Sally's bruised cheekbone.

Sally shook her head again. After he gave her the puppy, he'd made her promise not to tell what happened. He said that he might not have raised her, but he was her legal guardian, and he had a right to discipline her. An obligation even. Besides, he was sorry he'd hurt her. That was why he'd given her Tex. It was his way of apologizing. He said he'd make things right. Take her to the circus. Buy her popcorn, cotton candy. Anything she'd like.

"I had a daddy like that," Lena whispered.

Sally didn't often think of grown-ups as having mothers and fathers. Or their mothers and fathers having mothers and fathers. It was like trying to imagine infinity. Like holding a mirror in a mirror. It made her brain feel like it was collapsing in on itself.

"Like what?" she asked, feeling her cheek pulse, the bruise going deeper than her skin, deeper even than her bone.

"*Mean,*" Lena said. She stretched one long and elegant arm out, examining it as if it didn't belong to her.

Sally stared down into the shimmering blue water.

"Drunk. *Nasty,*" Lena added, and the word was like a hush. Like a secret inside a secret. She studied Sally's face and then dipped her hand into the water, trailed her fingers through the cool blue. "Maybe," she said quietly, "touches you in places you aren't s'posed to be touched until you're married?"

Sally shook her head, but her eyes widened in wonder. How did Lena know this? It was like she had peeked inside the trailer window, or a window in Sally's mind. Like she was a spy. Was it possible she was a spy? What if *Lena* was with the FBI?

"Don't worry," Lena said. "I won't go telling nobody your secrets. But I will tell you one thing. Ain't nobody got a right to touch a little girl like that. Especially not your own daddy."

Sally felt her throat close in around all those words she wasn't allowed to say.

"You should come with us," Lena said, a smile spreading across her face.

"What?" Sally asked.

"Join the circus! We're all *unusual* in the circus." Lena threw her head back with laughter and then stood up and walked around the edge of the pool, ignoring the stares of the other residents as she climbed atop the diving board and executed the most graceful dive.

Lena came back to where Sally was now sitting with Tex curled up in her lap. She wrapped herself in a threadbare towel and leaned down, whispering in Sally's ear. The cold chlorinated water dripped onto Sally's bare leg and onto the puppy, whose eyes were still sealed shut. "We're headed to Texarkana next. Making our way east. You just say the word, sweetheart."

East. She'd studied the maps in Mr. Warner's glove box, memorized the route that would take her back home, knowing even as she committed the highways to memory that it was a futile endeavor. That home was wherever Mr. Warner, *Frank La Salle,* took her.

"What about Tex?" Sally asked, motioning to the brown little puppy.

"Well, he'll come along, too, of course," she said.

Then Lena was gone, swinging her hips and tossing her hair, blowing kisses at the bitter-faced lady who gawked at her as she walked by.

That night, Mr. Warner took her to the circus. They walked from the Good Luck to the field down the street where the giant tent was set up. They could see it all the way from Commerce Street, its red and white stripes illuminated in the night. He insisted on holding her hand tightly as they crossed the busy streets, though she knew it wasn't for her safety. She wasn't a little girl anymore.

They walked past the sideshow tents with their painted signs: THE AMAZING LOBSTER BOY, THE HEADLESS WOMAN, WINSOME WINNIE, FAT AND PRETTY. It took her a moment to realize that MAGDELENA, THE BEARDED LADY OF LUXEMBOURG, was Lena.

"Step right up!" the barker at the main tent's entrance said. He was wearing a bright red shirt and a faded velvet coat with tails.

Mr. Warner handed him some coins, and the man motioned grandly for them to go inside.

Outside, the sky was dark and filled with stars, but inside the tent, it was as bright as daylight. Without letting go of her hand, Mr. Warner led her up the bleachers until they were peering down at the spectacle below.

He called the boy over, the usher selling

paper bags stuffed with buttery popcorn and candy.

"We'll take one of each," he said. "Popcorn and some Chuckles. You like Chuckles, Sally? And a Budweiser for me, if it's cold."

"No beer. Just Coca-Cola," the boy said. "Cold as ice."

Frank scowled, but it didn't matter; she knew he had a flask in his pocket.

The paper container of popcorn had an illustrated giraffe imprinted on it. She wondered if there would be giraffes. It seemed like anything might be possible here.

Another vendor came stomping up the bleacher steps hollering, "Peanuts, peanuts, live chameleons!"

Sally's eyes widened as she watched the little boy in front of her hand over fifty cents. In exchange, he was given an actual living lizard. Around its neck was a thin red ribbon, at the end of which was a gold safety pin. She watched as the vendor demonstrated how to pin the ribbon to your shirt.

"That way, he can't git away from y'all," the usher said, and nodded smugly.

"You want one of them, Sally?" Frank asked, nudging her.

She shook her head, feeling sick.

But then the lights began to flash, the spotlight seeking out the little man in a tall top hat named

Oscar. "Ladies and gents, boys and girls!" he boomed. "Welcome to the Big Top!"

Mesmerized, she didn't know where to look. Overhead, trapeze artists swung like glittery birds in the sky. Below, there were three rings, something magical happening inside each. In one, a giant elephant (Peanut's mother?) balanced on a tiny pedestal. In another, three clowns tumbled in circles, throwing cream pies at each other's faces and honking each other's bright red noses. She looked on with wonder and amusement, afraid she might miss something if she dared to blink. When the lights dimmed, a spotlight shone on the center ring, a tiger inside a giant cage. It was pacing, pacing back and forth as Oscar taunted it. She held her breath as she watched Oscar release the latch, setting the tiger free, covered her eyes as the animal lunged, teeth bared, at Oscar. Something inside her nearly snapped when he cracked his whip, taming the beast into submission again.

She had to look away, but when she did, she saw the boy who'd bought the lizard. The tiny chameleon had crawled up onto his captor's shoulder. She had read a book once in Mrs. Appleton's class about chameleons, and she knew they were supposed to change color, to blend in to their environment to protect themselves. But the boy's shirt was white, and the chameleon was green, bright green, almost like he wanted to be found.

Later that night, when Mr. Warner yanked at her clothes, at her hair, at her body, she dreamed she was on a trapeze, flying high above the clouds, *with the greatest of ease:* the breeze in her hair, her shimmering glimmering body awash in lights. Sparkling and beautiful. A living firefly.

Maybe this *was* the answer. Lena had invited her, asked her to come along. She could slip away in the night, ride the circus train to wherever they were going. She could learn to walk the tightrope, to swing from the trapeze. She could wear the seamed fishnet stockings, the sequined leotards. She could learn how to ride atop the elephants. She could swallow swords or breathe fire.

When he collapsed, breathless and heavy, stinking of cigarettes and liquor and the sour awful smell that she suspected was the scent of his awful soul, she began to dream her escape.

In the dark, all through the night, she schemed. Soon when Mr. Warner was gone to work, she'd go to Lena. Tell her everything. It was terrifying, but she trusted Lena. She loved her. And Lena would take care of her, take her away. She couldn't go home, maybe not ever, but she didn't have to stay here. As she drifted off to sleep, she dreamed the sharp razor edge of the tightrope stretched between here and anywhere else. Underneath a glittering, big top sky.

SAMMY

This time when the police showed up at Sammy's place in Baltimore, they had a warrant in hand. And even though Frankie and the girl were long gone, Sammy was trembling when he answered the door.

He sat at the kitchen table as they searched the rooms above him; he could hear their boots and muffled conversation. He heard them climbing higher, up to the third-floor attic room, and he felt his lunch turn in his stomach.

After Frank and Florence left, he'd cleaned out the attic room. Filled a trash bag with the things Frankie left behind: matchbooks, swizzle sticks, a broken watch, and dull razor blades. The girl's drawer, though, made him pause. He didn't know what he thought would be inside. She was just a little girl; maybe candy wrappers or a windup toy? A tangled Slinky or a rusty tambourine? But when he pulled the drawer open, swollen with the humidity, it was empty, save a tin with two or three rubbers inside.

He hadn't known what to do; he'd nearly thrown them across the room in disgust. Reeling, he'd gone to the bed and yanked off the sheets, gathering them in his arms, disgusted by whatever Frank had been doing in that room. Repulsed that he'd allowed it.

When the cops came downstairs again, empty-handed, he could have shrugged, seen them out. He could have sent them on their way. But it was what he'd found in that drawer that stopped him. That dusty drawer, empty now as if she'd never existed at all.

"Thank you, Mr. DePaulo," the older officer said, tipping his hat.

The other followed behind, shoulders stooped.

"Wait," Sammy said.

Sour bile crept up the back of his throat, and he went to the sink. As the cops waited for him, he turned on the faucet and filled a smudged glass with water.

"They were here," he said, swallowing hard. "Course I didn't know anything about the girl. Who she was. He told me she was his kid. His stepkid."

"And?" the stoop-shouldered cop said, straightening. "Where did he go?"

"You might see if you can track down some-body named Joey Bonds," he said. "That was the name he mentioned. Before they left."

"Bonds?"

"Yeah. Somebody he knew from the pen."

"And where might we find this Joey Bonds?"

The realization that he'd just ratted Frankie out hit him.

"Well?" the tall one demanded.

Sammy nodded. "I heard there was a reward? Five hundred dollars?"

"Yeah, that's right," the older man said, scowling. "But we're not in the business of giving rewards to people who harbor fugitives."

"Tell us where to find this Bonds character," the tall one said. "Or we might come back with a new warrant. One for your arrest."

Sammy sighed. And he thought about Frankie, that sick bastard. "Out west somewhere," he said.

"How far west are we talking? Pittsburgh or California?" the older one demanded.

Sammy sighed. "Texas, I think."

"That's a big state."

Sammy nodded. "Not that big."

LENA

I t was true, what Lena had told Florence. About
her own daddy. Lena knew it the second she
saw him, that old man Frank with his skinny
ass and bowlegs. His long jaw and shifty eyes.
Goddamn sex pervert. People might call Lena a
freak, but that wicked man was a true freak if she
ever saw one.

Lena had been a normal girl once, just like
Florence (a name that sounded made up to her,
but who was she to talk . . . she herself had been
born Lorraine). Twelve years old with a freckle
face and red hair, scabby knees, and nothing but
sweetness. And she'd had a pervert daddy, too,
who had his way with her while her mama turned
a blind eye. Though of course nobody would
suspect a minister of being a monster.

But then when she turned thirteen and breasts
started to bloom on her chest and hair started
to sprout from between her legs, it began to
grow from her chin, too. And he'd thought
that the devil himself had come to live inside
his daughter. When he'd called upon God to
cast her out, she'd spat in his face and said
maybe he was the one that put that demon seed
inside her. Secretly she thought it might just be
Mother Nature's way of protecting her. Because

the second her voice deepened and she grew whiskers, her daddy wouldn't touch her with a ten-foot pole. Of course nobody else would, either. Her mama spurned her. Her brothers and sisters suffered the most (the cruelty of children is notorious but still always mystifying). And so she packed up her bags and headed west, didn't look back even once.

She began with a small sideshow circuit but got snatched up by the big-time, big-top folks when they got a look at her gams. She had legs that went on for miles.

Over the years, she'd made it her business to welcome the newcomers: her fellow freaks who flocked to the circus like penitents to the cross. She became the mother her own mother never was. Her arms were as long as her legs, and she used them to embrace the whole damn damaged world.

Someone knocked at her door. She thought it might be Florence, but when the door opened, it was just Oscar.

"Hey, Lena, time to skedaddle," he whispered. He was a three-foot-tall silhouette, the moon just a sliver behind him.

It was the middle of the night, which meant trouble. An altercation between one of the circus folks and a rube, probably. They weren't supposed to leave for Texarkana for another week, but they were a family, and they moved along together. Time to get out of town. Ready or not.

She thought about going and waking Florence, but how could she with that man standing guard like a dog baring his teeth? There was no way she could get past him, no way to save her. Not tonight.

"Hurry up," Oscar said, tapping an impatient foot against the dusty ground.

She gathered her clothes, her few belongings. She tidied up the trailer as best she could in the dim light. It pained Lena to leave Florence there; her heart ached as she walked past the LaPlantes' trailer. The only comfort she had was the certainty that the circus would come back (they always came back), and if that poor child was still here with her bruised cheeks and sorrowful eyes, she'd snatch her up next time.

Before she left, she glanced up at that glittering sky and made a wish, for Florence, on the brightest star.

RUTH

Florence came knocking on Ruth's trailer door not five minutes after Hank took off for work the next morning. She was frantic, banging her knuckles against the door.

"Sweet Jesus," Ruth said, ushering her into the trailer. "What's the matter, honey?"

Florence paced back and forth across the floor.

"Where did they go?" the girl cried.

"Who?"

"The circus people," she said, her gaze shifting frantically from Ruth to the door and back again. *"Lena."*

"Well, I assume they all are headed on to the next town by now."

"Texarkana?"

"I suppose?" Ruth said. "Why?"

"I was gonna . . . I was hoping . . . ," she started, but then her expression turned from disbelief to resignation. "I didn't get a chance to say good-bye."

Ruth had seen Florence with Lena by the pool a few times. She figured the woman was just being friendly. Lena had found out that Ruth did hair and had come by just the other day to get her hair done. Ruth had asked her if she might like to have anything waxed or plucked, and she'd laughed so hard she said she needed to use her little girls' room. Ruth didn't judge people. "Live and let live" was her motto.

"Will they come back?" Florence asked, sniffling a little.

"Next summer, I suppose," Ruth said.

"Oh," Florence said softly. Sadly.

"She's your friend?"

"Yeah, she's real nice. She let me try on her high heels once. We wear the same size. She said I'd make a good flyer, you know, on the trapeze? On account of how brave I am." She stuck her chin out just a bit when she said this, and it made Ruth's heart ache.

"You *are* brave," Ruth said. "Just like that girl Francie in the book I gave you."

Florence's eyes lit up. "I am?"

"You are."

Ruth invited Florence to stay for supper. She'd heard arguing coming from the LaPlante trailer the other night and had a bad feeling that Frank was responsible for that bruise underneath Florence's eye. She also had a sneaking suspicion that Florence didn't want to talk about it. The men were still at work, so the two sat out at the picnic table and ate the oven-fried chicken Ruth had learned how to make when she and Hank first got married.

It was quiet now without the circus folks here.

Summer would be over before she knew it, and with the changing of the seasons would come the harvest. Normally, she and Hank would be hitching their trailer to their truck following the crops, but he had a steady job now, plus she liked it here and hoped that for once, they might just stay put.

"Florence, you know you need anything at all, you can come to me," Ruth said. "I know I ain't nearly as glamorous as that girl Lena, but I got a soft shoulder to cry on. If you ever need it."

Florence nodded, her chin dimpling.

"I also got a nice cold steak to put on that bump you got there. It'll take the sting out and help it heal faster."

"Thank you, ma'am," Florence said, and Ruth stood up, grabbing their empty plates to go inside. She reached into the icebox and found the steak she'd planned to cook up to send to work with Hank tomorrow. She brought it outside and helped Florence apply it to that damaged eye.

"And you tell your daddy . . . ," she started. "You tell him you ain't nothing but a little girl. He ain't got no right. What kind of daddy . . ."

"He *ain't* my daddy," Florence said, and then her hand flew to her mouth as if she might be able to catch the words that just flew out.

"What do you mean, he ain't your daddy?" Ruth asked. Her stomach felt leaden, sinking.

"Nothin'," she said, standing up quickly. "I

only mean, I don't call him that." The steak fell to the ground, and Ruth quickly picked it up and brushed off the grass and dirt. But before she could press it to Florence's eye again, the girl had stood up.

"Thank you for your hospitality. I best be getting home. My father will be home from work real soon. Plus, I wanna keep reading that book. I really like it."

Ruth didn't sleep at all that night. Her ears were trained on the sounds of the night. Without the lowing elephants and the accordion laments, the trailer court was quiet enough to hear the hissing of both the snakes that lived at the edges and the snakes that lived among them.

SALLY

It felt to Sally like the author had written her life on those pages. Francie Nolan was from Brooklyn, not Camden, of course, but the streets could have been the same. New York wasn't far from New Jersey at all. And even though it was 1949 now, and Francie was alive at the beginning of the century, their hearts were the same. They both had musician daddies who drank too much. Both of their families had to struggle to just get by. Sally's mama sewed, and Francie's was a janitress. Like Sally, Francie's daddy died when she was still just a girl.

The women in the story could be so unkind to one another. So cruel. When that poor young unwed mother went out to walk her baby and the other women started throwing stones at her, it made Sally think of those girls back home, their secret sisterhood and their cruel taunts. She thought about the way they'd left her there when Mr. Warner caught her with the notebook. The fact that not a single one of them stuck around. She ached with every sentence. Every truth it seemed that the author had captured.

She found herself holding her breath as she

read, sometimes for several pages. It wasn't until she started to see stars that she'd suck in a breath. Then she got to Chapter 33, and she didn't breathe at all. The scene where the bad man attacked Francie and pressed his nakedness against her in the hallway of the tenement building made her heart beat so hard and fast she thought she might faint. *"He had a beaked nose and his mouth was a thin crooked line . . ."* She looked toward the trailer door. *My God, my God,* she thought. *"Francie stared at the exposed part of his body in paralyzed horror."* Sally felt her skin growing hot with shame and rage. Then, as Francie tried to call out for her mother, Katie Nolan was there, holding a gun under her apron. And then, the explosion, and then, and then . . .

"Nose stuck in a book again," Mr. Warner said, stumbling into the trailer. "What are you, some sort of bookworm?"

Sally was suddenly in two places at once. Here, now with Mr. Warner. And there, with Francie, as her mother shot the man so he couldn't hurt her. *"Francie thought the revolver looked like a grotesque beckoning finger, a finger that beckoned to death and made it come running."* There was a gun here in the trailer, too, though like Francie, Sally knew nothing about guns and certainly had never shot one before. Francie's mother had used the gun to save her from that

305

awful man. *Mama,* she thought. But her mother wasn't here. There was a gun, but she was all alone. No Sister Mary Katherine to help her, no Lena.

Only Ruth.

SALLY

"I ain't supposed to leave the trailer park," Sally said, feeling nervous.

"It's okay," Ruth assured her. "It's not far. And you're with me. Your daddy trusts me."

It was a blistering late-summer afternoon. Only a week left until school started, but it was so hot, it could have been the middle of July still. The air was swimmy with the heat; both of them were perspiring as they rode on Ruth's bicycle east on Commerce Street toward the Trinity River. The pool was being cleaned at the Good Luck, and so Ruth had told Sally they'd find another place to cool off. The river was close to the trailer court, and Ruth promised they'd be back long before Mr. Warner got home from work.

Ruth pedaled the bike standing up, and Sally sat on the leather seat, gripping onto Ruth's waist. She pressed her cheek against the cool cotton of Ruth's dress and breathed in the sweet scent of her. Listened to her lungs inhaling and exhaling. Felt the hard certain rhythm of Ruth's heart in her back.

When they got to the edge of the woods, Ruth stopped the bike and they both got off. It was already about ten degrees cooler in the shade of the ash trees. It felt strange that only moments ago they'd been so close to the city, and now it felt like they'd stepped into a fairy tale. Everything was shady and green.

"Follow me," Ruth said, leading Sally by the hand through the woods along a limestone path. In the clearing, Sally gasped. The river was quiet and still as a pond, surrounded by high grasses. Yellow and green. Floating all along the water were lily pads. It was one of the most beautiful things she'd ever seen.

"Well, you comin' in?" Ruth asked, slipping her dress over her head. She was wearing a red-and-white polka-dot halter swimsuit underneath. Her skin was white as milk, a constellation of freckles across the smooth expanse of her back. Sally peeled off her own dress, slipped off her shoes.

The water was blessedly cool. Ruth was a graceful swimmer, and she could hold her breath forever. She made Sally think of the Esther Williams movies she loved, the aqua-musicals with the women who were like mermaids. Sally swam in the cool water among the lily pads until her fingers pruned up. The water felt so good; she didn't ever want to get out and go back to the trailer again.

They sat on a blanket at the water's edge, soaking up the sun, and ate the lunch that Ruth had made, and afterward, she felt sleepy, her limbs tired from the swim, her eyelids heavy.

"Go ahead and take a nap if you want," Ruth said. "We got all day until your daddy comes home."

Sally felt her body tense.

"It's okay," Ruth reassured her, and motioned for Sally to put her head on her lap, where she stroked her hair. It was hypnotic, and Sally felt herself falling asleep, sucked under as though sleep were an undertow. She fell into a deep slumber—a Technicolor water ballet playing out around her. Everything bright and shimmering.

"Wake up, hon," Ruth whispered. "Somebody's here."

Sally bolted up, squinting against the bright sunshine. She could hear the sounds of voices nearby, the crushing of branches. Had Mr. Warner somehow tracked them here? Her body grew rigid.

"Shh . . . ," Ruth said, pointing downstream.

Two boys Sally recognized from the trailer park were doing something at the water's edge. She sighed in relief. When her eyes had adjusted to the light, she could see they had a turtle in their hands. A big snapping turtle. Sally had seen a couple of turtles at the Good Luck, figured they must have wandered away from the river. She always hoped they wouldn't find themselves on Commerce Street having to navigate in the traffic.

"What are they doing?" Sally whispered.

Ruth shook her head. "I don't know."

The older boy, who must have been about fourteen, reached into the pocket of his jeans and pulled something out. He fiddled with it for a minute, and then a flame leapt from his fingers. It startled Sally. Maybe they were going to smoke a cigarette?

But then she watched as the younger boy set the turtle down on its back, and the older one leaned over, the flame burning bright in his hand.

Ruth was on her feet and running along the water's edge, before it registered with Sally that they were going to set the snapping turtle on fire.

"Stop!" Ruth said. "Y'all put that fire out and leave that poor turtle alone."

Sally watched as the boys looked up at Ruth in her swimsuit barreling toward them. Before either one of them could react, she had a handful of the older boy's hair and she was pulling him away from the turtle that lay helpless on the ground, aflame. She then quickly scooped up the snapping turtle, smoke coming off its shell, and submerged it in the water. The boys stood, stunned, at the river's edge.

After a couple of moments, the younger boy backed away, and Ruth turned to them, her hands on her hips. "What's the matter with you? That's a living creature, a helpless living thing. What would your mama say?"

At this the boys took off, their legs pinwheeling as they ran through the high grass.

Ruth returned to the water. Sally got up and ran quickly to where she was now squatting at the river's edge.

"Is it okay?" Sally asked, kneeling down next to her.

Ruth shook her head. Tears streamed down her face, and Sally felt her heart heave.

"Goddamn little bastards," she said. "Helpless creature like that."

"Is it going to be okay?" Sally asked again, looking at the blackened turtle, lying still under the water.

Ruth stood up, shaking her head. "I was too late, Sally. I couldn't save it." Her chest lurched. "I'm sorry, sweetheart. I didn't get to the poor thing in time."

AL

Detective Vail? This is Al Panaro again. Listen, it's been two months since we got any sort of update on Sally. I don't mean to keep bothering you, but—"

"Mr. Panaro, I'm sorry to interrupt. But are you aware of the situation in Cramer Hill?"

"No?" Al said, confused. Cramer Hill was a neighborhood in Camden, over on the other side of the river. Was it possible Sally was back in Camden? How? When? No matter. His heart started to pound with the possibility that Sally was home again. Safe.

"You haven't read the papers today?"

"No—"

"Guy named Unruh shot up his whole neighborhood." Vail cleared his throat. "Killed thirteen people. Three of 'em were kids."

"Oh my God," Al said.

"The local departments are pretty focused on this right now. We've got a community that's just wrecked."

"I can't imagine," Al said, stunned. "But Sally—"

"What I mean to tell you, sir, is that Mrs. Horner isn't the only one grieving a lost baby right now."

312

• • •

Grief blanketed the city like an early snow that September. Al knew that if Sally were still there, if she'd never left on that bus with Frank La Salle, Ella might have held her a little more closely that night, clinging in the way that parents do when tragedy strikes. When there is that *knock, knock* on someone else's door reminding you that all of this, every last thing is precarious, perilous.

How sad it was that grief had a shelf life, he thought. It's only fresh and raw for so long before it begins to spoil. And soon enough, it would be replaced by a newer, brighter heartache—the old one discarded and eventually forgotten.

Just over a year ago, it seemed to Al the horror of Sally's abduction had resonated with every mother, every child. Women in Camden clung to their prepubescent daughters, seeing them not through their own eyes but the eyes of a fiend. What would that monster see as he gazed at their rosy-cheeked girls? They must have comforted themselves with the differences: Sally had curly light-brown hair. Their daughters were blond or redheaded. Sally was plump, but their daughters were skinny. Besides, he hadn't just snatched her up; Ella had practically handed her over. (*Put her on a bus with that fellow, what was she thinking? And that girl, that poor fatherless girl. Hadn't her father been the one they found dead on the train tracks several years ago? The drunkard who was always stumbling out of Daly's Café?* Al had heard the whispers.) She was not like their girls. What happened to her would not happen to their bright-eyed daughters.

But a year later, it was clear that Sally had already begun to slip from their collective memory. Women clung just a little less tightly to their children. Not every man sitting alone at a lunch counter was a possible kidnapper. And now the next monster had arrived, stalking the streets. There wasn't enough room on the shelf for this old, tired sorrow. *Maybe we can only suffer so much,* Al thought; communal capacity was a shallow well.

Al thought of those innocent children, the ones gunned down by that madman. One of them, he later heard, had gone to school with Sally before her family moved across the river. Little blond girl named Irene. He wondered if Irene's mother had also once taken comfort in the differences between her daughter and Sally, and if she cursed herself now for her smug complacency, for her false sense of security.

SUSAN

Autumn came again, bringing with it the first bitter winds and icy frosts that would destroy the plants and gardens the greenhouse's customers had so lovingly tended to all summer. Susan and Al's own garden would suffer from the crystalline blanket, which snapped stalks and anesthetized the nightshades. Only the root vegetables would survive.

Susan woke up that September morning and felt a distinct chill run like ice water down her back. Her first waking thought was of Sally. This is how she'd woken every morning for over a year now. Not with the soft ascent from the depths of a dream but with the sharp bite, that cold blade of the truth. This is the cruelty of grief. The way it gathers strength in the night, blooming again and again and again. There was nothing she could do to combat it other than allow its icy fingers to dig in and then to move on. Normally, she would tick off a list of things she needed to do for the day: work-related items, domestic chores, all those maternal obligations. Dee's first birthday had come and gone, and now she was walking. It was her intention to go through the house today and safeguard it against the curiosity and clumsiness of a toddler. She also needed to consider the distinct possibility that Ella might need to move in with them soon. Ella hadn't asked, would never ask, but Susan knew that she was getting worse, not better, and that every day that Sally was gone seemed to cripple her more.

Susan bolted upright and shook Al from his own slumber.

"What's the matter?" he asked.

She shook her head, unable to articulate the ominous feeling she had. Outside the wind rattled the windows in their frames. She shuddered involuntarily.

"I don't know."

"Is it the baby?" he asked, rubbing sleep from his eyes.

"No," she said. "Something else is wrong."

ELLA

Ella herself woke that morning to the lacelike patterns of frost on her windows and for one brief and horrifying moment thought that she had somehow slept through an entire season. That autumn had come and gone while she slumbered. But then she wondered if, perhaps, that might not be such a terrible thing.

She'd taken a Sominex the night before to help her sleep, and when she woke in the morning, staring at the icy filaments spread across her windowpane, she first felt etherized, numb and oblivious in her bed. When she tried to move her arms, her legs, at first there was no sensation at all. Nothing. If she hadn't felt her heart beating in her chest like a drum, she would have thought she was dead.

She was able to move her head; the rheumatism, thankfully, had not yet crept into her neck and spine. She saw then that the window was cracked open; when she'd opened the window to cool the hot flashes that made an inferno of her body, she'd forgotten to close it and the chill had crept in. Slowly, her limbs started to prickle and sting, and she pushed herself up to sitting.

She began to shake, a shiver that emanated from her gut and moved outward. The chill gripped her limbs, shaking her like a leaf-bare tree in a bitter wind.

But it wasn't sadness that gripped her this morning. It was *terror,* a fear more profound, more chilling, than any she'd experienced before. More horrifying even than when the policeman knocked on her door to tell her they'd found Russell's watch, his hat at the tracks.

And she thought five simple words:

Something is wrong with Sally.

RUTH

"Mama!"

Ruth bolted up out of bed. It was 3:00 A.M., and the trailer court seemed to reverberate with the child's cry. Ruth had been dreaming of carrying a baby in her arms. Her own nameless, faceless baby. When the cry rang out, the dream baby opened its mouth, which became a beak, and the wings beat against her as the bird took flight.

Ruth quickly put on her clothes, an old housedress and her robe. It was sticky, humid still. Septembers were brutal in Texas. The heat relentless. Even at 3:00 A.M.

She made her way from her trailer across the dirt lot to the LaPlantes' trailer. She was terrified of what she might be interrupting, but her conscience took over where her own will faltered. She remembered the turtle at the river.

But just as she was about to knock, the door hurled open and Frank poked his head out. He didn't appear startled to see her. Instead, he seemed grateful that she was there, that she was awake.

"Something's wrong," he said. "We need to get her to a hospital."

Ruth felt faint as she wondered what he could

have done to her, what horrific things he might have done to her, that sent him barreling out of that tin can looking for help.

"Where is she?" Ruth asked.

"In the back. I'll get the truck started, and maybe you can help me get her in."

It was dark in the trailer, and smelled of motor oil and liquor and smoke. What kind of place was this for a child?

"Mama, Mama!" she cried out again, and Ruth quickened her step. She felt her way through the darkness to the back of the trailer where the beds were.

Florence was on the floor, curled up into a ball, clutching her belly.

Ruth dropped to her knees and put her arm around her. "It's okay, sweetheart. It's me, Ruth. Your daddy and I are going to get you to the hospital.

"My mama . . . ," Florence said, her voice just a thin river of breath. "She don't know where I am."

"What?" Ruth said.

"You gotta tell them that."

"Who?" she said. "Florence. Tell who? You said your mama was dead."

"Please," she said, and she gripped Ruth's hand. "Tell her I'm sorry. And I just wanna go home."

Frank came back into the trailer. Ruth's heart

was beating so hard, she was sure he'd be able to hear it.

"I think it's her appendix," Frank said. "Can she get up?"

Ruth recoiled as he put his hand on her back.

"Mama!" Florence cried.

Together they helped her stand up, and she clung to them both as they made their way out of the trailer and into the cab of Frank's truck.

"I'll come with you," Ruth said to Frank. "Let me go tell Hank."

"No. We're fine," Frank said, reaching across Florence and slamming the passenger door shut.

Florence pressed her face against the glass, her palm splayed there. Ruth reached out her hand and touched the window as Frank backed up.

When the truck was gone, Ruth went to the trailer. She knew that there were answers inside, answers to questions it made her sick to ponder, and so she reached for the door handle. Locked. She yanked hard at the handle, shook the door until it felt like her arm might fall off.

Bastard.

SALLY

For two days, Sally slipped in and out of sleep. The pale green walls and the buzzing fluorescent lights above her made her feel like she was at the bottom of the swimming pool. The sheets were cool, the pillow soft. Medicine dripped down a long tube into the back of her hand, and it made her feel sleepy, but not the groggy sort of feeling of the Lix-a-Col Mr. Warner gave her. *Peaceful.* And no one bothered her save for the nurses who came in to take her temperature, to change the bandages. The sounds of the hospital at night were so strange. There was a rhythm to them, as though the walls were breathing. As if the building itself had a heart that was steadily beating. She dreamed of mermaids.

"You're healing up nicely." The doctor nodded, examining the wound that traversed her lower abdomen.

"You'll be good as new before you know it," the nurse agreed, after the doctor turned on his heel and went to check on the child in the next bed.

"How long am I gonna be here?" she asked.

"Another couple of days, I imagine. I know your daddy sure is ready for you to come home. Calls to check on you twice a day."

"Where is he?" she asked. She hadn't seen him since he'd brought her to the hospital.

"Visiting hours are Wednesday nights and Sunday afternoons," she added.

"People can come and see me?" She thought of Ruth, vaguely recalled Ruth helping her into Mr. Warner's truck the night she got sick.

"Only parents, of course," she said. "Immediate family."

"Oh."

Mr. Warner came the following night with gifts. Bars of chocolate she was too queasy to eat, and a single red balloon. The nurse fastened the string to the radiator, and it bobbed in the window.

"Gave me a real scare, kid," he said, rubbing a hand over his head again and again.

She nodded. She'd been scared, too. When she first woke up in the hospital, she didn't know where she was. If she was dead or alive.

He was sitting at the edge of the seat he'd pulled up next to the bed. His gaze darted toward the other children who were engaged in their own visits, and then leaned toward her. His breath was hot on her ear. Her stomach roiled.

"You say one word to these people about who you really are, they'll keep you here. Put you up in the mental ward. You know what that is?"

Sally shook her head.

"They won't believe you, Sally. They'll think you've lost your mind. They'll put you in the

323

loony bin, lock you up and throw away the key."

Sally shook her head, heard her mother's voice ringing in her ears. She'd told Russell the same thing once. Threatened to drive him to someplace called Greystone Park. Sally had pictured a beautiful grassy field where children flew kites until she asked her first-grade teacher what Greystone was, and the teacher told her that it was a hospital for people who were sick in the head. For crazies. The only crazy person she knew was the man who wandered up and down Federal Street mumbling to himself, striking his forehead again and again with the palm of his hand. Why her mother thought her stepfather should go there was a terrifying mystery.

"No one will believe you, Sally."

With that, he stood up, donned his hat, and leaned over to kiss her forehead. His dry lips felt like razors against her skin. "I'll be back tomorrow to settle the hospital bill and bring you home."

After he left, the nurse helped her get up to use the restroom. She was still sore, and her legs were wobbly. When she sat down on the commode, she saw stars. She was still feeling unsteady as the nurse helped her back to her bed. She was just starting to drift off when the nurse shook her shoulder. "Florence? Wake up, you've got another visitor."

Why would Mr. Warner come back? Or could it be someone else? No. Only parents were allowed. The nurse had been firm about this.

"There's only ten minutes of visiting hours left, but I didn't have the heart to turn her away."

Sally cocked her head curiously.

"It's your mama."

Mama? Sally's heart throbbed inside her chest; she felt it pounding in the place where they'd split her open. Had her mama finally found her?

But then the door opened and it wasn't her mama at all, but Ruth. She came in, rushed to Sally's side, and leaned over her, hugging her tightly. Sally held on to her, tears soaking her pillow.

"I thought you were my mama," she said, her chest heaving. "I thought she came for me."

Ruth stiffened and stood up.

"But your mama, she's *passed*." A question. An accusation.

Sally shook her head.

"Florence?" Ruth said, reaching for her hand and squeezing it, but Sally could think only of what Mr. Warner had promised. That if she said one word to Ruth—a single word about who she really was—he'd make Ruth pay.

"I didn't mean that. I'm just confused, is all."

"Florence," Ruth said firmly this time, imploring.

How she longed to tell, for her own name to come from her lips. *Sally Horner. Sally Horner.*

"I just want to go home," Sally said. At least this was the truth.

SALLY

After she came home from the hospital, Mr. Warner didn't touch her. At first, she thought he was just being considerate. Letting her heal. Instead of leering at her as she changed her clothes, he turned away. And instead of putting his hands all over her whenever he pleased, he kept them to himself. Eventually, the wound healed. The doctor clipped out the dark black stitches, and she was left only with that ragged reminder across her belly. Still, Mr. Warner kept his distance. But after a while, she realized it had nothing to do with the surgery and everything to do with all the other changes her body was going through. Her body was transforming, almost daily. Her breasts went from the painful, marble-sized bumps on her chest into fleshy mounds that made her buttons strain and embarrassed her. She grew hair under her arms and between her legs. Once, in the small bathroom, she'd tried to use Mr. Warner's razor to shave it away. It made her think of Lena. Would she start to grow hair on her chin? On her chest? Her appetite grew as well; she couldn't seem to get enough to eat. Mr. Warner mocked her, snorting like a pig as she devoured her supper each night.

"Maybe I should just pour some slop in a trough

for you," he said, as she wiped her mouth gently with her napkin. "Disgusting pig," he muttered under his breath.

He didn't touch her, but his revulsion, his bitter insults stung almost as much as his angry fists.

"What am I supposed to do with you now?" he said, sloppy drunk. "It's like living in a goddamn barn. If you were really a pig, you know what would happen to you come winter?"

She shook her head, and he took one crooked finger and made a slicing motion slowly across his neck.

It might not have been as frequent anymore, but when it happened now he was always angrier, drunker, meaner. He called her fat, pinched the places on her body that had started to swell. He said she sickened him, asked where his sweet little girl had gone. She shook her head, thought of little Sally Horner, that girl she used to be. She'd disappeared a long time ago. Just a little bit at a time, so she'd barely noticed. In the undertow of the crashing waves at the shore, in the vaporous heat of a Baltimore summer, with the tumbleweeds along Route 66. Part of her had disappeared with Lena and the circus, in the mournful lament of the elephants.

"Hey," a girl from her class said to Sally during recess. "Where'd you disappear to?"

Sally had only been at Our Lady of Good

328

Counsel for a couple of weeks that fall before she got sick. She'd been out of school for as long as she'd been in attendance.

"I was in the hospital," Sally answered. "Appendicitis."

"Do you have a scar?" the girl asked. She had freckles like brown flecks of paint spattered across her cheeks. She was always getting in trouble with the sisters for cracking gum or passing notes to the other girls.

Sally's gaze darted to the playground, where the other children played a game of hopscotch and marbles, before she slowly lifted her blouse. The girl hooked one finger into the waistband of Sally's skirt and gently yanked it down. Sally's fleshy belly was exposed, white as a fish's. Flaccid and loose. The incision ran in a six-inch line, diagonally across her lower belly.

"Did it bust open?" the girl asked. "My brother knows somebody whose appendix busted and he almost died."

"No," Sally said. "They got it in time. Five more minutes and I woulda been dead, though."

That was what the doctors had told her. That if she and Mr. Warner been just five minutes later to the hospital, her appendix would have perforated, sending poison throughout her body. She thought of it as a time bomb that no one knew was there. The idea that your own body could one day detonate filled her with dread.

"Can I touch it?" the bold girl asked, already reaching her finger out to touch the scar.

Afterward, the two girls stood wordlessly appraising each other until the other girl broke the silence. "I'm Doris. What's your name?"

Sally hardly knew her own name anymore. She'd been so flustered trying to remember what to call herself that she'd said "Florence Planette" instead of "LaPlante" when Mr. Warner registered her at school.

Doris's face was earnest, friendly.

"I'm Florence," she said, and then feeling oddly bold herself added, "But you can call me Sally. Everybody does." She felt like she might throw up. But saying her name felt so good. Like coming up for air after holding her breath forever in the pool.

Sally didn't tell anyone at the trailer court about her new friend, Doris. Certainly not Mr. Warner, and not even Ruth. Ruth had been acting strangely since she went to the hospital. The times she'd come to visit her, she'd looked like she was on the verge of tears.

Sally could barely remember what she'd said the night she got sick. She remembered crying for her mama. She also remembered Ruth finding her curled up on the floor. But after that her memories were like broken bits of glass: riding in the truck, feeling like she might vomit as they wheeled her through the brightly lit hallways of the hospital, the rough hands of the nurse who reprimanded her when she lay in the bed and felt as if the mattress were falling away from her (the sinking, dropping feeling of her belly, her hands slipping from the bar of the trapeze). In the hospital, she'd dreamed about Francie Nolan from her novel, about that burned smell in the air after the bullet passed through Francie's mama's apron and into •that bad man's private parts. When Ruth came to see her, she'd almost told her everything.

But now that she was back at home, back inside that trailer, back inside her secret, Ruth looked at her with a sort of pity in her eyes. The first week Sally was home, she brought food to their trailer almost every day: fried Spam sandwiches and sloppy joes. She checked in on her every afternoon when Mr. Warner was at work and she was convalescing.

And then one day, out of the clear blue sky, Ruth had abruptly gotten stern, put her hands on her hips, and said, "Florence, we need to do something about this."

It felt like Ruth knew her secret. Sally shook her head. Had she said something about her mama to Ruth that night she went to the hospital? Was that why she was acting so strange?

"There's got to be somebody you could call?"

"What do you mean?" Sally had asked, even as her chest ached.

331

Sally didn't know whom she could call, or what she would even say. She was an outlaw, a troublemaker who'd been lucky enough to stay out of juvenile hall. This life, these bad things, were the price she had to pay for her freedom, a freedom that wasn't really a freedom at all. Besides, Mr. Warner had legal custody, he said, and if he was telling the truth, then her mama didn't want her back. Though no matter how hard she tried to believe that, *accept* that, she just couldn't. Every time she tried to make sense of it all, her mind went back to those photos she'd found in his valise. The news clipping. *Kidnapping*. But that article had said the man's name was Frank La Salle. His name was Mr. Warner. Or Mr. LaPlante. Or, if he truly was her daddy, Bobby Swain. It was too hard to keep track of the lies, and so she kept her mouth shut. She was careful not to say another word to Ruth. She didn't say much to Mr. Warner, either. To the other girls at school, she kept her lips zipped. But Doris was different. Doris seemed to understand her. Without saying a word, Doris *accepted* her. She didn't look at her with pity the way so many others had. She was her *friend*. Maybe the first true friend her own age she ever had.

RUTH

Ruth had picked up a little gift for Florence for Christmas: a hairbrush with a wooden handle and real boar bristles. Florence came over to get her hair done for the Christmas pageant at her school, and Ruth presented the brush to her tied in a red ribbon bow.

"This is for me?" she asked.

Tex was jumping, jumping, trying to see.

"It is," Ruth said, smiling.

Ever since Florence got sick, Ruth had felt truly troubled by what she had said about her mama. About her not knowing where Florence was. What could she have meant by that? She'd been delirious, granted, but something didn't sit right with Ruth. And then there was the way she'd reacted at the hospital when she thought her mama had come for a visit. Even as she watched Florence outside, playing happily with Tex or scooting him away from a solitary game of jacks, it troubled her, like trying to read small print from too far away; no matter how hard she tried, she couldn't make sense of it. Luckily, since she got home from the hospital, Florence hadn't shown up with any more bruises, and she hadn't heard any outbursts coming from the trailer. Maybe her getting sick had knocked some sense into Frank. Maybe he'd leave her alone now.

"You doing okay?" she asked Florence as she used the new brush to work through her tangled curls. "You haven't been coming by so much lately."

Florence shrugged.

"Must be hard without your mama and Christmas coming so soon," she said.

Florence's mouth twitched. Ruth pressed on.

"I lost my mama when I was about your age, too. Hardest thing in the whole world was the holidays."

Florence nodded but still wouldn't speak.

"You know, I would have given up every Christmas present I had just to hear my mama's voice again back then. Sometimes, I wish I could just pick up the telephone and talk to her."

Florence fidgeted.

"You know, I'm here for you, sweetheart. I mean, if anything's bothering you. Stuff you don't want to share with your daddy."

She was certain now there was something going on, something Frank didn't want anyone to know and that Florence was too scared to tell. If she could just get her to open up, then maybe she could help her.

"Listen here," Ruth said gently, and slowly untied the ribbon from the hairbrush. "How about this? See this ribbon?"

Florence nodded.

"It's actually a very special kind of ribbon," she said.

"It's pretty."

"Well, it's more than pretty. It's also a way for us girls to stick together," she said. "See how I can see your window from here?"

Florence peered out through the curtains at the trailer across the way.

"Let's say maybe you're feeling sad, or lonely, or scared. Or maybe you're in trouble? All you got to do is to open up your window just a little crack, and hang the ribbon out. If I see it, I'll know you're needing me. And I'll come to you. Would you like that?"

Florence studied the ribbon in Ruth's hand. "You can know all that if I just put that ribbon out there?"

"Yes. I promise I'll be there quick as can be."

"And won't nobody know what it means except for you and me?" she asked.

Ruth held it out to her. "Nobody at all."

ELLA

That's a lovely shade of red," the salesgirl said.

Ella nodded absently as she studied the bolts of fabric, touching them with her fingers, gauging the softness of each.

"Making something for Christmas?" the girl persisted. "A nightgown?"

Ella shook her head and moved down the aisle. "Silver Bells" played through the speakers overhead. Christmas music haunted Ella. Everywhere she went it seemed there was the jingle and jangle of Christmas bells, the *ba-ba-ba-boo* of Bing Crosby crooning about a white Christmas. She used to love Christmas; she'd always loved shopping and cooking and decorating the house. When the girls were young, she'd found no greater joy than watching the sisters' faces light up at the sight of a stocking filled with treats. She and Russell had never had a lot of money to spend on gifts, but she'd always set aside a little each year to splurge on one special thing for her daughters (a new doll, a beautiful barrette). Each year she'd sewn matching Christmas nightgowns for them to wear, flannel with yoke collars and tiny bows at the neck. Now as she walked through the fabric store, her knobby fingers grazing the bolts of fabric, she wondered if Sally even liked red anymore.

This year, she thought of baby Dee. She was old enough now to wear a nightie, and this winter was predicted to be a brutal one. Though she couldn't remember a single winter in New Jersey that hadn't been cruel.

When she was a child, she had loved winter. Loved the snow that fell from the sky. Her mother had told her that each snowflake was an angel and that if you caught one on your tongue and swallowed it, the angel would protect you. She'd told this story to her own girls and took pleasure as she watched them running about, mouths gaping wide, trying to catch the angels on their tongues. She wondered if it was snowing wherever Sally was.

If there were any angels there who might keep her safe.

RUTH

Two days before Christmas, Hank came home early from his shift.

"What are you doin' home so soon?" Ruth asked as he walked through the door.

Hank, with his white-blond hair and fair skin, was even paler than usual, if that was possible. He looked like he'd not only seen but *swallowed* a ghost, his Adam's apple bobbing up and down.

"Somebody got shot," he said.

"What?" Ruth asked, feeling her pulse start to thrum.

"Gangster named Green. Every time he comes into the Sky-Vu, there's trouble."

Ruth knew that the Sky-Vu where Hank worked was frequented by gangsters. That all sorts of nasty things happened behind the Sky-Vu's closed doors. She'd heard the rumors, about the back room where Hank's boss, Joey Bonds, hired underaged girls to do the things those men's wives would never do. Some of the girls with their baby teeth still. It made her sick just thinking about it.

"What happened?" she asked.

"I don't know exactly. Green was at the bar, chatting it up with some other fellas. Then he walked out into the alley and somebody shot him."

"Is he *dead?*" she asked.

"As a doorknob," he said. "Folks were running outta there like roaches when the lights come on. Saw our neighbor hightailing it . . ."

"Our neighbor?"

"LaPlante," he said, gesturing with his thumb toward the LaPlantes' trailer. "He comes into the Sky-Vu a lot. Real cozy with my boss."

"Frank is friendly with Joey Bonds?" Ruth asked, mystified. Frank had said they didn't know a soul in Dallas. Why would he lie about that?

"Sure. I thought you knew that. He's the one who set him up with the trailer. Anyway, place is crawling with cops. They shut us down, sent everybody home."

Ruth's mind spun with what all of this meant. Frank LaPlante knew Joey Bonds, well enough that he'd arranged for him and Florence to live at the Good Luck. What kind of man was he that he was affiliated with shady types like Bonds and Green?

"What's the matter, Ruthie?"

"They gonna open up again tomorrow?" she asked as Hank poured himself a beer.

"I sure hope so," he said. "I can't afford any time off."

Ruth nodded, but she was distracted. How on

earth did some widower mechanic from back east know a guy like Joey Bonds?

On Christmas Eve, Ruth had put up a tiny fake Christmas tree. Pink branches. Glittery and soft. She found a radio station playing Christmas carols and made Hank's favorite meat loaf. She was feeling full of Christmas cheer when Hank came home from the restaurant at 2:00 A.M. (They'd reopened just a day after they cleaned that man Green up off the pavement in the alley.)

She'd asked Florence to spend Christmas dinner with them the next day, planned to make her famous chocolate crinkle cookies for dessert.

"Ruthie," Hank said, slumping down into his chair at the kitchen table.

"Yeah, hon?" she said, scooping a healthy slice of meat loaf onto his plate. The twinkling lights on the tree made patterns across his face.

"They let me go," he said. "At the restaurant."

She felt the joy suck away from her like water down a bathtub drain. "Why?" she asked. "I thought everything was back to normal."

He shrugged. "Hell, if I know. Said they're making some changes, got rid of the entire kitchen staff. We're gonna need to move on. Way I figure it, we can head to California or Florida for the citrus harvest."

Ruth shook her head. *Florence*. She couldn't leave Florence. Besides, she'd hated Florida the one winter they spent there. The mosquitoes and humidity just about did her in. She'd thought that maybe they were settled here for a bit. That the restaurant job, while tiring, wasn't the backbreaking work he was used to. But here they were again. How could she have been so foolish?

"I talked to another dishwasher about a citrus farm in San Jose. California. Nice little motor court where we can park the trailer."

There was no way she could leave that little girl here alone with Frank. Florence needed her, and she needed Florence. "There must be something else you can do here? Another restaurant in town? Now that you got kitchen experience—"

"I already asked everybody I know. Nobody's hiring."

Ruth felt her heart fragmenting. She couldn't leave. Not now.

"When?" Ruth asked.

"Tomorrow. First thing in the morning."

"It's *Christmas* tomorrow."

"And I still ain't paid the rent yet for December. If we stay here, there won't be nothing left to get us situated anywhere else. Manager's going to be at his mother's house tomorrow, won't see us go."

"But what about Florence?" she finally managed.

"She's got her daddy," Hank said.

"I got a bad feeling, Hank," she said, desperate

now. She couldn't leave Florence here. "About that man Frank. A hunch he ain't who he says he is."

"You and your hunches. It's a bunch of hoo-ha."

"I think he's lying about her mama being dead," Ruth said, wondering even as she said it if she should have.

Hank raised an eyebrow. "What makes you think that?"

"It's not just that, Hank. She had a bad bruise on her eye earlier this fall, and the way he keeps her on such a short leash. Never plays with any of the kids here. Plus, you shoulda seen how she was when she had the appendicitis. She was curled up in the corner like a frightened little critter."

"Course she was terrified. You'd be terrified, too, if your appendix was about to blow up."

Ruth shook her head. "And how on earth does Frank LaPlante know Joey Bonds? Doesn't that seem strange to you? We gotta do something. I don't know what, but I can't just leave her here. Daddy or no, that man Frank . . . somethin' about him ain't what it seems."

"Ruthie," he said. "I'm real sorry. I am. But we got to get on the road. First thing tomorrow."

SALLY

Sally heard Mr. Warner come lurching into the trailer at 2:00 A.M. on Christmas morning. She curled herself into a tight ball at the edge of the bed and prayed that he was drunk enough to just pass out. But he didn't come to the bedroom, and in the kitchen he kept cursing and smashing into things. Each slam and bump felt like a blow.

On nights like these, Sally prayed. But the prayers were no longer the foolish prayers of a child or even a penitent. And most of the time, they were not even directed at God. (Who was God now? *Where* was He? He had abandoned her just like her stepfather had the night he staggered across the train tracks and howled at an unforgiving sky. He was long gone.) When Mr. Warner lay panting next to her, she curled up at the edge of the bed and prayed to be somewhere else, some*one* else. She was Irene with her beautiful corn silk hair. She was Bess with her pale shoulders and overbite. But most nights she was Vivi. Vivi and her untroubled sleep. Sally dreamed herself into their respective beds. Worn cotton sheets as soft as flesh, fresh nightgowns, and the lingering taste of Pepsodent.

It was Christmas Eve, and tonight she thought of Vivi. Dreamed herself into her life.

Tonight Mother and I made oyster stew for Father. When we came home from caroling, it was so warm and delicious. It took my cheeks forever to warm up, though, even with my brand-new scarf Mother made for me. I don't believe in Santa Claus anymore, but I hung my stocking on the mantel anyway. Mother gets wistful about me growing up.

She smelled him before she saw him: liquor and gasoline.

"Ho! Ho! Ho!" Mr. Warner shouted.

Father let me put the star at the top of the tree; he had to lift me up, the tree is so tall!

"Santa has a gift for you." He was standing in the doorway now. Sally could see his silhouette, listing to one side. He held on to the doorjamb to keep from falling over.

At church, we prayed for those less fortunate. I said an extra prayer for poor Sally Horner.

He pitched forward, and she caught her breath. She squeezed her eyes shut, and when she opened them again, he was kneeling at the bedside, his face just inches from hers. The vaporous fumes coming from his breath, his skin, made her sick.

"Well, what do we have here? Looks like a fat Christmas goose," he said, laughing.

Dear God.

"Roll over," he said, grabbing her shoulder. "On your stomach."

After, as he lay sprawled and snoring, Sally inched out of the bed and went to the dresser where she kept the brush Ruth had given her. She untied the ribbon, which felt like a wish in her hands. She walked quietly to the window and gently pushed it open just the tiniest bit, and slipped the ribbon partly out before lowering the window again.

Please, God. Save her.

RUTH

As the sun rose on Christmas morning, Hank hitched the trailer up. The air was sharp; it felt like blades in Ruth's chest.

"Ready?" he said.

"Just a minute. I need to go say good-bye to Florence."

She walked briskly over to the LaPlantes' trailer. It was quiet; everyone was asleep. Feeling her pulse quicken, she pressed her hand against the trailer and patted it gently, as if she were patting Florence's hair.

Knock, knock.

"Who is it?" a voice barked from inside.

"It's me, Ruth," she said. Her own voice sounded like shattered glass.

"Come on, Ruthie!" Hank said, leaning out the open truck window. It was cold, and his breath came out in puffs. She knocked again.

"Frank?" she said loudly. "I need to talk to Florence!"

"Ruth!" Hank said from the truck. "You're gonna wake the whole park up."

The trailer door swung open, and Frank stood there in his boxer shorts. Shirtless. Concave chest exposed. "What the hell, Ruthie? It's Christmas morning."

Ruth tried to see past him into the trailer, but it was like looking into the depths of a starless sky.

"Hank and I . . . ," she started, tears welling up in her eyes. "We're heading out. San Jose."

Frank stepped out of the trailer, shutting the door behind him. "You don't say," he said, frowning. He put his hands on his hips and shook his head. "Whatever for?"

"They let Hank go at the Sky-Vu. After the shooting, Mr. Bonds let half the kitchen staff go," she said, studying his face for signs of recognition. Of anything that might explain who he was.

But his expression was blank. "Well, we certainly will miss you. Especially Florence."

"Here," she said. "Can you please give this to her?" Ruth handed him the note she'd drafted after they'd finished tying down their meager belongings. In case this happened and she didn't get a chance to say good-bye.

"Sure thing, Ruthie. We'll really miss you two," Frank said, scowling. "Merry Christmas!"

Ruth backed away from the trailer reluctantly. The sky was starting to fill with light as she got into the passenger seat of the truck.

"Alrighty then," Hank said. "Off we go."

Ruth leaned against the passenger window, wiping at her tears. When they drove slowly past the LaPlantes' trailer, her stomach turned. Then it dropped at the sight of a bit of red sticking out of Florence's window.

SALLY

Sally stirred awake, her head pounding. She could hear Mr. Warner outside and so she reached up and touched the ribbon. Why hadn't Ruth come to her last night? She'd promised her if she saw the ribbon, she'd come help her. But it was still there, tucked through the small crack in the window. When Sally pulled it back in, it was cold to the touch. Stiff, almost icy.

She sat up, and her body was aflame with what he'd done to her. The pain was so shameful, it made her want to curl back up under the covers and never get out of bed again. But she knew that he would keep coming back, that he would never ever leave her alone for long.

She conjured the little brass angel chimes her mother always put on the mantel. She thought of the flame that somehow, miraculously, caused the little angels to go around and around, hitting the tiny bells as they went. She recalled the carousel, the brass ring, thought of the endless circles. Angels trapped forever, painted carousel ponies circling forever.

Christmas morning. She imagined her mother in the kitchen making coffee cake. She could almost feel the soft flannel of her Christmas nightgown. When she held her breath she could even hear

348

her stepfather singing "White Christmas." She dreamed herself down the stairs to the living room, where her Christmas stocking was hung. Where the tree twinkled, and gifts in shiny paper lay waiting.

"Florence!" Mr. Warner's voice pulled her out of her daydream.

He was outside, standing just below the window where the ribbon had been. *Knock, knock.* He rapped against the glass and she startled. *"Sally,"* he hissed.

She got out of bed, limped to the kitchenette, and stepped down out of the trailer.

She was confused. Had they traveled while she was sleeping, moved to a different trailer court? She rubbed her eyes and looked again. The space where Ruth's trailer had always been was empty. Tex was running around, yipping in the vacant space.

"Look at that," Mr. Warner said, shaking his head. "Left without saying good-bye, huh? Looks like it's just you and me again, Sally."

Stunned, Sally tried to make sense of what he was saying, what she was seeing. She scooped Tex up into her arms and ran down the drive toward the canteen, peering at the other trailers all dolled up for Christmas. None of them were Ruth and Hank's.

"Where'd they go?" she asked when she arrived back at their trailer.

"Hell if I know," he said.

"She didn't tell you nothing?" Sally asked.

"Nope," he said, shrugging. "I woke up and they were long gone."

As she stood there in that empty space, Tex yipping at her feet, she realized she couldn't count on anybody. Not her mama, not her teachers, not Lena, and not even Ruth. Lena was gone. Ruth was gone. Mr. Warner, for once, was telling the truth.

RUTH

The trailer park in San Jose was filled with migrant workers. No one spoke English. The women here stayed inside their trailers all day, and when they did come out (to hang their laundry or yell at their gaggles of children), they didn't acknowledge Ruth. She wished they spoke the same language; she walked all the way to the market just for conversation, lingering in the aisles, at the register, if only to exchange pleasantries with the cashier.

She missed Dallas. She missed Florence.

As she watched the mothers at the motor court, gathering their children at the end of each day, scooping them up into their arms for kisses or in order to swat their behinds, she felt a longing so deep and strong, it sometimes made her wince, as if it were a physical pain instead of heartache.

She wrote letters to Florence. Sent them off, but she knew that in all likelihood they'd never reach her. Not if Frank got to them first. Every day that went by without a response, she became convinced that he was confiscating them. Hiding them from her. And the more time she had to ruminate on everything that had happened in Dallas, the angrier she became. She grew bitter with Hank even for pretending as if everything

351

were back to normal, when nothing at all was.

Then one day in February, when Hank went off to work, swinging his lunch pail, whistling "Dixie," she felt overcome. As soon as she watched the truck carry him and the other men off to the orchards, she knew she had to do something before she lost her mind. She closed the door to her trailer and picked up the phone. Asked to be connected to the Dallas Police Department. This phone call was long distance, would probably cost them a day's wages. But she couldn't stand it anymore.

"There's a man, name Frank LaPlante," she said to the woman who answered the phone at the Dallas Police Department. "Hangs out with Joey Bonds at the Sky-Vu. Lives at the Good Luck with his daughter."

"What's your complaint, ma'am?"

She felt her body shudder. Helpless. "Please," she said. "God, please do something."

SALLY

In February, Doris pulled Sally aside to a small grove of persimmon trees at the edge of the playground. Sally was learning how to do cat's cradle with a shoelace she'd pulled from Mr. Warner's old pair of shoes.

Doris had a mischievous look on her face that Sally was coming to recognize. Doris had surprised her before with cigarettes stolen from her mother's packs, with lipstick pilfered from her older sister's drawer, with chocolates and once, a single gold earring. But when Doris pulled the pocketknife from her skirt pocket, Sally gasped.

"Where'd you get that?" she said.

"From my daddy," she said, shrugging as if it were no big deal. But Doris was still smirking; Sally knew it was a *very* big deal. Girls weren't allowed to have knives at school.

"Give me your hand," Doris said, and Sally thought maybe she was going to give her the knife. She trembled. But when she held out her hand, Doris simply opened the knife and took a quick swipe at the soft pad of Sally's index finger. The blood took a moment before bubbling out of the razor-thin incision. Doris then cut a thin slice in her own finger and pressed it hard against Sally's.

"We're blood sisters now," Doris said somberly. The impish smirk was gone. She leaned forward and touched her forehead to Sally's. "This is a sacred bond. No lies and no secrets between us. Together, forever. Through thick and thin."

Sally nodded, her finger stinging.

Doris stood up straight again and reached for Sally's hand. The cut on Sally's finger was deeper, and still bleeding. Doris pulled Sally's hand closer and leaned over, enclosing her finger in her mouth. She sucked at Sally's finger, and Sally felt her body go warm and soft. Her finger came out with a sucking pop. But it had stopped bleeding.

Sisters, she thought. *Through thick and thin.*

"Let's go to your house," Doris said.

Sally had never brought a friend home before. Not in Camden, not in Baltimore, and certainly not here in Dallas. She couldn't imagine what someone might make of her and Mr. Warner's living arrangements. She was ashamed to imagine the small trailer through Doris's eyes. Still, Doris seemed like the kind of person who wouldn't care that she lived in a motor home.

And so when Doris invited herself over, Sally hesitated but then nodded. "Okay."

Mr. Warner wouldn't be home until suppertime anyway. He wouldn't even have to know. Now that Ruth was gone, there wouldn't be anybody else to see her and ask questions. Since Ruth left, Mr. Warner didn't have anybody to keep an eye on her after school anymore, but it hardly mattered. He told her if she so much as thought about taking off he'd hunt her down again. Like she was just one of the swamp rabbits that wandered into the trailer park from over by the river. The only hope she had left was that Lena might return with the circus that summer, though she wondered sometimes if she'd only dreamed the tightrope walkers and acrobats. That little bit of magic and sparkle was hard to recall now. She might be here forever, she thought. She might never, ever get free.

Sally and Doris walked home, kicking rocks and swinging the satchels in loop-dee-doops until their shoulders ached.

"Step on a crack, break your mother's back," Doris sang, stomping on every crack while Sally carefully avoided them, recalling the pain in her mother's face when her rheumatism flared up.

When they got to the trailer park, they were breathless from skipping down the sidewalk.

"Which one's yours?" Doris asked.

"That one," Sally said, motioning to the trailer, which looked gray and dull in the sparkling sunshine.

"Swanky!" Doris said, giggling, and skipped ahead.

"Wait," Sally said, regretting this decision.

"For what?" Doris said, crossing her arms.

"Never mind," she said, and moved toward the door, plucking the key from under the mat.

Inside the trailer, Doris flitted about, picking things up and putting them down. In the kitchen she opened drawers and studied the contents inside. She lifted a spoon from the silverware drawer, studied her reflection, and then put it back in. She sat down at the kitchenette and jumped back up again, opening the oven door and peering inside.

"You can just hitch this soup can up and move along whenever you want?" she asked.

"I guess," Sally said.

"I'd pay a million bucks to live like this."

Doris continued on her self-guided tour through the small trailer, making her way to the bedroom.

Sally felt even more breathless than she had been before. The most private and awful place in the world, and here she'd just gone and let Doris in.

Doris went straight to Mr. Warner's bed and sat down, swinging her legs. She leaned over and opened up the drawer to the nightstand. She rifled around, plucking out one item at a time: a crumpled pack of cigarettes, some loose change, a condom in a square cellophane wrapper.

Sally swallowed hard.

Doris tore open the package with her teeth,

studied the rubber, and then blew it up like a balloon. When she released it, it flew about the room. Sally waited for her to make some comment, though she hoped that maybe she didn't know what they were for.

Doris yanked harder at the drawer until it pulled almost all the way out, and the gun came sliding toward the front of the drawer.

"Well, looky here at this," Doris said, picking up the gun.

"Put it down," Sally said, glancing around the room as if Mr. Warner might just walk in. "Please, Doris."

Doris held the gun out in front of her the way the cops always did in the movies. Like Humphrey Bogart as Sam Spade in *The Maltese Falcon*.

In all this time with Mr. Warner, Sally had never once picked up the gun. She usually knew where it was, but she'd never so much as touched it before. "You better put that down," she said. "That's Mr. Warner's."

Doris lowered the gun and turned to Sally.

"Who's *Mr. Warner?*" she asked.

"He's the man I live with here," she said; her body was vibrating and her skin hot. She thought of the promise they had made, the one made of blood and blades. She looked at the door again, then turned back to Doris, whispering. "The one that took me from my mama."

Doris was smiling, but her grin disappeared.

"What do you mean? You said you live here with your daddy. That your mama's dead."

Sally shook her head and looked down at the gun in Doris's hand.

"I lied."

"About your mama?" Doris said.

"About everything," Sally said, words tumbling. "We're on the lam. 'Cause I got caught shoplifting, and he woulda taken me to the courthouse, but he said that if I did what he said, he wouldn't make me go to jail. He said he was FBI." The rush of words, her secrets spilling, felt strange. Out of her control.

"What?" Doris said, her jaw slack. "What did you steal?"

"A notebook," she said. "From the Woolworth's in Camden." Her heart was beating nearly as hard and fast as it had when Mr. Warner caught her up by the elbow at the Woolworth's.

Doris looked at her, incredulous. "Kids can't go to jail," she said, shaking her head. "Not unless they killed somebody."

"Well, now I know he ain't with the FBI. He says he's my real father. But I think that's a lie, too. There's a reward out for me. He took another girl once, too. *Kidnapped.*" The word felt odd in her mouth and hung in the air between them like the smell of something rotten.

Doris's eyes were wide. She sat down on the bed and waited for Sally to continue.

"At night . . . ," Sally's words came forth like waves crashing against sand. "He does bad things. To me, I mean."

"Like hit you?" Doris asked. Her voice was softer now. Maybe even a bit scared. " 'Cause lots of daddies do that. Mine's got a belt that hangs on a nail by the door. When he gets home from work, Mama tells him what we all done wrong, and we get the belt."

"No," she said, shaking her head. "Dirty things. *Nasty* things." She gestured to the bed, feeling like she might faint. It was like she'd been carrying around an anchor and it was sinking, sinking.

"You mean . . . ," Doris started, then spoke in disbelief, *". . . intercourse?"*

The word sounded wrong. Like a foreign language. She felt the same way she had when she read those words in Sammy's books. In *A Tree Grows in Brooklyn.*

"I guess?" Sally said.

Doris shook her head, as if trying to make sense of what Sally had just said. "You'll go to hell for that, you know. Y'all will."

"No, I didn't do nothin' bad. He . . ." She paused, shook her head. "He makes me."

"Well, you can't let him do that no more. And you gotta go to confession."

The anchor dug into the deep, deep sand beneath the watery surface of this awful sea.

Suddenly Sally regretted everything. She regretted letting Doris come home with her; she regretted the promise made when they pressed their bloody fingertips together. She'd sworn to tell the truth, but now here she was worse off than she was before. There was no way she was going to kneel in that cold confessional and tell Father Rogers what Mr. Warner had done to her. She barely had the words. That word that Doris had used, *intercourse,* felt like medicine. Bitter and chemical.

"If I was you," Doris said, standing up from the bed and smoothing the blanket flat again, "I would tell him he best stop messin' with me or else I'd blow a hole through his skull." Doris aimed the gun at the pillow where Mr. Warner's head rested on those nights after he crawled off her and back into his own bed. "Bam!"

SUSAN

The call came in the middle of dinner at Ella's house. Susan excused herself and went to answer. She shivered as a gust of cold air came through the cracks around the front door. It was early March, but it could have been the middle of January. The winds were howling, mournful, and the air had a bite to it. Her mother refused to run the furnace, the cost of oil not in her budget.

"Is Ella Horner there?" the man asked, his voice gruff.

"May I tell her who's calling?" Susan asked, peering into the dining room. Al and her mother were sitting at the table. The baby was in her high chair, shoving green beans into her mouth. Al ate quietly, but Ella wouldn't touch her food. They'd had to plead with her to come downstairs for supper.

"This is Detective Vail from the county sheriff's office," the man said. "Regarding her daughter, Sally Horner."

Susan felt her knees liquefying, folding under her. She gripped the edge of the telephone table.

"This is her other daughter, Susan. Mother's not well. Can I help you? Do you have news? About Sally?" Her words seemed to float in the air before her face. Her ears buzzed. She could barely hear him through the static.

"We've received some information from the Dallas Police," he said. "There's been an arrest made."

"Oh my God," Sally said.

"A man named Joseph Locurto," he said. "Goes by Joey Bonds."

"What was he arrested for?" she asked. "Did he do something to Sally?"

"No, no, ma'am. He was arrested on unrelated charges. There was a murder at his nightclub around Christmas. During the investigation, he was found to be running some illicit operations in his back room. With underage girls."

"Sally?" she asked. "Oh my God."

"No, no . . . however, some evidence recovered during the investigation linked Bonds to Mr. La Salle. Ledgers and receipts. During questioning, it came to light that he is, indeed, affiliated with him. We believe that Mr. La Salle and Sally may be staying somewhere in Dallas."

"Who's on the phone?" Al hollered from the dining room.

She covered the earpiece. "Just a minute," she said, her voice trembling. The wind outside howled, and tree branches scratched at the windows.

"Oh my God. What happens now?"

"Local authorities as well as the FBI are

362

collaborating," he said. "We'll keep you posted if we get any more information. Can you please pass this along to your mother, ma'am?"

"Of course," Susan said. "Thank you," she added, but he had already hung up.

She stood in the hallway for several moments, collecting her thoughts and trying to recall exactly what the detective had told her about Sally. She needed to figure out a way to tell her mother without getting her hopes up. Sally was still gone. Still missing.

"Sue!" Al hollered again. "Your chicken's getting cold!"

Susan straightened her skirt and took a deep breath, and put on a careful smile.

"Who was that?" her mother asked, grimly pushing the chicken around on her plate.

Susan reached for her mother's hand, and Ella looked up at her and her face filled with terror. She shook her head.

"Is it Sally?" she asked.

"It was the police, Mama. They have some information. They think that man La Salle may have taken her to Dallas. There's someone, some man who owns a nightclub? The police there, the FBI, are looking for her."

"Was it Vail?" Al said, standing. "Is he still on the phone?"

Susan shook her head.

"She's never coming home," Ella said. Not a

question, but an awful certainty she now seemed to have.

"Don't say that, Mama," Susan asked. "Why would you say that?"

"But it's true," Ella said, shaking her head. She turned and looked straight into Susan's eyes. "Don't you understand? It's just like with Russell. Don't you see?" Her words hung there, in the air. Suspended.

ELLA

When Ella plumbed those terrifying depths, the dark murky waters of her memory, this was what she recalled: the smell of rosemary and thyme, steam fogging the kitchen windows. The mournful sound of Lester Young playing "Sometimes I'm Happy" on the phonograph. It was spring. The tulips Russell had planted had begun to burst from the earth, their blooms like swollen hearts.

Ella was making chicken noodle soup, the chicken thighs creating greasy swirls. Russell hadn't gotten out of bed in a week. She'd put the record on, cooked his favorite soup, and hoped that it might entice him to come back to the land of the living.

Sally was six years old, a bubbling bright child full of questions. "Is Daddy sick?" she asked each time Russell retreated. "Does he have a temperature? Can we make him chicken soup?" And today, because Ella was tired of making excuses about what was wrong with Russell, she nodded and began to gather the ingredients from the pantry. As she chopped the anemic celery and limp carrots, salvaged from the icebox, she wondered if it was possible. If there was a cure for this. If he would *ever* be well.

Susan was upstairs getting ready to go out to a picture show with some girlfriends. Some Gary Cooper flick. She was sixteen. Her whole life ahead of her. Ella watched her sometimes, and envied her youth. Not her unlined skin or silky hair. Not even her untroubled bones. Instead, it was the *optimism* of youth. That carefree, trouble-free *trust*. The breezy obliviousness to all the ways the world can, and will, conspire against you. What Ella wouldn't have given to have even a single day in which she once again believed the world to still hold promise.

She assumed it was Susan coming down the stairs, the light spring in her step, and so she was startled to see that it was Russell. He was wearing a clean shirt, pressed pants, and she could still see the comb marks in his pomaded hair.

She turned to the stove and studied the noodles, fat as fingers spinning lazily in the broth.

He came up behind her and nuzzled his clean-shaven chin in her neck. She could smell liquor on his breath already. God, did he have a bottle hidden upstairs? She felt her shoulders stiffen.

"Thought I'd go out for a drink or two," he offered, as if this were a gift. As if this were her reward for holding the house together for the last week while he retreated into that private melancholy.

She turned to face him, holding the wooden spoon in her hand.

A slow grin crawled across his face, the only evidence of his travels to the land of misery in the lingering dark pockets beneath his warm brown eyes.

"Dance with me, El?" he said, as the needle in the record moved to "Empty Hearted."

He reached around her waist with one hand and grabbed the hand holding the spoon with the other, and the spoon clattered to the floor. But instead of allowing him to whisk her away, instead of giving in to the smell of his skin, the softness of his hands and his eyes, she pulled away from him. She picked up the spoon from the floor and held it out like a weapon.

"You can't do this anymore," she said.

"*Come on.* I just wanna dance with my girl," he said, and reached again for her, lowering his chin and looking up at her like a little boy in trouble with his teacher.

She shook her head. Her eyes burned with the smell of pepper, onions.

He pulled at her, the cheerful sounds of the music mocking the sadness that gripped her. As if he'd passed it along to her. Infected her.

She knew what would happen. He would leave her here alone in the kitchen. Susan would skip out the door with her girlfriends. Even Sally would retreat to her own little world. And she would remain. Caught inside these four walls. Pots to scrub, sheets (stiff and stinking with his sickness and sweat) to wash. While he went out and drank himself into happiness, maybe even into other women's arms (she didn't know, how could she ever know?), she'd be left alone. Again.

"Stop it," she said, pushing him as hard as she was able. He stumbled backward, knocking his hip against the kitchen table.

"Jesus, El," he said, laughing. "You tryin' to hurt me?"

"Hurt *you?*" she blurted. "I'm the one. *I'm* the one who hurts."

And as she said it, it became true. The pain she ignored knocking at her door like the church ladies who came on Sundays. *Knock, knock.* But this time, she answered it. Let the pain in, and it settled in her bones. In her aching chest, her breaking heart.

"You go out tonight, you don't come home," she said.

"Aw, Ella." He still must have thought she was teasing. How could he think she was joshing with him?

"I mean it," she said, summoning the words she'd tried to say a hundred times. "You leave me now, you might as well be dead."

His smile disappeared. He backed away, hands up in surrender. Then he stood in the foyer, hands lowered, shoulders slumped. For a moment, she thought he might just simply walk back up

368

the stairs, return to bed. But he stood still and stared into her eyes. "Might be easier," he said, shrugging.

"What?" she asked, the words catching on the lump in her throat.

"If I was dead?"

He reached for his hat on the hook, his coat.

"Yes," she said, her body aflame. Her heart a crimson tulip blooming in her aching chest. "It would."

SALLY

Where are we going?" Sally asked. She clung to Tex, who was wriggling in her arms, his sharp little claws digging into her skin.

"Get in the truck," Mr. Warner said.

"But I like it here," she said quietly, shaking her head. "I'm doin' good in school. My teachers all say so. I'm practically getting straight As. And I'm the one who got picked for the May crowning; I'm supposed to put the wreath on Mary's head. Only one girl gets picked by the sisters, and it's me. I can't miss that. And Doris wants me to join the Girl Scouts with her next year, and I told Lena I'd be here this summer when the circus comes back, if Ruth . . ."

He laughed.

"Please. Why do we gotta leave?"

"Get in the truck," he said. "I won't hear another word out of you."

She looked at him, felt the words bubbling up in her. Acidic. She never talked back to him, never argued. She'd been doing what he said for almost two years without complaint. She'd been too afraid. She'd also believed that if she did as she was told that he'd eventually let her go home. That he couldn't keep her forever. That if she was a good girl, he'd *have* to let her go. She couldn't get in that truck again. Couldn't let him take her even farther away from home. When would it stop? When would she be free?

"I don't really belong to you," she said, the words escaping. "I don't care what you say. You ain't my daddy."

He struck her, and it nearly knocked her off her feet. She dropped Tex, and he yapped at Mr. Warner's feet. She touched her split lip with her finger, staring at him with disbelief as she tasted the blood.

"No," he said. "I *ain't* your daddy. Your daddy killed himself rather than spend a minute more in the house with you and your crippled mama."

Tex growled, baring his sharp teeth at Mr. Warner, who lifted his boot, connecting with the little dog's ribs. The dog flew at least five feet across the dirt, howling loudly.

"No!" Sally cried. She ran to Tex and dropped to the ground, cradling the whimpering dog in her hands. "How could you hurt a helpless little dog? Doris was right, you're a bad man!"

"We're leaving," he said. "Now. And the dog stays here."

SUSAN

Maybe I should go," Al said.

"To Texas?" Susan asked. "God, Al. We couldn't find her when she was just in Baltimore. We don't know anybody in Texas. And how would you even get there? Never mind who's going to run the greenhouse if you're gone. Let the FBI handle this, Al."

Susan pictured Texas as the Wild West of Hollywood movies that Al loved. Gunslingers and sunrise showdowns. Audie Murphy as Billy the Kid. But no matter how hard she tried, she could not imagine Sally there. (Perhaps she knew, in her heart of hearts, that by the time the police got there they'd already be gone. Tumbleweeds constantly moving, blown by that monster's whim.)

Al was pacing up and down the rows and rows of tomato plants at the greenhouse, hands buried in his hair. The air was thick with the heady scent of the plants, a smell she'd always found promising before.

"Your mama's about to lose her house," he said.

Susan nodded. He was right. Ella had stopped sewing. The phone had gotten shut off. Al had to pay her last water and electric bills so her utilities wouldn't get turned off, too. Susan knew they'd need to move her in with them shortly. The thought of that filled her with a quiet and shameful dread. They were just starting their family. Dee was just beginning to get a little easier to care for. She and Al had some semblance of their life back. Well, as much as they could be given everything that had happened. A small awful part of her believed that Sally wasn't coming back, ever, and that it might serve them all well to just accept it and allow themselves to grieve. But her mother's anguish was endless, and she, like Al, knew that until Sally was home, Ella would never be well. Even then, there was no guarantee.

"I'm thinking we could use the reward money. I could even take a plane down there."

She nodded. "Okay. Because she can't . . . Mama, I mean . . . I can't live with her, Al."

She expected he would come to her, comfort her. She even reached for him, imploring. But the look on his face was not the one he usually wore of concern and understanding. He was angry. She could count the times he'd been angry with her before on exactly one finger.

"What if it were Dee?" he said.

"What's that?" Susan said.

"What if somebody took the baby away from you? What if somebody stole her right out from under your nose and you didn't know where she was, or what was happening to her?"

Susan shook her head, the thought too painful to even allow registering. "I only meant—"

"That poor woman, your *mother*, hasn't got anybody but us to help her anymore. It's been nearly two years, Sue. Newspapers don't care about Sally anymore. Neighbors don't care. Police say they're looking, but they seem to be a day late and a dollar short. *Somebody's* got to do something. For Sally. For *Ella*. She's your mother, Sue."

As tears welled up in Al's eyes, Susan felt sick. She'd never seen Al cry. Not even once. He was someone who never raised his voice, never lashed out, and certainly never wept. It made her feel uneasy, like her world was tilted somehow.

She nodded, and felt a sickening turn of her stomach. Al was right. She was a terrible daughter. A terrible sister. She was the one who'd fled that house as soon as she was able, leaving Sally alone with her mother and her pain. If she'd been there, maybe Sally wouldn't have gone off with that man. Maybe she'd be home now, and her mama wouldn't be drowning in grief.

SALLY

The gun was in the glove box of the truck. This was a fact that brought both fear and solace to Sally as they drove across the endless desert, Route 66 stretching forever and ever in front of them, behind them. The terrain made Sally think of the moon, like some lunar landscape, pocked with craters and desolate. They were so far away from home now, it might as well have *been* the moon. She studied the door handle, thought of escape. But escape to what: this vast nothingness? She looked longingly at the train tracks that ran parallel with the highway. So many miles of tracks, but not a single train.

Tex had run after them, so close to the truck's wheels Sally feared they might run him over. She didn't say a word to Mr. Warner for a whole day after that. No matter what he said to her, no matter how many times he explained that somebody at the trailer park would take him in. She hoped that was true, but she also hoped it wasn't the mean little boys who lived in the trailer closest to the canteen, the ones who set that poor snapping turtle on fire. She tried not to think of Tex at all as they hurtled across the southwest, but she also knew she'd never forget the sound of him yipping at their tires. And she'd never forgive Mr. Warner for this.

He gripped the steering wheel tightly.

"They still got a reward out for me?" Sally ventured, but he only stared straight ahead at the road. "I just mean, I don't know why we gotta leave unless they're still looking for me."

"*Goddamn it.* Why do you ask so many questions?" he said, looking at her. His mouth was smiling, but his eyes were angry.

"I miss Tex," she blurted, the knot in her chest coming undone.

This time, he didn't motion for her to slide across the bench seat, and so Sally pressed her body as close as she could to the door. She splayed her palm against the glass, which held the heat of the sun. Outside, there was nothing but rock and sand and tumbleweeds, which made Sally impossibly sad. How they cartwheeled, at the mercy of the gusts that swept across the highway. She curled herself into a ball and imagined she was made not of bones but of sticks. Twigs. Gnarled and brittle limbs broken off from their roots. She and the tumbleweeds were no different, both at the whim of a terrible wind.

Texas, New Mexico, Arizona. They all looked the same until soon they were surrounded not by sand but by tall pines, standing like guards along the sides of the road, a mountain looming large ahead of them. The air was thin and so dry her split lip opened again, and she had to wipe the blood on a paper napkin she found on the floor. *Flagstaff, Arizona.* The window glass was cold now. The setting sun was bright, but there was snow tucked between the trees at the edge of the road. Then they were on a busy street with motels and restaurants on one side and train tracks on the other, the scream of the whistle as the train passed loud. They drove slowly, in traffic for the first time since Albuquerque. It was twilight, and the neon blinking sign was of a horse-drawn wagon, wheels flashing, spinning endlessly, but the wagon still. THE WESTERN HILLS MOTEL.

"Please, can we stop here for the night?" she asked. They'd stopped after only seven hours the first day, staying in Amarillo at a small motel at the edge of town. But today they'd already been driving for eight or nine hours, only stopping to gas up and to eat and to use the restroom. She felt dirty; the sand from the desert had made a fine layer, a second skin. She wanted a bath. She couldn't remember the last time she'd had a proper bath. Was it in Atlantic City? In Baltimore, there was no lock on the door at Sammy's and she'd been too afraid to take a bath and have someone accidentally walk in. The trailer only had a stand-up shower. The closest thing to a bath she'd had was swimming in the Good Luck swimming pool. When she thought of that, she thought of Lena, and her eyes burned with the remembered chlorine sting.

Mr. Warner shook his head. "Not much longer."

"Where are we?" she asked.

"Near the Grand Canyon."

She'd heard of it before, of course. It was one of the Seven Natural Wonders of the World, according to *National Geographic Magazine*. She recalled that the article had said that the rock at the bottom of the canyon was around two billion years old. Facts like that made her feel small. Contemplating the center of the Earth or the stars in the sky made her head ache.

"Think we might be able to park the trailer there," he said.

"That where we're going to live now?" she asked, and then felt that same sinking, diving-bell feeling. Plummeting. The Grand Canyon was almost a whole mile deep. If she were to fall into the canyon, she wouldn't survive, and she certainly would never be found. Crying, she said, "I still don't know why we had to leave the Good Luck . . ."

He banged his palm against the dashboard. The loud smack of it startled her, and she held her breath. He leaned across her and threw open the glove box. She saw the gun, and felt a sob rise up. Her nose ran, hot snot running down, stinging her split lip.

But he only grabbed a crumpled envelope, which he shoved at her.

"Read it," he said.

She took the letter with trembling hands.

Dear Florence and Frank,

I am so sorry it's took so long to write. We been on the road following the work.

The reason I'm writing is that we're in San Jose now, and we got a nice spot at a trailer park, kind of like the Good Luck. Hank's found a job picking oranges at a citrus orchard here. There's plenty of work, Frank. Maybe even some garages where you might find a job. We saved you a spot at the trailer court. They've got hookups and the rent's cheap.

I put the address on the envelope. I know y'all don't have a phone, but I put the number here anyway. 6-4151

Much love,
Ruth

"What's this mean?" Sally asked, her breath catching. *Ruth.* She hadn't forgotten her like he said.

"We're headed to California."

"California?"

"It was gonna be a surprise, but you had to go and spoil it."

Her heart snagged, and she returned to the letter:

> P.S. We sure do miss you two. (And Tex of course!) Florence, you been like a daughter to me. Maybe if you come, I can give you a nice new 'do. I got the prettiest red ribbon.

Shaking, she looked at Mr. Warner to see if he understood what this meant. The ribbon. It was a message inside a message, like those little wooden nesting dolls. But what did it mean? What was Ruth trying to tell her?

As the sun set that night at the Grand Canyon, and the sky filled with stars, Sally grew dizzy looking up at them. They looked close enough to touch here, not hidden behind the clouds like they were back home. There was a whole universe out there she didn't understand. All those bright heavenly bodies. Sally thought of her mother and sister as well. Of Lena and Ruth. Of Doris and all those other girls back at home. All of them looking up at the same sky. How could it be, how was it possible, when she felt like she was so far away, that the sky was the same?

She didn't sleep that night; instead she watched Mr. Warner sleep. Studied the way his chest rose and fell. Inside was a heart that beat like hers.

Inside his head a brain that thought and dreamed and wished. Inside his veins blood flowed. He was just a man. Just a man. As he tossed and turned in the small bed, he was vulnerable. He trusted that he would wake in the morning. That she would not run, not leave. He was as stupid as she had been, she thought. As foolish and blind.

She thought of those bright stars overhead, and that vast canyon below. Both more limitless and terrifying than this single, awful man sweating and sleeping before her. She thought of Ruth; the letter like a promise. She thought of the glove box. She thought of the gun.

San Jose, California
March 1950

ELLA

Before Al could set out for Texas like he planned, the detectives called Ella and told her that they'd located a trailer park in Dallas (*The Good Luck,* couldn't they have spared her the cruel irony of its name?), but that man and Sally had already left.

"Where did they go now?" Ella asked.

"We believe they're headed to California," the officer said.

California. As far away as they could possibly be from Camden, New Jersey. It might as well have been the other side of the world.

"You're never going to find her," Ella said, feeling the pain gripping her shoulders, her hands. Her fingers curled into fists, balls of hurt. "You'll keep chasing, and he'll keep running. Don't you see?"

"Ma'am," he said. "I assure you. We're going to find them. We interviewed the neighbors at the trailer park. They knew her."

The pain that gripped her joints quickly took hold of her heart.

"They knew Sally?"

"Yes, ma'am," he said. "Said she seemed like a happy girl. She went to school and liked to swim in the pool. She had a little dog she called Tex."

Could this be Sally? A happy girl who liked to swim, who had a pet dog? How could it possibly be? For two years, she'd been away from her mother, her home, living with a monster. A child molester. A rapist.

"Neighbors said the dog followed her everywhere. They found him sitting in the empty spot where their trailer used to be, like he was waiting for her to come back."

Ella choked back a sob. "California?"

"Yes, ma'am," he said. "We'll keep you updated, but you just need to stay positive. Let us do our jobs. She's alive. She's healthy. She's being taken care of."

Tears rolled down her cheeks as she thought of that dog sitting in the empty space, waiting for her to come home. Wondering what on earth he'd done wrong to be left behind.

That afternoon, Susan came over with the baby for lunch. Ella was in the kitchen, hunched over a loaf of bread, but she wasn't making the sandwiches. She was gripping the Formica, her knobby knuckles white. She barely recognized her own hands anymore. They made her think of roots, like the bare roots of the rosebushes Susan brought her from the greenhouse.

"Mama?" Susan asked, setting Dee into the high chair. "Are you okay?"

When Ella looked up, for an odd moment it wasn't Susan she saw, but Sally.

"Mama, what is it? Are you having pains?"

Yes. Yes. Nothing at all but pain.

"Come here, sit down," Susan said, taking Ella by the elbow and leading her over to a chair. "Is it about Sally, Mama? They'll find her. This is just another setback."

At Sally's name, Ella let out a mournful sigh.

"I forgive her," Ella said, nodding. "I really do."

"Who's that, Mama?"

"Sally. I forgive her for what she done with that man."

Susan released Ella's arm and scowled at her. "Mama, Sally didn't do anything to be forgiven. That man, he was wicked. He made her do those terrible things. You can't possibly blame Sally?"

Ella shook her head. "No, no. Of course not . . . ," she said, waving her hand as if she were simply confused. Had misspoken.

"Mama," Susan repeated. "Ain't nobody at fault here except for Frank La Salle."

At the sound of his name, Ella winced. Just the mention of him like a sharp blade. She squeezed her eyes shut, but the only thing she could see was Sally, playing with a puppy. Splashing in a pool. A happy little girl, living thousands of miles away from her crippled mama. Maybe forgetting all about her by now.

RUTH

"They should be arriving soon," Ruth said to Hank as she packed his lunch pail. She was a bundle of nervous energy. "Frank and Florence."

Hank was bent over, lacing up his boots. He grunted.

"It sure will be nice to have her around again," she said. She closed the lid on the metal pail and latched it shut. The silver box always made her think of a coffin.

"What time will you be home?"

Hank sighed. "When the pickin's done, Ruthie."

Ruth wondered sometimes how the men did it, how Hank and the others survived those fields, those groves: the daily picking or cutting or gathering or plucking of berries or lettuce heads or sugarcane or fruit. The bloody hands, the aching backs, the endlessness of it, and for what? Collecting baskets or boxes or barrels of another man's garden. The mindless hours, the harvesting of fruit that would only serve to make another man rich. Ruth, at least, made something beautiful. When the women from the trailer park (mostly the other migrant wives) came to her, she was able to transform them. To take their limp tresses and inspire them, to take their willful curls and tame them into submission. The women who came to her trailer left *changed.* She was an artist. This was what she thought as she pulled the cool shears from the waistband of her housedress. *I am creating beauty in this ugly world.* What was Hank creating but another dollar in a rich man's pocket?

Still, each day he headed off to work the groves with the *braceros,* those weathered, dark-skinned men. They must have been leery of Hank with his fair skin and hair, his white-blond eyelashes and brows. She'd been teaching herself Spanish so that she could at least exchange a few words with their wives as she cut their hair. The women were warming up to her now. She knew that the men only spoke Spanish as well, and so Hank must have gone entire days without speaking, or understanding, a single word. She tried to imagine his loneliness: the endlessness of the trees, the heaviness of the ladder on his back, the sun on his skin.

At least he got to keep as many oranges as he could carry; any that had fallen from the trees were his for the taking. He brought home the best ones. She squeezed them for their juice, sent them in Hank's lunch kit, even spritzed the citrus into her own hair before sitting in the sun; the juice bleached highlights into her clients' hair. Everything here in California was golden.

"I'm hopin' it'll be in the next day or two," she tried again.

"What's that?" he said, distracted.

"Florence," she said, and the girl's name felt like a puff of dry cotton in her mouth.

"Have a good day, Ruthie," he said, and kissed her head as he did every day. "Stay outta trouble."

He was only teasing, an old joke. He didn't know her real reason for inviting Frank and Florence here, that this was just the beginning of her plan. He would have said she was meddling, that it wasn't her place. Still, she'd written a letter inviting them, convinced the owner of the auto court to reserve a spot for their trailer, offered to do his wife's hair for free in exchange. She didn't tell Hank she felt somehow responsible for Florence, that she thought of her as she might her own daughter. She didn't tell him about the way it felt to braid her hair. The way tenderness overwhelmed her sometimes. That when Florence confided in her, she'd felt for one strange moment that her whole life had been leading to this. That perhaps her destiny had been not to be a mother but to be this girl's protector. Hank wouldn't have understood this. He was so focused on the single orange, the single head of lettuce, the single cane of sugar, he couldn't see beyond his own hands. He couldn't see the field, the grove. He couldn't see beyond the green leaves of those orange trees.

Frank had called, said they were coming, though Ruth knew it could take weeks to drive from Dallas to San Jose. Their own truck had broken down in the desert, somewhere just east of Barstow, and they'd been stuck there waiting for a new clutch for over a week. Luckily, Frank was a mechanic. They likely wouldn't find themselves stranded, not because of car troubles anyway. It was only March; the desert was hot but not deadly this time of year. They'd be here soon; she had to believe it. Because the alternative was unbearable. She just needed to get Florence here. Then she'd quietly and perfectly set her plan into motion.

VIVI

Vivi fell in love with a boy that spring of 1950. His name was Lawrence. He was new to Camden, in her class at school. He was tall and thin and soft-spoken. He had a bit of a stutter, just the tiniest impediment, but it made him vulnerable. This was what she was drawn to. This gentle weakness. It made her want to protect him.

She'd felt this way about Sally once. God, had it been two years already? A sort of lifetime. She could barely remember who she was two years ago. She'd been a little girl then. Now, she was thirteen, practically grown. She'd gotten her period. She'd grown breasts. The boys who once annoyed her now stirred something inside her, made her blush with shame at these longings. But the feelings she had for Lawrence weren't as simple as this. When he spoke to her, his shy eyes downcast, she felt like she was getting a second chance. That this boy had been put in her life for a reason. He seemed to give her purpose.

After school instead of running with the crowd of girls she used to, she and Lawrence walked together to the Woolworth's. What had happened to them? Those blood sisters of hers? Last fall, they'd read about Irene in the papers, went to her funeral where they could barely look at each other; whatever bond they'd forged with razors and blood seemed to disappear. Allegiances, alliances, and pacts nothing more than silly childish wishes. She had been earnest then, believed in the power of a promise.

At the Woolworth's, she and Lawrence sat at the counter and spooned cold ice cream from the silver malt cup they shared. Every now and then she would glance to the end of the counter where that man had sat, eating pea soup, that afternoon. He was a ghost who haunted all their lives, but Vivi's especially.

She thought about telling Lawrence. About sharing with him the truth of what happened that day. That the girls had tricked Sally. Had led her here to humiliate her. That the other girls had no intentions of including her in their stupid club; it wouldn't matter what Vivi said. That she hadn't done something to stop it. She could have whispered in Sally's ear, told her the girls were only letting her get her hopes up. She could have saved her from that man. The fact that she hadn't ate away at her every single day.

"You know, Vivi . . . ," Lawrence said, staring into his ice cream.

"Yes?"

"I think you're . . . swell."

The heat that rose to her cheeks seemed a

contradiction to that cold ice cream. "Thanks," she said.

"You're n-n-not like all the others."

She shook her head. *Yes, I am,* she thought. *I am no different at all.*

Suddenly, she knew it was time to do what she should have done nearly two years ago.

On the way home, she told Lawrence to walk down Linden Street rather than the direct way home.

"Sure," he shrugged. "Whatever you like, Vivi."

When they reached the house where she'd watched Mrs. Horner collapse on the pavement, she had second thoughts. The house looked run-down, abandoned. The patio furniture was overturned; the walls were shrugging off their paint. A mangy-looking black cat looked up at them with mild annoyance. Still, she climbed up the stairs, Lawrence staying behind on the sidewalk, and knocked on the door.

A young woman answered, and Vivi wondered if perhaps she'd gone to the wrong house.

"Is this the Horner residence?" she asked.

"Yes," the woman said. "I'm Susan. Mrs. Horner's daughter."

"Oh," Vivi said, and smiled. "My name is Vivi. Vivi Peterson."

Her name seemed to spark something in the

394

woman's eyes. "You're the one," she said. "The one Sally said she was with. At the shore."

Vivi nodded, tears filling her eyes.

"I just wanted to let you know how sorry I am," Vivi said.

The woman nodded. "Everybody is," she said almost bitterly.

"No," Vivi said, shaking her head. "I mean to say, I *apologize.* We tricked her. It was a terrible thing to do. We told her she could be in our club, blood sisters, if she passed the initiation."

The woman's eyes widened.

"That's how he got her. He caught her stealing a notebook at the Woolworth's." Her chest ached. "It was because of what we told her to do."

She recalled Irene and Bess fleeing from the counter, saying, *Come on.* And how she'd lingered a few moments longer. Stood listening as he told Sally that she was in trouble, under arrest. She could still recall the smell of pea soup, the scatter of saltine cracker dust where he'd sat. She remembered ducking behind the seed packet display as he marched Sally out the front doors.

"Ma'am?" Vivi had said to the waitress behind the lunch counter. "Who was that man?"

The waitress shrugged. "One of those fellas who live over at the YMCA, I think. Think he said his name's La Salle."

"Is he a policeman?"

The waitress snorted. "Pretty sure he's on the *other* side of the law."

At the time, she hadn't known what that meant, but after Sally disappeared, when her story was in all the papers, she'd realized her error. She had failed Sally not only by not telling her what the girls were up to, but by not going to the police. Telling them right away who that man was. She'd harbored that secret for nearly two years now. It had planted in her like one of those seeds, vines slowly creeping up, circling her neck, blooming in her throat. If she'd said something right away, maybe they could have kept him from taking her.

"He tricked her," Vivi said, and then took a deep breath. "We all did. It was cruel. And I'm so sorry. I want you to know I pray for her every night. I hope she comes home soon." She was flustered, felt her cheeks warming, too hot in her wool sweater. "I just wanted to say that, and to let you know that if you need anything . . . you or your mama—"

"You take home economics?" the woman, Susan, said abruptly.

"Home economics? You mean at school?"

"Yes. Did they teach you how to sew yet?"

"Sure," Vivi said. "Just this year. I made an apron. With rickrack trim for my mama."

"Come in, then," the woman said. "I need you to help me sew this piecework."

She nodded and looked to Lawrence, who stood waiting at the bottom of the steps, hands shoved into his pockets. "Go on," she said. "I'll call you later."

Lawrence nodded and took off down the sidewalk, and Susan added, "And I need you to explain to my mother that Sally didn't go with that man willingly."

ELLA

Ella was restless. That girl Vivi had taken over all her sewing, leaving Ella with little to do but sit around with her misery, staring out the window waiting for the phone to ring. Vivi had told her what happened at the Woolworth's that day. About how the girls tricked Sally, and how the man pretended he was with the FBI. And she thought about how scared Sally must have been. How terrified. It was a small consolation, but it oddly eased her mind to understand how it was that he got her to go with him. That Sally wasn't a fool, only a scared little girl.

Today as Vivi worked in the other room, Ella peered out at Russell's garden and noticed the tulips were back. Those flowers were so damned insistent. Ella's beheading of last year's crop provided no deterrent, and with the spring another dauntless batch had emerged along with all the other flowers: the vibrant pink and red of rhododendron and azaleas. The forsythia bush like a blazing sun. Even the roses that Susan and Al had bought seemed somehow filled with purpose. *It's spring,* they seemed to announce. *Chin up!*

But Ella scoffed at the garden's optimism. After the police came up empty-handed in

Baltimore, when they started talking about Texas, she withered inside. They'd promised they were closing in on him, that he was in Dallas, somewhere, and that they would follow their leads to find him. To find Sally. Al had been hell-bent on getting down there, too. But she'd known they wouldn't find them there; that this man, this monster La Salle, was smarter than all of them. He'd been smarter than Sally, smarter than she. For nearly two years now, he had outwitted the police and the FBI. Now they were on a wild-goose chase to California.

And so as she sat gazing out the front window at Russell's garden, the flowers did not cheer her. They were like flowers at a funeral, she thought, a never-ending funeral. Her grief a needle stuck in the groove of a record playing the saddest song.

"Mrs. Horner?" Vivi said from the other room.

"Yes?"

"I've finished with this week's sewing. Is there anything else I can do for you?" She stood in the doorway to the parlor now. What a sweet girl. She'd once been friends with Sally, she said, though Ella knew that this was just kindness, just words meant to soothe that incessant ache. Ella would never admit this to anyone, but sometimes, she imagined that Vivi was her daughter. As she listened to the steady rhythm of the treadle, she allowed herself to imagine that the girl was not a stranger, but a child she'd raised herself. When she looked at that silky hair, she imagined running a brush down its length, unknotting the tangles.

"No," Ella said. "Go on home. Don't forget your coat. Is that boy comin' to get you?"

Vivi nodded and pulled on her spring coat. She came to Ella and touched her shoulder gently. Ella reached up and put her own gnarled fingers on top of Vivi's hand, closed her eyes, and tried to remember what Sally's skin felt like.

SALLY

In the motel room somewhere in California *(Needles? Barstow? Bakersfield?)* Sally lay on her back and crossed her arms over her naked chest, staring at the ceiling, at a water stain shaped like a heart. Mr. Warner said they were going to California, to see Ruth, but she didn't know if she should believe him anymore. They'd been on the road forever, it seemed. What if this, too, was a lie? He could be taking her anywhere. They might never settle down again, she worried, moving endlessly back and forth across the country. Running, running forever.

In the bathroom, she could hear him using the toilet. A sliver of light under the door was the only light in the dark room.

She studied the motel door, deadbolt fastened, chain secured. The walls were paneled wood, and the knots looked like eyes.

On the nightstand next to her was a telephone. It was black. Solid.

She heard the water turn on, and the song he sang whenever he got in the shower. "The Girl That I Will Marry," that Frank Sinatra tune. Then the rumble of a cough.

Sally rolled over, put her hand on the phone, felt the cold plastic in her palm. She touched the dial, put her fingers in each hole of the rotary. *1, 2, 3, 4 . . .*

He was singing about the girl's painted nails and gardenias in her hair.

Steam from the shower seeped out through the crack under the door. Everything smelled of rust. Of wet towels.

Slowly, she lifted the handset, pressed the cold receiver to her ear. She put her finger in the 0, felt her heart quicken. She'd memorized the number Ruth sent in her letter. She only needed to give it to the operator to be connected.

He hummed when he forgot the lyrics.

Slowly, she dragged her finger in a circle, dialing.

Suddenly, the water in the shower abruptly shut off, and the bathroom door flew open. Frank stood naked in the bathroom doorway. Half of his face was lathered in shaving cream. He held a straight razor in his hand.

She threw the handset as though it were on fire, leapt from the bed, and ran to the door.

But he was quick, and she felt her arm being yanked behind her back before she could reach for the chain.

When the scream escaped from her mouth, he caught it. His fist, clutching the razor, pressed against her mouth. She could taste the soap, and her eyes stung. *The blade, the blade.*

"Listen up," he said. "You try that shit again,

and I will slice you in two. Do you understand me?"

She nodded, tears streaming down her cheeks.

"Promise," he said, lowering the blade until she felt its cold press against her trembling neck.

She nodded again.

"I'll kill you first, and then I'll go back to Camden and kill your whole damned family."

ELLA

Susan held Ella's arm as they slowly made their way to church on Sunday. Something about this made Ella feel incredibly old and infirm. She jerked her elbow, signaling for Susan to release her, and immediately regretted it. It was still cold, the streets slushy from a late storm. When she hit an icy patch, she reluctantly put her arm out again, and Susan took hold.

They didn't speak the entire way. By the time they reached the church doors, her joints felt like rusty hinges. She wondered if she would have the energy or fortitude for the return trip home.

A few ladies from the neighborhood stood by the front doors, chatting and smoking. They stopped when they saw her, leaned closer together, whispering as she passed. Determined, she kept walking, chin held high, clutching the folded piece of paper in her hand.

Inside, Susan released her arm and gestured to an empty pew near the back, but Ella shook her head. "I'll be right back," she said.

Leaving Susan behind, she marched purposefully through the buzzing hum down the aisle to the reverend who was speaking to the ladies who occupied the front row. (They were the widows of East Camden, a group to which she technically belonged but had never been invited to join.)

"Reverend Bailey?" she said, interrupting them.

"Yes?" he said, taking a moment before his own recognition set in. "Mrs. Horner, how lovely to have you here . . ."

"I have a prayer request," she said, summoning every bit of courage she had and thrusting the sheet of paper at him. "When it comes time for that, during the liturgies."

He took the paper from her and nodded solemnly.

The last time she'd spoken to Reverend Bailey was when he came to her home to comfort her after Russell's death. Russell had cleaned both St. Paul's and the rectory where the reverend lived for years. She'd asked him then if he would be willing to officiate at the funeral services, and he'd shaken his head sadly.

"Oh dear, I'm so sorry. Suicide is a mortal sin. One who takes his own life does not respect the sanctity of life, nor the sovereignty of God. As a man of God, I cannot condone . . ."

"What about his burial then?" she had asked, feeling the heat rise to her ears.

"There are consequences to taking one's own life, Mrs. Horner," he said, his face reddening. "He cannot receive a Christian burial."

"He can't be buried with his *family?*" she said, her voice loud, her disbelief and horror nearly overwhelming her.

"Unfortunately, that is one consequence," he said, nodding sadly. "Though of greater concern are the *spiritual* repercussions."

It was then that she realized the reverend had just condemned her husband to an eternity in hell. Russell Horner, the man who stayed up all night long with Sally when she had scarlet fever, who climbed up on their elderly neighbor's roof to string Christmas lights after her husband passed away, who gave a bandmate the trumpet he'd had since he was a child when old Charlie Horton had to sell his own horn to pay his house note. "How else is he gonna play?" he'd said when Ella called both him and Charlie fools. Russell Horner was a drunk, and he was tortured by the world, but he was a good man. The idea of him burning in hell was ludicrous.

Now, Reverend Bailey unfolded the paper, and his eyes scanned the request Ella had agonized over for nearly an hour: *Please pray for my daughter, Sally Horner, that she is safe and unharmed and will be returned to her loving family soon.*

He looked up at her, but before he could speak, she said, "Don't tell me you've damned my twelve-year-old little girl to hell, too?"

Then she took a seat in the front pew, right where he would have to see her face through the whole sermon.

RUTH

Ruth heard the truck pull up before she saw it. *Florence.* She was here. Hank was at work, and she'd had back-to-back appointments all morning. She hadn't even had time to sweep up the hair that littered the floor of the kitchen in shiny black and blond curls. But when she saw Frank LaPlante's truck pull into the park, she threw the door open and went running outside.

Frank rolled down the window and leaned out. He looked even more weathered than usual: dusty, his hairy greasy.

"Well, ain't you a sight for sore eyes, Ruthie!" he said, grinning.

She couldn't see Florence behind the glare of the California sun in the windshield. *No, no, no.* Where was she?

Her heart stuttered as Frank pulled the truck and trailer farther in, rolling to a stop in the empty space next to Ruth and Hank's trailer. She was holding her breath as she walked toward the passenger side where, as she blocked the sun, she could, finally, see the little girl sitting on the other side of the glass.

Ruth tapped her fingers gently against the window, but Florence didn't roll it down. Didn't even turn to face her. Maybe she was just sleeping? She tapped again. "Florence?"

Florence turned to look at Ruth, indeed as if waking from a dream, and slowly reached for the handle to roll the window down.

"Florence!" she said, feeling overwhelmed at the sight of her.

The child, too, looked worse for the wear, her clothes and skin both ashen, as if they'd carried a fine layer of dust from the desert with them from Texas. She sat upright, her hands clasped in her lap. She was plump still, healthy at least, with a little bit of color in her cheeks. But her hair. What a mess. Her curls had grown out since Ruth had given her the haircut back in Dallas, but they were matted, tangled, pulled back in a frayed braid. She was just a child, a child left to care for herself.

Ruth's hand shot out instinctively and opened the truck door. Florence tentatively stepped out, her legs longer, Ruth noted by the higher hem of her old skirt.

"This the spot, Ruthie?" Frank bellowed. He stood in the empty space next to Ruth and Hank's trailer, hands on bony hips as he surveyed the space.

Ruth nodded, speechless, and opened her arms to Florence, who fell into them. Ruth buried her nose in Florence's curls, smelling the weeks they'd spent on the road in one quiet inhalation: fried food, sweat, sunshine, gasoline. Florence clung to her, her hands gripping Ruth's housedress, her desperation so profound and palpable, Ruth could feel it. Smell it.

When she pulled away, Ruth felt her knees weaken. Dangling from the end of Florence's braid was the red ribbon.

"It's okay, honey. It's okay," she whispered to her. "You're safe now."

Frank came back over and hopped into the truck, pulling forward to position the trailer in the right space.

Florence's body was shaking, just a little, not perceptible to the eye but certainly to Ruth's fingers as she stroked her back. When she began to shake harder, Ruth pulled back and gripped her shoulders. Peered into her sweet face.

Frank got out of the truck and moved behind it to start to undo the hitch.

"Everything is going to be fine, sweetheart. I *promise* you," she whispered.

Florence's eyes were wide. Terrified.

"What is it, hon?" Ruth whispered. Florence hadn't said a word.

Both of them glanced at Frank. He was crouched down, examining the hitch. The knees of his trousers were worn thin.

"He's gonna . . . ," she started to say, and her voice sounded brittle.

"What?" Ruth whispered.

Florence trembled.

"He's gonna kill me."

AL

W hat are you doin', Al?" Susan asked, feeling a sudden and inexplicable chill.

He was rifling through the drawers where she had carefully folded his shorts, meticulously rolled his socks.

"If I drive, I can be in California in less than a week." He opened up the closet door and pulled out the suitcase they hadn't taken out since their honeymoon. "I'll just sleep in the car, save money that way. If I don't stay at any motels."

Outside, it was a bright spring day. Birds were chirping hopefully in the trees. Sunlight streamed through the window, bathing the room in a soft warm light.

"Al, honey . . . ," Susan said. "They don't even know for sure he's got her in California."

Al threw the suitcase down on the bed next to her and released the metal clasps keeping it shut.

"How long have I known you, Sue?" he said.

"Why, since I was in second grade? Course, you were in the fifth grade then. Older boy." She smiled.

"Since before Sally was born. I've practically been a part of your family since I was ten years old. I used to love to come to your house, wished I lived there."

"You did?"

Al's face softened. "My house was always so loud. Eight of us kids. It was like a zoo. But your house was always so . . . peaceful."

Al had never talked about this before.

"Course, your mama never said much to me, but she made sure there were snacks for us to eat. Cookies, what have you. Remember the time I busted my knee open playing Red Rover?"

Sally nodded. She remembered helping Al up the steps to her house, her mother ushering them inside and into the powder room, where she silently tended to Al's ravaged knee.

"She gave me a little nip of whiskey before she set to cleaning the gravel out." Al smiled a little at the recollection. "Took every last bit out with a pair of tweezers. Kept asking to make sure I was okay."

Susan nodded. She'd forgotten this. She'd forgotten her mother's tenderness. She'd been taking care of her mother for so long now, she could barely remember when her mother had taken care of her. Hearing Al speak of her with such fondness filled her with a guilty sort of melancholy.

"Nobody cared for me like that before. That had happened at my house, I'd still have those bits of gravel in my knee."

Al reached for Susan's hand.

"You're too hard on your mama sometimes,"

he said. "Her life's been nothing but heartache, Sue."

Susan nodded, and she thought about her mother's pain. About the permanence of it. About her anger and frustration and impatience. She thought she'd been hiding it. But Al could see through her.

A sob escaped her lips, and her hand flew to her mouth.

"I've got to take care of a few things at the greenhouse first," he said. "Make sure my brothers don't run it into the ground while I'm gone."

Susan wiped at her tears.

"You really think you can find her?" she asked.

Al shook his head. "I don't know," he said. "But if I do . . . what he's done to our family, to Sally . . . I swear to God, I'll kill him."

RUTH

Florence was here now, but Ruth knew from the wild desperate look in Frank's eyes and the way that Florence clung to her that the girl wasn't safe. She'd told Ruth he was going to kill her. She'd *said* that; Ruth hadn't dreamed it. When Ruth had sent the letter to Frank in Dallas, urging them to come to San Jose, her plan had been simply to get Florence back to where she could keep an eye on her, hopefully get her to open up, to tell her what was going on. But Frank hadn't left the girl alone for a single minute since their arrival. It had been three days, and Frank had been practically glued to her side. She needed to find a way to get Florence alone.

Ruth pulled her shears from her apron pocket and turned the chair so that her neighbor, Gert, was facing her. Gert was the only other woman who spoke English at the trailer park, but she was decades older than Ruth. Ruth studied the soft gray curls that framed the elderly woman's face. Her eyes were milky blue, cataracts most likely. It was difficult to tell if she'd ever been beautiful. Gert had been at the trailer court in San Jose since she was Ruth's age. Almost forty years now. She'd raised two children here, but only one of them had made it to adulthood. *Boy*

and a girl, she'd said. *My daughter . . . influenza.
She was five years old.* Her son never came to
visit. He was a lawyer in Sacramento with his
own family. Gert spent most of her time listening
to her stories on the radio or tidying up the tiny
trailer. She and Ruth went to the market together
on Sundays, and every month Ruth cut her hair.
Gert's husband, Ben, was an electrician by trade,
a handyman by necessity.

"Where's Ben working these days?" Ruth asked
today, pulling a curl on either side of the woman's
face, making sure they were even length.

"He's still working odd jobs over at
Normandins'," she said. "That car dealership
near the Lucky Supermarket?"

Ruth caught her breath.

"Normandins are a real nice family. They've
always got something for him to do."

"That right?" Ruth asked, wheels spinning
fast. "Hey, do they happen to have a services
department over there? A repair shop?"

"Sure. Something wrong with Hank's truck?"

"No, truck's fine. I actually got a friend looking
for work," she said, feeling her throat close
around the word "friend." "Maybe Ben could put
in a good word?"

"I don't see why not," she said. "Always happy
to help you out, Ruthie."

As Ruth clicked her shears, trimming Gert's
curls, her mind raced. She needed to get Frank

away from Florence. Just a few hours would be all it took, she hoped.

Later that afternoon, Ruth stood outside Frank and Florence's trailer. Frank leaned one hand against the doorway, the other running across his unshaved chin.

"Ben's put in a good word for you, said you're a hard worker, a good mechanic. All you need to do is show up." She tried to sound as casual as she could. Just a friendly neighbor helping a fella out.

She'd brought oranges for Florence, used them as an excuse to come over to the LaPlantes' trailer.

"Want one? They're real sweet," she said, holding the bowl out to Frank. He grabbed one and grinned at her.

"I don't know nothing about foreign cars," he said.

"Foreign cars?"

"Imports," he said. "Those cars made over in Europe."

Ruth shook her head. What was the difference? Weren't all cars made the same way? She hadn't thought to ask Gert what kind of cars they serviced.

"I'm sure they work on American cars," she said, nodding as if this were a fact. She scrambled to come up with something to convince him.

415

"Hank brought our pickup in after we got here. It's a Ford," she lied.

Frank sighed. "My truck's clutch is startin' to slip. I shouldn't be driving it far until I can fix it."

"Oh, that's no trouble. Ben says you can take the city bus in at lunchtime, that's when his boss can give you an interview. He'll give you a ride back to the trailer park after work."

"You're a real peach, Ruthie," Frank said then, and leaned forward, kissing her cheek. She felt her body tense, the hair on the back of her neck rise as his bristly cheek brushed against her skin. But she smiled and waved her hand.

"I'm happy to help out," she said.

"You keep an eye on Florence while I'm gone?" he asked, tilting his head.

Ruth nodded, her heart fluttering. "Of course. Like she was my own."

SALLY

W hat's the matter with *you?*" Mr. Warner said. "Cat got your tongue?"

The next day, Sally sat in a lawn chair in front of the trailer, writing in her composition notebook. Her handwriting was still small, though not the microscopic etchings it had been when he first took her. She was braver now; it showed in every loop and letter. She never went back to the early pages; it was too painful to reread the musings of her eleven-year-old self. Too difficult to see how stupid she'd been. How hopeful. This document was proof of so many things. Of what Mr. Warner had done, yes, but also what a fool she had been. He was right.

But she was tired of being a fool. Tired of being fooled.

"I said, what's the matter with you?" Mr. Warner asked again.

Sally stared down at the lined pages of the notebook. They'd only been in San Jose a few days. Mr. Warner hadn't even mentioned school yet. She wondered if he had any plans for her to finish out the school year. Thinking about school made her think of Doris. She imagined her in the classroom back in Dallas, wondering where Sally had gone.

"You gone deaf on me now, too?" he asked, leaning down. "Huh, deaf *and* dumb."

A tear dropped to the page, blurring the ink.

Mr. Warner buttoned his shirt and said, "I'm taking the bus into town this afternoon to look for work. I'll be home by supper. You tell Ruth to help you cook up those chicken thighs in the icebox. A couple of potatoes, you just got to cut the eyes out. You stay with Ruth today."

Her eyes burned. *Ruth.*

"Something wrong with your ears?" he said, louder this time, and cuffed her ear softly.

Still, she refused to look at him.

"Goddamn deaf-mute," he muttered, laughing as he walked across the dusty lot toward the bus stop. "Fucking Helen Keller."

As soon as the bus lurched away from the bus stop, Sally stood up, threw the notebook down, and went inside the empty trailer. Shaking, she paced up and down the narrow trailer hallway. She wasn't sure what she was looking for. Where to go, what to do. She hadn't been alone in so long, she hardly knew what to do anymore. She remembered the valise then. Those photos. It had been so long since she'd found them, sometimes she wondered if she'd dreamed them.

She went to the bed and dropped to her knees. There it was, right where she'd left it back in

Dallas. She reached under and grabbed it by the handle, sneezing at the dust that had gathered there. The clasp was still broken, and so the lid lifted easily. She pulled out the envelope and shook the photos onto the bed again. There was that girl Dorothy, *Dot,* just as Sally remembered her. She wondered where she was now. If she was grown. She started to put the envelope back and then noticed a silky pocket in the valise she hadn't noticed before. She reached her hand in, felt a couple of loose bobby pins (Dot's?), and then a folded-up piece of paper shoved way over in the corner. It was also a news clipping, yellow, fragile. She unfolded it carefully and smoothed the wrinkles out, her breath hitching.

POLICE SEEK GIRL, 11, MISSING WITH FORMER CONVICT. It was her own face pictured beneath the headline. That photo taken of her in Atlantic City. She barely recognized that little girl on the swing anymore. Fingers trembling, she sat down on the floor and read the horrific truths in black and white.

> Thursday, an eight-state police search was under way for blue-eyed Florence (Sally) Horner and a convicted 52-year-old rapist who persuaded her mother to let the child accompany him to Atlantic City, New Jersey by posing as the father of Sally's school chum.

He was not her father. He was a stranger. A convict. A liar. Nothing he'd said was true. Her hands shook so hard, she had to press her palm to the floor so she could read the article.

"I don't think my little girl has stayed with that man all this time of her own accord," Mrs. Horner said.

Her mother. She could hear her voice as she read her words. She *hadn't* known.

Sally glanced at the door as if he might just walk back in, catch her here holding on to his lies. But the trailer was still. He was gone. And so she gathered the photos and the clippings, put them all in that yellow envelope, shoved the valise back under the bed.

Knock, knock.

She jumped, felt her skin tingle with fear.

"Florence?" Ruth called out.

"Just a minute!" she answered. She ran to the bureau and threw open the top drawer, but the gun was gone. She rifled through his undergarments, but it was not there. Which meant that he had it with him.

Clutching the envelope, she made her way to the door of the trailer and stepped out into the blinding sun, where Ruth was waiting in a pair of bright yellow pedal pushers and a crisp white sleeveless blouse, knotted at the waist. Her hair was in curlers. Her eyes looked frantic, but she was smiling.

"I just made some lunch, sweetheart. You hungry?"

MARGARET

The girls at St. Leo's sometimes ditched school at lunch. Instead of going to the cafeteria, they snuck away to the park. They walked together arm in arm, plaid skirts swooshing against bare knees. Margaret Howard followed behind them, invisible. At the park, they'd gather around the picnic table, smoking cigarettes or flirting with the boys who were never far behind. They didn't notice Margaret. Not today, not ever.

And so she sat alone on a bench, eating a peanut butter sandwich and pretending to study her primer, listening to the squeals of delight and the cries of frustration (sand in the eye, a lost toy) of the children on the playground. She watched the little boys chasing each other, shooting with imaginary guns. She observed two little girls climbing the octopus-shaped contraption that emerged from the sand like some prehistoric beast, its eight arms reaching from the subterranean depths from which it came. Had she ever been carefree like this? Shouting and laughing with other children? Or had she always been this lonely?

The three girls from her class sat huddled together at the picnic table, poring over a magazine, heads pressed together, the locks of their hair (three indistinguishable shades of blond) intertwined. Clean white bobby socks and saddle shoes, Catholic school plaid and cardigans buttoned tight. In uniform, she might look like the rest of them, but she felt so terribly different.

When a gap opened up in the huddle, and one girl looked up at Margaret, smiling with something close to recognition, if not invitation, Margaret boldly stood up and walked toward the girls.

"Hi," she said, but her voice didn't even seem to register, the smoke from their cigarettes more substantial than her vaporous words, which blew away in the breeze, and the girls' circle grew tighter, a fortress shutting her out. So she walked away, kicking at rocks with her scuffed brown shoes. Staring at the ground, quivering chin to chest, she slipped into the shadows of the eucalyptus trees.

"Hey!"

Margaret looked up to see an old man jogging toward her.

"Excuse me!" he hollered, smiling, breathless.

She studied him quizzically.

He bent over, hands on knees, to catch his breath and looked up at her, smiling. "You haven't seen a loose dog running around, have you?"

She shook her head.

"Normally, she doesn't run off," he said,

shaking his head, looking toward the grove of eucalyptus trees, shielding his eyes from the sun. "But she saw a rabbit and took off after it."

"Oh no," Margaret said. "What kind of dog is she? I have a collie at home. Her name's Rusty."

"*My* dog is a collie," he said, incredulously. "She's only a few months old."

"A puppy? Oh no! What's her name? I can help call her for you," she said.

The man smiled, his teeth long and yellow. He had a long scar on his cheek.

"Her name? Why, it's Sally."

SALLY

Come inside," Ruth said. "I made those sandwiches you like."

Sally followed Ruth into her trailer, which, unlike Sally and Mr. Warner's, was bright and cheerful. Her hands continued to tremble, and heat spread through her body. She wiped away the droplets of sweat forming at her temple.

"Sit down, hon," Ruth said, motioning to a chair at the small kitchen table. "Let me get you a glass of water. You look like you seen a ghost."

Sally obeyed, sitting down on the cool vinyl seat cushion. The table was covered with a blue-and-white gingham oilcloth, and at the center of the table was a Corningware cornflower bowl filled with oranges. This bowl was the same one her mother had at home: white ceramic with delicate blue flowers. It was something Sally had hardly noticed before: the way you can walk across the same floor every day and never notice the pattern and color of the linoleum. But still, it must have registered somewhere, deep in her memory. She could see her stepfather sitting across the table from her, scooping a spoonful of mashed potatoes from this bowl. A cold glass of beer in his hand and a plate piled high with roast beef. She could see him winking at her mother as she hurried from the stovetop to the table with a small matching gravy boat, steaming gravy inside. She remembered her mother sitting down, sighing and smiling, as she stole a sip of her father's beer. Sally could recall having to sit on a Sears catalog to be able to reach the table, the pages cold on her bottom.

"Here," Ruth said, pushing a plate in front of her. Deviled ham and yellow mustard on Wonder bread with the crusts cut off. Pickles. "Eat something. You look about to faint."

Sun came through that window as well, illuminating the table in a clean, warm pool of light. Across from her, Susan would have been chattering on about something she'd read at school, or a joke she'd heard. *Knock, knock,* she might have said.

"Are you okay, sweetheart?" Ruth asked. "Listen, I was hoping we could talk about Frank. I know there's somethin' you ain't tellin' me . . ."

Sally hesitated and then pushed the envelope toward Ruth, who looked at her quizzically.

Ruth picked the envelope up and released the contents onto the table. Her brow wrinkled as her eyes scanned the photographs, the news clippings. When she saw the clipping with Sally's photo, her hand flew to her mouth and she cried out.

"My real name's Sally Horner," she said. "And I want to go home."

MARGARET

S ir?" Margaret said. They had been looking for Mr. O'Keefe's lost dog for at least twenty minutes (walking along the edge of the woods, calling, *Sally! Sally!*), when she realized they'd wandered away from the park along the winding trail that ran beside the Guadalupe River, the woods on either side growing thicker and thicker.

"What time is it, sir?" she asked, feeling like a sleepwalker startling awake from a dream.

"Not sure," he said, shrugging.

Her mouth twitched; something about the man suddenly made her feel uncomfortable. He was grinning at her still; he'd been grinning at her the whole time, even though it looked like maybe he'd lost his dog for good.

"I should probably be getting back," she said, starting to back away, but he reached out for her elbow.

She yanked her arm back, and his smile disappeared.

"I'm expected at school, sir," she said, feeling her body grew rigid. Ossifying.

He peered back over his shoulder at the woods, still holding on to her elbow. Above them, the sky was dusky, ashen. He pulled at her arm, and she resisted, and so he yanked again, this time hard enough to hurt.

"You're hurting me, sir," she said.

"Listen to me," he said, leaning in close to her. "You come with me, there won't be any trouble. But if you so much as think about running, I'll go straight to your mama and make sure she knows all about those cigarettes you were smoking back there at the park."

"But I wasn't smoking," she said, and yanked her arm again. She felt like a rabbit in a trap.

Then she saw the gun in his waistband.

The scream rang out like an alarm. Had it come from her own mouth? Mr. O'Keefe held on to her arm but stepped backward, confused.

A young woman with bright red curls came running out of the woods, looking over her shoulder as if being chased. She squealed again, but this time, it was obvious that it was not a cry of terror but a playful shriek of delight. "I'm going home, Nicky Tremain!"

When the woman saw Margaret and the man, she stopped, and following behind her was a young man running, tripping, laughing. He nearly knocked the young woman over as he came tumbling out of the woods, his hair and clothing mussed. He stopped, stood next to her.

The redhead pointed, at Mr. O'Keefe, at Margaret. The young man with his flushed cheeks stood dumbly next to her.

"Are you okay?" the young woman asked Margaret.

The man turned to her, squeezing her arm tighter.

Margaret's gaze darted back and forth, between Mr. O'Keefe and the young couple.

"I don't know him," she said, shaking her head. Terrified.

The young man in the khakis stiffened, throwing his shoulders back.

"Is he hurting you?" he said, stepping closer, chest puffed out.

She nodded, tears searing her cheeks.

She felt Mr. O'Keefe's grip release. He let go, muttering something under his breath, and backed up. Then he turned and ran, dust from the trail kicking up behind him.

"Who was he?" the redheaded lady asked.

Margaret shook her head. "I don't know. But he had a gun."

SALLY

It was heavy. That was what Sally thought as her hand closed over the cold receiver of Ruth's phone, that it was unbearably substantial. She thought of the motel phone, the way she'd thrown it against the wall, the sound of the dial tone buzzing in her ears for so long afterward.

"Go ahead, doll," Ruth said. Her voice reminded Sally of a string tethered to that red balloon at the hospital. Tight and shivery.

"I'm scared," she said.

Ruth nodded and squeezed Sally's free hand. "I know, sweetheart. I know that."

Sally looked at the bowl of oranges, closed her eyes. She thought of Mr. Warner. Of the blade, the taste of shaving cream.

"Do you remember the number?" Ruth asked.

Sally nodded. In the first grade, they'd had to memorize their telephone numbers, their addresses. They had to recite the directions home. She remembered standing before the class, her mind going blank as she tried to recall which way her house was. Until he died, her stepfather had always come to collect her from school. She never paid attention to which way they walked. She'd always been too busy chatting with him, avoiding the cracks, making wishes on dandelions gone to seed. Her classmates chuckled as she began to cry. She couldn't remember the directions, but luckily she'd recollected her phone number. Her mother had made her recite it again and again, just in case she was ever lost.

"It's long distance," Ruth said. "A toll call. We'll need to dial the operator."

Sally pressed the phone to her ear and remembered holding a gift shop conch shell to her ear in Atlantic City just two years ago. Listening to the hollow empty shell mimicking the ocean.

When the operator came on, she did as Ruth had told her: "I'd like to make a long-distance call, please. To Camden, New Jersey."

She rehearsed what she would say when her mother answered, tried to remember the sound of her mother's voice. Her palms were sweating so much, she could barely hold on to the phone in her hand. She tried to picture her mother; where would she be in the house? How long would it take for her to make her way to the ringing telephone?

She could hear the muffled sounds as the operators connected her call. It took forever, and then the operator came back on.

"Ma'am?" she said.

Was she talking to her?

"Yes?"

"I'm sorry. That phone number is no longer in service."

"What do you mean?"

"Ella Horner in Camden, New Jersey? That number is no longer connected."

Sally thrust the phone at Ruth, shaking her head.

"Mama's phone isn't working anymore," she said. Had her mother moved? How on earth would Sally ever find her then? God, what if something had happened to her? Her stepfather was gone, had just disappeared one night. Had she been so foolish to think that it couldn't happen again?

"It's okay," Ruth said. "There must be someone else you can call. Do you have grandparents? Aunts and uncles?"

Sally shook her head. Where was her mother? Maybe Mr. Warner was right. Maybe they had forgotten her. Moved on. But to where?

"My sister," she said. Susan would know what had happened. Susan and Al. But they wouldn't be able to come to California for her. How would she get home?

"Do you know your sister's phone number?"

She tried to think where Susan would be. At home with the baby? But the baby would be nearly two years old now: her niece or nephew, she thought, growing up without her. She knew that California was three hours behind the

432

East Coast. It would be almost five o'clock in New Jersey. They might still be at the greenhouse. They stayed open most nights so people could stop by on their way home from work. The greenhouse would be busy. It was spring. People would be beginning to plan their gardens. Sally closed her eyes again and thought of her stepfather's garden. Remembered the strawberries that crept onto the sidewalk from their tangled vines. The tulips, erupting from the earth with their purposeful and alarming beauty every spring.

She heard tires on the dirt drive outside the trailer and stopped breathing. Could it be Mr. Warner coming home already? No. He'd gone into town on the bus, said he wouldn't be home until suppertime.

Ruth left Sally and ran to the window, peering out through the curtains. Her hand pressed against her chest, she turned to Sally. "It's just Mr. Ramirez," she said. The neighbor on the other side.

"Do you need me to call the operator again?" Ruth asked.

Sally shook her head and dialed the operator. "I'd like to make a long-distance call. To Florence Township, New Jersey, please. The Florence Greenhouse." It had always felt strange that there was a town that shared her given name.

She listened this time to the operators at their switchboards, the clicks and mutters and hums. So many people all over the country making calls. So many connections. As she waited, she wondered how many of them were about to change someone's life with their voice. How many of them would deliver news, good and bad, to the person answering at the other end of the line. Her heart ached with the thought of all those people, waiting for their voices to be heard.

"Florence Greenhouse, this is Al."

"Al?" She looked at that bowl, filled with oranges, and her eyes stung. "Al, this is Sally."

"Sally?" His voice sounded far away. But it was *Al.* "Oh my God. Where are you?"

Sally looked at Ruth, who was sitting at the table, her eyes wide and expectant.

"I'm with a lady, my friend. In California," Sally said, and the tears spilled, running in hot streaks down her cheeks. "Tell Mama I'm okay, and don't worry. I want to come home. I've been too afraid to call before."

"Where are you exactly, Sally?"

"Do you want me to talk to him?" Ruth asked.

Sally shook her head.

Ruth pushed a piece of paper at her where she had written the address of the trailer park.

"Send the FBI after me, Al. Please," Sally said. "I am so scared."

"I'm calling them as soon as I hang up. Stay exactly where you are, Sally. Are you safe?"

Sally nodded. "Yes, but please, Al. Please send them right away. He'll be coming home soon."

AL

Al knew the local police would be of no help. The Baltimore Police, the Dallas Police. None of them had managed to do a damned thing to help Sally in almost two years. It was like some Abbott and Costello sketch, "Who's on First," and all that. Nothing more than a bunch of silly Keystone Kops locked in a futile and ridiculous chase. This guy, Frank La Salle, had outsmarted them all. Maybe Sally was right: the FBI. He should go straight to the FBI. He could hardly believe this was happening. Just this morning, he'd called the Triple A to inquire about maps for the cross-country trip.

The operator connected him quickly to the FBI headquarters in New York City, and he recited the address where Sally was. Sally. God, that poor child.

He could barely feel his legs beneath him when he stood up. As he made his way from the front office out to the greenhouse, where he knew Sue was tending to a customer who was looking for ground cover, he tried to think how to break this news to her. How to tell her that her sister *was* in California like they thought. That she was *alive*.

"Where's Sue?" he asked his kid brother Joe, who came to help out after school.

Joe shrugged. "Outside with a customer, I think?"

Al rushed past him through the rows of plants, the scent of soil and greenery so heady and fragrant, it made him feel almost dizzy. He made his way to the rear entrance and spied Susan standing in the back lot, talking to Mrs. Hoffmeier, one of their regular customers. Sue was holding the baby on her hip. His heart nearly stopped at the sight of his wife, his child. The idea that someday his daughter would be Sally's age, would be vulnerable, would no longer be nestled safely in her mother's arms once again overwhelmed him.

He recalled the long walk up the walkway to Bobby Lee Langston's mother's door, his dead shipmate and friend's blackened boots in his hands.

"Sue!" he said, calling out to her, his voice breaking along with his heart.

Both women looked up at him expectantly.

"Al?" Susan said.

He watched as the realization arrived. She seemed to know exactly what he was going to say before he said it.

Mrs. Hoffmeier, too, seemed to intuit the news and reached out to take hold of the baby. Everyone knew what had happened to Sally. Their heartache and tragedy had become the heartache and tragedy of the entire state of New

Jersey. Not a day had gone by in the last two years without a customer asking after Sally. Susan handed the baby to Mrs. Hoffmeier and ran to him.

"Where is she?" Susan asked. "Oh my God, Al. Where's Sally?"

SALLY

"Pack your bag, quick as you can," Ruth said.
Sally thought about what she should take with her. What from this life would she possibly want to bring back home? Two years ago, Sally had packed a suitcase and told her mother she was headed to the shore. So much had happened since then, so many moves. Even that little red suitcase had disappeared, abandoned in the Atlantic City rooming house. She wondered sometimes about that girl carrying it as well.

She stood inside the trailer and looked around. Her heart clanged like loose change in a tin can as she thought of Tex, the way he liked to sleep on her pillow during the day. Never Frank's. As a matter of fact, he'd torn up one of Frank's pillows, left a mess of feathers all over the bed. Frank had threatened to take the puppy to the pound over that. Poor little Tex. She ached at the thought of him.

Even most of the clothes she had now were almost too small: skirts inches too short, buttons straining against buttonholes. And everything she'd left behind belonged to that other girl.

She rifled through her drawer, looking for something her mother would approve of, because surely she would get to see her mother soon?

Maybe her old school uniform from Our Lady of Good Counsel? It was the nicest thing she had.

"Hurry up, Sally," Ruth said, poking her head into the trailer. "They should be here soon."

"I don't know what to take," Sally said, staring at the open drawer.

"I'll pack for you," Ruth said. "Go to the canteen and wait there. In case Frank gets back here before the police arrive."

"I'm afraid, Ruth," she said.

Ruth came to her and pulled her into a hug. The brass ring that rested against her sternum was so cold. *Please don't forget me,* she thought.

POLICE CHIEF
JOHN DARLING

The call had come in to the Santa Clara County Sheriff's Department just as Police Chief John Darling was coming back in from lunch. He knew something big had happened the moment he walked through the station doors. Everything was abuzz. Phones were ringing. People were chattering. There was electricity in the air. *Horner, Horner,* the secretaries whispered. Before he knew what had happened, he thought they were saying *hornet,* and indeed, the station felt like a buzzing hive.

But the drive out to the trailer park in San Jose was quiet, the air between himself and his partner, Officer Alvarez, charged yet remarkably still.

The girl.

He wasn't sure what he expected, but it wasn't this. He, like everyone else, had read the articles in the papers, seen the shots of both Sally Horner and Frank La Salle. They'd seemed like characters in the books he liked to read. Dashiell Hammett. Raymond Chandler. The guy's mug looked like the gangsters he'd only read about in the papers, seen in the movies. But now, here she was, not some black-and-white damsel in distress. No noir fiction. But a *girl*. A young, somewhat homely, but very real, teenaged girl.

All alone. Standing, shaking, quaking, clutching an envelope in her hand, she couldn't have been much more than four feet ten in her dingy bobby socks and wrinkled skirt. Her hair was a mess of tangled curls, and her eyes were swollen and pink from crying. Her blouse was buttoned wrong as well, with one edge hanging longer and a single empty buttonhole. She was not dirty, but disheveled. For some reason, it reminded him of the time he'd taken his son to the circus, and they'd seen a chimpanzee dressed up in a little tuxedo. The monkey had been screeching wildly, manic inside that stupid suit. A wild thing that was supposed to look human. His heart had gone out to that poor beast, as it went out to this poor wild creature now.

"I'll go to the girl," he said to his partner. "You keep an eye out for La Salle."

As he got out of the cruiser and approached her, the girl backed up against the side of the canteen building, shaking her head. "Please help her."

He was confused. What was she talking about?

He walked slowly toward the girl with his palms up, in some strange surrender. As if approaching a wounded wild thing.

"Miss Horner," he said, and she shook her head. There was a strand of hair, wet with tears,

442

clinging to her fat white cheek like a single parenthesis.

"Please, Officer, you gotta help Ruth."

"Mrs. Janish? The lady that called in? Where is she?"

But before the girl could answer, there was a scream, and a gunshot from inside one of the trailers.

RUTH

Ruth had heard the city bus pull up but hadn't thought anything of it. Frank was supposed to get a ride home at the end of the day with Ben. She and Florence had at least an hour before they should be coming home.

Ruth had sent Florence to the canteen, where she knew she'd be safe in case Frank did come back, and told her to wait there. Then she had gone into Frank's trailer herself to gather the rest of Florence's things. Nauseated, she'd made her way to the bedroom, trying not to cry as she considered everything that had been going on in there for the last two years and for all that time at the Good Luck, right next door to her. Her heart ached with all the ways she'd failed Florence. But she wouldn't fail her again.

She threw open the drawers and grabbed Florence's clothes, the hairbrush she'd given her, her composition notebook, her stomach clenching as she considered what secrets were written inside.

When she heard the trailer door open, she thought it was just Florence come back from the canteen.

"Sweetheart, I told you . . . ," Ruth began.

But the shadow that filled the doorway wasn't

Florence, and the stink of him, that gasoline-and-pomade stench, burned her nostrils.

"Well, looky here," he said calmly. "Looks like we've got a burglar on the premises."

"Frank," Ruth said.

"You know, it's fully within my rights to protect what's mine."

The dusty sunlight at his back, he was only a silhouette, but it didn't take long before she realized that he was holding something, and that something was a gun.

A body either cooperates or defies you, Ruth knew. And while in the past, her own body had failed her when she needed it the most (she considered her inhospitable womb, the blood that appeared predictably, nearly religiously month after month), she willed it now to obey. *Calm,* she thought. *Keep calm. Do not show him how afraid you are.*

"You're home early," she said, forcing a smile.

"What are you doing in here?" he said. "You think you can just trespass in a man's home?"

Home. God, she had never, ever thought of her own trailer as *home.* Home was a place she dreamed of, a little house with shutters and green grass, a waist-high fence and a chimney exhaling cotton ball puffs of smoke. A backyard with a tree for climbing, with a bedroom for her and Hank, for that baby girl that never was. Home was a phantom. A chimera.

445

"I said, what are you doing in here, Ruth?" Frank said, throwing his small shoulders back, thrusting that skinny chest forward in some semblance of intimidation. Something about this made her pity him. He'd become a monster in her mind, but here he was, just flesh and bone. Just ribs and jaw and ragged breath.

"I know what you done to Florence," she said softly. "To *Sally*."

"What's that supposed to mean?"

"Listen, Frank. I don't know why you done it, but you're a decent man. A hardworking man."

She knew that when Hank was angry, when he felt defeated, flattery went a lot further than you'd ever think. One of the ladies whose hair she cut once told her that the way to a man's heart was not through his stomach, as the old saying went, but rather through a pat on his back.

He didn't seem swayed, however. What was it they also said about flattery? *It's like cologne, better to be smelled than swallowed.* And he wasn't swallowing it.

"I don't want any trouble here, but it's time you let her go home," Ruth said, keeping her voice calm and even. "You still got time."

"Time for what, Ruthie?" he asked, moving toward her now. The gun was raised, pointed directly at her chest.

"Time to get out of here," she said, stunned

by her body's stillness. Peace. "Before the FBI arrives."

"FBI?" he said, chuckling a little, and then his laughter turning into a racking cough.

"You can get right back on the city bus and be at the depot in twenty minutes. Connect you to anywhere you want to go," she said. "You need money, I got some in my trailer. But you got to let her go, Frank. She don't belong to you. She ain't your daughter, and she surely ain't your girlfriend."

At this, Frank stopped short, the gun inches from her chest. She'd never been this close to a gun before.

Instinctively, her hands rose over her head. She could feel and smell the perspiration that now stained her blouse.

"I seen how good you been to Florence. How much you care for her," she tried again. "You just got caught up in this thing. It don't mean you're a bad man."

He pressed the gun against her skin in the small gap between her buttons. Her blood pounded in her temples, in her ears, against the cold metal barrel.

She thought of Florence. She'd gladly sacrifice her own life if it meant that sweet child might be saved. Ruth closed her eyes, waiting for him to shoot, but then her hand, as if with a mind of its own, reached down and grabbed Frank's wrist.

When the gun went off, she felt a warm splatter. Was it her own blood? Was this odd buzzing thrumming feeling *death?* But there was no pain. Only the smell of gunpowder and the odd, sharp scent of citrus.

She opened her eyes and saw the bowl of oranges she'd brought over the day before, shattered into a thousand pieces. The pulpy remains on the Formica counter.

A voice had boomed as though through a loudspeaker outside the trailer: "Come out with your hands up."

Ruth figured that Frank would kill her now. His eyes were dead as he aimed the gun at her again.

"Frank," she said. "If you shoot me, they'll come in and kill you."

Frank looked over his shoulder at the closed door of the trailer.

"But if you do as they say . . ."

The door of the trailer flew open then, and a police officer stormed into the trailer. Smirking, Frank set the gun down on the kitchenette table. He winked at Ruth, then raised his hands in surrender.

After they had pulled Frank outside, Ruth walked tentatively out of the trailer, and it made her think of walking out of a dark movie theater into a bright afternoon. It took her eyes several moments to adjust. Two other officers had Frank on the ground, his arms yanked behind his back. The air was murky with a cloud of dirty dust. Frantically, she scanned the lot, searching for Florence. For *Sally*. Finally, she saw her cowering at the picnic table in front of her own trailer. She ran to her, embraced her. The child was trembling so hard, it made Ruth think of the night she went to the hospital for her appendix. But this time, she wrapped her arms around her. Held her tightly.

A police cruiser peeled into the motor court followed by two more. They parked cockeyed in the drive, and the doors flew open.

"You're under arrest for kidnapping and transporting a minor across state lines," one of the officers with Frank said, like he'd rehearsed these lines for a play.

Frank lifted his chin. "I don't know what you're talking about, Officer. You mean Sally? Sally's my daughter. Well, my stepdaughter, but I raised her up from the time she was just a baby."

"I think her mama would beg to differ," the officer said, handcuffing Frank's wrists behind his back.

"Her mother?" Frank scoffed. "Ella Horner? She the one that sent you after me? I'm married to that woman. You can check the records. You think I'm some sort of criminal?"

"Yes, sir," the cop said. "And we been looking

for you for almost two years. Had our guys looking for you in Baltimore, in Dallas—"

"I'm a businessman, and I had business in Dallas. I got business *here*. I always registered my truck in my name. If you were doing your job, you coulda found me easy."

"Ma'am?" An officer loomed over Ruth and Sally, blocking the sun. "You and the girl. You two okay? Should we call an ambulance?"

Ruth felt Sally quaking inside the cocoon of her arms.

"We're okay," she said. "Everything is okay now."

She closed her eyes and pressed Sally's head to her chest, felt Sally's tears dampen her blouse. Inside her chest, Ruth's heart tumbled, cartwheeling with relief and something like sorrow.

Camden, New Jersey
April 1950

ELLA

They brought her his watch and his hat.

The officers, when they came to Ella's door that night. *Found by the tracks,* they said. The only evidence that it was Russell who had walked out in front of the train as bystanders watched in horror.

"I don't understand," she'd said. "What does this prove? Where is he?"

They had tried to explain that the impact, the blow of the locomotive, had left nothing recognizable behind.

She left his shoes by the door. His side of the bed tightly made. His aftershave in the medicine cabinet. As if she might get a call at any time telling her it had all been a terrible mistake. But after a while, she knew he wasn't coming home. That his watch, hands stopped at the time of the impact, was all the proof she'd ever get.

By the time they called to say Sally was coming home, she'd felt a similar sort of resignation. She'd begun to believe that the little red suitcase, the photograph of Sally on the swing, were the only traces of her daughter that remained.

But Al had insisted. Held both of her crippled hands in his and looked her in the eyes.

Sally was coming home. The impossible somehow suddenly possible. Ella felt like her world had been turned right side out after being inside out for the last two years. *Her little girl was coming back to her.*

It was past midnight, and the house was still. Susan and the baby were staying the night again. They had been staying with her since the FBI had found Sally. The baby had fallen asleep after a warm bath, and Susan had gone upstairs to sleep hours ago. Now Ella sat at the sewing machine, her body aching but the machine humming. As she sewed, oddly it wasn't Sally she thought of but Russell. The night the officers came to Ella's door to tell her that they'd found Russell's remains on the tracks, she'd been sitting in the dark, sewing as well.

Ella could never sleep when Russell was out, and if she did manage to fall asleep, she'd jolt awake, reaching for him on the other side of the bed only to find it empty still. And so, on those nights, she sat up. Waited for him to come home as if he were a teenager instead of a grown man.

That night Susan had come home from the picture show, *For Whom the Bell Tolls*, that's what it was, and gone upstairs after mooning over Gary Cooper for several minutes. Sally had gone to sleep hours before. The house was still. She had figured she might as well use her time to get ahead on her work. She was still tense from the argument they'd had, and so when she heard the footsteps coming up the front porch steps, her shoulders relaxed. He was home early. Daly's stayed open until 2:00 A.M., and so usually he stayed until they kicked him out, stumbling home by 2:15. But the grandfather clock said it was only midnight.

She didn't get up to answer the door. It was unlocked. He could let himself in.

Knock, knock.

Damn it, she thought. *Fool's so drunk he's forgotten how to turn a doorknob.*

She stood up from her work and made her way slowly to the front door. But when she peeked through the small window, it wasn't Russell but two police officers standing there. And just like that, the fissure, that fault line that she'd been straddling forever opened up. The firmament cleft, and the world swallowed her whole.

"Is Daddy home?" Sally had asked, standing at the top of the stairs, rubbing her eyes.

Might be easier, he'd said. *If I was dead.* It was her fault. She'd handed him a one-way ticket on that train. Put him on those tracks, just like she would put Sally on board that bus five years later. Only a fool makes the same mistake twice. She was a *fool,* a goddamned fool. She deserved every ounce of heartache she'd suffered.

For that reason, it was nearly impossible to believe that Sally was coming home. That this time, Ella was getting a second chance.

• • •

"Mama," Susan said now, standing in the doorway. "It's late."

The room was scattered with the fragile whispery paper of the pattern pieces. Scraps of fabric. Bits of ribbon and lace all over the floor. Susan had taken her to the fabric store, where she had chosen a pretty pink dotted swiss. The decision had been easy. But deciding on the pattern size had been nearly impossible. Ella had no idea how big Sally was now, how tall. How much she weighed. And so she'd chosen a pattern a size smaller than her own, the size she herself had been at thirteen years old. Vivi had offered to help, but she'd sent her on home to her own mama.

"You should get some sleep. Sally will be home tomorrow," Susan insisted, hands on her hips.

"I'll be up soon," Ella said without looking up from her work. Begrudgingly, Susan went up the creaking stairs alone.

Ella hadn't sewn in months and months, but it was like riding a bicycle, the way her fingers remembered. She ran the swath of fabric beneath the presser foot, watched as the stitches tethered the soft pink pieces together. Her joints were diseased, but she still had a remarkably steady hand, and she only had the hem left to do. She could hear Susan above her, the groan of the bedsprings in her old room as she lay down. The small sounds of Dee stirring.

She positioned the cloth and lowered the foot, pressed her foot to the treadle to finish the dress. Sally was coming home, and she'd need a dress to wear to Sunday services.

SALLY

Sally had never flown on an airplane. The lawman, Mr. Cohen, sat next to her, nose buried in his newspaper. He didn't seem to notice that she was shaking with fear. She should have been happy—they were headed back to Camden finally—but instead she felt like she might be sick.

After the police took Mr. Warner away, after she clung to Ruth, still afraid, the officer made her sit in the backseat of the police cruiser. Ruth had released her slowly, squeezing her hand, kissing the top of her head. "You go on now, Sally. Your mama's waitin' for you at home."

Home. It was all she'd dreamed about for almost two years now, but then why did it feel like her heart was being torn in two? She'd sat in the backseat of the police car all alone, the window down. Ruth leaned in and touched her hair. "I wish we had time for me to give you a nice trim before you went home," she said wistfully.

It wasn't until they were pulling out of the trailer park, her hand pressed against the glass as Ruth watched her go, that the officer told her she actually couldn't go home right away. No matter that she hadn't seen her own mama in nearly two years, she couldn't go back to Camden until Mr. Warner was charged in the court. She had to be there, they said. And so she'd spent the night at the county detention home for juveniles, where a friendly nurse took care of her before the doctor performed his medical exam, which she wept through, ashamed and horrified as she answered his questions about all the things that Mr. Warner had done to her. But he'd only nodded and scratched down illegible notes on his clipboard.

That night she hadn't slept at all, even though they gave her her own room away from the other children who lived there. Every time she started to fall asleep, something would startle her awake again. When the prosecutor came to pick her up and take her to the court, she felt like she was in the middle of some sort of peculiar dream.

In the courtroom, she'd sat in a hardback chair as they brought in Mr. Warner, *Frank La Salle,* his hands and ankles shackled. She fought the tears that welled up in her eyes.

He wasn't an FBI man. And he wasn't her real father. He was a *criminal.* All of this had been a lie, and she'd been so stupid. So gullible. All she'd had to do was pick up the phone and call home. Any time, and she would have been free. This was what Mr. Cohen had explained to her. Frank La Salle was a con man, a predator, and she wasn't the first young lady he'd taken advantage of. She thought of the photos in his valise, and wondered what the other girls' names were. If they'd been scared like she was. What else they shared in common. She wondered if they'd ever met—she and these girls—if they might have been friends.

But those girls were long gone; she'd never know them. Sally was alone in her grief and agony and shame. She wanted Ruth to be there with her, to hold her like she had when the police came for her. But as Mr. Warner had shuffled into the courtroom and winked at her, she knew she was completely and absolutely alone.

"Is this man your stepfather?" the judge had asked her.

She'd thought of her stepfather, remembered the song he used to sing. Her mother had been right, it was Russell, not her real daddy she was remembering. After a few too many drinks some nights, he'd wander into her room and sit at the foot of her bed.

"You awake, Sally?" he'd ask.

"Yes, Daddy," she'd say, and he'd sing his favorite song, "Waiting for a Train."

Sally loved when her father sang; his voice was as pure and sweet and steady as his trumpet. Even when he'd been drinking, his words were clear and sharp.

His voice always grew softer at the part about Texas with its wide open spaces, the moon and stars above, like he was sharing a secret with Sally. A beautiful little secret.

"Miss Horner? I asked you a question. Is this man, Frank La Salle, your stepfather?"

"My stepfather died when I was six. I never saw this man before that day at the Woolworth's."

The pilot came onto the loudspeaker and said they were flying over Chicago now, and that it wouldn't be long until they arrived in Philadelphia, where her mother would be waiting. They'd given her a new outfit to wear: a navy blue suit and a polka-dot blouse, a brand-new pair of black shoes and a bright red coat. It had brought tears to her eyes, as she remembered Sister Mary Katherine trying to give her that beautiful red coat from the lost and found.

They'd also given her a perky straw cap, which one of the ladies at the detention center affixed to her hair. "What lovely curls you have," she'd said, and Sally had thought of Ruth. Of her curls collecting on the floor of Ruth and Hank's trailer.

Suddenly, the plane bobbed and dipped, and her stomach roiled in waves of nausea.

"I think I might be sick," she said, eyes wide and teary as she bent over, light-headed. Mr. Cohen reached into the seat pocket and pulled out a flattened paper bag, and because it was too late to stand up and run to the restroom, she threw up into the paper sack, both mortified and relieved.

"It's okay," he said. "It's just a bit of turbulence. It should steady out. Try to breathe. You'll see your mother soon."

ELLA

It was nearing midnight, March 31, 1950, and Ella waited in the backseat of assistant prosecutor William Cahill's car at the airport, watching the planes land. In only moments, it would be April 1, April Fool's Day. Part of her still believed this could possibly be just part of an elaborate hoax, a cruel joke.

"Is that her?" she asked, leaning forward toward the front seat as a small plane taxied toward them.

"No, ma'am," Mr. Cahill said without looking back. "Not yet. She'll be here soon. They said there's just a small delay."

Susan also sat in the backseat. Dee was asleep in Susan's arms. Al sat up front with Mr. Cahill, smoking.

"Why doesn't it come?" Ella asked no one in particular, peering out the glass at the tarmac, the smoke making her eyes tear.

She turned back to Susan and studied the sleeping child in her arms. Already nearing two years old. Where had this time gone? Every time she looked at Dee she was reminded how very long Sally had been away. She was like a wall marked up with a child's height, a stunning reminder of time's insistent and inevitable passage.

Abruptly, Al stubbed his cigarette out in the ashtray and reached for the door handle. When the door opened, a cold breeze rushed into the car. Ella trembled.

"What is it, Al? Is it her?" she asked, but he was already striding across the tarmac, and in the distance, she could see the lights of the plane guiding the way for her daughter to come home to her.

SALLY

The photo that would be in all the newspapers was the one of Sally descending the steps of the airplane as her mother waited for her, Mr. Cahill gently holding Ella's arm. In the photo, Sally's face was anguished, her eyes wet. But what Sally felt as she walked down those steps and saw her mother standing there, waiting for her, was so much more complicated than anything those photographers with their popping, blinding bulbs could capture.

Her mother looked older. Sally knew, of course, that *she* herself would appear older to her mother. It had been two years; she was still a little girl when her mother last saw her. But she hadn't expected that her mother would have changed, too. That the lines that had just started to appear at the corners of her eyes, her mouth, would have deepened. That the sadness she'd seen pass across her mother's face before would have settled there, in the downward turn of her eyes and lips.

Ella, like Sally, wore a dark suit, and a dark little cap with a net veil that covered her forehead. It looked familiar, and it took Sally only a moment to realize it was the same cap that she had worn long ago to her stepfather's funeral.

This more than anything made Sally's heart feel wooden. Too heavy to stay suspended in her chest.

Ella reached for her, pulling away from that man, and Sally began to cry.

"I want to go home, Mama."

Her mother held her as they made their way past the journalists barking out their questions. The flashbulbs were like fireworks.

Are you worried about La Salle getting out? Did you know he'd raped those other little girls? Did he make you share a bed? Sally, Sally, Sally. He says he was like a father to you. Sally, did you love him?

She and her mother were ushered to one car. Al and Susan were escorted to another.

"Can we please just go home?" she asked her mother, whose mouth twitched, eyes narrowed.

The man driving the car turned around and said, "Real sorry, Miss Horner, but you can't actually go home just yet. We've got to take you to Pennsauken. To the Camden County Children's Center. They'll take good care of you there, just until the trial's over."

"I can't go *home?*" This felt like one of those nightmares she had sometimes, the ones where she was trying to go somewhere but her legs refused to move.

"Sorry, sweetheart, it's the law."

Her mother reached for her hand. "It won't be

long," she promised, but Sally felt like she'd just been fooled. Like everybody was playing tricks on her. Even her own mother.

"I'll come see you," Ella said. "It's going to be okay."

Sally shook her head and then leaned against the cold window, letting the hot tears stream down her face.

ELLA

Ella sat so close to Sally in the courtroom, she could feel the heat coming off her. Thankfully, they'd brought that awful man straight back to Camden, shackled to two lawmen on a train, they said, so Ella only had to spend a couple of nights away from Sally, though those two nights somehow seemed longer than any she'd spent over the last two years.

The pink dress she'd made fit Sally, but somehow it didn't seem right. Like a grown woman wearing a child's smock. Sally fidgeted inside it, fussed with the hem, the collar.

Ella's body ached; her joints were swollen. It felt like she might just burst. She was a balloon filled with too much breath.

When that man, Frank La Salle, entered the courtroom, she felt Sally's body stiffen next to her. Ella squeezed her hand.

Frank La Salle didn't look at either one of them as he took the stand. His head bowed low, he sat down, and the judge asked him how he pleaded.

"Guilty, sir," he said, and Ella gasped. The lawyers told her that he would likely put up a fight. But here he was, this sad old man, admitting what he'd done to her child.

Ella could hardly hear what was being said for

the buzzing in her ears. It was as if a swarm of bees had taken up residence inside her brain.

"Mr. La Salle, you, sir, are a moral leper. I sentence you to thirty to thirty-five years in state prison. You'll serve the sentence for the abduction concurrently."

Ella watched his face for any sort of reaction to what the judge had said. But he remained stoic, unflinching.

The judge looked directly at Ella before returning to Frank. "Mothers throughout the country will give a sigh of relief to know that a man of this type is safely in prison."

It was only then that Ella noted a shift in Frank's expression. He was smiling. Smiling at *her*.

SALLY

The newspaper folks came to the house on Linden Street, wanted another photo for the papers now that Sally was settled back at home. They asked her to sit and pose with the phone to her ear, pretending she was calling home. Her mother's phone service had been cut off, however, so as she lifted the receiver and pressed it to her ear, it connected to nothing.

"Perfect!" the reporter had said, winking at her. "Welcome home, Sally."

Later she offered to help her mother make supper. Sue and Al were coming over with the baby.

"Mama?" Sally said.

Her mother was at the counter, assembling a meat loaf. The ground beef was pink, with a bright yellow egg floating on top.

"Get me the bread crumbs," Ella said, without looking up from the bowl.

Sally reached into the cupboard where her mother kept the staples. Everything was where it had always been. Flour, sugar, oats. What did she expect? That everything had changed while she was away?

Her mother sprinkled the bread crumbs into the

bowl, worked the egg and crumbs into the meat.

"Ruth makes hers with Quaker Oats," Sally said. "Instead of bread crumbs."

"Ruth?"

"Mrs. Janish, she was our neighbor at the Good Luck. Remember, the one whose telephone I used to call home?"

Her mother flinched.

Sally hadn't talked to her mother at all about her time away with Mr. Warner. But she wanted her to know about the good things. That it wasn't all terrible. That in a way she'd been taken care of by so many people. Sister Mary Katherine. Lena. Ruth. She thought of Ruth, asking her to grab the container of oats and shake some into the bowl when her hands were covered with the hamburger and eggs. *Tap a couple of drops of Tabasco in there too, would ya?* she'd say. *Gives it a bit of a kick.* And then Ruth would kick back her bare foot behind her.

"I cooked in Baltimore, mostly hamburgers and eggs. But Ruth taught me how to make chili and meat loaf and we made pork chops once, but I burnt them so we had to feed 'em to Tex. Oh, Mama, you woulda loved Tex. He was the sweetest dog ever. He slept on my pillow every night, liked to put his nose in my hair . . ."

Her mother's hands flew to her ears, like a child trying to block out the sound. It didn't matter that there was hamburger and egg on her hands; she

471

pressed her ears against her head, and the raw meat stuck to her skin.

"Mama," Sally asked, scared. "What's the matter?"

Her mother lowered her hands from her face then, and looked like she was just waking up from a dream. She shook her head and quickly cleaned the mess from her cheeks with a dish towel.

"It's nothing, Sally. I'm sorry."

ELLA

I'm going out to get the mail," Sally said.

Ella was at her sewing machine. Al had finally convinced her to see that specialist in Philadelphia, who prescribed some medicine to help with the pain in her hands. While the pain was still there, of course, it was dulled. Deadened a bit. Enough so that she'd been able to get back to work, send that sweet girl Vivi back home to her own mama. She knew she needed to start making money again on her own if she and Sally were to stay in the house on Linden Street.

Ella wasn't sure what she had expected if Sally were ever to come home. On those rare occasions when she allowed herself to entertain that weak flicker of hope, she hadn't thought past the reunion. She'd imagined the moment that she took her daughter in her arms. She'd dreamed the scent of her hair, the way it would feel to hold on to her. The sound of her voice. What it would feel like to hear her say "Mama" again. But beyond that she hadn't dared (or even known how) to imagine.

What she hadn't known, couldn't have known, was that Sally would be so different. Of course, she was *recognizable*. Her pale blue eyes. Her curls and her soft smile. Her voice was the same.

But she was also changed. Physically, of course, she was more woman than child now. But it was so much more than that. Where she had once been such a bright, shimmering light, there was a certain dullness, a darkness now. All that light that used to dance in her eyes was dimmed a bit. Where she had once been interminably curious, she was now somehow shrewder. As though she already knew everything there was to know about the world, and the burden of this knowledge exhausted her. Her endless enthusiasm and eagerness had been replaced by wariness, *weariness*.

Ella felt like Rip Van Winkle, like she'd closed her eyes and woken up with two years stolen out from under her. She might have gotten her daughter back, but those two years were gone. Ella could barely consider what had happened in her child's life in the last two years. She was a girl trespassed upon, violated in unthinkable ways. Ella tried so hard to put those thoughts out of her mind, but it sometimes seemed as if Sally's skin still bore the imprints of that man's hands. She was jumpy now: she flinched and winced, stiffened. Her left eye had taken to twitching nervously. Even when she seemed to be enjoying herself, that trembling lid betrayed her.

When Sally tried to talk about her life on the road with Frank La Salle, Ella felt her ears begin to buzz. She saw stars. That woman, Ruth, who had helped her escape. She spoke about her with a fondness that felt, oddly, like a betrayal to Ella.

"Ruth sent another letter," Sally said, coming in from outside.

"That right?" she said, and pressed the treadle.

That woman had written letters nearly every other week since Sally came home. Sally had offered to let Ella read them, but it had been too difficult.

Sally pored over the paper in her hands, her eye scanning the words.

"Oh, Mama!" she said, looking up, her eyes oddly bright though filling with tears.

"What is it?" Ella asked.

"She's gonna have a baby. She just found out! Oh, how I'd love to go see her. Do you think? I mean, is there any way . . ." Sally's words trailed off, like unraveled stitches.

"Of course not," Ella snapped, snipping them off like the blades of her shears. "What's the matter with you, wantin' to go back there?"

"Oh, Mama," she said. "I didn't mean . . ."

"You'd think you missed it there. Living in squalor with that monster. What's the matter with you?"

The second she said it, she felt the same way she had when she snapped at Russell that night. Her bitterness something she couldn't control, and the bile of her words burning her tongue afterward.

AL

S he loves you," Al said to Sally.

"Sue?" Sally asked, distracted.

He'd given her a watering can and asked her to water the annuals that he'd arranged earlier in tidy rows along the long tables in the greenhouse. She seemed to marvel at the delicate spray of water, the simple task of watering the thirsty soil.

"Your mama," he said. "She's just struggling."

"Her rheumatism's better since she saw the specialist."

"Not that, Sally," Al said.

He watched her as she moved down the aisle, shuffling her feet like an old woman instead of a teenaged girl.

When he thought about all the things she must be carrying around inside that head of hers, that heart, it took everything he had not to punch something. Someone. If he'd made it to California before the police got to him, he's pretty sure he could indeed have killed Frank La Salle. Even with him safely in prison now, justice supposedly being served did little to quell his rage.

And Ella, Ella who'd been offered this *gift,* was acting like a damn fool. Here was her daughter.

476

Alive. Saved. But he'd seen her barely able to look Sally in the eye.

"Can I stay with you and Sue?" Sally said, carefully dribbling water into some geraniums. "Maybe go to school here in Florence this fall? I'm behind at school now. None of my friends from Camden will be in my grade."

Al rubbed his hand across his face. As much as he wanted to tell her that she could stay with them, live with them, he knew it wasn't right. The girl had lost two fathers already; he wasn't about to let her lose her mother, too. Ella owed her this.

"You can stay with us this summer," he offered. "But you need your mama. And she needs you."

Camden, New Jersey
1951–1952

SALLY

Sally was a year behind in school. In the fall of 1951, those girls she once knew—Vivi and Bess and the others with their shiny hair and untroubled eyes—moved on to high school, but she was left behind in the eighth grade, her life somehow stunted. Towering over the other children, more woman than girl, she stuck out. An aching, throbbing thumb.

Everyone knew who she was. Everyone knew what Frank La Salle had done to her. Yet no one said a word. It was as if they all shared the same awful secret. But she could feel it in the way their gazes held too long: the girls assessing, and the boys? God only knows what they were thinking.

At school, she sat in the back, never raised her hand. It didn't matter, because the teacher never called on her anyway. She listened, of course, her mind thrilling still at the amazing world and all that there was still to learn. At how much she had missed while she was away.

"Who can tell me the phases of the moon?" the teacher asked, her eyes expectant.

Silence. Sally's arm itched with the desire to lift.

"Anyone?"

New moon, waxing crescent, first quarter . . . Her mind hummed. *Waxing gibbous.*

"It's right there in your textbook. Didn't anyone study the lesson?"

Full moon! That bright full moon that hung overhead, casting its brilliant light through the window in the rooming house in Atlantic City. She'd stared at her pale skin in wonder as it bathed her in its cool light. Marveled at its tidal pull, the sound of the waves crashing against the sand through the open window.

"Waning . . . ?" the teacher prompted.

In Baltimore, it waned, dimming the dark corners of that attic room. The world, the world of that locked room had been made of shadows, and she'd felt betrayed by the heavens.

The girl in front of her raised her hand.

"Yes, Abigail?"

"Crescent?"

"Not yet. Waning gibbous, third quarter, then . . . ?" The teacher sighed, disappointed in all of them.

Waning crescent, Sally thought. That sliver of moon that sliced the sky the morning she realized that Lena and the circus had left. She'd walked through the empty lots where Lena and the others' trailers had been. The dirt littered with sparkling sequins, like scattered stars in an upside-down sky, the only evidence they had ever been there.

AL

Al studied Sally's face. On Sundays when they went to Ella's for dinner, he couldn't help but notice how different this Sally was from the little girl he'd once known. She was sweet and kind, as she had always been, but instead of chattering away, legs swinging beneath the table, instead of interrupting their conversations with her questions, rather than squealing with delight at the simplest things (a piece of chocolate cake, a song on the radio), she was reserved. Polite. *Quiet.*

"Sally, I hear you won the spelling bee this year? That's just terrific!"

Dee, sitting on a stack of books to reach the table, said, "I hate bees! I got stung by a bee! Right on my bottom. I sat down on it."

Sally smiled without showing her teeth.

"That's a different kind of bee," Susan explained.

"What was the winning word?" Al asked.

"Transmutation," Sally said softly. "T-R-A-N-S-M-U-T-A-T-I-O-N."

"Well, look at that!" Al said, clapping his hands. Dee followed suit, clapping her tiny hands together as well.

Ella hadn't eaten anything on her plate; she

483

simply pushed the food from one side to the next.

"Never even heard of that word before," Al said.

"It means to change from one thing to a different thing," Sally said. "Like alchemy. Turning base metals into silver or gold." Her eyes widened a little. Just the tiniest spark.

"Fascinating, Sally. Ella, did you go watch the bee?" Al asked.

Ella stared at her plate.

"Mama? Al asked if you went to the bee," Susan said firmly, reaching for her hand.

Ella withdrew her hand and clutched it to her side, her eyes wounded.

Sally spoke louder, her chin jutting out. "The alchemists believed that they could transform something as simple and plain as lead into a higher metal. That it had the potential inside it to become something of value. Something special." Her eyes were brimming with tears now. Al felt his heart begin to sliver.

"I'm feeling so tired. Think I'll turn in early tonight," Ella said, but made no effort to move from the table.

Susan nodded. "Okay, Mama. Sally and I can clean up."

Sally put her hands on the table, shaking her head, tears running down her cheeks. "But they were wrong," she said. Her voice was trembling.

"It doesn't matter what you do to it, lead *cannot* turn into gold. It can never, ever change."

Ella looked up, and Al noticed the pain cross her face. He'd seen it a thousand times. Watched as Ella endured. But not once had he ever seen anything but her usual scowl, the hardened response of someone accustomed to suffering. But now, her face softened.

Al and Sue sat motionless, and even Dee seemed stilled, as Ella set her fork down and reached slowly across the table. Her fingers, knotted and gnarled like tree roots, curled around Sally's wrist.

Sally looked startled by her touch. She looked down at Ella's hand and then back up at her mother's face.

Neither spoke a word, but Ella held on, tears rolling down her powdered cheeks.

"I'm sorry," she said to Sally. "I'm trying so hard."

Beneath the table, he felt Sue's own hand clutch his knee, and in that single gesture he felt something like hope.

ELLA

S ally was right, of course, Ella knew. People don't ever change. Not really anyway. Everyone is always fundamentally the same. No alchemical process in the world could change who a person was deep down inside.

That monster Frank La Salle had proven that he would always be the same: sick inside his soul, feeding off the innocence of girls like Sally, one after the other. The police had revealed that Sally was just one in a long line of children he'd violated. The years he'd spent in prison didn't change that, didn't deter him or rehabilitate him.

Russell, despite the titanic shifts in his mood from one day to the next, was predictable. Ella knew that she, too, remained unchanged; she would always be that child she'd once been, staring at her empty palm after her favorite marble was stolen, standing at Russell's empty grave, sitting stunned on the sidewalk when she realized her daughter had been taken. She'd always been and would always be a trusting fool. But without trust there was no hope, and without hope, what was there?

And no matter what it might seem, Sally wasn't truly changed, either. She might look like an imposter on the outside, a woman now, more reserved and shy, but Ella knew that inside she was still that same bright-eyed little girl that Ella had put on the bus that day. That sweet child in love with the world. No amount of evil could destroy that. A light like that is something that cannot be purloined. The fact that she was able to find brightness among the horror of those years with La Salle was something to be honored, not resented. If only she had that ability herself.

"Mama?" Sally said. She stood in Ella's bedroom doorway in the dress that Ella had pressed for her the night before. Her hair was brushed smooth, shining in the sun that streamed through the window. "I'm ready for school."

"Come here, sweetheart," Ella said, motioning for her to come closer. "Your hem's coming down a bit. Let me sew it up real quick."

She reached to the nightstand for her sewing kit and threaded a needle, pricking her finger. A little drop of blood beaded up on her finger and she studied it a moment before she put it to her mouth to stop it from staining the hem of Sally's skirt.

"Oh, Mama," Sally said, reaching for her hand. Studying the wound that was gone as quickly as it was made. "Are you all right?"

"I'm fine, Sally. I'm just . . . ," she said, "just so glad you're home."

SALLY

That following spring, Sally got a weekend job at a local restaurant. It made her feel grown-up, all that responsibility. Earning her own money. She even loved the pinstriped uniform with its stiff collar and buttoned front. She was the youngest waitress on the staff; most of the others went to the high school, while she was still just in junior high. The older girls ignored her, except for the one named Gloria who was also new. She was sixteen and had just moved to Camden from Trenton. She wore red kitten heels with her uniform and winked at the boys who brought their girlfriends there on dates.

The first time they spoke was on Saturday when they ran into each other in the break room. Sally was clocking out after a lunch shift, and Gloria was clocking in.

"What's your name?" Gloria asked.

No one had asked her name in so long. She hesitated. Who was she now? *Florence Fogg? Florence LaPlante? Florence Planette?*

"It's Sally," she said.

Gloria wore red lipstick that matched her shoes. Her face was milky white, her cheeks tinged with dime store blusher.

"I like your shoes," Sally said. "I had a coat that color once."

"They're all yours," the girl said, slipping them off and pushing them toward her.

"You sure?"

"Sure as sugar," Gloria said.

And so Sally quickly slipped out of her loafers and exchanged them for the red shoes. Those ruby slippers. *There's no place like home.* The heels were a perfect fit. She could be someone else in these shoes. "Thanks."

"You got a cigarette, Sally?"

"We aren't allowed to smoke in here," Sally said, feeling her cheeks get hot.

Gloria rolled her eyes and smacked her gum. "Well, let's split then," she said.

"But you just got here," Sally said in disbelief. First, at this girl's audacity. Ditching her shift? And second, that Sally was the one she had approached. *Why Sally?* Sally had done her best since her return to Camden to become invisible.

"Well?" the girl asked, arms crossed against her ample chest.

"Sure," Sally said, nodding and nodding again, thrilled.

"We could maybe go to the Woolworth's and get an ice cream float," Gloria said.

"Aren't you worried about getting fired?" she asked.

"They can't fire me, the owner's my uncle."

Sally nodded again, grabbed her purse and looked down at her new red shoes.

"What's that?" Gloria asked, pointing at the brass ring that pressed against Sally's chest, and Sally's fingers flew to her neck, fingering the cold metal reminder.

Wildwood by the Sea,
New Jersey
August 1952

SALLY

S ally knew her mother would never let her go. She didn't blame her, of course; she was only trying to keep her safe. She was fifteen, going to high school in the fall. No longer a little girl. Still, her mother worried.

She and Gloria were thick as thieves—*joined at the hip,* her mother said, and sighed, though Sally could tell she was quietly delighted that Sally finally had one true friend. Instead of telling Ella her real plans, Sally simply asked to stay at Gloria's house for the weekend. They planned to go to the Farnham pool, maybe catch a movie *(they were both just dying to see that new Marilyn Monroe flick),* enjoy the last few days of the summer before school started again. After Gloria came and picked Sally up, they didn't walk to her house but to the bus stop.

As she stepped through the accordion door onto the bus, she couldn't help but recall that afternoon just four years—but also a lifetime— ago. She remembered that kind woman, Miss Robinson, who met her at the bus stop. She knew now that Mr. Warner must have tricked her, too. Sally thought of the diving horses, wondered if Miss Robinson ever got a chance to see them.

"Wanna read a magazine?" Gloria asked, reaching into her straw bag and pulling out the latest movie magazines. Marilyn Monroe was on all the covers. They had talked about trying to find a theater in Wildwood showing *Don't Bother to Knock*.

"No, thanks," she said, leaning back in her seat. "I'm feeling just a tiny bit queasy."

Gloria shrugged and flipped open the *Movie Life* magazine.

When they arrived at Wildwood, they went straight to the beach after asking a young couple to take their picture by the Wildwood sign, the marquee letters with the bright red arrow. She and Gloria with lipstick smiles and bright eyes.

On the beach, they spread their blanket out and rubbed their skin with suntan oil, their noses filling with the scent of cocoa butter. They played in the waves, holding hands and rushing into the surf. Sally collected shells, making a little pile. She thought she might bring the prettiest ones home for Dee.

When the boys approached them, Sally had fallen asleep in a warm cradle of sand, the lapping waves a sort of summertime lullaby.

"Hey, you girls, wanna come walk the boardwalk with us?" One boy's lanky body cast shadows across their legs. Another boy stood at his side.

A quick glance at each other behind their magazines. The language of best friends. A shrug. A *why not*.

"Why not?" Gloria said.

Both of them, these pale and smiling boys, had just come back home from Germany. The Army. They might as well have said they'd just arrived from Mars, for all this meant to the girls.

"Use a made-up name," Gloria whispered in Sally's ear. "I'm Marilyn," she said, scrambling to her feet and holding out her hand to the tall fair boy with the dimples.

"And what's your name?" the handsome, dark-haired one said, looking down at Sally.

Slowly, she sat up and peered at him.

"I'm Vivi," she said, and even as she did, she felt herself changing. Transmutating. "Vivi Peterson."

All afternoon they rode the carnival rides. The girls clung to each other in the line for the Hell Hole and held hands on the roller coaster before throwing their arms over their heads, screaming. The boys tagged along, spending all their pocket change on carnival games and ice cream. When the sun went down, each couple climbed into a separate Ferris wheel cart and lifted off the ground. From the highest point, Sally could see the entire boardwalk below, the lights on the piers and the phosphorescent sea. When she looked up, the constellations sparkled like sequins above them.

Afterward, back on Earth, Sally peered up into the heavens again.

The blond one, Nick (Gloria's boy), said, "Hey, you know, we've got a room at the Rio. We could have some drinks? I make a mean sloe gin fizz."

Sally felt herself stiffen, but Gloria nudged her.

"Sure," Gloria said. "Why not?"

The boys' motel room had sliding doors that opened to the pool. The walls of the room were aqua blue, the same color as the chlorinated water. Sally and Gloria sat dangling their feet into the cool blue, and Sally thought of Lena, her golden gams. Where was she now? Did she wonder what had happened to Sally when she and the circus arrived at the Good Luck again that summer? Had she read the papers? Thinking about Lena made her think about Tex, and her heart snagged at the memory, his tail wagging expectantly whenever she was near.

"Here ya go," Eddie said, handing her another drink, red with grenadine in her plastic cup. She'd lost count of how many she'd already had. The whole world had a soft sort of glow to it. The water was shimmery, illuminated from below.

Gloria and Nick were necking on a lawn chair. She watched his hand as it crept up Gloria's bare back.

"Hey, lovebirds! How about we take this party inside?" Eddie said, and they all filed into the room after him through the sliding glass door. Gloria tripped and giggled, "Oh, shit!" as her drink spilled on the carpeted floor.

When the lights went out, Sally felt herself slipping, diving, plummeting beneath familiar deep waters. The ashtray, chlorine, chemical scent of the motel room. The familiar lullaby of the crashing waves. She closed her eyes, allowed herself to be unmoored. This world slipping seamlessly into another.

This felt familiar, though she didn't tell him so (this fresh-faced boy with his eagerness and wanting). They lay face to face on the hard mattress in the dimly lit motel room. Her shoes, the red kitten heels her mother still didn't know she owned, lay discarded on the carpeted floor. (Those scarlet secrets she kept deep in the back of her closet at home—so afraid of what her mother didn't say, the words as dangerous as blades.) She had taken them off to walk on the beach earlier just after the sun went down. Her hair was gritty with sand now; it cracked and ground in her teeth and between their tangled tongues.

It was dark here except for the pale pink light from the neon sign outside, blinking, blinking, keeping time with the metronome of sighs coming from Gloria and Nick in the other bed:

"Marilyn," he whispered to Gloria now. "You're so pretty."

Sally tried to think only of her own breath, her own heart. And her boy, Eddie, breathed hotly in her ear, his hands pulling her closer until she felt his pelvis pressing against her own hips.

His want was raw, familiar. Eddie was hungry in an almost angry, entitled sort of way. She knew this, too; it was what her body understood. His longing was palpable, suffocating. He whispered in her ear that he'd been waiting for this, for someone like her, and she knew what it felt like to be wanted.

From across the room, there was the sound of metal teeth unzipping.

"Hey now," Gloria said, laughing first. "Slow down, buddy." Whispers and the sound of skin against skin, then the shushing of crinoline, of sheets and the sharp sudden snap of a slap. "I said stop!" (Boys at the restaurant called Gloria a tease.)

"Come on . . . ," her boy said.

"Vivi," Gloria said loudly, her voice close. "Let's go."

Gloria was standing at the foot of the bed where she and Eddie lay frozen, and Sally sat up, dizzy, spinning. Her tongue was numb.

"Wait," she said, but Gloria was already slipping on her own shoes, grabbing a cigarette from a discarded pack on the table by the door.

There was the tick and hiss of a match, the smell of burning tobacco, the shining tip of her cigarette punctuating her every word. "I said, Let's go. *Now.*"

Gloria opened the motel door, and Sally could see her silhouette in the doorway.

Gloria looked like a stranger. Like someone she should know but didn't. This happened sometimes. People becoming things they were not. Transmutating.

"Stay," Eddie said, and it was not a plea but a command. "You go on ahead," he said to Gloria.

"Well, I think that's up to her. Do you want to stay or come home?" Gloria asked Sally.

Sally's voice didn't seem to work. She had been here before: pressed ribs to ribs with someone in a dimly lit room. Perhaps she had been here her whole life. Perhaps she was born on this mattress, birthed on these starched, anonymous sheets. Everyone wanting something of her. Everyone aching. She wondered where home was. If maybe she was already there.

"You go on. I'll take her home in the morning," Eddie said.

"I'll stay," Sally managed to say.

"Fine," Gloria said. "I'll call you tomorrow."

Then Gloria was slamming the door, and Nick was scrambling after her, drunkenly tripping over Sally's red kitten heels on the floor.

"Ah, come on," he called after Gloria. "Wait!"

Now they were alone, she and Eddie bathed in pulsing pink light. She knew what would come next: hands, hips, lips. She clung to this understanding as if it could save her. As if her bones and his skin moored her somehow. Breathless, she floated on this raft, which bobbed and dipped on this violent sea of pale pink sheets.

"Vivi," he cooed in her ear.

But then she stopped, pressed her hands against his chest. Shook her head.

"No," she said, sitting up. She reached over to the nightstand and clicked on the light.

Eddie shielded his eyes. "What'd you do that for?"

"My name's not Vivi," she said.

"What?"

"My name. I lied."

The boy's hair was tousled, his face and chest red with sun. "Ah, come on, stop yanking my chain."

Sally felt herself ascending, rising from the ocean floor. She was dizzy as she surfaced, as the air above filled her lungs. She took a deep breath.

"My real name's Sally," she said.

He laughed and moved toward her, stealing a kiss on her neck. "Okay, Sally. Or whoever you are."

She pushed him away, sat up taller. It mattered who she was. It mattered.

"Sally Horner."

"Sally Horner," he said, as if he were searching for something he'd lost in the sand.

Her heart was an anchor again, tugging her under. She shook her head.

"Wait," he said. "You said you're from Camden? Do you know Elizabeth Knightley? She's my cousin."

Bess. Bess Knightley. Tears ran hot down her cheeks. She could taste the salt.

"Wait a minute," he said, recognition creeping into his voice.

He sat up, pulling away from her as if he'd been burned. It was too dark to see his features, but she didn't have to see his face to know the way recognition sets in. When he realized who she was.

"I *do* know you," he said. "I read all about you in the papers."

The world tipped and tilted. The raft she was on began to sink. Her mouth was full of salt water, of sand.

"Holy cow," he said, flinging the covers off her, staring at her half-naked body awash in pink light. He scrambled out of bed and ran to the bathroom. The fan clicked on, but she could still hear his body heaving, and so she curled her knees to her chest. Sally had been here before, in a motel room with a man who both loved and despised her all at once. Neon dreams and the distant hum of the highway.

He came out a moment later as she was getting dressed, gathering her things. She wondered if she'd be able to find Gloria at the bus station.

"I'm sorry," he said softly. "I drank too much."

She nodded, though she knew he was lying to spare her feelings. Mr. Warner was with her; perhaps he would always be with her. She'd carry the memory of him in her skin. He had, somehow, become a part of her.

"I didn't know," he said. "If I did, I never would have . . ."

She shook her head. The bus was probably long gone, she realized.

"It's okay. Can you just take me home?"

She had been here before. Racing along an unknown highway in a car with a man she barely knew. She absently played with the necklace as he shifted into higher gears at the insistence of the revving engine.

"Sally Horner," he kept saying again and again.

Sally stared at the road ahead of her, illuminated by the two weak beams of Eddie's headlights. Her body hummed and buzzed as the car accelerated.

"What was it like?" he asked. "I mean, you must have been so scared. You were just a kid."

She looked at him, felt herself soften.

"I'm sorry. I just mean, a lot of people wouldn't

502

have been able to survive that. You must have been really brave."

She was transported back into Ruth's trailer. *You are brave,* she'd said. Just like the girl in that novel.

"I'm sorry. You probably don't want to talk about it. Especially with somebody you hardly know."

As Eddie drove, she closed her eyes and leaned her head back. She could almost smell the shampoo-and-citrus smell of Ruth's trailer. Feel Ruth's fingers playing with her curls.

"What was that?" Eddie said, leaning forward and peering up through the windshield.

Sally opened her eyes and saw something shooting across the sky. And then it happened again.

"A shooting star?" he said, looking at her, grinning like a little boy. "Are we supposed to make a wish or something?"

She touched the brass ring. Suddenly, the sky was streaked with light.

"I think it's a meteor shower," she said. "Perseids."

"Wow!" Eddie said again.

"Pull over," she said, touching the dash. She wanted nothing more now than to be out of the car. To stand beneath that sky. To hold her arms out. To embrace the night.

"Here?" he said.

"Yes! Pull over, so we can watch."

Eddie shrugged, then turned the steering wheel sharply, directing the car toward the shoulder. They were going fast, and the tires spit gravel behind them. Hurtling like a locomotive down the shoulder, Eddie stepped on the brakes and the tires squealed.

Sally kept peering at the heavens, thrilling as three more meteors shot across the sky. It looked like fireworks. Like the Fourth of July.

"Shit!" Eddie said, jerking the wheel again, but Sally was spellbound.

"Sally," he said, and she finally looked away.

The truck was parked on the side of the road, barely illuminated by the low beams of their headlights. Her heart stilled at the understanding, but she was no longer afraid. *You are brave.* And she looked back up. Because she knew now that all of the answers to all of her questions resided in that luminous sky.

Camden, New Jersey
August 1952

VIVI

After the funeral, inside the Horners' musty living room, the girls stood in a huddled circle around the platters of deli meats and whispered. Only Vivi stood outside the circle. Had she once been one of them? One of these gossiping girls, these vicious little magpies? She felt sick as she watched their heads bent together, heard their cackling chatter.

"They'd been drinking, I heard," one said. "At some cheap motel in Wildwood. She didn't even know him. Can you imagine?"

"Was he really your cousin, Bess?" another said. "I heard they took him off to jail but they set him loose after he sobered up. Think they'll press charges?"

"I heard her sister's husband had to go identify her, but the accident was so bad, the only way he knew it was her was from a scar she had on her leg."

Vivi thought then of the scar fading in her own flesh, the slivered line from those blades. They didn't know, of course. There was no way for them to understand what they were about to set into motion that day they took Sally to the Woolworth's: the inevitable and irrevocable consequences of their quiet cruelty. They were

507

just kids, just girls then. They didn't understand that a single act of careless unkindness would have repercussions long after poor Sally tagged behind them as they giggled and whispered secrets they would later be unable to remember. Though for all these years, Vivi could still recall the sound of her loafers scuffing along the pavement behind them: *Wait! Wait up!* They were too young to know that they were somehow, in that moment, both powerful and powerless. That this is the blessing and the curse of being a girl in the world. *The girls*. What had become of them while Sally was away? Irene, of course, was buried next to her father now. Bess and Vivi barely spoke to one another anymore. In the years that had passed, whatever bond they'd all forged with blades and blood had weakened. The certainty they'd once had that their friendships would prevail seemed silly now. Childish. Sally herself was proof, wasn't she? And Irene, too. That the world would always conspire against girls? Wasn't all of this evidence that no matter what sort of allegiances were promised, what sort of pledges made, in the end they were all on their own? Alone?

Vivi went to find Sally's mother. Mrs. Horner was now sitting in a chair by the front window in the parlor, a blanket spread across her lap, a paper plate loaded with tiny sandwiches and baby gherkin pickles balancing on her knees. A teacup filled with red punch sat on the table next to her.

"Mrs. Horner?"

Ella didn't turn from the window. She seemed to be studying the garden growing out there, the fleshy dahlias and bloodred poppies.

"It was a lovely service," Vivi said, and watched her hand as it reached out and touched the woman's arm.

Purple asters and sunny daylilies.

"He sent flowers," Ella said.

"Excuse me?" Vivi said, and sat down in the chair across from her. She continued to hold on to Mrs. Horner's thin arm.

"That man. He sent a spray of flowers for Sally."

"The boy from Wildwood? The one who was driving?" Vivi asked.

Ella shook her head.

"Red roses," she said. "Can you imagine? Like it was Valentine's Day."

Vivi realized that she must have meant Frank La Salle.

"I told Al to throw them away," Mrs. Horner said, and Vivi nodded, her mouth twitching. Ella looked at her then for the first time, and it was as though she were looking for something. Some*one* in Vivi's face. Was she looking for Sally, for her lost daughter?

"There were almost three hundred people,"

Vivi said. "That called at the funeral home last night. Someone counted."

"Three hundred people?" Ella's voice was so filled with want, with longing, that Vivi had to bite her cheek so she wouldn't cry.

"Yes, ma'am," Vivi said, offering the only thing she had left to give. "She was truly loved."

SUSAN AND AL

That night, after the funeral, Susan put Dee to bed and crawled in next to Al. She laid her head against his shoulder, that solid wonderful shoulder, and cried. She cried until her chest ached and she felt empty. He stroked her hair and knew somehow not to offer her any words.

"Thank you, Al," she said. "For bringing her home to us."

Al nodded, though he couldn't help but feel the same way he'd felt after he delivered those empty boots to Bobby Lee Langston's mother. When he walked away, leaving her with the last effects of her child.

"I'm sorry," he said.

But Susan shook her head.

"I love you, Al. And she loved you, too. Sally did."

"Mama?" Dee stood at the foot of their bed, rubbing her eyes with her tiny fists. The sight of her there, the moon glow from outside illuminating her, was almost too much to bear. She was luminous. Like an angel. And for a single moment, Al and Susan both felt an odd calm wash over them.

"What's the matter, sweetheart?" Susan asked, her voice breaking.

"I had a bad dream," Dee said.

"Well, we can't be having that now, can we?" Al said, sitting up and motioning for Dee to come to them. He hoisted her up and she crawled under the covers between them. Her body was warm, as if she carried the moonlight in her flesh.

"Shh," Susan said as she stroked Dee's hair out of her eyes. "You're safe here. Go to sleep. Both of you, get some sleep."

Only Al knew that he wouldn't sleep right away. His heart was broken, but it was also unbearably full of gratitude and love.

ELLA

*S**he's in a better place. She's with the angels now. She's at peace.** All these offerings were meant to comfort her, to ease her mind. Ella didn't begrudge her neighbors these meager, empty platitudes. But what did they know of heaven? What did anyone know of where her child had gone? Her husband?

For months after Russell's suicide, Ella had agonized over where his soul had flown to when it rose from those tracks. She conjured the stories from her own childhood religious education: of the odd in-between of purgatory, a listless limbo. She hadn't dared seek counsel from Reverend Bailey, who would have her believe that Russell now resided in some fiery corner of hell.

Reverend Bailey hadn't known (couldn't know) about the sweet notes, that lovely melody that accompanied most of their days together. He hadn't felt the bristly scruff of Russell's cheek as he pressed it to hers, hadn't heard the sweet soft crooning of "Summertime" in her ear. He hadn't watched Russell as he hoisted Sally up onto his shoulders and took Susan by the hand as if they were his own children at the waterfront park when the Fourth of July fireworks burst above them and the crackling speakers played

"The Star-Spangled Banner." He hadn't seen the way Russell held on to Sally's fat little ankle at the side of his head while he pointed to that sky with his other hand. He hadn't seen the way the explosion of colors reflected in all of their eyes. Her children, her husband sharing in this small miracle.

"It's so pretty!" Sally had squealed, delighted. "It looks like colored stars!"

There would be no way to explain to Reverend Bailey that Russell was not a reprobate but a *saint*. That, if only for a brief period of time, he had brought her joy. That he might have been troubled, but that he loved her. Loved her girls. That sometimes, life was simply too much to bear. Both its pain and its beauty.

And so that night after everyone had left, she was certain, as certain as she had been of anything in her life, that Sally and he were together now—perhaps if not in heaven, then in the heavens. Among those luminous stars.

LENA

"Look, Lena! Look, a goddamned shooting star!" Oscar hollered, jumping and gesturing to the wide Texas sky.

Lena, sitting in a lawn chair outside the trailer, unhitched again at the Good Luck that August night, studied the constellations, and thought about that girl, Florence. *Sally.* Was it just three summers ago they'd sat here together under this same sky?

She'd read the papers, heard the rumors confirming all those terrible things she'd once suspected. Her heart had broken at least a half-dozen times thinking that she should have taken her with them when they fled to Texarkana that night.

Sally's dog still lived here, at the park. Taken in by one of the migrant workers' wives who fed him a steady diet of black beans and rice like he was one of her babies instead of a dog. Her husband wouldn't let him sleep in the trailer, though, so Tex roamed about the park now, looking for affection wherever he could find it. Tonight he sat in Lena's lap and she stroked the soft fur behind his ears.

Maisy, in torn fishnet stockings, was crab-walking across the dirt lot. She peered through her legs at Lena and winked.

Oscar put his hand across his chest as if in reverence to all that beauty above them.

"It's *luminous,*" Lena said, smiling. "Make a wish."

SISTER MARY KATHERINE

In Baltimore, the news of Florence's death brought Sister Mary Katherine to her knees: first in grief and then in prayer.

Of course, by then it had become her mission to save girls like Florence, like *Sally,* the ones with secrets written in their crumpled clothes and sad eyes. She became an expert in the art of detecting sorrow. She also learned that the way to protect those poor lambs was not by whispering her suspicions to whatever priest sat on the other side of the latticed confessional wall.

At first she made her anonymous calls to the parents themselves, and finally, she'd go straight to the social workers and police officers herself. Her life was threatened more than once, by angry fathers usually waving fists and once, a pistol, but she never ever felt again the profound sense of failure she felt about Florence Fogg, the brume of shame and fear lifted.

Her true calling, if not God, was this.

And Sally Horner was that bright shining star who led her there.

RUTH

The letter had arrived that afternoon. It bore the tragic news, of course, but it also offered this:

Dearest Mrs. Janish, Thank you, Ella Horner wrote. *For taking care of my daughter all that time. You were like a mother to her.*

The new baby was coming soon, only two years after her daughter was born. It was August, too hot to sleep; she hadn't slept well in nearly a week. Most nights lately she tossed and turned as Hank snored softly and the baby moved quietly inside her. But tonight, heart aching, she rose. She pulled out the black-and-white composition book she'd salvaged from Frank's trailer and stroked the cover, as soft as a child's curls. She took the notebook, the one she hadn't touched since the police took Florence away, *Sally* away, and forced herself to read her story, the pages marked with a tattered red ribbon.

When she was done, she quietly made her way outside. Funny thing. *California, Washington, Idaho.* It didn't matter where they went, the stars followed. A map of the universe spread out before her.

Tonight, as she studied the constellations, she thought of Sally, and wondered what happens after a star dies. Does the light just fade away? She hoped not. What she wished for, under that reliable sky, was that it was a brilliant explosion.

A detonation first, and then all that beautiful brightness would shatter and scatter across the heavens into so much luminous stardust.

AUTHOR'S NOTE

In the summer of 1948, when Sally Horner's name was in the headlines of newspapers all across the country, Vladimir Nabokov was struggling to write *Lolita*, the book he called his "little time bomb." *Ticking, ticking.* Something about it must have troubled him, though he had never been afraid of detonation before. Of the spark and its consequences. Still, on three separate occasions he purportedly tried to burn his notes, stopped by his wife and collaborator, Vera.

I imagine them on that early August morning in Ithaca, Nabokov feeding his notes into the garden incinerator in the backyard while Vera, oblivious, worked inside the cavernous and drafty rental house. I picture her sitting at the desk, where he dictated and she transcribed his dreams. Perhaps next to her was a stack of newspapers—the ones they'd gathered for research, filled with stories that served as fodder for the debauched Humbert Humbert. Was it the girl that troubled him? Was it Lolita, as elusive as the winged nymphs he hunted?

And then, one of life's little serendipities:
Florence "Sally" Horner. Eleven years old.

I wonder, when she read the headline and studied the photo beneath it, if her heart had fluttered restless in her chest, like the tiger swallowtails that darted about in their garden. That flittering girl in her white dress, alight on a swing. Perhaps she studied the girl's face, the bright wonder of her eyes, the way her hair caught the sunlight. I envision Vera running outside to Vladimir feeding that dangerous little book to the flames, waving the newspaper at him. *I found her. Volodya,* stop! *I found Lo.*

Without Sally Horner those pages might have been nothing but ash.

My initial encounter with Sally Horner was when I was nineteen years old and reading *Lolita* for the first time. Though I must admit, the name *Sally Horner* barely registered in my consciousness, as her story was relegated to one of Nabokov's famous parenthetical asides: "(Had I done to Dolly, perhaps, what Frank Lasalle, a fifty-year-old mechanic, had done to eleven-year-old Sally Horner in 1948?)" It took more than twenty-five years before I found her again. This time, I happened upon Sarah Weinman's riveting long-form essay, "The Real Lolita," published in *Hazlitt,* where I learned the true-crime story hinted at inside those parentheses. I am tremendously grateful and indebted to Ms. Weinman for this introduction to Sally.

At the time that I read this story, my youngest daughter was eleven years old, the same age as Sally when she was abducted. Perhaps for this reason, I originally found myself drawn to the story of her mother, Ella Horner, a seamstress raising two daughters alone after her second husband's suicide. Those classmates, those girls, who convinced her to steal the notebook and likely witnessed the confrontation between Sally and La Salle, also fascinated me. I was consumed by all of those people in Sally's life who were left behind. But most of all, I was captivated by Sally, though for a long time she remained as elusive to me as one of Nabokov's butterflies.

I spent more than a year learning everything I could about Sally and her family, about her abduction, from newspaper archives, census records, yearbooks, and other scholarly articles that speculated on the role Sally's true-crime story played in Nabokov's novel. I studied the places she lived: from the row house where she lived in Camden, New Jersey, to the trailer park where she and Frank lived in Dallas. But mostly, I imagined. I dreamed myself into Sally's life.

Of course, no one but Sally and Frank knows what occurred as they traveled from Camden to Atlantic City then on to Baltimore, Dallas, and, finally, San Jose. And so this is *not* a true-crime story in the traditional sense. And that was never my intention. While I drew heavily on Sally's heartbreaking story, this novel is ultimately an imagined rendering of the years that she spent on the road with her captor and of the impact of her abduction on those she encountered along the way as well as those she left behind.

I am not a biographer, nor am I a true-crime writer; I am a novelist, and this is, in the end, a work of fiction. While the series of events and the settings in which they occur *mirror* history, the characters and their inner lives are entirely fabricated. In most instances, I have used the actual names of the real characters involved, but some of the names have been fictionalized. I have meticulously researched Sally's ordeal, but I have also dreamed up both the horrors she must have experienced and the friendships and moments of joy that, perhaps, enabled her to survive. I have taken many, many liberties with both character and plot. Sister Mary Katherine, Sammy, Lena, Vivi, and several other characters are figments of my imagination, speculations based on the places where Sally was known to have lived and gone to school. Sally *was* enrolled in Catholic school in both Baltimore and in Dallas; Sister Mary Katherine was born of this truth. The trailer park where Frank and Sally lived was, indeed, where the circus workers stayed when the circus was in town; Lena and Oscar materialized as I dreamed those long summer days of 1949. The mass murder by

Howard Unruh is a true crime, but Irene (who lives only in my imagination) was not one of his actual victims. There are many other instances in the novel where, inspired by history and place, I spun both characters and events from these delicate threads.

While the timeline and sequence of events reflect history, there remains (for me) much mystery regarding Frank's motives and the logistics that enabled him to transport Sally across the country without getting caught by law enforcement. I constructed the relationships with Sammy in Baltimore and Joey Bonds (a real-life character) in order to both understand and dramatize the sequence of events leading up to Sally's eventual rescue. The confrontation between Ruth and Frank in those final moments is also pure fiction. So, too, is the encounter with the boys in Wildwood, though the car crash and Sally's ultimate demise is, tragically, absolutely true.

This was the most challenging novel I have ever written. And while I didn't ever burn it in a backyard bonfire, there were times when I felt the itch to light a match. For saving it from the ashes, I first need to thank Rich Farrell. Without your words of encouragement, it would certainly have been incinerated. Jillian Cantor, I cannot express my gratitude for the almost daily reassurance you gave me as I struggled to bring these characters to life. I am so grateful for your generosity of time and spirit. Amy Hatvany, Mary Kubica, and Caroline Leavitt, you were all there exactly when I needed you. *Thank you.* I offer humble gratitude to my agent, Victoria Sanders, for taking this project (and me!) on and for forcing me to dig deeper and work harder. I am so lucky to have you in my corner. Bernadette Baker-Baughman, Jessica Spivey, Benée Knauer, and Deborah Jayne, you are an unbeatable team. Thank you to Henry Dunow and Peter Senftleben for years of support. Thank you to my editor, Hope Dellon, for your enthusiasm, insightfulness, and *kindness.* To Lisa Senz, Hannah O'Grady, and Nancy Sheppard for such a warm welcome to the St. Martin's Press family, and to Amy Schneider for her keen eye. Thank you to Olga Grlic as well for designing a cover that makes my heart swell.

And thank you to my friends and family who listened to me talk about this story ad infinitum (Heather Anderson, Miranda Beverly-Whittemore, Melissa Clark, Toni Donk, Janet Dunphy-Brown, Neal Griffin, Nina Hall, Cecilia Meyer, Tricia Ornelas, Shannon Roberts, Jim Ruland, Danielle Shapiro-Rudolph, Esther Stewart, Teri Stumpo, Beya Thayer, and Nicole Walker). To my parents, Paul and Cyndy Greenwood, and sister, Ceilidh Greenwood, for always believing in me and my work. To my husband, Patrick Stewart, and my girls, Mikaela and Esmée, for your endless patience and love. I love you three more than I have words to express.

In 1953, when Nabokov finally finished the novel that would become one of the most celebrated, and most reviled, books in American literary history, Sally was dead. Of course, Sally Horner lives on inside those dangerous pages, little bits of her life borrowed and changed. *Dolores Haze, Dolores Haze.* Funny, how a whole beautiful and sad life can become the footnote to someone else's story. How this luminescent girl (like so many girls) could be, until now, just an adjunct, captured and preserved inside a parenthetical cage.

Books are produced in the United States using U.S.-based materials

Books are printed using a revolutionary new process called THINKtech™ that lowers energy usage by 70% and increases overall quality

Books are durable and flexible because of Smyth-sewing

Paper is sourced using environmentally responsible foresting methods and the paper is acid-free

Center Point Large Print
600 Brooks Road / PO Box 1
Thorndike, ME 04986-0001 USA

(207) 568-3717

US & Canada:
1 800 929-9108
www.centerpointlargeprint.com